LAST OF DAYS

www.lizerneventura.com

Summary: A barista discovers she belongs to a bloodline that wields superhuman abilities to preserve Earth and prevent its untimely demise.

ISBN: 979-8-9931023-1-3
ISBN (ebook): 979-8-9931023-0-6
First Edition

Cover illustration © 2025 by JV Arts
Book design by Jamie Ryu

LAST OF DAYS

THE LUMEN SAGA: BOOK ONE

Lizerne Ventura

For my mom Lorna, my dad Herman, and my loving husband Jon Mark—without your endless love and support, this novel would've never seen the light of day

CHAPTER I

DAWN SLAMMED THE muffin containers on the counter of Maizel's oversized coffee cart, groaning as she shook out her aching arms.

"G'mornin'," a short, squat woman said to Dawn with a smirk. She stood at a table next to the cart arranging scones, profiteroles, and colorful macarons, which matched her headwrap—elaborately tied to resemble a bow atop her head.

"I'm so sorry, Maizel," Dawn said as she darted behind the coffee cart, removed her coat and crossbody purse, and threw them in a cubby.

"Don't be," her boss said dismissively. "The rush wasn't so bad."

Dawn's apron caught on her already-messy topknot as she put it on, loosening long strands of her sleek, dark brown hair—she had her Filipino and Korean genes to thank for it. She snuck a glance at Maizel.

Her round face was exuberant with a rosy blush on her cheekbones and her lips curved upward slightly at the corners in a perpetual smile. "Your apron's inside out. For someone named after the sunrise, you're definitely not a mornin' person."

"Believe me, I know," Dawn muttered, fixing her apron so the gold "M" monogram faced outward.

Thank heavens her boss was understanding. Today was the first day back at the film studio since the winter break.

Maizel's android wheeled toward her, its dome-shaped head displaying circular, blue-pixel eyes in her direction. One of its metallic arms and pincers extracted a mug from its cylindrical body, placing it before Dawn with perfect precision.

"That oat milk latte is yours," Maizel said, eyeing the mug as a plume of steam wafted in Dawn's direction.

"Oh, you are the best," Dawn said, gingerly lifting the mug to her lips.

She closed her eyes, relishing the pleasant aromas of freshly brewed coffee and pastries, mixed with the sound stage's smells of sawdust and paint. What she considered the liquid of life slid down her throat and warmed her up.

Someone cleared their throat, and Dawn nearly spit her coffee out. Her friend with pink-tipped hair stood in front of her.

"*Annyeong!*" he greeted her in Korean with a sing-song voice and unbridled enthusiasm.

"Hey," Dawn coughed with less gusto. "Sparkle, how many cups have you had?"

The robot had moved to the side of the counter, where Maizel was helping it unbox the sweet-smelling blueberry muffins and place them on circular trays.

"Just two," he said, fingers up like a peace sign. "Can you make me a flat white, please?"

Dawn stared at the slim-figured man she had known since high school. He bounced ever so slightly on the balls of his feet, barely containing his energy.

"Sure," she said slowly, drawing out the word, then turned to the espresso machine to prep his drink. "But we're cutting you off at three drinks, remember?"

Ignoring her, Sparkle sashayed to the table and helped himself to a macaron. "Let me fix your hair," he called out over the sound of grinding beans.

Dawn blew out a breath. "Be my guest. I got a little windblown on my way here. I took the airlift."

"In this stormy weather?" Maizel asked. The bot, now loaded with the muffin trays, rolled away to offer them to the sound stage's cast and crew.

"Someone had a death wish," Sparkle teased, mouth full.

"Well, the rain stopped, but it still felt like flying through a hurricane," Dawn conceded while she finished steaming the milk.

Deftly handling the small jug, Dawn moved to the counter where Sparkle's cup of espresso was, then poured the milk, creating a traditional latte heart.

"I can't," Sparkle said, walking back to the counter. "I can't let him see you like this." He fished a few bobby pins from his pocket and started pinning Dawn's dark brown locks. "I would die of embarrassment for you."

Dawn flinched at her friend's well-intended hair remedy but didn't wave him off.

"Can't let who see her like this?" Maizel asked, rounding the counter and wiping down the espresso machine.

"The Stallion," he scoffed, as if she should've known. "Code name for Logan Pines."

Maizel snorted. "Wasn't it Double-O-Seven or Mr. Darcy before?"

"It changes every month per his fan club," Dawn quipped. Pain poked her temple. "Ow!"

"It's a secret club," Sparkle emphasized, shoving the last bobby pin into her hair.

Dawn swatted his hand away. "If it's so secret, then how come everyone knows?"

He rolled his eyes and crossed his arms. "The Stallion doesn't know. And I'll have *you* know that today's the day he finally makes a move." He took a step back to survey Dawn's hair, then nodded and smiled, as if congratulating himself on a job well done.

Dawn arched an eyebrow. "What are you talking about?"

Sparkle picked up his flat white. "Oh, nothing," he said before taking a sip. "I just may have orchestrated a little something. You're welcome." He gave a sly wink to Maizel before spinning around. "Oh!" he whispered behind the cup. "Something sexy this way comes."

Dawn peered around Sparkle and saw Logan at the far end of the sound stage, his long strides bringing him closer to her by the second.

"Look at those pecs!" Sparkle cackled, waltzing away.

Dawn watched as Logan passed by the crew members, each of them waving their hellos. Of all the sound stage coordinators, he was their favorite—a natural at coordinating schedules, deliveries, vendors, and all the ins and outs of his assigned stages at Stardust Studios.

Dawn's heart rate doubled as he approached, his phone in hand. It didn't help that he was smoldering. Moving heavy equipment around the sets like a workhorse (and probably some other non-work-related activities) had evidently earned him his most recent nickname. She tried to maintain her composure as he put his phone away and gave her his full attention, flashing her his crooked grin.

That smile. It could melt her.

"Your usual cortado?" she asked, peeling her eyes away from him to reach for a cup.

4

"Let's change it up today. Surprise me," he countered, swiping his black hair away from his eyes. It had gotten longer over the break. "I missed our morning chats. I missed . . . you."

The forward comment made Dawn's face grow so hot, all she could do was return a shy smile.

Maizel ignored them, casually looking through a checklist on the far side of the counter but staying within earshot.

Before the studio closed for the year-end holiday break, Logan had stopped by almost every morning, struck up a conversation, and learned tidbits about Dawn, that she'd studied abroad in London, she was a polyglot, that she'd had basic firearms training, and had gone skydiving once—the latter two were things he pointed out they both had in common. She'd welcomed his flirtations, *if* that's what they were, believing she didn't stand a chance against the gorgeous actresses who vied for his attention.

"How was your holiday?" Logan asked as he watched her weigh espresso grounds.

"Simple, cozy, and . . . lazy," Dawn grunted, pressing hard to tamp the grounds. "My dad's a climatologist, and he travels for work a lot—he flew out to the Global Climate Summit in Japan this past weekend. So we usually spend our holidays at home and have a relaxing dinner."

Their week of festivities had consisted of lounging in the living room dressed in sweats, drinking bottomless mugs of hot cocoa, and listening to her dad's tall tales and riddles. He was notorious for concocting brain teasers that stumped anyone with ears for days on end.

Dawn drifted back to the present as she prepped the espresso, pumped a bit of syrup, and slowly poured the milk over it. She loved making coffee—the grinding beans, the aroma, the hot cup in her hands, and the delicate art of pouring milk. She almost forgot she had an audience.

Something that sounded a lot like a snort came from Logan. "That's it?"

"Well, I also filled out some job applications." Dawn shrugged as she sprinkled dried peppermint leaves on top of the macchiato. She passed the cup to him. "I'm still figuring out what I really want to do."

"Just don't open up a rival coffee cart," Maizel muttered as she passed by, wiping down stray coffee grounds. "I'll head out soon to check on the other craft services. You good to handle the rest of the day here?"

"Of course," Dawn said.

"Filming in five!" someone yelled from the other side of the stage.

"How 'bout you, Logan?" Maizel asked, with mischief in her voice, "You think you can handle this one here?" she said, elbowing Dawn.

"As long as I've got my morning cup, ma'am," he replied, raising the cup that Dawn had just put in front of him.

Maizel shuffled away to finish up the table spread and gather her belongings.

"It's a peppermint macchiato," Dawn whispered after he sipped and nodded in approval. "You didn't tell me what *you* did on vacation."

He leaned in closer to speak quietly. If anyone were watching them, they'd have thought they were trading secrets.

"I went sightseeing with the crew and explored the hiking and nature trails you recommended. I have to say, even with the weather fluctuations, those ocean vistas were incredible."

Dawn recalled her suggestion to visit the bluffs off the Palos Verdes Peninsula—and was surprised that Logan took it seriously. He had mentioned growing up near Colorado Springs and talked at length about his favorite national park, The Garden of the Gods. Its celestial rock spires had once been surrounded by a forest of oak and juniper trees hundreds of years ago. It was hard to imagine that now, as a couple of devastating wildfires ravaged the vegetation before they were born; only the rocks had remained. She found his fascination with rocks endearing.

"You thought I'd forgotten about that, didn't you?" Logan said, seeing her facial expression. He continued to sip his coffee. "You should've come with us; even Sparkle came."

"I . . . didn't know I was invited," Dawn said, fiddling with the crystal pendant around her neck. "Did you do anything else for your holiday?"

"I've been training for a marathon in March, but I took a break to see my parents. I also spent time with a buddy who I was in the Air Force with—"

"Before your injury?" Dawn blurted out. She regretted the words as soon she spoke them, recalling the story from Sparkle's gossip a month earlier. "I-I'm sorry. I shouldn't have said that. I heard that's part of the reason you came to work here . . . but I would like to hear it from you."

"I guess word really gets around. I'd be happy to tell you all about my *battle scars*," he joked, "another time."

"That sounds like a great idea," Maizel jovially interrupted as she appeared beside Dawn. She reached out to Logan offering a small, folded piece of paper.

Dawn looked at her, her eyes asking, *What do you think you're doing?*

"Here's her number. You two should get together after work sometime!"

Dawn's eyes went wide, and her jaw dropped.

"Uh, Maizel, that's not necessary," Dawn said as her hand went up to take the paper from her. But Logan was faster and taller, snatching it so quickly that Dawn ended up grabbing air. Before Dawn could protest, Maizel bolted for the door.

"Gotta run," she whispered loudly without looking back. "Hubs is at the gate!"

After Maizel fled, Dawn turned to look back at Logan, closing her mouth. Her brain was still processing what just happened.

He wanted *my number?* she thought incredulously.

He had pulled out his phone, and it was obvious he was adding her number to his contacts. He looked up at Dawn just as her phone buzzed in her pocket.

"There. Now you have *my* number." He smiled sheepishly. "I swear I was going to ask for your number today. Maizel beat me to it."

Dawn pulled out her phone, seeing that she just received a message from him.

"Thanks," she managed. Before she could read his message, her phone buzzed again in her hand and both of them peered down at it—an incoming call from Howel Farringdon. "Oh, it's my dad. Er, excuse me for a moment. I should answer it."

Logan nodded, taking another sip of his coffee, and Dawn whipped around for a little privacy. As soon as she answered her phone, a voice talking over what sounded like aircrafts zinging past came through.

"—SHOULD BE FINE! I'M RINGING HER RIGHT NOW!" her dad said to someone else. "DAWN? I'M AT JETT PIERCE'S HANGAR AT THE BURBANK AIRPORT."

Her phone wasn't on speaker, but he was so loud, she held it away from her ear.

"Dad?" Dawn whispered loudly. "Is everything al—?"

"YOU NEED TO COME MEET US HERE."

"Right now? I'm at the studio. Maizel left and I—"

"IT'S AN EMERGENCY," he said, talking over her. "I CON-TACTED MARION, AND SHE'S WORKING OUT DETAILS WITH MAIZEL. I NEED TO LEAVE TO . . . YOU NEED TO MEET MY, UM . . . ASSOCIATE."

There was a tinge of panic in his voice.

"Okay, okay," Dawn assured him, untying her apron. "I'm coming now."

"GET A RIDE—I'LL HAVE MARION PICK UP THE AIR-LIFT," he yelled over someone else talking in the background. "YES, YES, SHE'S ON HER WAY TO—"

The call ended. Dawn's heart raced. What kind of emergency he was dealing with?

"Is everything all right?" Logan asked. Dawn wheeled around to face him, having forgotten he was there. "I didn't know your dad was British. I mean, I'm assuming because of his accent."

"Oh, yes—I think I need to leave," she said hurriedly, folding her apron and tucking it under the shelf. "And yes, he's British, and I'm part White, er, also British, but I was raised here—and a little bit of everywhere."

"Did he say Jett Pierce? *The* Jett Pierce of Clean Energy Tech and Transportation?"

"Yup, he's a . . . family friend," Dawn said, crouching to grab her coat and purse.

Apparently, Logan had heard their whole conversation. The interest he showed in her was elating, but worry over her dad was beginning to gnaw at her. She fought the urge to sprint for the door.

"I'll get you a ride," Logan whispered, as he put in an earpiece. "Steve, can you call a cab at the front gate? . . . No, for Dawn Farringdon . . ."

As he paused between responses she couldn't hear, Dawn inhaled slowly, attempting to steady her racing heart. He had just said her name—her *full* name—which made her giddy and embarrassed at the same time.

"Burbank Airport," he said, looking at her, his eyebrows up, asking for confirmation.

She nodded.

"Your ride will be at the south gate in two minutes."

"Thank you, I really appreciate that," she said quickly, not knowing what else to say.

She rounded the counter, and they both headed to the tables of breakfast foods. Dawn started placing covers on top of the trays.

"I'd walk you to the gate, but I gotta run in the other direction. I hope everything works out," he waved, then bolted toward the exit.

"Me too," Dawn whispered to herself as dread twisted her insides.

CHAPTER 2

"CAR NAVIGATION HAS been overridden by CETT security," an automated voice announced when Dawn's ride approached the restricted area of Jett Pierce's private hangar. "Please stay in the vehicle."

Clenching her jaw, Dawn stared at the rain pelting the window. The car slowed to a maddening crawl as it traversed the restricted area, frazzling Dawn's already frayed nerves. Finally, the vehicle stopped near the open hangar entrance, right beside a thin-haired man in an argyle vest, pudgy around the middle—her dad.

She jumped out of the car, flinging herself into his arms wide open. They embraced, but only for a moment before Dawn released him. Out of the corner of her eye, she saw the car driving itself away.

"I was so worried about you. What happened? Why did you leave the summit early? You couldn't just tell me over the phone?" she huffed.

The hangar bustled as androids and CETT personnel scuttled around them, inspecting the airlifts and running diagnostics.

Her dad sighed, his concerned expression changing to one of relief. He seemed in dire need of caffeine as he looked at her with bloodshot eyes.

"I'm all right, but a lot has happened," he said, his voice low and discreet, "which is why I needed to come back and talk to you. First, let me introduce my associate."

Howel turned and beckoned someone to join them.

A man in a stark white long-sleeved dress shirt approached, a noticeable limp in his step. Wrinkles lined his face, and his brown mustache and goatee twitched as he smiled cordially; if it weren't for his chestnut, feathered hair, tossing about freely in the wind, he might've looked overdressed and out of place.

"Lopple Fitch," the man said with a nod. He spoke with slurred words and an unfamiliar accent. "Pleasure to meet you."

Dawn tensed, suspecting he was drunk, yet she hadn't scented the slightest hint of liquor on him. He seemed perfectly amicable, maybe a little *too* friendly, like a salesperson whose only goal was to meet a quota. "I'm Dawn." She returned the nod, but not the smile.

Howel motioned them to follow him just as a gust of wind further ruffled Lopple's hair. They were led to one side of the hangar, out of everyone else's way, and formed a small huddle.

"Lopple is a good friend of mine. He's going to help you meet a few more friends who are part of . . ." Howel paused, searching for the right words. " . . . a clandestine council of sorts. And you will represent me."

"*That's* what was so urgent?" Dawn squeaked, her voice pitching higher than intended. She had bailed on work, and her dad had left the climate summit to attend another meeting?

"The council is meeting *today*," Howel emphasized. "It *is* an emergency. The weather fluctuations will be devastating. They verified developments yesterday during the summit, which is why they're meeting soon—"

"At a different venue," Lopple added, placing his hand on her shoulder.

Dawn glowered at Lopple. What made him think he could encroach on her personal space? It took every ounce of effort to not recoil.

Finally, he took his hand off her shoulder and whispered to Howel. "I apologize, but I must go now. They're almost here."

Her dad nodded curtly. "Meet at 1:00 p.m. You'll enter my study. That should give you enough time to prepare."

"Dawn," Lopple acknowledged her, inclining his head, "You'll need to change your attire. I'll see you soon." Then he turned to Howel with a meaningful glance before exiting the side door.

"Dad, I've never represented you at any meeting before," Dawn protested, once Lopple was gone. "What's going on? And who is that guy? I've already met all your associates."

"Sharp as always." He smiled, but it didn't reach his eyes. "These associates are from a *different* but related field. I wanted to introduce you to the council myself, but I didn't quite anticipate things would turn out this way. In any case, I've made *some* preparations, and my friends on the council are expecting you."

"Expecting me to—"

A man with a deep voice cleared his throat behind Dawn, cutting her off. She wheeled around to face Jett Pierce.

"Howel!" Jett bellowed as they exchanged greetings.

Dawn peered up at the completely bald man wearing a stylish trench coat over his purple-embellished suit. His tawny skin pulled taut, giving way to a wide, toothy grin.

For a man of his age, Jett Pierce was still impressively built. Behind him, a slender, mousy assistant stood in flats, making Jett appear even taller. A hefty bodyguard in a black suit and sunglasses stood off to the side, despite the fact that Jett didn't *need* a bodyguard. Everyone knew that the CEO of Clean Energy Tech and Transportation could hold his own in a fight.

"Dawn!" Jett's voice softened as he turned toward her. "My assistant alerted me that the airlift prototype we gave you malfunctioned this morning. I assume you were the one riding it?"

"Oh, right," Dawn said. Her dad's perplexed stare bore into her.

"Gita is summoning the replacement right now," he said, thumbing in his assistant's direction.

The petite young woman stepped forward and thrusted a mobile device in front of Dawn.

"Please enter your address and the prototype will be on its way shortly," Gita assured.

Dawn entered the family doctor's address out of habit. Hikaru Kawasaki, who they fondly referred to as their "healer," had been their on-call physician for ages, his house conveniently situated a couple blocks from theirs. Because Howel traveled for work frequently, they relocated often, including Hikaru, residing in Jett's properties around the globe. Although Howel would never admit to it, he was paranoid about privacy. Graciously, Hikaru had let them use his address for mail and deliveries throughout the years.

"Your phone," Jett presented, extending his hand that held a new, sleek device.

"You're replacing mine right now?" Dawn asked, hesitantly handing hers over.

All the tech her family used—gadgets, vehicles, computers, and AI—was manufactured by CETT.

"Yup, just copying over your data," he said, placing her old phone directly on top of the one he held. He went on to say Howel's housekeeper would stop by later to get new devices with all the bells and whistles, data copied over, and something about beefed-up security and anti-tracking. It was the same spiel every time. Then he ended by promising they could "contact Gita any time. Her info is on the devices."

Dawn looked at Gita sympathetically. Working for Jett Pierce must have its perks, but being on call twenty-four hours a day did *not* sound like fun.

A chirp indicated the process had completed, and Dawn pocketed her new device.

As a rumble of thunder and lightning lit the sky behind them, more rain pounded the hangar's roof. Jett frowned at the dark clouds.

"Shall we send you on your way?" Jett nudged Howel. "Your vehicle's ready. I observed the inspection myself."

"As always, thank you, Jett. Can you give me a moment to have a word with Dawn?" Howel asked.

"Absolutely. Gita, let's go over the rest of my appointments this afternoon," he said, heading to the front of the hangar.

Once Jett wasn't in earshot, Dawn turned to her dad. "You just got here!"

"Don't worry—I asked Jett for his best weather-proof vehicle for the flight."

"You're going to *fly*?" Dawn grimaced but remembered she had also been crazy enough to fly in this inclement weather.

"I have many things to tell you—some of which I wanted to tell you sooner but couldn't. Marion will let you in on a few secrets. I hope you'll forgive me," he said in a somber tone usually reserved for their housekeeper when tasking her with something outside her purview.

Howel stuck his hands in his pockets and teetered on the soles of his feet, a nervous tick of his.

"I wanted to see you . . . in person." He shrugged. "I'm setting up a lab and don't know how long I'll be away."

"You won't tell me where you're going?"

Ignoring the question, he pulled something out of his pocket, reached for her hand and pressed a tiny key—no longer than her fingernail—in her palm.

"This is for my journal in my study."

He closed her fingers over it. Without saying it, Dawn knew he wanted her to keep it out of sight. She stashed it in her purse.

As soon as it was secured, he hugged her and whispered, "The council is part of a secret society. They call themselves *Lumen*."

Dawn pulled away and narrowed her eyes at him, waiting for an explanation that never came. He turned to look beyond the hangar's opening and Dawn followed his gaze. Something zipped by—it almost looked like a giant bird, silhouetted by a flash of lightning.

"I trust Lopple," Howel said slowly. "He'll help you navigate the path set before you."

Typically cryptic of him, Dawn thought, like he was telling a riddle during dinner. What was it that he so desperately wanted to tell her yet couldn't? She stood beside him, his arm around her shoulder, as he admired the steady downpour. He loved the rain, welcomed the dreary weather that reminded him of London.

In their silence, Jett and Gita made their way back to them.

"Let's see Dawn off first," Howel said to his old friend. "I have a few questions about the vehicle you'll be loaning me."

Jett nodded in agreement and confirmed the new prototype car for Dawn was on its way.

They walked toward the hangar entrance, and soon after, a shiny, silver vehicle pulled up near the front. Jett's bodyguard tapped the door with his black-gloved hand, and it slid open. Ducking inside, Dawn searched her dad's eyes.

"Can you at least call me when you get to wherever you're going?"

"I'll be in touch," Howel said with a wave. As the door began to shut, he reminded her to meet Lopple in the study at 1:00 p.m.

Dawn watched from the window as the car shuttled her away from the hangar, Jett, and her dad.

By the time the car pulled up to Hikaru's contemporary cottage, the rain was pouring as if the skies held a grudge against their Beverly Hills neighborhood. Dawn made sure to turn off the navigation completely before putting the car in manual mode. Then she drove it two blocks down, to the house with the white, wrought iron gate—the sprawling property Jett was letting them occupy. She parked in the garage and went through the side door that led to the reception room.

Their large Siberian husky's paws padded the hardwood floor as he ran to greet her, his gray and white tail wagging furiously.

"Hey, Hiro. Marion's not home yet?" Dawn absentmindedly asked the faithful canine.

He looked up at her with his piercing blue eyes, tongue hanging out of his mouth. She gave him a scratch behind his ears before running upstairs to her room. Dawn hung her coat and put away her purse before heading to the kitchen. Her stomach growled loudly.

On the counter, a tray with a glass of water and a covered plate caught her eye. A mix of sweet and savory smells made her salivate as she lifted the cover to reveal a Filipino rice cake called bibingka, an apple, and a pizzant—a pizza-stuffed croissant, topped with melted mozzarella shreds.

"Miss M., you really do think of everything," Dawn said.

Grasping the tray in both hands, she made her way to the study. Dawn nudged the sliding door open with her foot, and the light automatically turned on. Crossing the room, she set her lunch on the desk while Hiro plopped down in the middle of the Monte Carlo rug.

Settling into her dad's swivel chair, she wasted no time inhaling the bibingka, peeling back the banana leaves it was wrapped in—its sweet and salty flavor profile melting in her mouth with every bite. She glanced at the door next to the windows, which led to their backyard. It was strange that her dad would want Lopple to meet at the entrance to his study. It meant he'd need to fly and land a vehicle in their backyard. Was it that much trouble to knock on the front door?

She finished off the rice cake, savoring the cream cheese, and leaned back in the chair, contemplating. Switching gears, she rummaged through the desk drawers, looking for her dad's journal. Not there.

Swiveling the chair, she scanned the opposite wall. Across the room were recessed bookshelves, a bed sheet draped over a cheval mirror, and a closet door. It would take forever to go through all the books on his shelves.

She spun the chair back around and scanned the surface of his desk, eyeing a stack of loose papers, a desk lamp, and an Ormolu clock. It was almost 1:00 p.m. Where would he hide a journal? Instinctively, she lifted the stack of papers—and there it was—a cognac, hardcover book.

Dawn carefully picked up the journal, running her fingers over the embossed leaf design. In the cover, where one would've expected a keyhole, was a deeply debossed design of a key—the same tiny size as the one her dad gave her. But there was no locking mechanism.

She opened the book and flipped through the pages, puzzled. Not only was it not locked, the pages were mostly blank. Mementos were taped to some pages—a long, black feather, a photo of Howel in his younger days with friends, and random news clippings.

Of course her dad would make his journal a riddle. No surprise there. She flipped back to the black feather, which was almost the full page length.

Curiously, she traced her fingers over the paper around the feather, feeling the indents and scratches on its surface. Switching on the desk lamp, she examined the page. There were marks a pen pressed into the paper would make—a pen *without* ink.

The key might give her more clues. She sprang up from the chair, ready to bolt upstairs and retrieve it from her purse, but something startled Hiro. He leapt to his feet a second before she did, growling at the opposite side of the room, his fur and ears sticking straight up.

Tap, tap. The sound of someone knocking on glass made her jump. It was loud enough to be heard even with all the rainfall. Dawn glanced at the clock, now 1:00 p.m., and slid her attention to the drawn window shades. Lopple must be outside.

Tap, tap. Her head snapped in the direction of the closet door. No, it was coming from the *mirror* under the sheet, Dawn realized, suddenly freaked out. Hiro barked a warning to an unseen intruder.

"Dawn?" Lopple ventured, his disembodied voice muffled beneath the sheet. "Don't be afraid. It's me, Lopple."

Hiro snarled, bearing his sharp canine teeth.

"L-Lopple?" Dawn squeaked. "Where are you?" She shushed Hiro and patted his head without taking her eyes off the mirror.

"At the bridge," Lopple said, clearer. "You'll need to open it so I can cross."

"At the bridge," Dawn repeated slowly. "I'm not sure what that means, exactly."

"Do you see a mirror anywhere?"

"Yes, I'm sure there's one under the sheet." *I just don't want to uncover it*, she thought but didn't say.

"If you remove the sheet, I can instruct you on how to let me cross the bri—er, come through the glass."

"Can you come through the door instead?" Dawn asked, unnerved.

"The mirror is more secure," Lopple insisted. "Howel and I always travel by bridge."

She knit her brows in confusion.

"The mirror is the fastest, safest way," Lopple said after a long pause. "And you'll be traveling by bridge to the council meeting. You still there?"

"Uh, yes. Just a minute . . . I'm figuring out how to . . ." Dawn trailed off, still processing what he just said. *I'll be traveling by bridge? What in the world . . .*

Her eyes flicked to Hiro, who was prepared to pounce.

She took a calming breath, then stepped toward the shrouded mirror. It stood a few inches taller than her and just wider than her shoulders. A cold, clammy sweat formed on her brow and palms. Heart pounding, she crouched down and took hold of the bottom of the sheet, and as she stood, gave it one strong yank.

The sheet fell to the floor and Dawn gasped as she took a step back. Instead of her horrified reflection, there stood Lopple, inexplicably behind the glass, hands clasped behind his back. It was like looking into a tunnel from a window. There was a soft glow to him, but his surroundings were dark and misty. He wasn't outside getting rained on. In fact, he looked dry—in the same clothes from earlier.

"May I come in?" Lopple asked politely.

Dawn rounded the mirror, peering behind it. Nothing looked unusual—it hinged on two oak legs and had a flat, silver backing. She stepped back in front of it, taking note of its oval shape and the antique metalwork that framed the top and bottom. Bright-colored gems asymmetrically embedded the metal, enhancing the adornment. A green-banded gemstone, the size of the golf ball, lay at the top of the frame.

Dawn moved to the other side around Hiro and noticed Lopple's eyes hadn't tracked her.

"Can you see me?" she asked.

"No, Howel's side of the bridge is closed," Lopple said, raking a hand through his hair. "It means I'm unable to view his side of the portal, and unless someone is there to open the bridge, I can't cross it."

"How is this even *possible*?"

"The energy from the embedded gem and crystals are inter-twined with stones on other portals, creating a vast network of bridges," Lopple explained patiently. "Some gemstones, such as the black agate that your father has on his bridge, counter the energies of others, essentially locking the bridge."

"Right," she drawled after he responded to her rhetorical question. He sure had a lot to say about gems. She skeptically scanned the frame and found a gleaming black stone that eerily resembled a glassy eye, nestled to the right of the centered green jewel.

"So, you're saying these are *magic* jewels? Which can open *magic* portals?"

"Well, no," he said, rubbing his goatee. "Basically, it's energy. Lumen need to harness their aura—which your people sometimes call *chi*—to control the energies of the jewels."

Dawn snapped to attention at the mention of Lumen. Her dad said something about them. Was Lopple a Lumen?

"How am I supposed to unlock this thing?"

"I can channel my aura through you if you place one hand on the glass and the other on the black gem."

She glanced sideways at Hiro, who had stopped growling and sat on his haunches.

"All right," she said nervously.

Lopple laid his palm flat against the glass. "Place one hand where mine is, and touch the black jewel with the other," he instructed.

Stepping closer to the mirror, she hesitated. "This isn't going to hurt, is it?"

"Not at all."

She placed her left palm where Lopple's was, the glass cool to the touch, then reached up with her right and placed two fingers on the black stone.

Lopple narrowed his eyes, and immediately, Dawn felt warmth in her palm. It was radiating . . . and pulsing. The heat traveled through her arm, across her shoulders and into her right arm, eventually reaching her fingertips on the stone.

The glass swirled, like mercury mixing with blue steel. She gasped as she felt Lopple's hand against hers, pushing her backward.

Dawn withdrew her hands and staggered back, bumping into Howel's desk. Hiro resumed his attack stance, growling at the stranger who limped through the liquid-like glass.

"H-how did you . . . wh-where did you come from?" Dawn stammered.

Thunder roared outside and shook the entire house. Lopple hobbled backward toward the mirror, nearly losing his balance. His wide eyes flitted to the window, then to Hiro's bared teeth and back to Dawn. She recognized the look in his eyes: fear.

Lopple swallowed and appeared to gather his wits.

"For starters," he said, straightening his spine, "I-I'm from a place that doesn't have crazy thunderstorms like this."

Two could play at this game. Dawn curled her fingers into fists and straightened herself as well. She wanted—no, she *deserved*—answers.

"Why haven't you or my dad told me what is *really* going on here?" she snapped. "What's this council meeting we're supposed to be going to? Are there going to be more Lumen people there, like—like *you*?" Whatever a Lumen was, surely he was one of them.

"*We* are not going," he said sharply. "*You* are going. And it has to be soon." He glanced at his wristwatch with two faces on a wide strap.

Dawn crossed her arms and glared at him.

"Please," he said, softening his tone. "Your *father* needs you to trust me. And you have my word—I'll explain what I can now, and the rest later."

The anger bubbling up inside Dawn faded, and even Hiro stopped snarling. Although she hated to admit it, Lopple was right. Her dad made it clear this emergency meeting was immensely important. A thought occurred to Dawn as she grappled with all she had witnessed in the last five minutes: There was so much she didn't know about her dad. She hadn't even known he kept a journal.

"Fine," she conceded. "How much time do we have?"

"Just enough time for me to brief you."

A gurgling sound came from Lopple, and he held his stomach in embarrassment. He looked at the desk behind Dawn.

"May I ask what that is?" he said, eyeing the desk.

Dawn followed his gaze to the tray.

"It's a pizzant, a pizza-stuffed croissant. It's yours if you want it," she motioned to the chair, inviting him to sit.

Before she could finish her offer, Lopple was already hobbling over to the desk. He flinched as he eased himself into the chair.

"Thank you," he said, and held up the morsel to take a giant bite out of it.

"You said you wouldn't be accompanying me. Why is that?" she pressed, watching him devour the pizzant in two bites. "How can you expect me to be prepared for this meeting?"

Lopple bit into the apple and chewed noisily. "All you need to do is make an appearance." Fishing a small flask from his pocket, he unscrewed the top, drained it, and continued to chomp down the fruit. "You will go alone. That was the plan."

"I don't see what my presence alone would accomplish. By the way, I have a vehicle with airlift capabilities from Jett, so both of us can travel."

Lopple shook his head. "The meeting place is in Tencho."

"Where's that?"

"East of Tokyo," he said, nibbling at what was left of the apple's thin core.

Dawn's eyes widened. "One of Japan's water-floating cities?"

Even if the weather permitted, there was no way Jett's commuter airlift could fly them halfway around the world.

"It's not quite a *water*-floating city, but it's *east* of Japan," Lopple burped. "Pardon me," he said, sounding surprised with himself. "Listen—I *cannot* go with you. I apologize for . . . withholding information." His voice dropped low. "You *will* encounter Lumen there. They have mastered their auras, they can read minds and communicate telepathically, they can change the form of their physical appearance. For reasons I can't say now, it is paramount to keep my identity a secret."

He punctuated every hushed word with a pleading tone, concern rippling over his face. Lopple was talking about people with super-powers—people who could hear them right now. The thought sent a shudder through Dawn. After seeing him walk through a mirror, how could she know what was possible or impossible anymore? Then another thought struck her. *Can he read* my *mind?*

"I don't mean to sound rude," he said, before she could dwell on the idea any longer, "but do you have another outfit? Your attire would draw attention."

Dawn narrowed her eyes at him.

24

"A warm shirt, trousers for cold weather, and comfortable shoes for fly—er, walking will suffice," Lopple said, slightly slurring his words again.

She told him to wait in the study, and a minute later she came back wearing a white, long-sleeved shirt, charcoal hiking pants, and black flats.

"That'll do," he said, taking one look at what she had donned.

He shuffled across the room and opened her dad's closet door without hesitation. A few coats hung inside. Lopple took a light gray one off the hanger and tossed it to Dawn, who caught it with ease. She held the soft fabric against herself in front of the mirror, its hem falling just below her ankles. The fabric was fascinating, changing color from white to gray, depending on how the light struck it.

She threw it around her shoulders and put her arms through the slits, realizing it had a loose hood and could be worn like a cloak or cape.

"Time to go," Lopple said, glancing at his dual-time watch, "or you'll miss your ride."

"My ride?" Dawn asked, whipping her phone out of her pocket. "I'm getting there through the mirror, right?"

"The bridge is the first part of the journey. Others will assist you to Tencho and back."

She quickly messaged Marion that she was leaving the house, and that dad's friend Lopple, was in the study.

"Oh, I almost forgot," Lopple said. "Your communication devices are forbidden."

Scowling, she placed her phone on the desk, knowing that Lopple wouldn't be able to access it without her biometrics anyway. As she approached the mirror with no cell phone, no identification, and no money, she traded frowns with Lopple in the mirror's reflection. She really *was* putting blind faith in her dad's associate—and others she had yet to meet.

"Miss Marion, our housekeeper, will be here soon," she warned, in case he had plans to ransack the house in her absence.

"I'll wait right here." His attention darted to Hiro. "Marion and I are acquainted."

With his fingertips, Lopple hovered over the green jewel at the top of the mirror frame. Dawn watched as her reflection, a light brown-skinned young woman with a worried face, faded in the swirls of silver and blue.

"You're just there to make an appearance," he said, as if that was supposed to help put her mind at ease.

Great advice, she thought, but only grimly muttered, "Thanks."

Dawn inhaled and held her breath as if she were going to jump into water, then she stepped through the bridge and into the unknown.

CHAPTER 3

THE SENSATION OF stepping through a magic mirror—or enchanted portal or bridge or whatever other name—was completely foreign to Dawn. The liquid-looking glass had swirled, but it wasn't in any way wet or sticky.

A biting wind batted at her. She pulled her hood on and clenched her jaw to keep her teeth from chattering. What had happened to the thunderstorm? Oh, right. It was on the other side of the world.

Fog was everywhere, thick and dense. A few yards away, ashen blobs the size of elephants moved ever so slightly, and they encircled her. Beyond the blob creatures was a blue sky with a hint of pink. She blinked rapidly, forcing her surroundings to come into sharper focus.

The creatures weren't elephants. They were feathered—birds, gargantuan in size—four of them, all varying shades of white, gray, and black. One was noticeably all black—even its hooked beak gleamed like oil. Its feet were hidden underneath the heavy mist, and it had matching straps across its body. Something stirred on its back.

Not something. Some*one*.

A striking woman, also cloaked in black, sat atop a saddle on the giant bird. She had an alluring look with dark fox eyes, but her cheeks brought a touch of color to her delicate complexion. Both coldness and warmth emanated from her. The woman turned to a man sitting atop the ash-feathered beast next to her, shooting him a look. Then they both turned to look at Dawn.

All the creatures had a cloaked rider—and everyone now had their scrutinizing eyes on her. They remained silent. Were they communicating telepathically?

The man on the ashen bird spoke to her, loud enough for everyone to hear.

Dawn's cheeks burned. She couldn't understand a word he'd said. Lopple had said nothing about knowing a foreign language.

"I—I didn't understand that," she stammered, "but my name is Dawn. I'm the daughter of Howel Farringdon . . ."

Maybe coming here had been a mistake. But then the man dismounted his ashen bird, jumping down onto an unseen platform. She watched, awestruck, as he took three effortless leaps to where she was standing. Gaping down at him, she realized he was an entire foot shorter than she was.

"Dalton Crimpletott, at your service," the man said in a cheery English accent, gazing up at her. He bounced slightly as he spoke, his blond curls peeking out from underneath his hood. "Come—you'll be riding with me."

He smirked impishly and spun around before she could respond, taking a couple of light-footed leaps toward his bird. Dawn ran to keep up with him. He really *was* floating while leaping, his fitted, white cloak billowing behind him.

When they reached his bird, he reached up with gloved hands to pat its wing.

"This is Fenno, my diurlax," he beamed with pride.

Fenno, who was slightly smaller than the other birds, was still enormous in comparison to Dalton. The bird bent down and nuzzled Dalton with its beak, which was large enough to swallow him whole.

"Wow, he's amazing!" Dawn said, unable to hide her excitement. "Can I pet him?"

"You may pet *her*," Dalton emphasized.

She cautiously stroked Fenno's feathers. At a distance, her plumage had looked like a blend of light gray and white, similar to her dad's cloak, but up close, it glistened with a metallic sheen. A grin bloomed across her face as she took in the magnificent creature—a *diurlax*. When the diurlax rose to full height, Dalton took one incredible leap to mount Fenno, and Dawn's mouth fell open.

Dalton encouraged her to hop on, but after searching for something like a rope to grip and finding nothing, she concluded he must've expected her to leap up the same way he had. She looked up at him helplessly.

"Come on, Fenno," he coached.

The diurlax instantly stooped down low enough for Dawn to climb onto her back. Dalton, who had his feet in stirrups about a foot apart, was leaning forward against Fenno instead of straddling, while his hands each gripped two hornlike handles positioned outside of his shoulders, as though he was doing a pushup. Dawn spotted two additional horns and stirrups positioned for a second rider. The dwarf instructed her to hold the horns and put one foot in the stirrup, then hoist herself up and place the other foot—much like mounting a horse.

Dawn did as instructed but missed putting her other foot in the stirrup on the first attempt. Her chin hit Dalton's back.

"Sorry," she whispered.

"I'm all right," he said. "You can put your weight on me—the harnesses were designed for tandem riders to be on our stomachs."

Dawn got her other foot in the stirrup and awkwardly rested her chin on his back. The diurlax rose to full height again, and Dawn felt a rush of giddiness being high off the platform. Now that Fenno was upright, they were both in more of a standing position.

She wondered if there were any belts or straps to hold them in, and must've done so aloud because Dalton replied, "Not on this harness, but diurlaxes are expert gliders. Don't be afraid, your father has never fallen off before."

She breathed a sigh of relief, remembering that these were her dad's friends. "How do you know my dad, Mr. Crimple—Crimpletott, was it?"

"Call me Dalton," he smiled while trying to crane his neck to look back at her. "Your father and I have known each other for a while. I was wondering when he'd let you meet us."

A sudden pang of resentment hit her. When did her dad plan on telling her about all *this*? Dalton must have sensed her discomfort.

He turned his head back and whispered, "I'm glad today's the day."

Despite feeling left in the dark, an overwhelming sense of assurance came over Dawn. She surveyed her view on top of the diurlax, no trees or buildings in sight, and she asked how high up they were. Dalton informed her they were high enough not to be discovered, then pointed to a tuft of clouds in the distance, their destination: Mount Tencho.

Squinting in the direction he pointed to, she only saw wisps of clouds. No mountain. He laughed at her and assured her, "You'll see it. When we cross the barrier shield."

Dawn caught sight of another rider who had leapt off his diurlax and flitted toward the bridge. Next to it, there was a recessed area in the platform where the fog parted.

"We're awaiting the last guests," Dalton said, also directing his attention to the rider who was unhooded, revealing his dark, medium-length mane and trimmed beard. He carried a gray bundle of cloth.

"See where the mist parts on the platform?" Dalton inclined his head. "It's a small pool with another bridge submerged in it. We have Aquavi representatives on the council."

"Uh-KWA-vee?" Dawn repeated.

Dalton nodded. "People of the water."

The bridge in the clear waters of the pool turned a shimmery, dark blue. A young woman passed through the mirror headfirst, then her upper torso, and lastly—where Dawn had expected to see legs—the girl's blue-green fishtail.

"She's a mermaid?!" Dawn's eyebrows shot skyward.

Dalton turned to see her shock and laughed. "You should see your face!"

Dawn shut her dropped jaw. The slender mermaid swam around the mirror once and then slowed to a stop, making herself upright. The mermaid was no longer a mermaid. In a moment, her tail turned into swaths of cloth, and in the next, she walked up the stairs from the small pool.

She emerged from the water, wearing a long, blue-green skirt, dark hair wound tightly atop her head, her tanned shoulders exposed from the heart-shaped bodice top. She watched in amusement as the cloaked man unraveled the cloth bundle he carried. It was two cloaks—one of which he wrapped hastily around her dripping body. He held out the other cloak behind the woman, just as a second

Aquavian—a lanky youth in board shorts and a cloth wrap around his waist—emerged.

"Who's the mermaid?" Dawn whispered, eyes straying back to her.

"Her name is Laurel. She's an Aquavian princess. The bony boy traveling with her is Reed, and their people prefer 'finfolk,'" he said matter of factly. "The man assisting her is an Etheran flier—like me. His name is Ezra, her betrothed."

Ezra wordlessly pointed to another flier, and Reed, who had followed Laurel from the pool, ran toward the rider Ezra had pointed to. The Aquavian princess turned to look directly at Dawn—their eyes met for a brief moment—before Laurel pulled her hood on.

Dawn continued staring, mesmerized by these strange people who could shift from mythical creatures into humans. Ezra turned his back to the princess and crouched down, letting her climb on his back and wrap her arms around his shoulders. Then he flitted back to his diurlax and the two of them mounted.

With everyone harnessed, two riders on each bird, except for the commander, the diurlaxes shuffled about, lining up for flight.

Then, one after the other, the birds began diving off the edge of the platform where the fog poured down like a waterfall. Fenno, who was last, jerked forward, awaiting her turn. Dalton turned his head to the side—a look of pure glee on his face—and shouted to hang on just before the feathered beast dove into the air.

Hands slick with sweat, Dawn shut her eyes, gripping the horns for dear life. She couldn't hold back her scream, thrilled and terrified at the same time. As Fenno started to level off and glide, the effects of zero gravity spawned a thousand butterflies in Dawn's stomach.

"Relax!" Dalton yelled. "Open your eyes. You're missing the view!"

How did he know my eyes were closed?

The butterflies-in-her-stomach feeling waned as Fenno soared, and Dawn slowly forced her eyes open. Dalton wasn't wrong. Beyond Fenno's wingspan she could see a layer of pink-hued clouds far below. The sky was a canvas painted with swaths of golds, yellows, reds, and all the blended colors in between, that glowed brighter as they approached the rising sun.

"What do you think?" Dalton yelled back again.

"It's . . . this is . . . I can't even . . ." Dawn sputtered.

"Unbelievable, isn't it?"

"Yeah," Dawn laughed, elated.

They flew in silence for a long stretch, and eventually, Dawn relaxed her grip. In perfect harmony, the small flock flew in diagonal formation, led by the commander's black diurlax. When it flapped its wings, the others followed like dominoes. When the black bird climbed higher, the others did the same. Then it banked left, but Ezra's diurlax didn't follow. The commander had rounded the flock and trailed Fenno, letting Ezra and Laurel take the lead.

As they approached the tuft of clouds Dawn had seen from the platform, the two diurlaxes ahead of them broke formation. They flew dangerously close, one overtaking the other, speeding toward the finish. Dawn's vision became obscured as they entered a misty patch, but she could hear the others laughing and whooping as they raced. Their energy was contagious, and she, too, found herself laughing and hollering with Dalton.

Soon the fog cleared and gave way to a towering stone mountain range, which appeared out of nowhere.

Laurel let out a high-pitched howl, just as her and Ezra's diurlax flew upward into a loop. In the corner of her eye, she saw the commander's black bird catching up to Fenno, nearly flying alongside them.

"Hang on tight!" Dalton yelled as Fenno jerked north.

But Dawn wasn't ready. The shift in weight was unexpected and she went from lying on her stomach to vertical in a heartbeat, her grip too relaxed. As the horns left the reach of her fingertips and her feet unmounted the stirrups, she fell backward. She cried out and grasped—in slow motion—for anything to hold on to but only clutched at air.

CHAPTER 4

HORRIFIED, DAWN WATCHED Fenno ascend without her. The bird's tail feathers were visible, but they were leaving her line of sight as she free-fell.

Dawn screamed, limbs flailing. She caught a glimpse of Dalton's shocked face as he turned back to see her completely out of reach. After that, everything became a blur—mountain, sky, diurlaxes—as she tumbled through the air.

Her survival instincts kicked in. She hadn't come here to die. *Straighten out and slow your fall*, she told herself, attempting to keep the panic at bay.

Dawn flung her arms out and arched her back, forcing her body into an *X* shape with her limbs. Immediately, the cloak took up more area and created drag. She stopped tumbling, and although she was dizzy, she was now falling like a skydiver, just like she learned the previous summer.

If I unfasten my cloak from the shoulder, she thought, *I could create more resistance.*

Now that she was accelerating, it was harder to move. She managed to unfasten her cloak in the second attempt, and, holding on tightly to the fabric, she stretched her arms open. It was working!

She could see the layer of clouds beneath her quickly approaching. But something suddenly tugged at her cloak. She glimpsed a diurlax's ashen body overhead, diving with her. Its claws wrapped around her upper arms, then its wings spread to stop its dive, effectively yanking the cloak from Dawn's body.

She cried out as the sudden jolt sent her flailing again. A second set of claws grabbed her upper arms—tighter, this time. Sharp talons dug into her skin as they yanked her skyward. Head throbbing, she looked up and saw jet-black wings flapping hard to ascend. Dawn's vision went blurry, and she fought to keep her eyes half open.

After drawing a shaky breath, she could see the mountain in the sky again. Her arms ached as the diurlax's grip on her tightened, but at least she was certain she wouldn't slip away. They neared the gray stone of the mountain, peppered with greenery and wildlife. Goats scaled the steep rock face. As breathtaking as it was, Dawn couldn't admire it as much as she wanted to, not with all her lightheadedness.

Ahead, Dawn spotted the foot of the mountain where the other riders waited, their diurlaxes already dispatched somewhere. The black diurlax descended to the area too quickly for Dawn's liking, and she let out a soft groan when she felt a flutter in her gut. Before her feet touched the ground, the bird flapped its wings hard, kicking up dust as it gently lowered her, then released her.

Dawn was only a foot off the stone-hard surface, but hitting it sent a shock wave from her feet that went all the way to the top of her aching head. The diurlax then maneuvered to her left and landed, sending up small dust clouds around them.

Falling to her knees, Dawn hunched over and threw up just as a few of the riders ran to her. She looked up and saw Dalton, who had worry written all over his face.

As the gentle breeze cooled her clammy forehead and sent a shiver down her back, Dalton uttered profuse apologies and wrapped her dad's torn cloak over her shoulders.

The commander approached, scowling at Dalton. She was clearly much younger than him, but he hung his head, like a young child being scolded. Dawn attempted to thank the intimidating woman for rescuing her, recognizing it had been her diurlax who had successfully caught her in midair.

The commander, however, kept her cold eyes on Dalton and barked orders through gritted teeth to clean up the mess. Then she flitted to the foot of the mountain and disappeared through an arched opening.

"I'm sorry," Dawn croaked.

"You shouldn't be the one apologizing, dear!" Dalton replied. "I'm the one to blame. I'll fetch something to clean up. You three go on ahead." Then he flitted away through the archway.

The Aquavian princess knelt near Dawn on one side, and her betrothed stood on the other side. She patted Dawn's back comfortingly and volunteered Ezra to help carry her.

Initially, Dawn insisted she'd be fine and waved them off, but as soon as she stood up, her legs quivered like Jello.

Laurel linked her arm through Dawn's, and Ezra—who was still cloaked—did the same on the other side to support their wobbly guest. Laurel's thin and slender frame made her seem deceivingly small. The princess was much taller than she'd thought and surprisingly strong.

They approached the same archway the commander had gone through. It was a dimly lit passageway lined with doors and branches to other passages within the mountain, but the couple didn't have any trouble navigating it. They took a left, and Ezra opened the first wooden door in the wall then let them file in.

The room glowed with white light. The low ceiling had recessed lighting—or so Dawn thought. She squinted at the lights, impressed they had electricity in this floating mountain range, but soon realized they weren't bulbs—they were white gemstones, the size of her fist, shining brightly to illuminate the room.

Laurel left Dawn standing where she was and disappeared behind a paneled partition made of wood and paper. A delicate cherry blossom design was painted on it. Dawn spun around and spotted Ezra on the other side of the spacious room, removing his cloak and hanging it on a hook in the wall. She quickly averted her eyes to give him privacy.

"Thanks for helping me," Dawn breathed, loud enough for both Laurel and Ezra to hear.

"Of course," Laurel called from behind the partition. "What's your name?"

"Dawn . . . Farringdon," she hesitated. "I'm really just here as a stand-in for my dad."

"Me too," Laurel said from behind her partition. It occurred to Dawn just then that Laurel, who was a princess, was likely the daughter of a king. Still speaking from behind the partition, she introduced herself as Laurel Benevis, then introduced her friend, Ezra Valedor.

Ezra poked his head out from his own partition, revealing his cedar-colored hair, slightly scruffy face, and tanned skin. "I'm her intended!" he scoffed.

Laurel snorted. Dawn could tell that their playful bickering was nothing new. They traded a few barbs, including one in which Laurel mentioned Ezra was old enough to be her father. Instead of taking offense, he replied with a hearty laugh and said that was a good one. (He wasn't *that* old, Dawn thought, but might've been a decade older than Laurel.) After their teasing died down, Dawn asked the name of the commander.

"The commander?" Ezra asked. He came out from behind the partition wearing black pants and a white, long-sleeved shirt with a kimono style V-neck that suited his medium build.

"Yes, the rider on the black diurlax."

"She is the ruling Lord of Mount Tencho," he said, putting on a thin, dark blue cloak that was more suited for indoors. "She is a direct descendant of the Valedorian bloodline."

Is everyone here royalty? It was probably safe to assume that—on top of everyone having superpowers. "Got it—my mistake," Dawn said, fiddling with her pendant.

"Don't apologize," Laurel interjected, popping her head out. "Her name is Angel Rockwood. We all know you're a groundling—er, new here. It takes a while to get adjusted. It took me some time as well."

"You may call her *Lord* Angel," Ezra clarified.

An awkward silence followed their exchange and Dawn took that as a cue to stop asking questions. She didn't know what it meant to be a *groundling*, nor did she have any clue how important this Valedorian bloodline was to them. She was grateful for a switch in topic when Laurel beckoned her to change into the extra dress she had.

With legs still shaky, Dawn made her way to Laurel, who was already dressed in a pale blue, wrap dress made of soft linen. It went down to her ankles, and the sleeves were long and wide, covering part of her hands. How she had managed to completely dry off without any towels remained a mystery. The princess's blue-green skirt and bodice were neatly folded and tucked on the shelf carved directly into the stone wall.

Laurel pulled out another wrap dress from the shelf and held the cream-colored cloth up against Dawn. It was half a foot too long since she was shorter than Laurel, but she hung her torn cloak on a nearby hook and put the dress over her clothes anyway.

When the three of them were ready to leave, Laurel hooked her arm through Dawn's and led her out into the dimly lit tunnel once again. Behind them, Ezra closed the door, and the light from the gemstones vanished, making the passage even darker. Still, Laurel had no trouble leading the way in the dark through the maze-like tunnels. Evidently, she had been to Mount Tencho enough times to navigate its complex labyrinth.

Dawn could barely make out the doors they passed alongside the walls. As her eyes continued to adjust to the darkness, she began to see that smaller jewels encrusted on the stone walls started to glow as they approached, lighting their steps.

"The gems on the walls are . . . glowing," Dawn half-stated, half-asked.

"Yes. I thought you'd like to be able to see where you're going," Ezra said behind her.

"You're *making* that happen?"

"Yes," he replied as if he was saying something as trivial as "cats say meow."

Laurel suddenly pointed and took a sharp turn to the right. This part of the passage had light at the end of the tunnel. Dawn squinted and held up a hand to shield her eyes from the brightness as they exited onto a wooden platform and courtyard. Laurel unlinked her arm and walked ahead as Dawn stopped to marvel at her surroundings.

The mountain rock itself had been cut into on multiple levels like an apartment complex, and the courtyard was where the floors opened up to windows and balconies. To the south, the rock jutted up higher into the distant clouds, which hid the mountain's peak. She imagined the entire mountain was tiara shaped, and they were somewhere near the tip of the circlet.

"Welcome to the Etheran realm," Ezra said, standing next to her. He must've found her expression amusing. "What do you think about our mountain in the sky?"

"It's definitely not a *water*-floating city," she scoffed, remembering Lopple's words. She had never imagined anything like this could actually exist—a floating mountain range, feathered beasts, mermaids, and magic mirrors. Sure, she had read about fantastical creatures and places in books and seen them in movies, but this was different. This was insane.

Am I going crazy?

"It feels like it's a dream, but I don't think I could ever dream any of this up," she said with a wild grin.

Ezra looked into her eyes, forming a connection that felt more real than anything she had witnessed in the last half hour. "This is better than a dream. It's real life."

"Are you coming?" Laurel called from across the serene, Japanese-inspired courtyard.

They caught up with her, then Ezra took lead and motioned for Laurel and Dawn to enter another dimly lit passage. This time, Ezra set a faster pace. After a few minutes of traversing the maze-like passages, they reached the bottom of a flight of steep, stone stairs that seemed to disappear through a nearly vertical tunnel. Dawn, who was struggling to catch her breath, took one look at the challenge ahead and slumped against the wall—it was all she could do to keep her knees from buckling.

Wiping the sweat off her forehead with the back of her hand, she breathed faintly, "I just need a minute."

"That wasn't very convincing," Laurel bluntly pointed out. "This place has its own atmosphere, but the elevation might be taking a toll on you. Let Ezra carry you."

Dawn hesitated but then nodded. Ezra, who didn't seem to mind one bit, turned his back to her and bent down. Dawn nearly fell on him but locked her arms around his neck to keep from sliding. As he stood and hoisted her up, Dawn wished she were less of an inconvenience. Up the steps he went, right behind Laurel.

Dawn counted the stairs as Ezra climbed, but after thirty, she lost track. Ezra hadn't slowed down at all. Perhaps he was used to the elevation. Maybe this mountain was his home.

A moment later, Laurel cheered as she cleared the last step. She ran off to talk to someone standing in front of the meeting room.

Ezra continued down the passage that started to glow. White gemstones on the ceiling lit their path like moonlight as they approached a door at the end of the hall.

"You can put me down now," Dawn breathed.

Ezra knelt at once, and Dawn steadied her feet on the floor.

"Are you all right?" Ezra asked, getting up as both of them walked toward Laurel.

"*Me?* Yes, I'm fine, thanks. Are *you* all right? That flight of stairs was endless." She checked his face. He hadn't even broken a sweat.

"Yes, well, when you grow up chasing goats on the crags for fun, going up some stairs is nothing," he shrugged.

"Ha! Is that so?" laughed the woman who had been chatting with Laurel. She was cloaked in white and had a dark brown braid that fell to her waist. "I always thought the goats were chasing *you*, brother."

Laurel snickered and Ezra waved off the jab.

"This is my sister, Stralla," he said with a playful smirk. "Don't mind her. She's but a lowly guard at the door."

Dawn said hi and waved—that was all they had time for—then quickly followed Laurel and Ezra into the council room, leaving Stralla outside.

Unlike the changing room from earlier, which had consisted mostly of stone, this one was fashioned in wood and had wide windows that spanned across the wall, opposite the door. The drawn paper shades made it impossible to see outside, but they filtered in the morning light.

The woman in black stood in front of a long, birch table where most guests were already seated. She wore flowy, kendo-like pants and a top with shoulder cutouts and the same wide sleeves as Laurel. Her straight, obsidian tresses flowed to her waist. The fiery demeanor she had displayed earlier was replaced with a calm visage. While she stood at the same height as Dawn, Lord Angel's impeccable poise gave the impression that she was standing atop a pedestal.

Angel welcomed the trio, introduced herself as the administrator of the council, then invited them to sit, motioning gracefully toward the empty chairs at the table.

The friendly chatter between guests in the room ceased. All eyes locked on the three of them, eager to get started. Dawn followed Laurel to the other side of the table where the backs of the chairs faced the window.

Laurel took the empty seat at the middle of the table, leaving the one near the end for Dawn. Ezra took the seat at Angel's right-hand side.

He has a higher rank, she guessed.

Laurel picked up the glass pitcher at the center of the table, next to a bowl of exotic fruits, and poured herself a tall glass of water. Then she poured another and offered it to Dawn.

Dawn watched as her newfound friend lifted her own glass, clinked it with hers in cheers, and proceeded to chug it down like someone who had wandered the desert for days.

Feeling thirsty herself, Dawn picked up her glass and raised it to her lips, side glancing at the others sitting at the table. All eyes were on them. She took a discreet sip, then paused. The water possessed a hint of sweetness and a refreshing coolness. She resumed gulping down more of it and tried to resist chugging it as Laurel had done but failed.

Laurel slammed her glass down on the table and exhaled, "Aaah!" for all to hear.

Dawn nearly choked on her drink, certain that Laurel had just broken a social norm. Those who were still balking at them were giving annoyed grimaces, and everyone else was too embarrassed to maintain eye contact.

Angel cleared her throat, drawing everyone's attention as she stood as still as a statue at the front of the room. Just then, the door at the other side of the room swung open to reveal a disheveled Dalton. He hastily shut the door and ran to his seat directly across from Dawn, who breathed a sigh of relief to no longer be in the limelight. Angel waited until Dalton seemed settled before continuing.

"Friends, I have summoned you here because of recent developments some of you may already be aware of." Angel turned to Laurel and Reed, addressing them in her velvety voice. "Princess Laurel and Reed Blackfin, thank you for coming on short notice as guests to our council. I am sure that your fathers, King Kameo and his chronicler, are tending to the matter we had previously discussed. This council has many questions for him and his representatives that we will delve into in a moment."

Laurel had flinched at being addressed as "princess," but she and Reed responded with polite nods. Angel continued speaking, this time to a teak-skinned woman sitting to her left, dressed in a gold and purple ensemble that Dawn thought resembled royal grapes.

"Rizza, I believe it is critical that we first discuss what your agents have uncovered . . ." Angel said in a more muffled voice, as if underwater.

Dawn looked around, wondering if she was the only one who was hearing the distortion. And then she heard someone else—a man's voice in her head.

Who let you pass through the bridge? the voice asked, ringing in her ears.

Whose voice is that? Dawn thought, her eyes darting around the table from Ezra to Dalton to someone sitting next to him—who looked familiar.

In fact, the girl sitting next to Dalton resembled Gita, Jett Pierce's assistant from the hangar.

It is *her*, Dawn concluded, distracted momentarily from the disembodied voice. The thin-framed girl had the same earthy skin, but now a black headscarf draped over her hair and shoulders. Angel stopped talking, and—to Dawn's surprise—Gita turned toward her.

She surveyed the table, seeing that everyone's eyes were on her for the umpteenth time today. *If only the floor could open up and swallow me.* She opened her mouth to explain the voice she'd heard, but Angel beat her to it.

"I am reminding all of you," Angel said, her voice no longer warped, "that for the sake of the groundlings in our midst, reading and projecting are prohibited during our meeting. Let us be courteous to our guests and refrain from conversing in Aquavian and Etheran languages."

Reading and projecting are prohibited? What does that mean?

Dawn didn't have a moment to ponder. As Angel finished her sentence, she, and everyone else's attention turned to a pale-faced man sitting at the other end of the table, adjacent to Dawn. Unsure why he had gone unnoticed up until this point, she stared at him now—at his sunken dark eyes and sagging skin with many lines, his shoulder-length moppy hair, and navy blue robe that was so oversized, it hung on his bony shoulders like a blanket.

"Forgive me," Pale-Faced Man said in the same voice that was in her head a moment ago. He did not look nor sound apologetic, but bowed his head slightly, closer to his knobby, steepled fingers resting on the table. "It was an honest mistake."

He said to Dawn in a measured tone, "I apologize to—Dawn, was it? Perhaps we can have a conversation afterward?"

"Very well," Angel cut in before Dawn could answer. Then the administrator paused, as if to smooth ruffled feathers, then began again in a more tranquil tone. "Dawn, yesterday, we learned that we are approaching the end of the Earth," she said, then continued, as if it were small talk about the weather. "We are at a crossroads, because if the groundlings continue on the same path, our Earth, our realms, our homes will become irreparable. Our fate will be the same, unless we change course."

"The Earth is ending?" Dawn blurted out, and scoffed, noticing how ridiculous her own voice sounded. "I just—I find that hard to believe."

"Of course you do," the woman named Rizza growled. The beads in her braids click-clacked as she spoke. "Groundlings never believe. Even as we speak, severe storms are ravaging the land and sea—a cataclysmic effect of groundlings' carelessness."

With every mention of "groundlings," Dawn heard the immense disdain in Rizza's voice.

"Rizza De Sol is correct," Angel said, her voice smooth as silk compared to Rizza's snarl. "She oversees the African continent and has seen first-hand how its inhabitants have suffered. You, like many groundlings, will have a difficult time accepting this. After all, you came here through a bridge, then flew on a diurlax, yet you still question whether what we're telling you is believable."

I am a groundling, Dawn realized.

"Howel does not believe you are a groundling," Angel continued. "That is the reason you are here."

"Whether she is a groundling or not remains to be seen," the one sitting next to Rizza said. She had a deeper voice for a woman, and short-cropped hair, red as flames. Her blouse resembled something between a black turtleneck and poncho. "Lord Angel, perhaps it is unwise to reveal our identities until we can confirm the nature of hers. I do not have the resources to protect yet *another* groundling from the soufors."

Protect another groundling? Dawn had so many questions. She pursed her lips to keep her mouth shut.

"Howel has sacrificed much. We should give our absent friend the benefit of the doubt," Angel countered. "If she is in fact a groundling, you know there are ways to alter one's memory."

As cordial as Angel sounded, that last part gave Dawn goosebumps. She didn't think it possible to forget about what had happened today.

"Dawn, this is Sidryl Crabtree," Angel motioned to her red-haired friend. "Sid hails from Eurasia."

Dawn offered a smile, but Sid gave only a glassy-eyed stare in return.

"Lord Asher, would you like to give yourself a proper introduction?"

Pale-Faced Man inclined his head to Dawn once more and his face contorted into something that hinted at a smile. It reminded her of Hiro, bearing his teeth.

"Lord Asher Elkhorn, my dear. Pleased to meet you," he said. "I am the head historian from the sky kingdom's capital, Etero."

It was all very important sounding, until she heard a snort coming from Reed. Dawn turned her head in his direction and caught Laurel elbowing him in the ribs.

When she looked back at Asher, his hideous grin had twisted into a sneer.

"If you ever hope to be a useful historian to your king, as I am to mine, you would take your training seriously, boy," he rebuked.

Reed didn't say anything, but a trace of a smirk played on his lips.

"You see, Dawn," Asher said as his gaze snapped to her, "the job of a historian is to help interpret prophecies. Do you happen to know what a *lumere* is?"

"No," she said quietly, wishing she could scoot away from him. "What is it?"

"People with aura abilities are Lumen. Our purpose is to preserve the Earth," he said as he leaned back in his chair, clearly enjoying the spotlight. "Lumeres are special. They are the chosen among the chosen. Lights to lead everyone else through the darkness. They can wield the power of sentient jewels—jewels with enchanted properties to enhance their aura. There were many prophecies about a lumere who will be the savior, and indeed, those prophecies have been fulfilled through King Malstrom Valedor himself.

"But there is one other foretold lumere, isn't there, Reed?" Asher continued, his voice dropping low. "One who is prophesied to be the lumere in the Last of Days to renew the Earth. There have been thousands of prophecies declared over time, and hundreds of those about the savior himself. How many prophecies of the last lumere do you suppose there are, Reed?"

"Hundreds as well, almost as many as the savior," Reed said, barely above a whisper.

"You are right, my boy," Asher said, as he watched Reed's smirk disappear. His eyes flitted back to Dawn's. "That brings us to *your* presence today, and the question the members of this council have in the back of our minds."

Laurel gasped excitedly and squeezed Dawn's arm not too subtly.

"Wait—what?" Dawn said as an unintentional smile crept over her face.

A giggle escaped from her mouth. It felt awkward. It felt *wrong*, like she was laughing during a funeral. But she couldn't control it.

The Earth is ending? Please. These people have a screw loose. Or two. I'm a barista. Just a barista.

"I told you she wouldn't believe," Rizza murmured. "Yet Earth won't survive another failed chosen one."

Dawn pulled her arm from Laurel's grasp and covered her mouth to stifle her snort.

"Are you . . . okay?" Laurel asked.

"Okay?!" Dawn said as she dropped her hands and guffawed uncontrollably. She looked around at everyone's serious faces, and then erupted in laughter so hard, she could barely speak.

"I feel—I FEEL—"

She paused, gasping for air in between giggles.

"I FEEL GREAT!" she finally managed to say, holding the aching sides of her stomach.

"She's hysterical," Asher said calmly.

"YES! YES!" Dawn cried, still unable to stop. "THIS *IS* HYS-TERICAL!"

Through her teary eyes, she saw Angel standing beside her, then something pricked the side of her neck. Eyelids drooping, Dawn fell silent immediately, instantly exhausted.

"Enough," Angel said, her voice echoing and sounding far away. "You had your chance, Asher. Now we're doing this *my* way."

The room started to spin into a blur, then it all went dark.

CHAPTER 5

DAWN SAT IN the middle of a long, wooden bench in a garden, basking in the sun's warmth. The saplings nearby gave just enough shade that she didn't have to shield her eyes.

A few gardeners were out and about, tending to the unique flora: colorful flowers ranging from bright pink to white, and plants with sweet fragrances and fruit. They'd put her housekeeper's gardens to shame.

A short distance away, a tranquil lake shimmered under the morning sun. What was she doing here? Movement on the other side of the water's edge caught her attention. A ram-like creature with fluffy, white fur lowered its head to drink, but a massive, gray diurlax swooped down, snatched it with its talons, and flew in the direction of the mountain cliffs.

Dawn gasped, jolted out of her nirvana. The ram was there a second ago, and now it was gone!

"They're called shepra," Angel said behind her.

It startled Dawn so badly she almost fell off the bench. Dawn craned her neck—realizing that it was sore—and saw that Angel was not alone.

She remembered Angel, the commander at the council meeting. But when did the meeting end? Where was everyone else? Only a pale-faced man accompanied Angel. Dawn had no recollection of him, but his presence made her uncomfortable.

"Beautiful, isn't it?" Angel continued. "This place, the balance of nature, the peacefulness of it all. This is my favorite garden, named Heisei. I often come here to meditate."

"It'sss lovely," Dawn said, finding her voice. Her tongue felt thick, and she was certain she was slurring her words, although she didn't know why.

"Thank you for patiently waiting here while the council convened. After an hour of discussion, you looked like you could use a breath of fresh air, so Dalton took you here to wait."

"Yesss," was all Dawn could think to respond with, her brain wracked with exhaustion.

Angel and Pale-Faced Man walked around the bench to face her. The elder man's navy-blue cloak dragged on the ground, collecting dirt.

"Before you go home, I wanted to formally introduce you to Lord Asher Elkhorn," Angel said. Dawn brought her head up clumsily and squinted at Angel, then at Pale-Faced Man. "He's a historian in Etero, the capital of our sky kingdom."

"Pleased to meet you, Dawn," Asher said, although he didn't sound pleased at all. "We'd like to ask you a few questions."

Without waiting for Dawn's response, they both took a seat on either side of her. Angel's fingers brushed against Dawn's hand, sending a surge of energy through her, like a splash of cold water on her face.

"We'd like to learn more about your background," Asher said, his smile too reminiscent of Hiro's bared teeth. "Please, tell us about your parents."

"My dad," Dawn began, surprised her tongue had lost its slug-gishness. Words tumbled out, as if she couldn't refuse answering. "His name is Howel Farringdon. He's a climatologist—"

"We know," Asher cut in. "Tell us about your mother."

"My mom . . ." Dawn furrowed her brows as she thought. "My dad said she died when I was only a year old. She developed a rare form of cancer shortly after she had me. Marion—our housekeeper—mostly raised me."

"I see," Asher said, clearly disappointed. "Did your father ever mention anything . . . unique about your mother?"

"Well, I thought her rare form of cancer was kind of unique." Dawn crossed her arms, recalling a framed photo of the beautiful Filipino Korean woman with Howel on her nightstand.

"Right," Asher said, softening his expression. "Forgive me—I do not wish to sound insensitive. We're just trying to piece together why Howel mentioned so little about you and your mother."

"I really don't know." Dawn shrugged. *I'd also like to piece together why my dad didn't tell me anything about you and this magical realm,* she thought sarcastically, but didn't dare say.

"Very well then," Asher said, clearing his throat. He narrowed his eyes. "How did you cross the bridge?"

"My dad's friend helped me," she returned, remembering that Lopple was trying to conceal his identity. She left it at that.

"What was the name of your father's friend?"

Dawn swallowed against her dry throat, somehow knowing he'd be able to tell if she lied.

"Surely you know the person who could manipulate the bridge?" Asher pressed.

"His name is Lopple," Dawn said, picturing his face as he scarfed down a pizzant.

"Lopple?" Asher echoed. He glanced at Angel and asked, "Do you know anyone by that name?"

"I do not," she replied.

"Very well," Asher said, getting up. "I must be going now. There is much work to do."

Angel stared blankly at him, but said nothing aloud, not even good-bye. The historian strode back through the garden and disappeared through a door that led into the mountain.

"You must send Mr. Lopple Fitch my regards. Come," Angel said, rising from the bench. She held out her hand to help Dawn up.

Dawn hesitated to take her hand, trying to remember something that felt amiss. Her brain was too slow, too foggy.

"Come," Angel said again in a voice that Dawn couldn't disobey. "Don't be afraid. We'll take a short stroll."

Dawn took her outstretched hand, and another undeniable surge of energy coursed through her veins. She got up, shaking the last traces of fatigue away. Angel led the way toward the lake, and Dawn followed, carefully lifting her dress so as not to dirty its hem or snag it on nearby branches.

"Everything in Tencho—and all sky cities—must maintain a balance. Between nature, our needs, and our wants," Angel said, checking that Dawn was keeping pace. "We have succeeded in maintaining that balance mostly through a very disciplined and simple way of life. The people of the water, the Aquavi, have done so as well, although they have suffered greatly. They are more susceptible to the damage caused by your kind's way of life."

Dawn mulled over those last words. *Your kind's way of life.* It was said as a matter of fact, without disdain or vitriol, unlike the others who spoke on the council about groundlings.

Angel quickened her pace, and Dawn lengthened her strides to keep up. It wasn't long until Angel stopped a few feet away from the glistening lake.

"Dawn, you know what a groundling's way of life is," Angel said. Coming from anyone else, it might've come off as accusatory, but Angel's voice carried a current of peace. "You've lived among them, and you would *be* one if it wasn't for Howel."

Angel held her arms close to her own body, hiding her hands in her sleeves. Then she closed her eyes, seemingly deep in meditation.

Dawn was confused. What were they doing here? Then she looked toward the lake and gasped. It had darkened, and a shadow that had surfaced in the middle of the lake spread rapidly, turning the water black.

She heard a voice—Angel's—in her head, blocking out all other ambient noise. She could no longer hear the breeze rustling the leaves or shepra shuffling about.

I and all of us who possess aura abilities are Lumen. We are tasked with protecting the three realms of Earth: the sky kingdom, the land, and the underworld, Angel said, her disembodied voice resounding in Dawn's head. *The land and the realm in which you live is what my kind call Eretz. Those* with *aura abilities who dwell on the land are called Eretzians. Those* without *are groundlings.*

Angel's eyes stayed closed and her lips still. The water had completely thickened like ink.

Earth's natural resources are being depleted, Angel continued.

As she spoke, the black water moved, rising and falling, forming shapes of people and images. Forests razed to the ground. Landfills overflowing with garbage. Factories pouring smoke into the sky. Every time the water rose, a new silhouette took shape, over and over again. Litter on the streets. Debris in the water. The arctic desert—with no ice in sight. Oil spills offshore.

The water twisted into uncontrollable fires, destruction from massive hurricanes, and the rubble of devastating earthquakes.

Earth will soon become uninhabitable unless our realms work together.

Suddenly and silently, as though all sounds were muted, the water dropped back into the lake, and all was calm. Dawn finally understood what Angel was trying to convey.

It didn't matter that there were few like Jett Pierce who promoted clean tech, or her dad who dedicated his life's work to the cause and went through great lengths to *not* contribute to the demise of the environment. There were simply too many people doing the opposite that it nulled the efforts of the few and far between.

A chill crept down Dawn's spine. Aside from grasping what Angel meant, Dawn could sense what Angel was feeling—resignation and acceptance that the world would indeed end. It wasn't a matter of *if.* It was only a matter of *when.*

In an instant, the lake returned to its former state—dark blue, shimmering in the reflection of the sun.

"I suspect the Last of Days are upon us," Angel said aloud. "It is an era that signifies the end of our kind and the end of the Earth. Those in the council that convened today believe we can prolong the Last of Days—if our realms work together. Time is passing quickly."

"Why are you telling me this? What does this have to do with me?" Dawn asked as a wave of fatigue washed over her.

"You need to get back home," Angel said, ignoring her questions. "Come."

Angel flitted toward another area of the garden before Dawn could protest. She jogged to catch up. They went through the garden following a narrow dirt path, which led to a part where the foot of the mountain jutted out like an exposed tree root. The rockface created somewhat of a partition, a wedge. Angel leapt to the other side of it where a hidden archway led into the mountain.

Upon entering the cavernous space, white gems gleamed on the walls and shone like bare bulbs—Angel's doing, Dawn surmised. The commander moved to the back of the cave, and for a moment, Dawn thought she saw other people moving toward them before realizing it was their own reflections. The cave wall was flat and smooth enough to act as a rough, dull mirror. Near the top, a handful of colorful stones sparkled, embedded into the wall.

"A bridge!" Dawn whispered.

"A long time ago, Eretzians forgot about their aura abilities," Angel said as the light from the glowing stones flickered upon her face. "With a new age of information, technology, advancements in medicine, and so much more, they simply thought it antiquated to rely on their auras. This resulted in them failing to teach the next generations how to wield their gifts."

Dawn felt lightheaded again, and Angel spoke faster.

"Your parents are one of the few Eretzians who held onto their abilities."

"I don't have any abilities," Dawn said breathlessly.

"That remains to be seen. Howel believes you do. You just haven't been taught."

"Where is he? Where's my dad?"

"It's better that you don't know his whereabouts. I promised Howel your safekeeping, and I did not make that vow lightly. Had it not been for your protection stone earlier . . ."

"Protection stone?"

Dawn's vision started to go in and out of focus. She squinted at the glowing stones, which seemed to brighten by the second.

"Howel is on an important mission," Angel said. "Dawn, you play a key role in this mission, which is bigger than any one of us. Howel believes you are integral to the Last of Days prophecy. As do I."

From the folds of her sleeve, Angel removed a hidden envelope and gave it to Dawn.

"Howel wanted you to read this after the council meeting today."

With a shaky hand, Dawn took the letter and shoved it into her dress pocket.

"This is where we must part. May we meet again someday."

"Wait, please!" Dawn fought off her dizziness. "What happens next? How am I supposed to contact you?"

Angel ignored the questions, but placed her hand upon Dawn's shoulder, and an inexplicable embrace of tranquility silenced Dawn.

She felt herself go sideways, like she was falling off a diurlax. Or was she being pushed? She couldn't tell. The extreme fatigue from earlier had returned, and she could no longer fight it.

Dawn closed her eyes, welcoming sleep. Disembodied voices echoed.

"She's falling through! I got her!" Someone's arms caught her.

"Is she all right?" a woman's panicked voice asked.

Someone forced her eyes open. All she saw was bright light and blurred faces. Then darkness again. Nothing made sense.

"She'll be fine. Let her rest," another said before she faded completely into unconsciousness.

CHAPTER 6

STIRRING BENEATH HER blanket, Dawn's fingers rubbed the soft fabric, and she pulled it closer to her chin. Shafts of sunlight crept in around the drawn shades, and twigs and leaves tapped on the glass as the wind hurled them. Dawn slowly opened her eyes to the dim light.

She hadn't slept like that in a long time. A deep, uninterrupted slumber. Still groggy, she shut her eyes and curled up to keep warm and cozy. But as she effortlessly drifted off for a few seconds, a piercing sound echoed downstairs. Marion's laugh. Boisterous chatter followed, their voices familiar. Dawn opened her eyes again, now wide awake.

That was Lopple's voice. And Laurel's!

She could no longer ignore what was flashing through her memory—the bridge, the diurlaxes, and the mountain in the sky. Her dad, whose whereabouts were now unknown. When she attempted to sit up, pain shot through her upper arms, shoulders, and neck as her muscles protested.

She hissed, sucking in sharp breaths against her teeth, struggling to get upright. Snatching her phone from the nightstand, she checked the date. Two days had passed. She frantically scrolled through her messages from Sparkle, Maizel, and Logan.

Throwing off her blanket, she scrambled out of bed, ignoring her aches and pains. Her ghastly reflection in the dresser mirror made her gasp. She was still wearing a long cream dress, slightly sullied, and her hair was a dark, knotted mess of tangles.

"I was there! And now I'm back," Dawn whispered to herself, incredulously.

She checked her phone and read her messages with one hand on her bed to steady herself.

Her heart somersaulted as she read Logan's get-well-soon message. Evidently, Marion had concocted a story that she'd caught the flu.

As she considered how she'd reply, her thoughts drifted to her dad, who was part of a secret, Earth-preserving council. It all sounded ludicrous. Except that she believed it. Every word of it. Maybe that was the crazy part.

She tapped a message into her phone. "Hi dad, how are you? Was your flight okay?"

As soon as she sent it, she got a reply. "Message undeliverable."

"X8," she said, activating the AI assistant, "where is my dad's phone?"

"I'm not able to trace it," the automated voice replied.

She sighed, knowing that if Jett had enabled anti-tracking on her device, he would've done the same for her dad. Anxiously, she hobbled to her bedroom door and turned the knob. The door creaked open, and the voices coming from the kitchen suddenly fell silent.

Dawn walked to the top of the staircase and called out loudly, "Miss M.?"

The aromas from the kitchen made her mouth salivate and her stomach grumble.

I'm so hungry, she realized. *But I desperately need a shower.*

"You can take your time freshening up," Marion yelled back from the kitchen in her strong South African accent, the sound of her voice familiar and welcoming.

Dawn yearned to run downstairs to see her housekeeper, to check that it was truly her and not a figment of her imagination. Hadn't she seen her the morning she left for work? It felt like ages ago. Realizing that she'd broken into a cold sweat and her knuckles were turning white from gripping the stair banister, Dawn released her hold. She *really* needed that shower. She decided she *would* take her time.

She walked slowly to the bathroom, wincing with every step. Her shower was every bit as therapeutic as relaxing, as she washed off the sweat and clamminess that clung to her over the past few days, as well as the uncertainty she harbored about her dad's mysterious plans.

After donning clean clothes, she felt like a new person, ready to face what may come. As she made her way down the stairs, she found herself smiling, passing the portraits on the wall of Howel and her late mother. *Everything will be okay*, she told herself. Upon reaching the kitchen table, she paused abruptly. She had expected to see Marion, Lopple, and Laurel, but she found only her housekeeper seated at the table with a full spread of food.

Marion, dressed in her usual vibrant headwrap and maxi dress, motioned with her hand for Dawn to have a seat, and Dawn did, but not before embracing her in a bone-crushing hug. Sounding as though all the air was being squeezed out of her, Marion wheezed, "I missed you too."

Dawn finally sat down and surveyed the mouth-watering feast before her. There was a pot of steaming tea surrounded by all kinds of colorful fruits and toasted breads.

Without hesitation, she grabbed a still-warm croissant and devoured it. She reached for her fork and pierced different slices of fruits, not bothering to put them on her plate before scarfing them down.

Marion sat there, hands folded, watching intently without uttering a word. Dawn didn't care. She was famished, and everything tasted as delicious as it looked. A thought crossed her mind as the previous events replayed in her head.

"How come you didn't wake me to eat anything?" Dawn asked between gulps of water.

"I tried, but you were so tired. I got you to take some broth and sips of water, but that was it. I got worried too and called the healer to come by again."

"Hikaru came by. *Again*? Does that mean he's aware of the situation? He's got an aura —and that means he's *Lumen*?"

"He's an aura *user*," Marion corrected, "as am I—and that makes us Lumen."

Dawn's eye caught her housekeeper's headwrap—a beautiful, bold cerulean, complimenting her brown complexion. Marion's mouth turned down at the corners, making her angled facial features look sharper.

"When I came home from the studio, I found Lopple in the study and he briefed me on a few things. We waited until you returned, unconscious and exhausted," Marion said with a slight tremor in her voice. "Hikaru was here and confirmed you were unharmed."

It was clear Marion had worried about her, but Dawn felt fine. The healer had said as much.

"Do you know where my dad is?" Dawn asked as she reached for another croissant.

"No," she shook her head. "I know what I *need* to know—enough to keep you safe. Lopple left and came back the next day. He wanted to talk to you, but you were still sleeping. The healer visited too, but only for a few minutes."

Marion stood up, cleared her throat and reached for the kettle.

"He said to let you rest. He wasn't too concerned. But you should drink your tea," she said, pouring Dawn a cup.

The teacup brimmed with steaming brown liquid and bits of dried, floating leaves; she recognized the atrocious smell of Marion's *kudzukan* tea. Her housekeeper grew the plant in the backyard greenhouse and used its leaves to brew tea and make elixirs.

Reluctantly, she lifted the cup to her lips and took a sip, trying hard—and failing—not to make a face when the bitterness hit her tongue. As bad as it tasted, it had actually worked in the past, curing Dawn's fatigue and alleviating physical pain to some degree.

Marion walked over to the sink and started loading the dishwasher.

"Does the name Malstrom Valedor mean anything to you?" Marion asked, looking over her shoulder at Dawn.

Dawn shoveled maple syrup-sweetened oatmeal into her mouth as she repeated the name.

"*Valedor* is familiar. Must be someone of royal lineage?"

"Malstrom Valedor is the ruler of the Etheran realm, the sky kingdom," Marion said, turning back to the dishes.

"I wasn't lucky enough to get an introduction, although I did meet some of his relatives, I think," Dawn shrugged and tasted a slice of mango.

It was sweet and juicy, like a bright orange piece of soft sugar cane. She was much more interested in the fruit than in discussing the Sky King.

"You may not have met him yet, but word would've gotten to him about you by now."

Marion dried her hands on a towel near the sink, then turned to face Dawn completely. She folded her arms, waiting until Dawn met her gaze to give her undivided attention.

Dawn finished off the mango slices and was finally feeling full— and a little drowsy.

"Valedor has sent his *soufors*, his hounds, to look for you," Marion said quietly, as if someone might overhear. "He's also on the hunt for Howel. He has spies everywhere, so we're not taking any risks with—"

A low rumble interrupted their chat and shook the entire house; the lights flickered. From the study, strange yelps that sounded like a cross between a cow's moo and a monkey's cry. Startled, Dawn turned to the direction it came from. The shaking stopped, and so did the peculiar sound.

"That was Lopple," Marion said, with an amused look on her face. "He's been uppity with the earthquakes."

"Really? That came from a human?"

Marion nodded, and then they heard someone else's laugh, if it could be called that. A loud, screaming cackle followed by wheezing, then another short burst of a high-pitched squeal. And possibly, a snort or two.

"And that was Laurel," Marion said after seeing Dawn's confused expression.

Who would've thought a sound like that could come from a mermaid princess?

After a beat of silence passed, Dawn thought it would be a good time to bring up her suspicions about Lopple.

"You trust him? Lopple, I mean?" Dawn whispered. "I know my dad does, but we just met."

Marion nodded, then moved from the kitchen sink and started putting the leftover fruit in the fridge. In a barely audible voice, she replied, "Howel trusts him, and I trust Howel. Lopple told me we met once a long time ago, but I don't really remember."

Dawn pondered on Lopple for a few minutes while Marion cleaned up. It was creepy watching him come through the mirror like a character from a horror movie. She shuddered at the thought.

How she felt about him was all over the place. Scared? No. Angry? At first, but not anymore. At ease? Not yet. He had never heard of a pizzant and was obviously not from here—*Eretz*, she remembered. He and the others were Lumen, otherworldly, powerful even. Curious—yes, she was certain that was the feeling that fueled her motivation to find out more about him.

Marion put her hand on Dawn's shoulder, nudging her back to the present moment.

"Dawn, now that you know what's going on, you can't leave this house until you master some basic aura abilities," Marion began.

"Is that why you told Maizel I got the flu?" she asked, unamused.

"Well, yes. I gave her a reason for you to miss a few weeks of work, but we'll likely have to think of something more . . . long term."

Dawn knitted her brows, uncertain whether she agreed with that and hating the fact that she wasn't given a choice. Then again, if there was anyone she *knew* she could trust, it was Marion, who took care of her as if she were her own daughter.

Marion added that they must take every precaution and went on to explain how Jett's security team had made a change to their facial profiles in the global tracking database. From now on, any tech and AI that captured their images or identifying data wouldn't be able to match them with their names.

Dawn couldn't hide her surprise; although she didn't quite know what soufors were, they sounded dangerous.

"Let's say I learn basic aura abilities. Then what?"

"Then you will complete the mission Howel has for you."

"And then I can go back to the studio?"

"That is what's on your mind right now? Making coffee at the studio?"

Dawn shrugged. "I like being a barista. I meet all kinds of interesting people at the studio. There's nothing wrong with that."

"Let us just take it step by step. First, master basic aura abilities. It takes time. It took me years before I could use my aura abilities on command."

"Years?" Dawn cried, shocked to see this new side of Miss M., who she had known all her life.

"For heaven's sake, you don't have *that* long. Howel mentioned he had a time-sensitive task for you. You'll need to get started training as soon as possible."

"Then let's start."

Marion pointed in the direction of the study. "They're waiting for you."

CHAPTER 7

UPON ENTERING THE study, Dawn was assaulted by the undeniably thick tension in the room. Despite their earlier shared reactions to the earthquake, Lopple and Laurel did not seem to get along. The Aquavian princess stood, leaning against the bookshelves, across from where Lopple sat, in the swivel chair with his back to Howel's desk. Dawn eyed them both—facing off against each other with arms crossed.

The cheval mirror was nowhere in sight, but the upholstered armchair and ottoman from the living room had been brought in. Marion carried in another chair, setting it down near Laurel and motioning for her to sit. The Aquavian ignored her.

Lopple was the first to speak, cutting through the silence. "We're so glad you're awake and well, Dawn. Why don't you tell us what happened after you left the council meeting? Princess Laurel explained everything up until the part where you left the room."

Laurel let out an exasperated sound. "Stop calling me 'Princess Laurel.' It's *just* Laurel."

Unbothered, Lopple stood up and offered the swivel chair to Dawn, then plopped down on the armchair, propping his feet up on the ottoman.

"I left the room?" Dawn repeated as she sat down slowly.

"You did," Laurel said, pacing the room while looking down at her bare feet. "You left with Dalton to get some fresh air."

"Right," Dawn said, unsure of herself. "I was sitting in a garden near a lake. And Lord Angel and Pale-Faced Man, whose name I can't remember, came and asked me questions."

"Asher was there?" Lopple asked, suddenly taking his legs off the ottoman and leaning forward in interest. "Asher Elkhorn? That slimy snake! Tell us exactly what they said. Picture it in your mind."

Dawn recounted all she could remember about Asher's questions, Angel's explanation of Eretzians and groundlings, the mesmerizing manipulation of the lake, the hidden cave, and the mirror bridge within its wall. By the time she had finished, she was breathless, as if she had relived everything through her memories.

Her fingers had found their way to her crystal pendant necklace, and she rolled it back and forth between her thumb and index finger.

"I'm impressed that Angel knew who I am," Lopple said, rubbing his scruffy chin, "yet she was able to withhold that information from Elkhorn. She also sensed your protection stone."

Dawn's fingers froze and she peered down at the pendant she was holding. Its aquamarine tint gleamed at her.

"That *is* a precious crystal," Marion said. "When charged with one's aura, it can be a very powerful source of protection."

Marion had told her long ago that the pendant was her mother's but had never said it was *magical*. Dawn continued to peer down at the stone's dainty, hexagonal shape; it was one of the few things passed down from her mother. If she were still alive, *she* would've taught Dawn about her aura abilities. Another thought crossed Dawn's mind.

"The journal . . . and the letter!" Dawn gasped.

"The journal is right there on the desk," Lopple said, pointing.

Dawn instinctively slapped her hand over it, as if to keep it from fluttering away. Immediately, she felt foolish. She resisted the urge to sprint up to her room to check whether the letter was still in her dress pocket and decided she would take a look at both today. Gingerly, she picked up the journal and slid it onto her lap.

There was an awkward beat of silence before Lopple took the opportunity to excuse himself and muttered something about checking Dawn's training progress in a few days.

"Where is he going?" Dawn asked after he limped out of the study.

"The bridge is in the bathroom next door to keep the water cleanup to a minimum," Marion said, as she snuck a glance at Laurel. "I'll be in the kitchen and minding the garden if you need anything."

"I thought Lopple was going to teach me today," Dawn said, confused.

"I'll be teaching you," Laurel chirped as Marion exited.

Although she and Laurel had become fast friends, she hadn't considered learning aura abilities from someone so . . . well, *young*.

"I brought your cloak back," the Aquavian said as she pointed toward the small closet. "I visited Angel yesterday, and she tasked me with teaching you aura abilities."

Dawn crossed the room and checked the closet, expecting to see her dad's cloak in shreds. But she found it perfectly intact—not a thread or stitch out of place.

"It's fixed!" Dawn said, surprised. "I thought it was beyond repair."

"Etheran seamsters are talented with their shepra fleece."

"How were you able to keep it dry?"

"We Aquavians have our ways." Laurel smirked.

"Thanks for bringing it back. It's my dad's."

"You're welcome. Can I ask a favor of you?" Laurel asked. "Could I borrow a set of your loose-fitting clothes," she said with hesitancy, then added, "similar to the ones you're wearing?"

Dawn looked down at her drab attire. "You mean sweats?"

Laurel's face lit up at the prospect of trading her lengthy dress with a gray hoodie and jogger pants.

While Laurel changed, Dawn checked that Angel's letter was in her dress pocket and stashed it away with the journal. The two then settled comfortably on Dawn's bedroom floor—a familiar place for Dawn that would suit her training, according to Laurel.

There was a moment when they met each other's gaze as they sat facing the other. *She's so photogenic,* Dawn thought, admiring how her sweats looked on Laurel's slender frame.

"Why, thank you," Laurel responded.

"Did you just read my mind?" Dawn asked. "I didn't, er, say anything."

"Not out loud, but you were *projecting* it," Laurel explained. "That's how we communicate telepathically. We can project our words, images, feelings, memories . . . all kinds of things."

"I must've been projecting all my thoughts in Tencho!" Dawn groaned, mortified.

"Some things, but not everything," Laurel confirmed.

She explained the lesson plan, which was to go over projections and shield thoughts.

Dawn nodded dejectedly. Surely, she had made an idiotic first impression to all those people—her dad's friends!—during the meeting.

"Now that I think about it, I remember they didn't like me— especially that woman with braids and another one with red hair."

Laurel's lips turned up at the corners.

"I also remember laughing. Something was funny to me, but I can't recall what."

Laurel cleared her throat, and her expression turned serious. "After you left with Dalton to get fresh air," she said, measuring her words, "the council discussed matters of urgency. Asher said King Malstrom ordered two of his soufors to find you—they got a lead that morning."

"SOO-ferz? Marion mentioned that earlier."

The silhouettes of two people appeared between Dawn and Laurel—dreamlike and translucent. Dawn reached out with her hand to touch the shadows but felt nothing.

"I'm using my aura—my life energy—to create a projection. You can see it, but only in your mind."

Dawn stared at the projection, mesmerized as the shadows took form and solidified. A man, hooded in black with a malicious sneer, and next to him, a woman with white, short-cropped hair.

They're hunters, Laurel projected.

The man removed his hood, revealing his neck, inked in tribal-looking tattoos. Without warning, the woman lunged at Dawn, slashing at her face with a small knife.

Dawn yelped and jumped back, but the projected blade went right through her.

"It's an illusion, it's not real," she breathed, trying to calm herself. "They're hunters? Like bounty hunters?"

Yes, but they don't treat their bounties kindly. These two in particular are known for their sadism toward Eretzians and groundlings.

The Inked Man in Laurel's projection crept closer to Dawn, his sneer twisting into a cruel smile. The woman pocketed her knife and drew a serrated blade from a sheath attached to her thigh. Grasping

Dawn's hair, Blade pulled her head back and held the tip of the knife right under Dawn's chin. Dawn gasped, startled by the whiplash and the sharp tug of her hair. She shut her eyes tightly, telling herself it wasn't real, but the tip of the blade pricking her chin told her otherwise. She cried out in pain, opening her eyes.

The menacing soufors were gone. She saw only Laurel, sitting in front of her with an intensity in her eyes. Dawn rubbed where the point of the knife had been, expecting there to be blood.

"There's no cut," Laurel said, "but I can trick your brain into thinking it feels pain, especially if you don't know how to shield."

The thought sent a shiver down Dawn's spine, and her eyes wandered to the window where she focused on the sound of rain pelting against the glass. There were soufors somewhere out there, hunting her. What would she do if they found her?

"Don't worry," Laurel said. "Angel commissioned a team of Elites, and they're working to keep you hidden. How about I project something less . . . intense?"

Dawn nodded and blinked. When she opened her eyes, she gasped. She was in the depths of the ocean with Laurel . . . or *as* Laurel. Her dark-brown tresses and mermaid tail swayed back and forth with the gentle current. The water was teeth-chatteringly cold, but it didn't bother her. All around her was the dark blue of the ocean, yet she could see clearly underwater.

Another Aquavian swam beside her, a mermaid with a beautiful, silvery tail. Her thick dark hair seemed alive with small, bluish-silver fish swimming in and around her locks. A stinging sensation on her arm caught Laurel's attention, and she turned her gaze to see a gelatinous creature's stringy tentacles at the site of the pain. Her mermaid friend pointed her finger, making a loop that surrounded them.

A siphonophore, her friend projected.

The creature's length was incalculable, and it glowed an array of colors like twinkling holiday lights. It encircled them from a distance, and neither of the mermaids could see where it began or ended.

"It's like I'm scuba diving, but a thousand times better," Dawn said.

In a split second, the ocean around her changed, a different projection. She could see what Laurel could see. This time, Laurel was younger; she was closer to the surface. She could feel what Laurel felt: scared, exhausted, and . . . hurt? Her fishtail had a gash and bled as she sprinted toward a different Aquavian, someone taller and more built. As the space closed in between them, his undeniable features came into view: a dark green fishtail, muscular, bronzed torso, and short black hair.

He outstretched his hand toward her, palm up, and a glowing orb of light formed in his hand. Laurel swam as fast as she could. Something was chasing her, and it was gaining speed. Her heart pounded in terror.

DO IT! Laurel screamed in her mind.

The ball of light from the man's palm burst into a beam, like a missile piercing through the water. It emitted warmth as it passed right by Laurel's head in a split second and hit the leviathan trailing close behind her.

The impact of the energy burst hurled the sea creature upward. It broke the surface, and a deafening roar erupted from its dragon-like jaws. Then its serpentine body crashed back into the ocean. Whatever the Aquavian had done to the sea monster had not harmed it, but only momentarily stunned it. The creature retreated, propelling itself away from its offender.

Young Laurel looked into her uncle's eyes and could feel the concern in them. He asked her something in their native language.

Even in a projection, she could hear his voice, and it sounded comforting. Reassuring.

Dawn blinked, and she found herself transported back to her room, still sitting on the floor across from Laurel.

"His name is Niro, and he's like an uncle to me," Laurel said, stretching her arms above her head.

Dawn glanced at the wall clock. A few hours had passed, although the projections she experienced were fleeting.

"The glowing orb of light you saw in his hand is called a *sumatok* in Orako, our Aquavi language."

"Su-MA-tok?" Dawn asked, committing the word to memory.

Laurel nodded. "A sumatok is like directing your aura as a burst of energy. Etherans can do similar things with their aura—which they sometimes call *en*—like create fireballs or aura weapons," she said, unbending her legs and leaning against the wall. "I need a break. It's your turn to share a projection—*intentionally*."

"Okay," Dawn said, standing up to glance around her room for ideas. On the other side of her bed, there was a glass chess set atop an end table, which the tidying bot was cautiously hovering over, dusting it. Immediately, Dawn sat down on the floor and closed her eyes, picturing her dad—his chubby middle, argyle vest, and joyful smile.

They sat outside on a beach-front property, staring at the glass chess set between them. The ocean breeze was chilly that day, but the sun warmed them. Dawn pursed her lips, thinking she was so close to saying "checkmate," but a glance at her dad's poker face told her otherwise. From inside the house, the wafting aroma of Marion's cooking—seared ahi tuna—made Dawn's mouth water. Howel's stomach growled loudly.

"Let's have lunch," he urged. "I'm famished. We can finish this later."

"No, wait," Dawn said, moving her queen across the board, forking his rook and knight.

"You've already won," he countered, getting up from his chair. "I forfeit."

"Dad," she whined, drawing out the word. "You can't do that! Finish the game!"

She called after him, but he was already shuffling through the house, remarking how delicious it smelled.

Dawn opened her eyes, surprised to find that Laurel was not sitting in front of her; she was standing in front of the glass chess set near her bed, inspecting the pieces.

Ezra likes this game. This is the same one you and your father were playing? Laurel asked voicelessly. *The pieces are in the same position as in your projection.*

"Yes, I had—"

No, Laurel projected, holding up her hand. *Project your words.*

Dawn thought of what she was going to say and said it in her mind, *willing* the message to be received.

I had X8, our virtual assistant, save the chess game at this juncture. It reminds me how my dad never let me win, never went easy on me. He isn't the type to give any hints to his riddles either. But that's why I'm fond of this chess match—I know I would've won because of my skill, not because he let me win.

"How was that?" Dawn asked excitedly. "Did you get everything I projected?"

"You projected about fifty percent." Laurel shrugged, and a smile curled her lips. "But I can see your memories, even if you don't project them. Aquavians call it *reading*."

"I only projected half?" Dawn asked, feeling deflated. She had given it her best shot.

"We'll work on it tomorrow." Laurel yawned. "Where I'm from, it's already late."

Dawn looked at the clock, surprised to find they had been practicing for hours. She found herself suppressing a yawn and asked if projecting was always this tiring.

The Aquavian explained that her aura hadn't fully awakened. "Until it does, experiencing and creating projections will take much longer than usual."

Dawn's stomach grumbled in response. Perhaps now was a good time to go downstairs for dinner. The aromatics of Marion's cooking—ahi tuna, coincidentally, and something garlicky—had reached her room. She invited her friend to eat, but Laurel curtly refused and bundled up her dress before heading to the bridge. She left so abruptly that Dawn wondered if she had committed a faux pas. Did the Aquavian diet include seafood?

CHAPTER 8

THE DINING TABLE was covered with a feast fit for royalty (at least in Dawn's opinion), yet there was no Aquavian princess to enjoy it. According to Marion, Aquavians mostly ate seafood—that was what was readily available to them. She had prepared seared ahi tuna, mushrooms and spinach sautéed in garlic, a variety of fresh bread rolls, cucumber salad, fancy sushi rolls she couldn't put a name to, and soup dumplings.

"But why prepare so much food? Laurel looked like she'd get full after one dumpling." Dawn asked before taking a big bite of seared fish.

"In case Lopple and Hikaru stop by for dinner. Besides, Laurel only ate seaweed for breakfast and lunch earlier."

"You made her seaweed salad earlier?"

"No, she brought her own seaweed and insisted on eating nothing else."

Dawn almost choked. "She *brought* her own food?" she sputtered.

"She might have something against me," Marion said as she put down her utensils. "Laurel has refused every food I've offered, seafood or not."

Laurel *was* peculiar. They had known each other for two days, Dawn thought, but already, they were becoming close. She had observed that the Aquavian was loud, rambunctious, and somewhat irreverent. On the other hand, their shared projections showed her a side of Laurel's mind that was no doubt reserved for family and Aquavian friends.

How *anyone* felt slighted toward Marion was a mystery, and Dawn was determined to get to the bottom of it. But first, her dad's letter and journal needed her attention.

"I'll ask her about it tomorrow. She said she'd be returning to train me to control my projections."

"I'm impressed with the progress you've made on your first day," she said, rising from her seat and walking toward the kitchen. She returned a moment later with a platter of assorted desserts and a hot kettle. "Finish up and rest," she said while filling Dawn's teacup with the steaming, brownish liquid. "The tea will help with your fatigue."

Dawn nodded. The dull ache in her temples from this morning began to settle back in.

"Why can't you teach me projection?" she asked, taking a sip of tea and adding a red bean sesame ball to her plate.

Marion picked up a mini chocolate chip cookie and took a bite, chewing thoughtfully.

"The Aquavi primarily communicate under the water through projection and reading. It goes without saying that Laurel has a propensity for it," Marion said, finishing off her cookie.

True enough, Dawn thought. Her housekeeper's schedule probably wouldn't allow enough time for training her anyway.

It was as though Marion read her mind when she added, "Laurel needs something to keep her busy. She has time for this."

Dawn sat in bed propped up against pillows with both the journal from her dad and letter from Angel in her lap. She also held the tiny key in her hand that her dad had given her—on the day she had last seen him. Reliving the memory of him leaving made her anxious. He said he'd *be in touch* but didn't make any promises or give specifics on when he'd return. Their interaction felt like a farewell, and she blinked back tears as she wondered when she'd see him again.

"Focus," she whispered, shaking her head to rid herself of negative thoughts.

In her open palm, the key gleamed with her slightest movement. It was like any flimsy, small key that came with a cheap journal, except this one had a tiny black stone at the center of its bow.

She sighed impatiently after examining the journal's cover for a keyhole; there wasn't one. All she could find was an indentation of the key in the area where there would've been a keyhole and latch, but it didn't matter how hard she pressed the key into it. It wouldn't stick, and the writing in the journal remained unrevealed.

"I give up," Dawn muttered, tossing the journal aside.

She unfolded the letter, hoping it wasn't blank like the journal, then breathed a sigh of relief when she saw her dad's familiar scrawl.

Dear Dawn,

Every choice I made when your mother passed away was to give you the best chance of finding your path in the way she wished. I've entrusted her journal to you. Use the key and activate it with your aura. There is much at stake and my whereabouts must remain unknown. My friends are helping me search for much-needed items to create a source that will renew the Earth's resources. It is my hope that in the process, we will bring peace to our realms. My associate—whom you've already met by the time you're reading this—is assisting us in finding these ingredients.

There is one coveted, rare ingredient, which must be retrieved when the time is right. It is rooted near the river where it's always night. Ripe for picking in the dark, but go not beyond the Ides of March. Past the maw and deep in the throat, it's hard to find and harder to grow. You've once been there long ago. You'll need a guide whose name you'll know. You'll need a guide whose name you'll know.

With love,
Dad
P.S. Remember Jack? I sure miss him. Let's visit him sometime.

After reading the letter, a woosh of air left her lungs, and she realized she had been holding her breath. She couldn't believe the journal was her *mother's*—the person she wished she knew—and here she was so close to, yet so far from, reading her mom's legacy beyond the grave.

Dawn scanned it again, scoffing at the part where her dad had written "much at stake."

What an understatement.

If renewing the Earth's resources was the mission, it hinged on some very lofty mini goals: 1. Find the rare ingredient to create the so-called source, which depended on . . . 2. Solving her dad's riddle and . . . 3. Mastering her aura abilities so she could leave the house. She also had to . . . 4. Complete everything before the "Ides of March" and . . . 5. Avoid the soufors.

She toyed with the pendant around her neck, her thoughts searching for a way out of this impossible mission.

Isn't preserving the Earth supposed to be a collective effort?

It is, another voice in her head argued back. *That's what the Lumen are for.*

But what about things that I want?

Well, what do you want?

I want things to go back to normal. I want my family—my dad—to be okay. I want my future to be a happy one.

Dawn's mind spiraled into the future, a fantasy in which she pictured herself and Logan happily in love.

Logan, I'd love to go out with you, but unfortunately, Earth will be in ruins if I don't master my aura abilities in time to find a rare ingredient my dad needs to help a secret society save the planet.

The constant rainfall pegging her window sounded like endless pellets from a shotgun. Her heart beat wildly, drowning out the sound of the rain, and the overwhelm of all that rested on her shoulders threatened to send her into a panic attack. She closed her eyes and took calming breaths, attempting to step back from the ledge she stood on. Her head throbbed.

I'm too young to have high blood pressure, she thought, massaging her temples.

Do not be afraid, a voice in her head said. *You are the key to the Last of Days prophecy.*

Her eyes fluttered open, and her shoulders loosened, releasing some of their tension. She reached for the mug of kudzukan tea on her nightstand and took a long sip. As the hot liquid traveled down her throat and warmed her insides, she reminded herself that worrying wouldn't get her anywhere.

You are not alone.

Whose voice was that?

A rap of knuckles on her door interrupted her thoughts, and Marion asked, "Dawn, may I come in? I brought you more tea."

"Of course," she replied, realizing that the voice—whoever it belonged to—was right. She wasn't alone. She had her family: Miss M. and Hikaru.

"Lopple will be here soon," Marion said.

And her new Lumen friends would help her too.

Dawn wearily smiled at her housekeeper, who came and sat on the side of her bed.

"Something on your mind?"

Dawn handed her the letter, which Marion read with a furrowed brow. "Are you worried about the mission?" she asked when she finished reading.

"Yes. What if I fail?"

Her housekeeper shook her head. "If you think that way, you will only succeed in crippling yourself. It is only your first conscious day back."

"But the Ides of March is—"

"Do not entertain those thoughts," Marion said gently, placing her coarse hand over Dawn's and effectively killing the words in her throat. "I have no idea what this riddle is, but we will figure it out together. Lopple and Hikaru will meet with me later. We'll discuss and plan for the mission while you train with Laurel. I promise . . . I will be with you . . . I will help you," her housekeeper assured her.

Dawn nodded and whispered, "Thanks, Miss M."

"Don't mention it. When did you get this letter?" she said, examining the type of paper Howel used. Marion rubbed the paper gently. "It is the kind of paper used for Etheran scrolls."

"Lord Angel gave it to me before she sent me back. Now that you've brought it up, I wonder why dad didn't give it to me himself at the airport."

"If he entrusted the letter to Lord Angel, maybe there was someone at Jett's hangar he wanted to keep this from. My guess is it's the same reason he wrote the riddle. He only wanted *you* to uncover the answer, and he wanted you to read this *after* the council meeting."

"I think I'm following. Since I can't control my projections yet, even if others hear my thoughts and gain access to the riddle, the answer is still encrypted."

"That is, until you solve it. He must think that by the time you solve it, you'll have gained some control of your aura abilities."

Dad knows me so well that he can anticipate the time it would take to solve his riddle.

"I have a question, though," Marion said, pointing to the post-script. "Who is Jack?"

Dawn chortled at the memory it brought to mind. Evidently, there were a few things her housekeeper *didn't* know about her. She explained to Marion that when she was a little girl, the nursery rhyme of Jack and Jill was the first she committed to memory. Unbeknownst to anyone else, Howel had cleverly turned it into their own secret message. If they knew others were watching or listening in, mentioning Jack meant safety; Jill meant trouble.

His letter was not sealed, yet Howel took precautions if prying eyes fell upon it. While anyone else would think Jack was a person, mentioning him was his way of assuring her that she needn't worry about him; *he was safe.*

CHAPTER 9

THE NEXT MORNING, Dawn ambled downstairs to find Hikaru, Marion, Lopple, and Laurel at the table with bowls of colorful fruits, toast, bagels, smoked salmon, and spreads. Hikaru's salt-and-pepper streaked hair swayed gently as he nodded and listened intently to Marion chatting animatedly beside him, holding her half-eaten avocado toast in one hand.

Lopple and Laurel were engaged in a heated conversation, with the former furiously chewing, his cheeks fully stuffed like a squirrel's, and the latter gesticulating in front of a plate of seaweed. Dawn brewed herself a cup of coffee and took a seat next to Laurel.

"Seaweed for breakfast?" Dawn asked while smothering a blueberry bagel in a cashew spread.

Laurel paused in mid-sentence about Aquavian history and turned to face Dawn. "I only eat food from the sea," she said with a flare of her nostrils.

Everyone at the table fell silent. Hiro continued crunching his dog food in the kitchen.

"We have smoked salmon," Dawn pointed out.

"It's nothing like the *fresh, wild* salmon our Aquavi fishermen catch," she said, shooting a conspicuous glare at Marion.

Miss M. narrowed her eyes at her and opened her mouth to say something, but Lopple cut in, oblivious to the tension around him.

"It is absolutely delicious!" he said, still chewing his food, while adding more smoked salmon to his plate.

Dawn caught Laurel rolling her eyes while Marion poured Lopple more water.

"I intended to stop by for supper last night but was a bit preoccupied and ended up missing dinner entirely," he explained.

"Too scared of a little rain and thunder, I bet," Laurel muttered under her breath.

Dawn, who had been thoroughly exhausted after their day of projection exercises, soundly slept through the thunderstorm. A glance at the window showed a partly cloudy sky, the morning sun rays streaming through in soft shafts of light.

"I'm not ssscared of thunder," he slurred. "There was sssomething that demanded my attention."

"Why do you sssound like that?" Laurel mocked, slurring her own words together.

Everyone at the table froze mid-bite, appalled.

Lopple finished swallowing his food and sat a little straighter, keeping his composure despite the slight. "I'll have you know my *slur* is due to a near-fatal injury."

Dawn's eyes grew wide as he tilted his head back to reveal an angry scar under his chin near the back of his jaw.

"A soufor named Silvers stabbed me with an aura blade," he said, snapping his head back down. "He tried to slash my carotid artery, that bas—"

Marion cleared her throat loudly to interrupt the unpalatable breakfast conversation.

"Laurel, Dawn—since you're finishing up, why don't you head to the living room to start projection exercises?" Marion urged. "I have important business to discuss with these two," she declared, eyeing Lopple as he had moved on to stuffing his mouth with juicy pear slices.

Laurel took a last sip of water from a rounded red mug and drifted out of the kitchen without a glance back. Dawn followed but took her plate and mug with her to the living room.

After settling into her favorite spot on the cream-colored, tufted sofa, Dawn opened her mouth to ask Laurel about being a grump, but the Aquavian spoke first.

"That's him! That's one of the soufors," Laurel said.

"Who?" Dawn replied, arching an eyebrow.

"The man Lopple mentioned." A projection of a menacing man with dark neck tattoos appeared between them. Laurel whispered, "That's Randen Silvers. Uncle Niro always talked about him."

"What about the female soufor? What's her name?"

"I don't know," she shrugged, "but the question we should be asking is why a soufor is after Lopple."

Did that mean the soufors were looking for him and *me?* Dawn considered that she hardly knew *anything* about Lopple, except that he's a trusted friend of her dad. Maybe Marion and Hikaru could glean more info about him after their chat.

"What else do you know about Lopple? Were you able to read his mind?"

Laurel shook her head.

"He's Lumen. He can *shield* his thoughts and *read* yours like the best of them. He's not Aquavian, but there *is* something he's not telling us," she said, pursing her lips. "You'll need to learn how to shield before I tell—"

Suddenly, the ground shook and someone shrieked loudly from the kitchen, followed by the shatter of a dish being dropped on the floor. Then the shaking ceased after a few seconds.

There was a whimsical clinking sound coming from the chandelier, its raindrop crystals swaying as it slowed to a stop.

"Don't worry, it's just a tremor," she said to Laurel.

They surmised that the yelp from the kitchen was most likely Lopple's.

"I'm not worried," Laurel said with a snort. "We get undersea earthquakes all the time."

"I guess that lines up with what my dad has been saying about more tectonic activity than ever last year. Anyway, since you can't reveal what's so suspicious about Lopple, why don't you tell me about the Aquavi and where you're from?"

A grin stretched across Laurel's face as though she'd been waiting for that question. "Perfect! I planned to go over Aquavian history today anyway."

Dawn's smile faltered. History classes were not her favorite, but she *had* asked for it. Picking up her bagel, she leaned back on the couch, expecting a lengthy lecture. She gasped and nearly dropped her food as the opulent living room morphed into Laurel's projection.

Armored war horses ran amok, and their Lumen knights hurled sumatoks and flaming aura arrows at one another. Some soldiers wielded swords and shields that glowed, fortified by aura, while others used their life energy to catapult massive boulders at their enemies.

Introducing the Etheran King, Malstrom the Merciful, Laurel projected sarcastically.

A lone knight wearing a gold helmet emerged from the gaggle of chaos and charged toward Dawn on his steed. A sumatok exploded nearby, its sudden wave of heat washing over them. Dawn flinched as Malstrom's horse reared up on its hind legs and let out a shrill neigh.

In one hand, Malstrom tightly gripped the reins, and with the other, he thrust his sword toward the sky as he bellowed a guttural battle cry. As his horse planted all its legs back on the ground, the sky king swept his sword forward, then continued charging toward her.

"I don't see how this relates to Aquavian history!" Dawn shrieked.

A deafening clang made her cover her ears as a flier on a massive diurlax swooped in from behind her and clashed swords with Malstrom.

It relates because Malstrom is one of the twelve lumeres, said Laurel's disembodied voice echoing in Dawn's head. *He murdered two of them, which led to the secession of the civilization that came to be known as the Aquavi.*

The flier screamed as the knight's sword came down on her shoulder in one blow, severing her sword-wielding arm.

"I don't even know what a lumere is!"

The projection vanished as Marion, Lopple, and Hikaru strode through the living room. They gave Dawn confused stares and raised brows as they walked to the bathroom, where the bridge still stood in the shower.

"You have cashew cream and bagel on you," Marion chortled. "I'll be back later. I need to run a few errands at the other gardens and properties."

Dawn watched her housekeeper disappear into the room, then looked down at her hoodie to find the bagel stuck to her front, with spread smeared on the side of her hair, cheek, and sweatshirt.

"I didn't know Aquavian history could be so . . . immersive," Lopple teased before vanishing with Hikaru.

An hour later, Dawn settled back into the living room, bagel-and-spread free.

"I'm going to take a step back and recap Lumen events," Laurel said. "I forgot that you didn't know what a lumere is. I thought Angel explained that to you."

"It sounds familiar, but my memory of the council meeting is fuzzy," Dawn admitted. She found it frustrating that she couldn't remember the details that occurred during the meeting.

"Never mind the council," Laurel said with a dismissive wave. "A lumere is basically a Lumen who can wield a sentient jewel—a jewel imbued with a person's aura. I was told that the ritual to create a sentient jewel, or *corgemma*—as the Etherans call it—is extremely complex . . . and fatal. The ritual was performed only once, over a thousand years ago, and it was deemed forbidden soon after. Are you following so far?"

Dawn nodded. "You're saying that Malstrom was one of the twelve lumeres, which are Lumen who can wield powerful sentient jewels. But the ritual to create the sentient jewels—or cor-GEM-mahz—was done a really long time ago. Wouldn't all the lumeres be dead by now?"

"All the *original* lumeres have died, except for one."

Malstrom's projection appeared once more, frozen before them with a deranged look in his onyx eyes, clad in blood-stained armor. His helmet was gone, revealing his disheveled hair, as dark as obsidian, partly matted. Although his skin was pale, his strong-set jaw and hint of a widow's peak strangely reminded her of Ezra. Malstrom held his sword, embellished only by the reddish stone set in the center of the cross guard. The stone, Dawn realized, was a corgemma.

Through the projection, she sensed Laurel's simmering hatred. "He stole the sentient jewels," she said through gritted teeth. "He draws power from them. That's why he's still alive."

Dawn shifted uncomfortably on the sofa, piqued by her curiosity of what Malstrom looked like *today*. She imagined a bald, ghost of a man, someone who was wrinkled and senile. *Surely, his beyond-advanced age would've left him wishing he weren't still alive, right?*

"He looks the same," Laurel replied as though she could hear Dawn's thoughts. "Ezra and his sister Stralla have seen him and confirmed he's of sound mind. Before present-day technologies, all were Lumen. We all dwelled on Eretz, ruled by twelve formidable leaders."

Eleven other regal Lumen appeared with Malstrom in Laurel's projection, and the living room suddenly felt crowded. Each person differed not only in appearance, but also in their unique armor, royal garb, or accoutrements.

"The Twelve underwent the ritual to become lumeres," Laurel continued, as a unique jewel appeared on each person—whether on a crown, necklace, ring, or the like. "The lumeres became more powerful in using their aura to lead their kingdoms, but the ritual left Malstrom a broken man; he lost his wife and their unborn twins."

Malstrom's eyes had dark circles underneath. Indeed, he looked like someone who'd been driven mad, to hell and back. That fevered look in his eyes was the same she saw in her dad's eyes on some nights, when missing his wife became unbearable. Dawn often wondered if that was the reason her dad threw himself into his work—to distract himself from the pain.

"He thirsted for more and more power," Laurel said, her eyes glassy. "He convinced three of The Twelve to ally with him; the others refused. So *Malstrom the Merciful*," she emphasized with scathing sarcasm, "*only* executed two lumeres and enslaved their kingdoms."

Two of the lumeres in her projection vanished from sight, and those remaining regrouped. The projection morphed into the battle scene from earlier as Laurel continued voicelessly.

A devastating war broke out . . .

Malstrom and his three allies, clearly superior in using their aura to fly, led their warriors against the six remaining kingdoms. Aura arrows whizzed by Dawn's head, causing her to duck with a horrified expression as they pierced the horses and Lumen armor of their foes. The smell of blood and burnt flesh filled her nostrils, and for a moment she thought she might vomit.

The war lasted four years as nation rose against nation . . .

Not a second too soon, the projection morphed into an archipelago's beach landscape with rudimentary battleships and diurlax riders descending on the natives' ill-equipped fighters. Blood-curdling screams mixed with war cries as Lumen murdered one another, lopped off limbs, or drowned in the crimson-tinged water.

. . . but Malstrom and his allies conquered all. The four lumeres— despite possessing impressive shifting abilities—were captured. They were forced to surrender their sentient jewels, then they were executed.

The battle scenes disappeared, replaced by an executioner wielding a scythe-like aura blade. Four lumeres kneeled on a scaffold, hands bound behind them, their heads covered with a black cloth bag.

"That's enough!" Dawn said, as the executioner raised his blade.

Just as the blade started to come down, the projection vanished, leaving Dawn back in her living room and Laurel sitting across from her with a smirk upon her face. Dawn breathed a sigh of relief and the knot in her stomach loosened.

"Can you keep the projections less . . . bloody?" she asked, rubbing her temples.

"Fine," Laurel said begrudgingly. "But it really happened the way I'm projecting it!"

"How do you know it happened that way?" Dawn eyed Laurel skeptically. "You said yourself that Lumen can create projections."

"They're memories of Lumen who were actually there. These projections were passed down through generations by Aquavian chroniclers," Laurel insisted crossly.

Sensing that arguing with her would be futile, Dawn switched topics.

"I get that Malstrom and the three lumeres who allied with him emerged victorious. How does that factor into Aquavian history?"

"The four kingdoms were a people of shifters—they could shift their aura at will to shape their bodies," Laurel explained.

A new projection appeared, showing thousands of shifters retreating into the seas—their bodies changing into ones that consisted of half human, half fish.

That was the beginning of the Aquavi . . .

The scene before them morphed yet again to show mountains, forests, and flatlands. The ground quaked as the earth split and fissured, then the mountains and other landscapes ascended to the skies.

. . .and also the beginning of the Etheran realm. The last two lumeres who remained alive on Eretz evaded capture and went into hiding. Eventually, Malstrom left the Aquavian and Eretzian realms alone, focusing his efforts on governing the sky kingdom. A century passed, and for a while, there was peace.

The projection vanished.

Dawn walked to the bay window bench where Hiro lay, his head resting atop a throw pillow. *What a sorrowful beginning*, she thought, as she absentmindedly peeked through the window slats to look into the backyard. Large puddles covered the desert scape and a light drizzle continued to fall from the gray clouds above.

"What do you think about Aquavian history? Not as boring as you thought, I gather?" Laurel remained seated on a luxurious armchair, her legs curled up beside her.

"It's *very* different from what I imagined. I mean, the Aquavi were essentially refugees," Dawn said, still overlooking the waterlogged backyard. The weather felt just as dreary as her heart. "I can only fathom the difficulties your people endured—learning how to communicate under water and dwelling amongst other sea creatures."

It was only early afternoon, yet Laurel nodded wearily. "The four Aquavian kingdoms appointed new leaders, and they each formed their own major underwater city—a *colaquas*. The Lumen who remained on Eretz scattered across the lands."

Laurel gracefully rose from her seat and stretched her arms above her head, her mouth wide open in an exaggerated yawn.

"How about we have a late lunch or early dinner and call it a day?" Dawn asked, aware that projecting had taken a toll on her friend.

"Nah, I'm done here," she said as she strode toward the bathroom.

Following her, Dawn thought about what Marion mentioned last night—how Laurel wouldn't eat anything aside from the seaweed she brought with her.

"Can I at least get you a drink of water?"

"Don't bother. There's plenty of water where I'm going," she returned as she stepped into the shower in front of the cheval mirror.

The gems on the mirror frame sparkled, activated by Laurel's aura, and the glass swirled in mesmerizing blue and metallic hues.

"Laurel, you and I are friends, right?"

The Aquavian turned to face Dawn, her back to the mirror.

"We are," she said as the portal's glow created an ethereal effect behind her. "What of it?"

"I'm grateful that you're teaching me all this stuff," she said, shifting her weight from one foot to another. "I don't know anything about Aquavian customs, but if I or anyone in my home made you uncomfortable or offended you somehow, I hope you'd let me know."

The Aquavian starred at Dawn with perfectly schooled features, her expression unreadable.

"Is there a reason you don't want to try any of Marion's cooking?" Dawn blurted out.

Laurel blinked. "I prefer to eat the food from my own colaquas. Is that a problem?"

"You can eat what you wish, however, Miss M. is practically family." After swallowing the dryness in her throat, Dawn pressed on. She hated confrontation, but she could not let this go; Marion was not *just* a housekeeper. "I hope you'll come to see Marion as I do—she's one of the kindest women I know—but even if you don't, you should treat her respectfully."

"Fair enough," Laurel said with a half-smile playing on her lips. "See you tomorrow."

Without another word, the Aquavian vanished through the bridge. Dawn had no doubt Laurel withheld what she really thought about Marion, but there was something else that bothered her. She stared at her perplexed reflection as the mirror returned to a solid state. Hadn't she expected water to gush out the moment Laurel crossed? That was the reason Marion moved the bridge to the shower, but the water never came.

Laurel didn't cross to an underwater bridge this time, Dawn realized, wondering where she would've gone. Wherever it was, she'd have to figure it out later. She turned on her heel to leave the bathroom when she heard a *clunk, clunk, clunk* on the glass.

Chapter 10

DAWN SPUN AROUND, surprised to see a disheveled Lopple leaning against the glass, his face contorted in pain.

"Help! Healer!" he called out, unable to see her, then gasped for air.

"It's me, Dawn," she answered immediately, scanning him to see where he was hurt but finding no visible injuries. She raised one hand to the glass and another on the black gem embedded in the frame. "Hikaru and Marion aren't back yet but come in—I'll call them."

Without hesitation, Lopple raised his hand to the glass—just as he had the first time she had seen him cross the bridge—and a tingling sensation pulsed through Dawn's arms and fingertips. It was fast like lightning, warm as a lit match. She took a step back as Lopple stumbled through and collapsed on the floor. He writhed and groaned, clutching his chest.

Instinctively, Dawn crouched down, arms outstretched, thinking she could drag him to the living room.

"Don't," he wheezed. Dawn froze, her hands just shy of grabbing hold of his arms. With difficulty, Lopple managed, "D-don't . . . touch . . . me! Poisoned."

Not one to stand and watch as someone injured lay before her, Dawn sprang into action.

"I'll call Hikaru and Miss Marion," Dawn said as she careened out of the bathroom.

Hiro, hearing the commotion, lopped from the bay window toward the bathroom, passed by her with his paws skidding on the hardwood floor.

"Hiro! Stay!" Dawn commanded.

"Hikaru! Hikaru!" Lopple groaned from the bathroom.

The husky had stayed put right outside the bathroom door, ears perked up on high alert.

In the kitchen, Dawn laid her phone on the counter. "X8, call Hikaru," she instructed the virtual assistant as she rummaged through the pantry and found a stash of dried kudzukan leaves. She figured the drink would act as a detox, as it had for her.

"Calling Hikaru," the AI responded a second later.

When the healer didn't answer, Dawn tried Marion while simultaneously prepping a pot of water on the stove, adding the leaves to it, and setting it to "quick boil."

The moment her housekeeper's hologram appeared, Dawn said very quickly in one breath, "Miss M.! Oh, thank goodness. Lopple's been poisoned and I can't touch him and he's asking for Hikaru—is he with you? Can you come ASAP?"

"I'll tell him—we'll be there soon," Marion replied, dropping whatever she was holding and setting off to get Hikaru. "Boil the kudzukan and—"

"I did! Should I 'quick cool' some of it and have Lopple drink it?"

"Yes," Marion huffed before disconnecting.

A minute later, Dawn knelt beside Lopple, who had paled and was sweating profusely as he clutched his chest while in the fetal position. He looked up at her from the floor with his hazel, pleading eyes.

"It's kudzukan," Dawn said as she put a squeeze bottle in his mouth and forced the cooled liquid down his throat. "Do you know what you were poisoned with?"

She saw his neck bob as he swallowed a few gulps, then shivered.

"Sangwor shamrock," he whispered, as he shivered again.

The mirror swirled not a moment too soon as Hikaru and Marion stepped through—both donning protective lab coats and gloves. Dawn backed out of the bathroom and ushered Hiro away. The intelligent canine had stayed at attention, observing near the doorway, but had not crossed the threshold.

"He was poisoned with sangwor shamrock," she said, watching Hikaru take vitals.

"Let's get him to the guest room," Hikaru grunted to Marion as he hoisted Lopple up by his arms; Marion carried Lopple's legs.

The next hour flew by as Dawn boiled more kudzukan and other herbs Marion had instructed her to add; the housekeeper ran from room to room, bringing medical supplies, towels, and Hikaru's healing crystals to the guest room. After doing all she could, Dawn paced the living room, wringing her hands, hoping that Lopple would pull through. She had never seen Hikaru tend to a patient with such care and urgency. It was obvious Lopple was a friend of his, and the situation was dire.

Minutes later, Marion emerged from the guest room with sweat glistening on her forehead. She looked at Dawn with a relieved smile, and a long exhalation left Dawn's lungs.

Lopple would live.

After finishing her errands and making sub sandwiches that no one had the appetite to eat yet, Marion joined Dawn in the living room.

They listened to the distant rumble of thunder and sporadic rainfall while waiting for Hikaru to ask for anything he might need. It was a rare moment of sitting and doing nothing, except contemplating what else needed to be done, yet deciding to put off any other tasks until later for not being able to focus.

Marion was first to break the silence. "You did well, Dawn," she said as she stroked Hiro's fur. "Sangwor shamrock is a type of Etheran plant poison used in aura weapons. It shuts down the respiratory system within minutes."

Dawn shot her a mixed look of concern and surprise. She had known that plants fascinated Marion, that her parents had financed Marion's studies in herbology and botany. She wondered whether her housekeeper's interest included poisonous plants and extended to those in the Etheran realm.

"What's the antidote?" she asked curiously.

"There isn't one. The only remedy is an aura cleanse and a detox, which is why it is fortunate you prepared and administered the kudzukan quickly. And Hikaru had a hunch it was sangwor shamrock."

The door to the guest room opened and Hikaru stepped out, looking like he had toiled in the sun rather than tended to someone's bedside.

"He'll be as good as new in a few hours," Hikaru said in a tired yet relieved voice.

"How long have you known Lopple?" Dawn asked, noticing the rose-colored healing crystals he held in a small bowl.

He gave her a puzzled look. "We only just met on the day you returned from the council meeting," he said as he removed his protective coat and folded it neatly. "Why?"

"It seemed like you were old friends," Dawn began, "the way you treated him . . . I mean, saved his life, er, never mind."

Perhaps she was overthinking it; Hikaru was just being Hikaru.

"I've healed many strangers, friends, and foes without discrimination—it is what we healers do," he said on the verge of collapse.

Marion rushed to his side. "Your care has exhausted your own aura," she said while helping him steady himself. "Go and rest in the other guest room."

She guided him while supporting his arm, but before they left, Hikaru turned back to Dawn and said, "There's a saying among us that I believe to be true: *heal one at death's door, gain a friend forever more.*"

The rest of the afternoon was thankfully unexciting and uneventful. Marion caught up on her house chores while Dawn spent time in her room, reviewing her dad's letter. His riddle about the rare ingredient dropped enough hints about its general location: "rooted near the river where it's always night," "ripe for picking in the dark," and "past the maw and deep in the throat." Certain this ingredient was in a cave—one that they had visited together—she asked X8 to reference her dad's travel logs and compile data on all the caves they had visited.

Then she caught up on her friend's messages and sent them long-overdue responses, assuring them she was steadily recovering from the flu. A swift reply from Logan sent her heart aflutter. "Get lots of rest. I'll send some soup tomorrow. Anything you like/don't like?"

Dawn couldn't hold back a grin as she messaged back. "Surprise me!"

"Is that a challenge? I'm up for it. Send me your address. G'night"

She returned a smiley face and—against her better judgment—Hikaru's address.

Later that evening, Dawn, Marion, and Hikaru—who had clearly gotten the rest he needed—met in the dining room for a quiet dinner. The healer checked on Lopple and reported that he was awake and enjoying his own Philly cheesesteak, "with extra onions" per his request. Miss M. asked Dawn to take more kudzukan tea to him while she and Hikaru took Hiro outside for a short nighttime stroll in the rain.

After gently knocking twice on the guest room door and hearing no answer, Dawn tiptoed in and set a mug of warm tea on the crowded bedside table. Lopple's plate with his half-eaten sub, a bowl of healing crystals, a dimmed lamp, and empty mugs also occupied the space. She cast a cursory glance at him and snorted when she saw him fast asleep in her dad's pajama tops, which sported a silly pattern of llamas. He seemed so much older as he slept. He could be her grandpa—the thought elicited another snort from her.

Lopple stirred. Dawn picked up the mugs and the plate with his half-eaten sandwich, making a beeline for the door.

"Where'd ya think you're going with that?" Lopple said thickly. "That'sss my sssandwich."

Dawn returned and was about to set the plate on the table, when he held out his hand and took it from her. She watched as he struggled to prop himself up on his pillows, then he took a big bite of the sub. Mouth full, he motioned for her to sit on the stool next to the bed.

She obliged him and sat, awkwardly keeping hold of the empty mugs.

"I guesss I have you to thank for yourrr quick thinking," he said after finally swallowing. He took a long draught of the tea she brought, grimacing before he swallowed. "Your en is stronger than you think."

He took another bite of his sandwich, slurping up an extra-long slice of onion that fell against his chin. He chewed thoughtfully, then continued.

"*En* meansss aura in Etherishhh and Orako," he slurred, then gulped down more tea. "Aurrra is an ancient concept. Other cultures refer to it by different names. I've heard groundli-lings call it *chi*, *chakra*, or *mana*. As far as aura abilities go, you either use it or lose it."

Dawn pondered his statement. If what he was saying was true, wouldn't she be at a disadvantage learning how to use her aura as an adult?

"I knowwww what you're thinking," Lopple said, then took another bite.

"Y-you do?" she asked, impatiently waiting for him to swallow and continue.

"Yesssss. You still have it. Your en is strooong," he said with a surprising bout of energy. "Y'must have a strong bloodline 'cause yer en is 'wakening . . . but you weren't taught from birth. Long ago, your kind thought they didn't need aura abilities because of their technolo-logical 'vancements. Your kind stopped teaching the next generations how to use their en. But those who still wielded their aura openly were looked down upon. Thought of as dangerousss. Called witches, wizards, sorcerers . . . mmmages!"

He paused with his forefinger in the air, then finished off his sandwich.

"Eretziansss were either hunted down . . . or they lost use of their aurrra. Not enough of them to protect themselvessss in the end. That's how you all became *grrroundlingsss*," he growled unintentionally.

Dawn chuckled quietly and watched him as he drained the rest of his tea. Lopple slumped back on his pillows and his eyes half closed.

"But Mmmarion, Hik-hikaru, and yyyou . . ." he said, closing his eyes a whole five seconds before forcing them open again, "You are Eretzian."

Lopple yawned before sleep overtook him, leaving Dawn wide awake to contemplate his ramblings.

CHAPTER II

DAWN TOSSED AND turned, unable to fall asleep. Despite the steady lull of the rain and comfortable bedding, she laid awake in the dark, mulling over the events of the long day. Malstrom's soufors were after her and, at one point, they had been after Lopple too—Randen Silvers had the intent to kill. Lopple's nasty scar hidden beneath his chin was evidence of that. But who poisoned him with sangwor shamrock?

How did she and her dad factor into all of this? Were the soufors after her dad as well?

Dawn sat up in bed, rubbing her eyes. Endless questions sprang up in her thoughts and she wished there was a way to still her mind. She had never been good at meditation and was not a fan of sleeping pills.

"Light on," she commanded the lamp on her nightstand, then grabbed her mom's journal and tiny key from the drawer and set them onto her lap. If sleep continued to evade her, now was as good a time as any to examine the items.

She flipped through the journal's pages. Still blank. Then she lifted the small key to eye level, squinting at the shiny black stone at its bow. Although it was miniscule in size, it looked similar to the black stone embedded atop the cheval mirror frame. She recalled Lopple saying something about the jewel acting as a lock—for a *locked* bridge—which is why someone on the other side had to activate it and allow him to cross.

The jewel itself could be a key, she considered. *How can I activate it with my aura?*

Thinking back to when Lopple passed his aura through her hands to unlock the bridge, she remembered the strange sensation. It was of radiating warmth, unlike anything she'd ever experienced.

Placing the key on top of the journal's cover, she brought both hands up and cupped them to her mouth, then blew her breath on her palms, vigorously rubbing them together. When they felt warm enough, she took her index finger and touched the key's jewel.

She held her finger to the key for a few seconds, then flipped the journal open. Nothing. The pages were still blank. She shut the book and tried a dozen more times, varying her approach. She summoned thoughts of fire, flames, and warm fuzzy feelings. Still, no success. She could ask Miss M. for help tomorrow but dismissed the idea; it was her mom's journal, and *she* wanted to be the one to unlock it.

A drawn-out yawn came out of her, and thunder grumbled across the sky. The steady pitter-patter of rain became a downpour, loud enough to drown out Dawn's pesky internal banter. Now that fatigue started to set in, perhaps unlocking the journal was something she could sleep on.

Just one more try before turning in, she told herself.

After taking a deep breath and relaxing her shoulders, she visualized the heat radiating in her palm like a glowing orb of light. Then she imagined the warmth traveling to the tip of her finger. It pulsed faintly. Certain that this time felt different, she concentrated on keeping that pulsating sensation at the tip of her finger. Slowly, she moved her finger to touch the key's jewel. When her skin made contact, the key snapped into the debossed imprint on the journal!

Dawn gasped at the sudden movement. It was as though the key had instantly become magnetized. The jewel glimmered. It worked—she had activated it! Ecstatic, she opened the journal and flipped to a once-blank page, now filled with writing.

Her jaw dropped as she leafed through the pages, marveling at her mom's delicate penmanship.

Some of the section headers read:

"Occurrences"

"Plants"

"Jewels"

"Languages"

"Colaquases"

What an odd way to organize a journal. It's more like a book of reference, she mused.

In addition to sections, random entries littered the pages throughout—some dated, some not. Notes were written in the margins and spaces between the lines, as though added as an after-thought. She took a closer look at some of the barely legible writing and recognized her dad's familiar scrawl.

He must've added to it after mom passed.

Turning back to the Occurrences section, Dawn scanned a few sentences that mentioned luxury aerospace giants that rivaled CETT. She turned to another page that brought her to "Plants." Amidst myriad sketches and descriptions of flora that were sure to enthrall Marion, the words "sangwor shamrock" jumped out at her.

Underneath the words was a drawing. Her finger traced the sketch of four leaves, shaped like the wings of a butterfly. Below, it read, *Touch leaves of four, breathe no more.*

There was an added description in her dad's writing. "Purple leaves. Poisonous. Fatal. See Sangwor."

Dawn shuddered. The warning sounded morbidly lethal, and she didn't think she was ready to discover what was in the Sangwor section.

She passed the page with a long black feather taped to it—now certain it was a diurlax feather—and another page titled, "Common Etherish Sayings." She arched a brow upon seeing "Nol timu—Do not fear" before skipping to the "Jewels" section. It was thick and detailed with names of lumeres, descriptions of gems, healing crystals, protection stones, and the like.

She turned the page and landed on a peculiar entry:

March 2, 2222

My dearest daughter,

Today, we found out you would be a girl! I can't put into words how excited we are. Marion was so happy for us as well. I've never seen her smile so big, from ear to ear. It has been the best news we've had in a long time.

Your heartbeat and aura are strong. Your dad thinks your heart sounds like a rhythmic war drum, but I think it sounds more like a rushing river. I can feel the current of your en. Vibrant. Unyielding.

You are so deeply loved, even before you are born. Even before we know your name. I can't wait to see you and hold you in my arms.

Love,
Mom

It was dated about six months before her birthdate. Tears traced Dawn's cheeks; her mom had written to her when she had yet to be born. She had never felt so loved by someone she wished she knew. With a light touch, her fingers ran over those last sentences; her own mother had once held the same book and written those words with her own hand. Dawn reread the page countless times well into the night until she fell into a dreamless sleep.

CHAPTER 12

"SANGWOR SHAMROCK?" LAUREL asked in an incredulous, high-pitched voice.

Last night's storm had finally blown over and the morning sun shyly peaked through the clouds, sending fractured rays of light through the kitchen window.

"Yes, sangwor shamrock," Dawn confirmed before hastily tying her dark brown hair in a ponytail. "I'm surprised Lopple got himself out of bed considering the state he was in last night."

"That poisonous plant is only grown in Etero and is primarily used by the *sangwor*—Malstrom's blood warriors," she said, pausing to drink from her stout red mug. "'Blood' refers to Malstrom's kin—they're merely Valedorian knights who share his bloodline."

"Sounds like nepotism," said Dawn while sprinkling furikake on her eggs Florentine.

"It has to do with the way Malstrom trusts the sangwor. He can see and feel through them because they are 'blood of his blood and flesh of his flesh.' That's how Stralla explained it, anyway." Laurel shrugged as she pushed around the stringy seaweed on her plate with a fork.

Dawn blinked, and when she opened her eyes, she nearly choked on her food—about twenty or so sangwor clad in all-white protective gear surrounded her and Laurel. They silently occupied almost every space around the kitchen table. What was most unsettling were the expressionless masks they wore—like ninjas in white. She closed her mouth after realizing it was hanging open.

"Do you recall meeting Stralla in Tencho? She is a sangwor," Laurel said, as the closest warrior next to the Aquavian removed her mask and hood to reveal Stralla's honey-tinted face.

The projection of Stralla pulled back a chair and sat next to Laurel. Stralla's striking cheekbones shimmered in the filtered sunlight as if she were actually there. The projection looked so real, Dawn was tempted to offer their new guest at the table something to eat.

Is that how you met Ezra? Through Stralla? Dawn attempted to project.

I didn't catch that. Reach out with your mind more, Laurel encouraged, her disembodied voice resounding clearly. *Try to picture what you're saying.*

Dawn tried again, this time imagining a scruffy-looking Ezra, standing behind Stralla.

How did you and Ezra meet? Was it through Stralla? Dawn projected as her eyes focused on Ezra, then his sister. She tried with all her might to *will* the message to reach Laurel.

That's better! the Aquavian said, unable to hide her surprise. *And yes, I met Ezra by way of Stralla, but it sort of started with my own sister. I should start from the beginning.*

The sangwor surrounding them vanished and a projection of another woman appeared sitting next to Laurel. Her hair and skin tone were similar to Laurel's, but her eyes were a deeper brown and her lips were fuller.

This is Kailani, Laurel projected, as if introducing her in real life, *my only sister.*

Dawn was surprised by how much older Kailani seemed—almost matriarchal.

When she was seventeen—my age, Laurel continued, *our father would take her on his trips to negotiate sharing seafood with the Etherans. She was married off to an Etheran Lord the following spring, and their union united our two tribes. It's only been a few years, but already, some sky dwellers have accepted our Aquavian clan almost as equals.*

Dawn studied the sisters. Kailani sat ramrod straight and dignified—a stark contrast to Laurel who hunched her shoulders forward and gripped her red mug, peering into its contents.

After Kailani married, my father was invited to attend negotiations in Etero, the sky kingdom's capital. Our whole family accompanied him. That's when I met Stralla, who was still a sangwor-in-training. Eventually, Stralla introduced me to the rest of her family, and that's how I met Ezra. Our parents negotiated a betrothal for us last year.

Laurel finally met Dawn's eyes as Kailani's projection disappeared. "My whole life has been planned for me."

Feeling compassion for her friend, and unsure what to say, Dawn thought for a beat and decided to ask a question that would elicit a positive response. "Since you met, were you and Ezra always good friends?"

Laurel nodded. "We've gotten to know each other better now that he's not a sangwor."

Dawn arched an eyebrow, wondering how one was stripped of warrior status.

"He wasn't expelled or anything. He and his two younger brothers were already sangwor. When Stralla officially became knighted, her father retired from his post as the head city planner. Ezra was able to step down as a sangwor and assume his father's position."

So, Ezra and his siblings are blood warriors, Dawn noted. Their ties to Malstrom aroused a worrisome train of thought: Ezra was betrothed to Laurel, who had been coming to the house every day for the past week . . . and it wasn't a stretch to assume Laurel was visiting him. That could've been where she went the other night after she crossed the bridge. What if Malstrom could see through Ezra and hear his thoughts? Hadn't Marion said Malstrom had a lead on my whereabouts?

"I know what you're thinking," Laurel began, "that there's a chance Ezra may have leaked info on your location to Malstrom. I can assure you he and his family are trustworthy."

"I understand *you* would trust Ezra with your life, but this is *my* life and my family's lives on the line," Dawn pointed out. "Isn't there a chance you're wrong? You said yourself that Malstrom could see or sense through his sangwor—and that includes Stralla."

"Ezra and his family have impeccable control over what they allow Malstrom to see. His father was searching for a way out of serving as knights long before Stralla officially joined."

Laurel pursed her lips and glanced over her shoulder at the window facing the backyard where Hiro roamed. "Ezra's family secretly plans to overthrow Malstrom," Laurel said, dropping her voice to a whisper. "Malstrom suspects it but has no proof; that's why Stralla was at the council meeting. She's a double agent. If there *were* a leak, it wouldn't be from Stralla or Ezra."

"I'll discuss this with Marion and Hikaru," Dawn said, clearing the table. She told Laurel she'd meet her in the living room in half an hour for a change of scenery; Malstrom's connection to the sangwor was a great risk, and she needed more time to consider it—alone.

What would be the cost if the sangwor or soufors discovered her whereabouts?

The afternoon passed uneventfully with Laurel trying to teach Dawn to project imagery with "barely a grain of sand's worth of progress." The Aquavian projected breathtaking waterscapes—chronicler memories of what they looked like centuries ago. Dawn found the Arctic tundra's beauty unparalleled but was once more reminded of her deadline to master her aura abilities—before the polar caps disappeared completely on Earth.

"Dinner's ready. Sushi tonight," Miss M. called from the kitchen as the projection dissipated and Dawn's body temperature returned to normal.

Marion had returned from her errands an hour ago, but Dawn decided to save the conversation about the sangwor until after Laurel left.

"I should get going." Laurel yawned, plodding toward the bathroom.

"Dawn, it looks like you have a visitor at Hikaru's house," Marion hollered again.

"See you tomorrow, Laurel." Dawn waved as she rushed to the kitchen.

Marion's mobile device projected video at Hikaru's front door—the address where she, Dawn and Howel usually sent all deliveries. It was one of their unspoken household rules, and recently, Dawn understood the real reason why they had always been secretive of their address.

At Hikaru's door, a broad-shouldered man clutched the handles of a large stock pot. He smiled at the camera, and Dawn's heart fluttered.

"Who's that?" Laurel squealed, looking over Dawn's shoulder and startling her.

"I thought you were leaving," Dawn said to Laurel, retrieving her phone to find she just received a message. "Logan really *is* at Hikaru's house! I thought he would have soup *delivered*."

Marion clicked her tongue. "Tell him to just leave it by the door. You know the rule."

"Can't Hikaru walk him over here to drop it off just this once?" *Please, please, please, PLEASE! I'm dying to talk to another* normal *person in real life,* Dawn wished.

"Dawn, it is not a good—"

"Wait. Did you hear that?" Laurel interrupted. "She projected four 'pleases' loud and clear. That's the best she's done all day. Look at her. She has stars in her eyes."

Marion deadpanned Dawn, then Laurel, clearly unimpressed.

"Obviously, she's infatuated, and her *arousal* is enhancing her projection," Laurel teased.

"That's ridiculous. He's just a friend from work." *I'm not* aroused! *There's nothing wrong with having a small crush on him.*

"I heard that!" Laurel gushed the moment Dawn finished the thought. The Aquavian folded her arms in triumph and looked to Marion. "Let's have a little experiment. Invite him over for dinner and see if Dawn's projections improve."

Marion shook her head. "We can't risk—"

"I'll stay for dinner as well. And I'll eat something," Laurel offered. Marion clamped her mouth, apparently intrigued by the promise of Laurel eating her food. "Hikaru could erase his memory if something goes wrong. There's no harm in it. He's an adult—it's only permanently damaging for children."

"Erase his memory?" Dawn echoed, wondering what kind of damage it could cause to a child. "Can that really be done?"

I want Logan to stay, but I'm not sure I want his memory wiped . . . or to be wiped from his memory.

Laurel snorted, and Dawn thought she muttered something about irony.

Marion looked from the video to Laurel to Dawn, then to Hikaru. *He is but one friend stopping by,* Marion's voice reverberated in their heads. Dawn got the sense her housekeeper was reminded of what it felt like to be head over heels for someone.

Marion's expression turned stern. "He can stay for dinner, on the condition that Hikaru erases our address from his memory afterward."

Shortly after Hikaru was briefed, he arrived with Logan, who was then awkwardly introduced to Laurel, a *distant* cousin. Then came the unexpected arrival of her *distant uncle* Lopple, who was delighted to be partaking in their spontaneous dinner party.

Dinner *was* interesting. It was also a disaster, or rather, Dawn interpreted it as such as she lay awake in her bed, recounting the most mortifying events of the evening. Small talk began with Logan bringing Dawn up to speed on the last two weeks of work at the studio. Everyone, including Laurel, tried the soup he made—a flavorful broth with mushrooms, veggies, and tofu.

Lopple praised Marion for the sushi, despite noting the lack of onions.

Then a three-second earthquake hit, and Lopple started choking on his food. Fortunately, Laurel roughly whacked his back until the lodged piece of fish was forced out of his mouth and back on his plate. After regaining his composure, Lopple (much to everyone's disgust) re-ate it.

The atmosphere didn't quite recover after that, and Dawn was somewhat relieved to eat in silence. She kept glancing at Logan, who seemed content with stealing glances of her too.

Later, Logan asked everyone, "Where are you all from?"

Dawn's breath hitched.

"Lopple, I assume you must've lived elsewhere—some place where earthquakes aren't so frequent," Logan added. "And Laurel, you have a unique accent I can't place."

Dawn shot Marion a panicked glance across the table as her fingers absentmindedly fiddled with the pendant on her necklace.

"You're extremely perceptive, Logan. I've lived in many places, but mostly in Calgary, Canada." Lopple smiled politely after his well-rehearsed line, then popped another sushi roll in his mouth to indicate that was all he wished to say.

It was Laurel's turn. "I grew up on a small Hawaiian island. I love seafood. All I eat is seafood," she said matter of factly.

She could pass for Hawaiian, Dawn thought, and wondered if the Aquavian had to tell other groundlings this same ruse.

"I grew up in South Africa," Marion chimed in, "but have worked with Howel for decades. He traveled frequently, and that is how I came to meet Lopple and Hikaru."

"We're all family friends. Just visiting," Laurel continued.

"Is this some sort of reunion?" Logan asked. "Or are you visiting Dawn's dad since he got sick?"

Not sure of how to respond, Dawn nodded. She felt a headache coming on and took a sip of the kudzukan tea.

Laurel agreed. "Yes, we came as soon as we heard. He's like a strange uncle to me."

Dawn coughed into her mug and linked her thoughts to Laurel's mind. *Do you mean* estranged *uncle?*

"I mean, *estranged* uncle," Laurel said a little too loudly. "Howel, Lopple, Hikaru—they're all estranged uncles."

Logan stifled his laughter.

Stop talking! Dawn projected, trying to kick Laurel under the table. But the Aquavian moved too quickly.

"Ow!" Marion cried.

"Can you pass the tea, Miss M.?" Dawn asked, hoping to mask her yelp.

She passed the teapot with a simmering stare as Dawn gave her temples a quick rub.

"Do you have a headache?" Logan asked, leaning closer so their shoulders touched.

"Y-yeah. It's the only symptom I've had since I've been recovering, but the tea helps."

"What kind of tea is this?" Logan asked, looking into his own murky cup.

"It's kudzukan tea—I made it with a blend of herbs," Marion said. "Try some."

"I think I'll try it too, Miss Marion," Laurel said, pouring some into her red mug.

Logan took a sip and blinked. "It's very strong. It must be an acquired taste."

Laurel raised her cup to her lips, and as soon as the tea touched her tongue, she sputtered it out—dousing her food and Dawn, who sat directly in front of her.

"Ew." Laurel coughed unapologetically.

Dawn wiped her face and hid her frown with her napkin at the same time.

"Well, I guess supper's done," Marion sighed. No one disagreed. "Go on and wait in the living room while I clear the table."

"What's for dessert?" Laurel dared to ask.

Dawn placed a pillow over her face to smother her words as she lamented, "Why'd you have to open your big mouth, Laurel? We could've had a nice, normal dinner."

"Am I interrupting something?" Marion said, peeking into her room.

Dawn sat up and groaned, tossing the pillow aside. "Logan's never gonna come back!"

Marion walked in and sat on the side of Dawn's bed. "I didn't take you for a simpering girl who cared so much about the affections of the so-called Stallion."

"*Not* funny. I didn't think I'd care so much about what he thought either."

"Dinner wasn't *that* bad. That spoiled Aquavian princess finally ate something I prepared. Lopple survived. And Logan would be crazy to not want to see you again, no matter how many times you get the flu."

Dawn cracked a smile. Her housekeeper knew exactly what to say to ease her anxieties.

"I saw the way he looked at you," Marion teased. "I know you like him too. Hearing your projections reminded me of when your mother taught me how to activate my aura. It is easier when one feels strongly about something. Hikaru and I think it's okay if Logan stops by for dinner now and then—especially since his presence is helping your projections progress."

"R-really? Hikaru is all right with this?"

"On a few conditions: Logan will meet at Hikaru's house. They'll walk here, then after dinner, they'll go back to Hikaru's. On the way there, Logan's memory will be modified slightly, so he won't remember this location. It will be as if everything took place at Hikaru's."

"Modifying his memory won't hurt him?"

"No. The side effects, which are fogginess and maybe a dull headache, are fleeting."

"You make it sound so simple," she said, then she decided to tell Marion what Laurel had revealed earlier. That Ezra's family were secretly planning to overthrow Malstrom. That their sangwor bloodline made it possible for them to be Malstrom's eyes and ears. And that this added another level of complexity since the Sky King had a lead on her whereabouts.

After Dawn finished explaining her worries, Marion conceded it was indeed something to be anxious about. "I wanted to talk to you about Lopple as well. The sangwor are after him. They've been trying to eradicate him since he led a failed uprising against Malstrom. Those sympathetic to his cause are still conspiring in secret. Lopple is aiding Howel for reasons unknown to me, but before Howel left, he made it clear that Hikaru and I were to keep both of you safe. We'll relocate soon, and when we move, there's no coming back to this place."

Silence followed while Dawn's brain swam in all the information her housekeeper had unloaded. She was supposed to be hiding from the soufors. Supposed to learn basic aura abilities. Supposed to focus on completing her dad's mission. And now Malstrom's sangwor—his blood warriors—were after a fugitive who could lead them directly to her.

Miss M. needn't explain the risks they were taking. With Logan and Lopple visiting, they took a gamble on keeping their location secret. Even after relocating, wouldn't Logan be in danger?

Dawn looked at her cozy surroundings. She had called this her home longer than any other place they had stayed at. Had their relocating and frequent trips truly been due to the nature of her dad's work, or had they had more to do with avoiding someone?

Not that it really mattered right now. The outcome would be the same. She sighed. Moving would help ensure their safety, but at the cost of no longer being able to enjoy Logan's company—or any groundling, for that matter.

"Get some rest. We'll talk more tomorrow," Marion said, getting up to leave.

"I'm going to miss it here," Dawn said just above a whisper. She knew Marion had been uprooted many times before. "Didn't this place feel like home to you, Miss M.?"

Before exiting, her housekeeper turned on her heel to face her. She said simply, "My true home has always been with the people I love."

CHAPTER 13

OVER THE NEXT few weeks, the stormy weather subsided, giving way to record-breaking high temperatures despite it being the middle of winter. This particular day was bright and sunny, perfect for a stroll in the neighborhood. From the living room window, Dawn could see little birds hopping around the backyard, peeking through the shrubs for bugs and insects. She wished she could go outside, although day-dreaming of Logan was the next best thing.

His casual smile frequently came to mind, and she admired how it sometimes turned into a playful, lopsided smirk.

"Focus," Laurel said for the hundredth time, while she sat reclined on the sofa.

"I *am* focusing," Dawn insisted, tearing her eyes from the window to face her relaxed instructor. "Thinking of Logan helps me focus. At least it did when I was projecting."

Dawn found that projections came easily after her initial slow start. She'd progressed steadily over the last three weeks and managed to conjure an impressive simulation of the Grand Canyon. It had taken hours of effort and practice, but she could now show Laurel a spectacular aerial view of the crevices and layered rock formations, which stretched out as far as the eye could see. Recalling details from her tour a few years ago, she appealed to all Laurel's senses with the sound of the wind rushing through the rock columns, the smell and chill of the crisp winter air, and the multitude of blended brown-red-orange-yellow hues at sunset.

If Laurel's gaping mouth was any indication, she was spectacularly enthralled with Dawn's projection (although she wouldn't dare say as much). Dawn knew that water had once shaped the layers of rock and that the Aquavian, in all her years of living in the deep blue, had never known that a landlocked place could be so . . . well, grand.

In turn, Laurel conjured immersive projections of biolumines-cent sea creatures and terrifying whirlpools that she and her Aquavian friends (mostly Reed, the skinny teen who had been with her at Tencho) took swirling thrill rides on.

In the evenings, when Logan didn't come by for dinner, Dawn continued research on her dad's riddle. X8 had returned an extensive list of hundreds of cave systems Howel had visited throughout his career. To narrow it down, Dawn filtered the list to show only caves they had *both* visited. Howel frequently went on cave expeditions first to conduct his research, then, if warranted, he'd ask Dawn to follow with a designated guide while he spent the next half of his excursion in labs and meetings, consulting his peers.

At the time, Dawn thought the purpose of her cave visits was to help her dad proofread his accounts of the sites. Now, she suspected his ulterior motive had something to do with her eventual introduction to the Lumen.

When she wasn't working on the riddle, Dawn enjoyed perusing the journal, reading colloquialisms in Orako and Etherish. It was fascinating to see that Aquavians had numerous words for types of water, and how Etherans could use their auras to link minds with their diurlaxes.

Despite how busy Dawn was with all her journal reading, training, and research for the mission, it could not mask the feeling of loneliness that kept her awake every night. She missed her friends, especially Sparkle, who she used to chat with nearly every day. So, against her better judgment, she contacted him via virtual chat last night.

He knew as much as Marion had told Maizel. Dawn had recovered from the flu but was currently occupied with helping her dad on a two-month-long project. Sparkle's jovial spirit—along with some studio gossip—helped buoy Dawn's dampened mood. Apparently, Maizel had hired a temp barista who made coffee that tasted like "sewer water," and her muffins were akin to "fresh-baked bricks." There was also a "new blonde bombshell" (Sparkle's words) who hung around Logan every chance she got, but Sparkle reassured Dawn, "Logan couldn't care less."

Marion was in excellent spirits these days, mostly due to the fact that Laurel was at least eating *some* of the food she prepared. And Laurel seemed to have boundless energy now that she expended less effort in reading Dawn's projections.

Laurel was so pleased with how well projection training had evolved, she'd decided to teach Dawn how to shield last week. And that was where Dawn's progress petered out.

While Logan's company every few days or so proved to be the perfect impetus to help Dawn improve her projections, he had the opposite effect on Dawn's shielding attempts. She could not bring herself to concentrate her thoughts on creating an impenetrable shield with him around.

"I said, focus!" Laurel huffed in irritation. She had instructed Dawn to visualize creating a tidal wave that would wash through her mind, clearing her thoughts like an empty sea cave, and securing her secrets in a tightly shut clam shell . . . among other random, ocean-related things.

"Empty sea cave, empty sea cave, empty sea cave," Dawn whispered pointedly with her eyes closed, convinced it was the dumbest mantra ever.

"That's it, let the waves wash away everything in the cave," Laurel soothed, then took a loud deep breath as if urging Dawn to do the same.

After deflating her lungs with a *swoosh*, the room quieted, and Dawn felt herself drift away, her thoughts fading to black.

Empty sea cave, Dawn thought as best as she could.

"Ugh! You're not doing it right," Laurel hissed.

I'm a closed clam shell.

"You're WIDE OPEN, and you're thinking about Logan again."

Tidal wave washing all my thoughts away . . .

"You're reminiscing about holding his hand," Laurel said, projecting the memory of him in the open space between them.

Dawn cursed in Korean as her eyes flew open. She glared at Laurel, angry that her instructor kept accessing her private memories. The last time Logan visited, they had a few moments to themselves in the living room while Hikaru, Miss M., and Lopple stayed in the kitchen to chat. She and Logan had enjoyed a quick snuggle on the couch, where his hand had found hers. What Laurel didn't know, however, was that his lips also found hers . . . and Dawn was not the type to kiss and tell.

She and Laurel had gotten along so far, but if the past week was any indication of how long their friendship would last, she might be better off finding a new instructor. Evidently, Laurel knew which buttons to push to piss her off.

Dawn covered her face with hands and groaned. "How can you keep reading my thoughts when I'm trying so hard to shield them? I can't even keep my secrets from you!"

Laurel nodded. "You love sweets, you have a fear of spiders, and you hate potted plants. That's weird, by the way." She then continued to rattle off Dawn's embarrassing moments and insecurities, which is what she had done *every* day to mark the end of their shielding sessions.

"This isn't helping me gain more motivation to shield!"

Laurel raised an eyebrow. "Really? Wouldn't you want to keep your shameless attraction to Logan a secret? You swoon every time he tells you a story of how he went hiking or rafting. You're smitten with him just because he's nice to look at."

Dawn's anger flared. "That is *not* true! I like him because he's kind and—"

"You like him because he's the *first* one to show you affection. He's literally nothing special."

Dawn fumed and was about to say something she might regret when Marion's disembodied voice interrupted. "Laurel! Dawn! Come down for snacks," she said through X8's speaker on Dawn's nightstand.

"How's shielding going?" Marion asked after watching them sit silently at the table across from each other, trading death stares.

Laurel lowered her eyes to the table, inspecting the immaculate rows of avocado and cucumber rolls plated before them. She was in no mood for conversation.

"Could be better," Dawn finally growled, after the awkward silence had gone on too long.

"I see," Marion said slowly, drawing out the last word. She eyed them suspiciously as Dawn picked at her bowl of dried fruit and nuts.

Dawn forced a smile to Miss M. before her housekeeper turned to fetch something from the pantry.

"What do you think of eel rolls and assorted sashimi for dinner?" Marion asked when she emerged holding a large container of un-cooked rice.

Laurel scoffed.

"What's your problem?" Dawn blurted out, failing to uphold diplomacy in front of Marion.

Eager for verbal sparring, Laurel responded quickly. "My problem is . . . You. Can't. Shield!"

"Well, I'd probably be making more progress with a *real* instructor because . . . You. Can't. Teach!" Dawn retorted.

"Your incompetence has nothing to do with my teaching abilities," Laurel said, her voice rising. "You don't care about shielding or your father's mission. You only care about when your next kiss with Logan will be."

"Excuuuuse me?!" Dawn interjected. She did not anticipate their conversation taking this turn, nor did she realize that Laurel had already seen the memory of her and Logan's kiss. Mortified and be-trayed, she snuck a glance at her housekeeper, who was conveniently putting away dishes, pretending to ignore what Laurel just said.

"You can't help but fawn over him because you're *soooo* infatuated!" the Aquavian added, emphasizing the last words for dramatic effect.

"I am not!" Dawn shot back. "Besides, when did *you* get all worked up about the mission? Every day you keep leaving early to go play with Stralla or your sham of a fiancé—Ezra, in case you forgot! Also, you're a terrible teacher!"

"You don't know anything about where I go after this!" Laurel seethed, pounding her fist on the kitchen table. "While you're busy locking lips, I'm meeting with Angel to report on your progress— WHICH IS NON-EXISTENT!"

Marion, who had ignored their bickering up until that point, stopped her task and turned her head toward them.

Laurel smirked at Dawn and taunted, "Shall I project your make out session?"

"Do you have a death wish?!" Dawn asked.

A wispy projection appeared in front of them. Dawn and Logan were in the air vehicle, facing each other on the reclined seats, just as Dawn remembered.

"STOP IT!" Dawn shouted, jumping up from her chair. She clenched her hands into fists, casting Laurel a glare that could cut glass, then she *willed* the projection to dissipate.

"AAAAAARRRGGGHHHH!" Dawn screamed in exasperation.

She raised her right hand instinctively, palm facing the image of herself and Logan, feeling her aura channel through her arm. She glowered at the projection while racking her brain to think of every type of thick metal wall going up, every security safe with bolts and lasers getting activated.

This is MY memory! Dawn projected to Laurel, biting off every word. *GET. OUT. OF. MY. HEAD!*

The memory projection flickered, then to everyone's shock, it disappeared.

Laurel smiled triumphantly. "FINALLY! I KNEW YOU HAD IT IN YOU!"

"GAH! You're still a lousy teacher," Dawn said, hands still curled into fists with her fingernails digging into her skin.

"You're the one wasting time," the Aquavian said, standing up from her chair, "daydreaming every chance you get!"

"That's enough," Marion said with her hands on her hips. She hadn't yelled or slammed her hand down on the table, yet her stern look and motherly tone proved enough to disarm Dawn.

"What gives *you* the right to take from the sea to your heart's content?" Laurel lashed out. "Overfishing is worse than ever! It's people like *you* who are the reason some of the Aquavi clans go hungry."

Dawn was angry but could see that Laurel was furious. Something within the Aquavian had snapped, and she was taking it out on Miss M.

Marion shook her head. "You think I don't know anything about your people or customs, yet you're welcome to come here every day? You think I don't know your father, King Kameo Benevis, or have been in contact with him more than you have in the past month?"

Laurel furrowed her brow, opened her mouth to say something, but closed it.

"You assume I don't know the rules of engagement for Lumen and groundlings," Marion continued sternly, "rules that you've been violating every day. Surely you should've figured out by now why you're tasked with teaching Dawn. Do you think it's because of your expertise? Or that your father didn't have the time to send any other qualified Aquavi?"

The princess walked around the table to face Marion head on.

"You have no right to speak to me that way, to speak of my father that way," Laurel said, her voice breathy from swallowing her surging rage. Her bottom lip trembled ever so slightly. Dawn got a kick out of seeing her so unnerved.

Marion took a step toward Laurel; they were less than an arm's length from each other, and while both their faces maintained perfectly polite facades, their auras were like two rams about to collide.

"Perhaps you should ask him yourself." Marion shrugged.

The princess ground her teeth as her schooled features faltered. Dawn thought she could see an angry vein popping out from the side of her delicate neck, but Laurel remained silent.

With nothing left to say, Laurel scoffed, then turned on her heel and stormed out of the kitchen. Dawn and her housekeeper listened as the princess trudged through the living room. Then the bathroom door slammed with such force that the sound reverberated back to the kitchen.

Dawn relaxed her tense shoulders as she and Marion shared a gloating chuckle. However, the taste of victory from their little spat was short-lived. Immediately, guilt settled in the pit of her stomach as she realized she lost her temper over something a seventeen-year-old had said.

"She'll be back," Marion assured her, seeing the emotions flit across her face. "Let us give her some time."

CHAPTER 14

DAWN TOOK THE rest of the afternoon to decompress, opting to spend time in the gym room practicing a sport she had long forgotten about: shadowboxing. Relying on muscle memory, falling into an old routine, and focusing on physical exertion helped to clear her head.

Hikaru came by and assisted Miss M. in harvesting her garden. Apparently, he visited the house often, and Marion ran errands with him; they spent a good amount of time together—something Dawn learned while in lockdown.

By early evening, gray clouds blanketed the sky. Hikaru and Marion picked up Italian food (one of Marion's favorite cuisines) for dinner, but the family healer didn't stay to eat.

Feeling physically spent yet relaxed, Dawn joined Miss M. at the dining table that night. Dawn stared at her empty plate and scraped up the last bit of fettuccine alfredo with her bread stick. As Dawn wiped the corners of her mouth with her napkin, Marion rose from her seat and started clearing the table.

"Did you bring the journal?" Marion asked Dawn as she disappeared into the kitchen with their plates.

"I did," Dawn answered, drawing in a breath. She surmised that since Logan, Lopple, and Hikaru were absent tonight, Marion was taking this chance to disclose information about her dad.

Dawn set the journal down on the table, opening to a page with a photograph taped to it. There were other pictures in the book, but this one seemed like it had a good story behind it.

Returning from the kitchen with tiramisu cups in hand, Marion placed one of the dessert entrees in front of Dawn and sat next to her.

"I always have room for these," Dawn said, salivating as she scooped a heaping spoonful.

"Mmm . . . such a shame Laurel doesn't know what she's missing," said Marion, digging into her own dessert cup.

Her housekeeper peered at the photo of four friends—youthful adults in formal attire whose arms were around one another's shoulders. They seemed to be at a luxe hotel or villa on a balcony overlooking the ocean. It was obvious to Dawn that they were close; her dad (with a full head of hair) and her late mother, and on the left, another couple—a pregnant woman and her spouse—that Dawn didn't recognize.

"You already know that's Howel and Imogen," Marion said, pointing to them with the tip of her dessert spoon. "Did I ever tell you who used to speak to you in Korean?"

"I think you told me once that my mom was the reason I picked up Korean so easily. I wish I could remember her more."

"Your mother *is* the reason why you know Korean so well," Marion said, her voice trailing off in a more serious tone. "I wanted to talk to you, because it's time you knew . . ."

"Knew what?" Dawn asked hesitantly, thinking she might not be ready for the answer.

"Howel and Imogen aren't your real parents," Marion blurted out. She pointed to the dark-haired man with light brown skin and the auburn-haired pregnant woman in the photo on the left. "*They* are."

Dawn's eyes widened and her eyebrows shot up to the stars. "W-wait, what?!" she squeaked, her voice an octave higher. "H-how do you know that?"

Mixed emotions bubbled up in Dawn's mind, but deep in her heart, she knew it was the truth. This was not something her house-keeper, who she had known all her life, would lie about. She couldn't tell if she felt more confused, betrayed, shocked, or amused. After all, who tells a twenty-five-year-old she's adopted?

"I took this picture," Marion said softly. "We were at one of Jett's events. This is—"

Dawn's spoon clattered onto the table. "I-I'm adopted. I'm adopted," Dawn repeated. Hearing herself say the words was like watching herself in a dream, only it wasn't. She abruptly rested her elbows on the table, buried her face in her hands, and blew out a shaky breath.

"I'm sorry we had to keep this from you for so long," Marion said just above a whisper, patting her back the way she did when Dawn was a little girl.

She lifted her head and turned to face Miss M.

"It all makes sense now. Every time I'd ask about my mom, it seemed that you and dad—er, Howel, I guess—would always say 'your mother this' or 'your mother that,' never really talking about *Imogen*. I thought it was odd we didn't have that many photos . . . All my friends had archives of pictures of them and their parents." Dawn took another deep breath, then kept going, letting her stream-of-consciousness thoughts gush out. "I didn't know how to shield yet. Is that why you couldn't say anything?"

Miss M. nodded slowly. Her yellow headwrap swayed back and forth.

"It does hurt a little," Dawn said, downplaying how deeply betrayed she actually felt, "being out of the loop." *Being lied to*, she thought, but didn't say out loud. "But I'm not surprised. A little shell shocked, yes, but after learning about Lumen, bridges, the Kingdom of Ether, finfolk, and everything else, I don't think I can say I was truly surprised."

"I was afraid this would unhinge you," said Marion, relaxing her shoulders a little. "You're just like your mother, Kathryn."

"Her name was Kathryn?" Dawn asked, gazing at the picture of her mom who had been nameless a few seconds ago. Kathryn looked elegant in her emerald gown, its flowy tulle draped over her baby bump that she cradled in her arms. Dawn didn't have to guess that her mom was pregnant with her at the time.

"Yes. Kathryn is of European descent, born and raised in South Africa. She adored your father, Mark, so much. He was Filipino Korean, and she embraced learning his languages and heritage. You could tell how much they loved each other by the way they looked at each other, by the way they spoke to each other."

Feeling parched, Dawn picked up her glass and drained it. Then she looked at her half-eaten tiramisu, wondering if Marion had any other photos of her parents.

A projection appeared in Dawn's mind, catching her by surprise. Her dad and mom were suddenly in front of her, posing for the picture that Marion had taken. Mark put his arm around her mom, who looked up at him with a grin. Mark gave her a quick kiss on the cheek before they both turned to look at Marion who was holding the camera.

"Miss M., you never told me you could project," Dawn said, marveling at the details in the ritzy surroundings and the sea breeze she felt on the balcony.

"Marion, were my eyes closed in that one?" asked Kathryn, her South African accent and pleasant alto voice carrying over the ambient noise and lively chatter coming from the main hall.

"No, Mrs. Kathryn," Marion answered, sounding much younger. "You all look flawless."

"Let's get back to the reception," Mark said. "I'm starving, and I know Kat's famished!"

Dawn blinked, and the projection vanished. She turned to Marion, who was dabbing her eyes with a handkerchief.

"I miss them—your parents," her housekeeper said between sniffles. "I think about them every day. They both passed before their time. I was devastated, you know. It was your mother who decided to take me in when I was fifteen. I was surviving on the streets at that time."

"I thought my dad—er, Howel—was the one who hired you," Dawn said, feeling her eyes go wide again.

"He did, but that was *after* your mother passed. She took me in first, knowing that I had aura abilities. I didn't even know I was using them to survive," Marion said, lost in a memory. "She didn't just train me. She fed me, she gave me a home, she treated me like I was her own daughter. Before she died, I promised her I'd take care of you as if you were *my* own."

Not knowing what to say, Dawn nodded. Miss M. had indeed fulfilled that promise. Dawn looked at Marion's fine lines near the corners of her eyes where tears trickled out before she could dab at them. Under the table, Hiro laid his head on top of Marion's feet—his own way of giving comfort. Miss M. always had a rock-hard exterior, a protective, impenetrable armor, and Dawn rarely saw this side of her.

"I can empathize with Laurel," Marion said, her expression changing as she furrowed her brows. "She has a family, but their customs and dynamics of how they express and show their love is different. Her father, King Kameo, is the ruler of all of Atlantis."

"You mean, The Lost City—under the sea—actually exists?"

"Yes, but it's not just a city. It's an entire nation. They have many underwater cities—colaquases—and appearing strong and confident before his people is necessary. His whole clan knows this. While Laurel has a sister, father, mother, I doubt she has ever experienced the familial bonds you have known your whole life," Marion explained. "Sometimes family has more to do with expressing love and less to do with blood."

Marion took a sip of her water as Dawn pondered the irony of having a biological family without knowing their love. *Could that be the reason Laurel gravitated toward Stralla, and the reason why she hated being seen as a princess?* she wondered.

"I don't understand." Dawn shook her head. "When did you ever meet her dad—King Kameo—and learn all this?"

"Howel is a long-time friend of King Kameo through his . . . work. I've been in contact with King Kameo ever since Howel left."

Marion outstretched her left arm on the table and removed her fabric wrist cuff, which so closely matched her skin tone that Dawn had forgotten it was there. It uncovered a gemstone beaded, double-row bracelet.

"See this stone right here?" Marion asked, pointing to one of the pale, blue-green gems. "It's called a communication stone—a *comm stone* for short. When stones like this one are charged with aura, then cut into separate pieces, they can remain connected. Lumen can pass messages through them using aura. And with a strong aura, you can deliver a message or a projection across great distances."

"It looks like a regular bracelet, like the chakra ones sold at farmer's markets," Dawn said, reaching out to touch the stone.

It gleamed suddenly, and its energy pulsated.

"To anyone else, it is." Marion removed the bracelet and passed it to Dawn. "To Lumen, these gemstones, jewels, and crystals serve different purposes."

Dawn held up the bracelet to her eye level, inspecting it. "How do you know when you have a message?"

"You'll feel the energy of the aura change. It's like a pulse. To receive the message, you must activate the comm stone with your aura, and you'll be able to hear and see the projection."

"Does that mean I'd be able to hear a message from King Kameo using the stone?"

"Not all messages can be read by anyone. Advanced aura users can encrypt sensitive messages so that only the intended person receives it. The message will remain until the aura is deactivated. It is an intermediate aura ability."

As Dawn handed the bracelet back to Marion, she thought about King Kameo, and then her mind drifted to the altercation she and Laurel had earlier. "Laurel said that Lord Angel tasked her with training me on aura abilities. But, obviously, you're more than qualified to teach me. You can read and project. I'm sure you can shield as well."

Her housekeeper put her bracelet back on and covered it with her wrist cuff. "We're actually babysitting—er, helping to keep an eye on Laurel."

"You're kidding!" Dawn snorted.

"King Kameo left for an excursion, and he asked Lord Angel to keep Laurel busy. The princess gets herself into plenty of trouble in the colaquas as it is."

"*That's* why Lord Angel asked her to teach me?" Dawn groaned. "But Laurel is an awful teacher! Don't you think I'd make much more progress if—"

"Now hold on," Marion put her hand up, halting Dawn's train of thought. "She was teaching you foundational skills—projection, shielding, and reading."

"But if we just—"

Marion cut her off again, holding up a finger with a single wag. "Think of it this way: Anyone can teach you how to crawl—even Laurel. It was only a matter of time before you learned to walk. You will eventually run, but it is up to you to learn to fly. You cannot blame Laurel for your lack of progress."

Dawn closed her mouth. *Easier said than done.*

"Correct," Marion said. "You projected that thought. Keep practicing. You will learn to accurately project and shield . . . in time to complete your mission. That reminds me—Laurel is not supposed to be reading all your thoughts. It is Lumen law to respect others' privacy, regardless of one's aura abilities. The next time she comes by, you can remind her of that."

Hiro shuffled toward the side door leading to the outdoor deck, wanting to be let out.

"Just don't tell Laurel we're babysitting her," Marion chortled. "That would royally piss her off."

Dawn snorted again. "She's bound to find out what you told me though. I can't even shield properly."

"You *can* shield. I've seen it, and you did it today." The woman looked at Hiro and waved off the husky, who was starting to whine. "You are very much your mother's daughter. She was a tiny woman, but she was stubborn, unyielding, and headstrong. *Eiesinnig*—was what everyone called Kathryn Aurelia."

"Ai-yeh-SI-nugh," Dawn repeated, saying the Afrikaans word choppily.

Marion nodded. "She and your father were Lumen, and the same blood that ran in their veins runs in yours. It is through your mother that you carry the Aurelian bloodline—a bloodline that descends from Eretzian lumeres. You, Dawn, are Aurelian through and through."

"Aurelian," Dawn whispered. The name itself sounded ethereal, carrying its own magical power to bestow on her.

"Now I'm going to take Hiro for a walk," Marion said with a pat on Dawn's shoulder. "I guess you haven't tried activating that amulet yet?"

Dawn looked down at the pendant she was absentmindedly twirling in her fingers. "You mean this? No, I didn't even think to try."

"It is a protection stone, but it has more than one purpose." Her housekeeper took it into her own hand and held it for a moment before letting the aquamarine jewel fall gently atop Dawn's heart. "It was your mother's. It would be out of character for her not to leave projections on it for her only child."

Dawn watched as Marion left the kitchen with Hiro. When she heard the door close, she took the pendant into her fingers again. Giddy with the anticipation of seeing a projection from her *real* mom, she squeezed her eyes shut and activated the pendant, channeling her aura to the tips of her fingers where she held the jewel.

Her mind spiraled into a dark room, the only light coming from the faint glow of a small white crystal. Kathryn—her mother—appeared before her, no longer pregnant. The light casted shadows on her thin, delicate features. Her auburn hair was tied back, and she was dressed in dark, fitted clothes and the kind of shoes meant for traversing rough terrain.

Kathryn, who stood at Dawn's petite height, took a step toward her daughter. Dawn gasped, feeling like she was in the same room with her mom, who looked to be a little older than her right now. Her mom lifted a hand to brush aside loose hair from face, and Dawn noticed her forearms were covered with protective cuffs that looped around her thumbs. It almost seemed like her mom was preparing for battle.

"Dawn, my love," Kathryn said softly. "I wish I could see you now, the person you've grown to be. The path ahead will present many challenges." Kathryn paused and looked down at her feet momentarily. "It always does," she said, a tinge of bitterness in her voice. "But I believe you will find the strength to rise above every challenge. Not just to walk the path, but to light it. You are an Aurelian, after all."

Dawn searched her mom's eyes with bated breath. Kathryn seemed to give her a long look. Background noise and indecipherable voices sounded far away. The ground shook with a sudden jolt, but her mother remained immovable.

"If we do not meet again, always remember that I love you."

Kathryn gave a fleeting smile before the projection vanished, leaving Dawn alone at the dining room table.

She sat there feeling strangely content that she had just heard "I love you" from her real mom, who was becoming less and less a stranger to her each moment. The silence of the expansive house enveloped her, but she was glad to be by herself as she pondered about what had been revealed. She was a lumere, an *Aurelian*.

The name sounded both foreign and familiar at the same time, and she couldn't deny that it was indeed something she felt in her bones.

Interlude I

WITH A SCOWL on her face, Laurel swam alone through the long rock tube that led to the living quarters of guardians in training. The white gems embedded into the wall glowed when she passed, casting warped shadows of her as she twisted and turned through the tunnel.

Reed's cabin just had to be at the very end of this maze, she thought, annoyed. Everything bothered her—the taste of the brackish water, the dimness of her surroundings, even the unnatural silence—which made her feel utterly alone.

No one seemed to have time for her these days, except for Dawn, but it wasn't like the clueless Eretzian had a choice. Laurel wished she could talk to Stralla, who rarely answered her comms these days. The double-agent sangwor was probably flitting about to serve Malstrom's every whim, Laurel seethed. She briefly entertained the thought of visiting Ezra but didn't want to get scolded. He did that a lot lately. Her frown deepened, thinking about what Dawn (who was as slow as a sea cow) had rudely pointed out—that her intended was a "sham of a fiancé."

Dawn was wrong of course, Laurel told herself, yet she couldn't understand why she got under her scales. Of the two of them, Laurel was the one with a *real* relationship that would lead to further unification of their tribes. Logan was just a groundling. Ordinary. A temporary infatuation. A distraction. Yet he and Dawn were so starry-eyed for each other. Just like her sister Kailani was. *Gross,* she scowled and shook her head as she swam.

Then there was that pesky Miss Marion. *How dare she disrespect me! After she's been stealing our seafood. All. This. Time.*

Laurel swam faster, her fin effortlessly propelling her through the last stretch of the corridor, as if she could outpace her feelings of loneliness. She longed to talk to someone who would listen to her vent about her infuriating situation. Other Aquavi teens had their own go-to clan to commiserate with—friends who'd grown up together.

Not her, though. She'd only had the privilege of private tutors, one of which was Reed's father, the head chronicler. *I wish I'd gone to the academy. I should've begged father to allow me.*

Reed, her skinny-as-a-needlefish childhood friend, was her last resort. Although he was four years her junior and they had slowly drifted apart over the years, their fathers still worked together closely. Not once had she visited him in the apprentices' quarters, but visitors probably weren't allowed anyway.

When she asked the half-awake surveillance guard where Reed's cabin was in the dead of night, he gave her directions to his cabin, no questions asked. *He must be an apprentice,* Laurel surmised, estimating he was around Reed's age.

She arrived in front of Reed's cabin. The thin slab of rock slid effortlessly aside, and she moved into the dark room.

What a sad excuse for a door, she projected, her mood worsening by the second. She used her en to slide it back into place.

She heard and saw nothing in the darkness but felt gentle ripples a few feet away. Reed was asleep.

Wake up! Laurel projected, more irked than ever. She pounded the side of the wall with her fist to send vibrations around the cabin, just for good measure.

A small white gem flickered near a lanky Aquavi teen—the extremely groggy-looking Reed was still lying on a loosely woven mat of kelp on the seabed.

Laurel looked around in shock at the illuminated austere space. Strapped to the rock wall were wide wrist cuffs, similar to the ones Niro wore on duty. On the other side of the room only a few feet away was another rolled up kelp mat tucked in a recessed area near the wall.

Kia! Reed projected in surprise, as soon as he sat upright and saw Laurel.

She flinched at hearing the Orako term, which meant "princess." Of all finfolk, he should know how she hated that word.

Don't call me that, she projected back, continuing their exchange in Orako.

You shouldn't be here, he said, sounding prickly. He rubbed his eyes and ran his spindly fingers through his dark brown hair. *You're betrothed, and if anyone finds out that you're—*

No one is going to find out I'm here, she returned, crossing her arms. *No one even cares.*

You shouldn't be in the guard quarters. What do you want? he demanded, rising to a vertical position.

My father reigns over Atlantis. I can be in the guard quarters if I want, she hedged. *Besides, it's important. I really needed to talk to you.*

Stingin' sea slugs! he said, unable to mask his irritation. *At this hour?*

Why is this cabin so small? she deflected, hoping he couldn't see her trying to compose her expression. She crossed the room to the opposite side from him in one fluid motion. *It's barely enough space for one person.*

If you must know, these cabins can house two trainees. My roommate is on surveillance duty tonight.

Ah, that explains how that guard knew exactly where your cabin was. She casually brushed her hair aside. *So, how are you doing?*

Reed rolled his eyes at her. *Why the formalities? You didn't speak one word to me during our trip to Tencho, but now you wish to know how I'm doing?*

I was busy. Laurel shrugged, feeling more slighted than annoyed.

It is my first year in guardian training, so I'm quite sore and tired with all the physical drills. And since my father is away on the expedition with King Kameo, I've been taking on more of his historian duties.

Laurel struggled to keep a look of indifference on her face, knowing she could not bring herself to apologize for interrupting his sleep. *I wouldn't have come here at this time to talk to you if it weren't urgent.*

Reed's irritation with her subsided a smidge. *Right . . . I didn't say you had nothing urgent to talk about. I was merely telling you how I was, since you asked.*

She looked him over as he stretched his arms, reaching for the ceiling. The cabin space was so confined that from fish tail to fingertip, he just barely grazed the floor and ceiling.

Could they put you in a smaller room? she asked sarcastically.

He frowned at her. *So what do you want to discuss that is so important? I heard you've been training the groundling on using en. Is that what you came here to talk about?*

She moved to the empty side of the cabin and faced him. *Sort of, but she's not a groundling. She's Lumen—and most likely an Eretzian lumere. The problem is that Lord Angel needed* me *to train her,* she said, clearly emphasizing her own significance. *It was fun at first, but now I'm not sure I want to keep doing it.*

The question plagued her: What was the *real* reason behind Angel tasking her in the first place? Surely her father had contacted Angel regarding this plan before his expedition—she figured that much.

Reed's silence urged her to continue.

I've been trying to contact my father to ask him to assign another Aquavian to train her in my place, but he hasn't been responding to my comms. I don't know when he'll be returning, and no one is telling me when he'll be back. Since your father went along on the expedition, did he tell you when they'd return?

No. He shrugged. *If you'd rather not train her, ask one of your former tutors to do it. I overheard my father suggest it to the king as a good task to keep you occupied.*

The words came like the shock of an electric eel. Laurel raised an eyebrow. *Is that so?*

Reed froze. If he wasn't fully awake before, he was now.

What I meant to say was, he said slowly, as if thinking of a way to backtrack, *I know that your father usually takes you on expeditions, but this one seemed to be more . . . confidential and dangerous. I was only told about some of the details because I'm preparing the records for it as a chronicler.*

Laurel's shoulders slumped. *Bilge scum! No one wants to tell me anything,* she muttered, overwhelmed by her friendlessness.

Even in the dimly lit room, Laurel saw Reed's demeanor change. She could read his every expression, the way he paced, fiddled with his own spindly fingers, and scanned every corner of the room—as if he was searching for a lost treasure—were all dead giveaways. He felt sorry for her, and his pity was the last thing she wanted.

Her eyelids twitched, which meant tears were coming. Clearly, her overactive tear ducts were due to spending too much time on land. If she cried, she knew he'd sense it by the change in vibrations or salinity. Shedding tears was an embarrassment for an Aquavian of her status. It wouldn't help matters anyway.

Thank you for telling me, she projected placidly, her voice quiet and emotionless. *You're the only one who tells me the truth, Reed. I'll be leaving now. Good night.*

Wait, he said as she moved toward the partition.

Reed reached over to the wall for his arm cuff and retrieved something from the pocket, then gently took Laurel's hand and placed a yellow comm stone in her palm.

I'll let you know as soon as I hear of their return, Reed promised.

Laurel looked down at the smooth jewel, recognizing it as the same one they had used in their youth. She had given it back to him so that Uki, Reed's younger sister, could practice sending him projections.

Isn't this Uki's?

She gave it to me because she didn't need it anymore, he said, holding the other comm stone in his hand for her to see. *I visit her and my mother from time to time anyway.*

He had kept something imbued with her en after all these years. When was the last time they'd had a real conversation? She was positive there were a few times he had greeted her in passing, and she had not even given him a glance of acknowledgment.

Thank you for this, she said, feeling undeserving.

Her gaze remained downcast, as she was still unable to look him in the eye. Her eyelids twitched again, so she shut them tightly; determined to keep her tears at bay, she turned and abruptly left the cabin, sliding the partition a little too hard.

As Laurel sprinted through the winding tunnels, her fingers curled tightly around the comm stone. Better he assume me unpleasant and disagreeable than seeing me turn to mush.

CHAPTER 15

FROM THE LIVING room sofa, Dawn lounged in a loose top and gym shorts while sipping her iced matcha. Cold drops of condensation trickled down the glass and fell onto her bare legs, making goosebumps rise.

Hiro lay at her feet, his long tongue uncurling as his mouth opened wide for a yawn. Although it was still morning, the heat beat down relentlessly on all of Southern California—and would continue to do so through the weekend, according to the forecast. Nonetheless, Marion was adamant about keeping the air conditioning on energy-saving mode.

Living underwater must have its advantages, Dawn realized as her thoughts drifted to Laurel. She was glad their shielding sessions weren't continuing through the weekend. It would allow time for tempers to cool, and come Monday, maybe it'd be as if nothing happened.

Dawn absentmindedly swiped the weather forecast and the projection switched to a news report about a raging forest fire. Despite the depressing news, Dawn was in a great mood. Last night, she'd watched more of her mom's projections on her comm stone. Kathryn had a soothing voice, light as a feather, and Dawn had fallen asleep listening to the sound of her mom's singing.

When Dawn woke up, she felt noticeably *different*. Or, at least, unlike herself. Today, her mind seemed . . . sharper. She could feel her own aura, similar to the way she felt the fabric of her clothes. And for the first time, she could feel others' distinct auras too. It was like looking at an object in her peripheral vision. Or like sitting in a dark theater with someone tiptoeing in and sitting behind you; you didn't need to see them to know they were there.

Marion's aura was like a solid brick. But there were *other* auras she could feel—Lumen auras—outside the house, like wispy, barely-there clouds. Driven by curiosity, she went to the window and peered between the wooden slats, but there wasn't a person in sight. She turned her gaze back to Hiro, still soundly sleeping. A whine escaped his mouth, and his tail twitched.

He must be dreaming. Maybe I can try reading him.

Dawn closed her eyes and focused on the canine's relaxed breathing, syncing her own breaths to its steady rhythm. Then she shifted her focus on Hiro's thoughts.

Darkness. Muted sounds. Blurred silhouettes. *Memories?*

A person. A woman. Her white sundress contrasted starkly with her dark skin. Bright yellow dress flats.

"Can you help me prepare lunch if you're not busy?" Marion asked.

Dawn startled. Her housekeeper had walked in and stood at the living room's entrance, watching her for who knew how long. "O-of course."

It wasn't often that Miss M. asked for help around the kitchen, but Dawn never minded making herself useful. She preferred to prep her own meals on the weekends anyway, since they were technically Marion's off hours.

In the kitchen, Marion placed a variety of produce on the counter. "You can wash those and chop them up for a salad," Marion said, walking to the fridge.

Dawn opened a cabinet to find a strainer, then put the lettuce, cherry tomatoes, and cucumber in to give them a rinse. "What's this thing with Laurel and food? Why is she so particular?" she asked while washing the veggies.

"Not sure. My guess is that she's angry that groundlings have always overfished while she's seen colaquases struggle to find food."

A memory flashed in Dawn's mind. "Colaquases"—the term for Aquavian cities—was a section in her mom's journal. When she'd reviewed it a few days ago, she'd found a few rough map sketches with Xs drawn in where there was ocean. She'd assumed they marked small islands. She reminded herself to take a look again later.

"Miss M., do you know how many colaquases there are?"

"Only the Aquavi would know that," she replied, laying out three artichokes and a lemon on the counter near the sink. "Do you know where I'm getting all the seafood we've eaten?"

"The store?" she guessed, taking her strainer to the cutting board Miss M. had placed there. She started chopping up the lettuce while Marion rinsed the artichokes.

"No." Marion smirked. "We have an informal contract with Aquavian fishers."

"Who's 'we'?"

"Hikaru and I," Marion said, her hands moving deftly to prepare the artichokes. "The fishers provide us with a fraction of their catch, which we're using for Laurel while she's with us. King Kameo knows of our agreement, but evidently, father and daughter don't speak much."

"Huh. So she's been making a fuss and practically starving herself here for no reason?"

"Almost. Laurel doesn't understand where we get the rest of our food. She thinks we're wasteful like the other groundlings I'm sure she's encountered."

Dawn thought for a while, carefully placing her chopped veggies in a big salad bowl. "But you grow most of the food yourself. Except for meat—I know you place orders, and they get delivered to Hikaru's."

Dawn wiped her hands on a kitchen cloth and looked out the window. There was a patch of the garden, small considering the variety of foods they had eaten over the past month. She was embarrassed to admit that she'd gone to the backyard only a handful of times in the last year, and it was to help Marion carry plants in from the greenhouse.

There was something calming about the way her housekeeper cooked, each step infused with intention and care. She watched as Marion gently lifted the lid from a tall stock pot on the stove, sending a plume of steam in the air. After adjusting the pot's settings, she placed her artichokes and lemon halves inside before replacing the lid. "Let's go take a look outside."

"I thought I couldn't go outside until I could shield."

"But you *can* shield." Marion smiled. "Come on. It is time you met some of the Lumen agents surveilling the property anyway."

Dawn's shoes crunched against the dirt path as she passed dozens of shrubs, succulents, and cacti. The red bark of manzanita trees scattered throughout accented the desertscape.

It'd be more beautiful if it wasn't so hot, she thought, sweat trickling down her back.

She clamped her mouth shut, swallowing her complaints about the sweltering sun. It was the first time she had been outdoors in more than a month, and she would *not* appear ungrateful for it.

"Here's where I grow berries, bell peppers, carrots and potatoes," Marion pointed out when they got to the garden patch. "And here's my herb garden," she said, walking past fragrant bushes that wafted of rosemary and other scents that Dawn couldn't place.

Dawn shielded her eyes with her hand and looked beyond the short boundary wall where the ground sloped upward and an avocado tree sat on the small hill.

"I need to check the greenhouse cooling system," Marion said, walking in the opposite direction. "Can you pick a few tomatoes and avocados? I'll meet you over there."

"Sure," Dawn said, walking past the row of trellised tomato vines, her eyes scanning for the red fruit. "Does red mean ripe? There's nothing red here," she muttered as she looked up and saw Marion disappear into the greenhouse.

The shade of the avocado tree looked promising, and she trudged over in that direction, hoping for respite from the sun. After walking up the slope, she stood near the tree trunk, hands on her hips, trying to catch her breath.

As sweat traced her temple, she took hold of the fruit picker leaning against the trunk. A light breeze made her shiver, the odd sensation giving her pause.

She felt it again. That rise of fine hairs on the back of her neck and arms, her skin tingling. The feeling that someone was watching her.

There were Lumen auras nearby. A sudden rustle of leaves sent her eyes darting about the tree. She yelped when a squirrel scampered across a branch. Then she looked higher into the tree's roof of leaves and branches, searching for someone who was watching her, knowing the Lumen could see her.

Closing her eyes, Dawn blew out a long breath. *I'm in a safe place,* she told herself. The thought of being home was enough to calm her. She opened her eyes and imagined an invisible dome forming around her, protecting her.

Hmmm, so the groundling can shield, a voice said from the branches above.

Dawn looked skyward to see where the voice came from, just in time to see an avocado hurling toward her head.

"Ah!" she winced, shutting her eyes and swinging the fruit picker in its direction. She expected to feel the rock-hard fruit hit her in the head, but nothing came. Derisive laughter filled her ears, and she opened her eyes, confused. *Was that a projection?*

She can barely *shield,* a deeper voice said from high up in the branches.

Dawn once again looked up, this time spotting a few hawk-like birds with brownish wings, a white-feathered front and head, and a brown stripe that went across their eyes. They certainly looked out of place sitting in an avocado tree.

You are an amusing sight, wielding a fruit picker like a weapon, said one of the birds. Or rather, Dawn *thought* she heard one of the birds say that.

Who are you? Dawn projected.

She took a step back, her attention still on the birds above, and hands gripped her shoulders from behind. She let out another yelp and wheeled around, swinging the fruit picker.

Marion ducked to avoid being struck.

"Oh—Miss M., it's you!" she breathed, clutching her heart.

"Will you cut it out?" the housekeeper yelled skyward.

One of the birds moved to a lower branch. *We were merely having a bit of fun,* the bird projected, its voice sounding familiar. As Dawn stared at it, the image of a woman with short-cropped, flaming red hair appeared in her head for a split second.

"Dawn, this is Sidryl Crabtree's *poru*, an extension of her aura," Marion motioned to the feathered creature, which had stilled. "She can see you and communicate with you through it."

A projection of the woman appeared in front of them, slightly transparent, but her vibrant, ruby-red hair came through clearly. Dawn stared, attempting to wrap her head around the concept a projection via poru. She remembered seeing the woman at the council of Tencho.

"Call me Sid," she said with a nod. "It must be your first time seeing an Etheran poru. I thought you'd be further along."

"She *just* learned to shield," Marion said defensively. "We're taking one thing at a time."

"I deduced that," Sid replied, without taking her eyes off Dawn. "Your aura has . . . changed. Keep practicing to strengthen your shielding. It'd do you better than shadow boxing."

"I—I *am* still practicing," Dawn sputtered, feeling self-conscious.

Sid took a bite from an apple she was holding, from wherever she was. "My agents tell me your groundling lover comes by often," Sid said while chewing. "You know, he wasn't part of our agreement. My team is to protect *you*, not anyone else."

Dawn's face reddened, knowing she was referring to Logan.

"He's not my . . . um, *lover*," she said, cringing at her own words.

Marion stepped forward. "Hikaru and I have the situation under control. There's nothing to be concerned about."

Dawn cut a glance to Miss M. and wondered if that meant they had already planned to erase all his memories for good. She turned her attention back to Sid's projection, whose eyes continued to bore into her.

"Just as long as the priority is still the mission," Sid said.

"All I've been thinking about is the mission," Dawn retorted, her voice sounding not nearly so confident as she intended.

Sid's presence served as a stark reminder of her role within the Earth-saving council that Howel was part of. The pressure loomed over her like the hot sun.

"The mission has always been the priority," Marion confirmed.

Sid nonchalantly took another bite of her apple. "Anyway, I'm making my rounds at the other safehouses . . . today."

During her momentary pause, Sid's eyes turned glassy, then she continued.

"I just got word of an intruder at one of the locations. Marion, if there's any disturbance here, you know where to go," Sid said, and the projection dissipated.

"So these birds are all porus?" Dawn asked as the handful of birds flapped their long wings, moving to higher branches.

"Yes, they're ospreys—a type of sea hawk," Marion nodded. "Etherans often choose them as porus for their ability to dwell on coastal land . . . as well as hunt over the water."

"I sensed a few of them earlier. Are there enough of them to fight off an intruder? If there'd ever be one, that is," added Dawn, her voice dropping low.

Marion studied her. "We're safe," she assured. "Sid activated a dome shield on this property. Any uninvited Lumen or porus will have a hard time stepping foot here, but in case anyone does, the porus are the eyes of Sid's team. They'd arrive at a moment's notice."

"I see," Dawn said, still feeling uneasy.

"Hikaru and I aren't old, defenseless groundlings just yet," Marion warned with a scoff. "We've still got a few Lumen tricks up our sleeve."

"Oh, I'd never think you weren't capable of defending yourselves," Dawn fibbed, wiping the beads of sweat from her brow. "Um, it's really hot out here. Should we go back inside?"

"Not empty handed," Marion said. "I saw that there were no more tomatoes. I've been using the gardens at the other properties to grow different produce. I'll go get some."

Her housekeeper turned and started toward the house, carrying a basket with kudzukan leaves and onions she had retrieved from the greenhouse.

"The other properties are hours away by flight. How have you been getting there?"

"By bridge, of course," she replied.

"When do I get to travel by bridge again?"

"Don't forget to pick a few avocados," Miss M. reminded, ignoring her question.

Dawn watched as Marion padded away, leaving her with the ospreys. She spent the next few minutes picking avocados when her phone buzzed. It was a message. From Logan.

A chorus of laughter and teasing along the lines of "*I can guess who that was*" and "*she's blushing crimson*" reverberated in her head—projections from the porus.

Dawn forced away the loopy smile that had crept up on her face, loudly cleared her throat that had suddenly gone dry and yelled, "GET OUT OF MY HEAD!"

CHAPTER 16

DINNER WITH LOGAN minus Laurel and Lopple was pleasantly uneventful. Dawn didn't miss Lopple's chatterbox tendencies and his sniffing at every dish, nor the princess' snootiness. Although the house was rather quiet without their raucous laughter, Dawn welcomed the friendly, relaxed conversation with Logan, Hikaru, and Marion.

As usual, Logan conducted himself as the perfect gentleman. Everyone enjoyed the homemade casserole he'd brought, which paired well with the leftovers from lunch.

After dinner, Dawn and Logan retreated to the living room to sip espressos and peruse weather reports. The extreme heat wave had wreaked havoc from California to Florida, and the worst of it was yet to come. Several stations touted the bushfires in Australia and showed clips of catastrophic fire tornadoes tearing through the east side, leaving a path of death and destruction.

"Fire season looks worse than last year," Dawn commented, remembering Angel's stark projection from the lake.

"Want to take a break from this and watch the basketball game?" Logan asked.

"Sure," she said, changing the channel.

They watched the game in silence, and she recalled the teasing from the porus earlier. No, Logan wasn't her lover, but it would be nice to imagine a future with him—cuddling on the sofa, watching the same shows, going for hikes, and traveling. Then her pragmatic voice spoke up:

You're not a couple. Just enjoy your time together. Hikaru might erase his memory soon. It's better not to get attached.

She drew in a long breath and let out a heavy sigh.

"You're different today," Logan told her. "Quieter."

"Yeah," she returned faintly, unsure of whether it was in a good way or not. As she forced herself to think of something else, Laurel came into her mind.

"I think I'm generally calmer without Laurel around," Dawn admitted. "We got into a heated argument the other night, and she kind of stormed off. I wish we could've resolved it."

He nodded, listening intently.

"I got *so* mad at her for something that seems petty now." Dawn frowned. "Then I chatted with Miss M. about how different our families are. Turns out, Laurel and I grew up in different . . . well, on opposite sides of the spectrum. I forget how young seventeen is sometimes. She's *still* growing up. She might annoy me to the moon and back, but I still care about her."

Logan had stopped watching the game and turned his full attention to her. "Of course," he remarked. "She's part of your family."

There was something about his statement that felt unsettling. Perhaps Logan was right—although Laurel wasn't part of her biological family, Dawn already thought of her as the younger sister she'd never had. The Aquavian had practically welcomed her with open arms when they'd first met, lending her a dress to wear and steadying her shaky steps on Mount Tencho.

Despite being a less than stellar teacher, Laurel was trying her best. Deciding then and there she would afford Laurel more patience, Dawn declared with a nod, "Yes, she *is* family."

Logan gave her a reassuring smile, and Dawn melted upon seeing it—the smile that not only made her swoon but also made her feel safe. She could be her true self in his presence, a feeling so strong that she was compelled to tell him what she had learned about her real mom.

"There's something else that's been on my mind," she added. "I found out a few things I didn't know about my mom before she died."

"Did she pass away when you were very young?" he asked, his voice thick with concern. "I sort of assumed that, since you haven't talked about her."

"Y-yes," she hesitated, because she realized Miss M. hadn't disclosed the cause of her mom's death, and it hadn't occurred to Dawn until then to ask. She made a mental note to find out from Marion the first chance she got.

"Miss M. knew my mom well," Dawn continued. "My mom took her in and basically adopted her. Recently, Marion started sharing more about my mom—her personality, how she and my dad loved each other."

Dawn pursed her lips as Howel, her adoptive dad, came to mind. She wasn't ready to share with Logan that she was adopted.

"Are you okay?" he asked, gently squeezing her shoulder.

She smoothed out her expression. "Yeah, but I don't know where I'm going with this."

Logan tightened his arm around her shoulders in response but said nothing.

"Learning about some of the traits I inherited from my mom has given me a lot of confidence," she went on. "I've been handling a critical project, a mission of sorts, for my dad while he's away. It's the first time he's put me in charge of something so important to him. I have to get it right—this one project will affect the trajectory of . . . his life's work," Dawn said, choosing her words carefully.

"If he trusts you with the responsibility, it means he has faith in you."

Dawn looked down at the pendant she was fiddling with.

"The mission I'm working on will need to be completed in the next few weeks," she said, hearing her own anxiety-ridden voice. "Even though I've been working on it every day, I can't help but feel so behind."

"You're right on time," he assured her as he lifted her chin up, and her eyes found his. "Whatever your mission is, just remember, you were made for this."

She managed a small smile. "You make it sound so simple."

Dawn leaned the side of her head on his shoulder. It felt right, being nestled against him.

"I guess that means you won't be back at the studio anytime soon since you're working on this major project now?"

"I'm not sure if I'll ever be able to go back," she admitted.

"What will you do after the project is completed?"

"I'm still figuring that out."

"Keep me posted. After my marathon next month, I'll return to Colorado for a few weeks. My dad is having surgery, and I'll be helping my mom take care of him while he recovers."

She blinked at him, slightly embarrassed. She had forgotten all about the marathon he was training for and never thought to ask about his family or how he was doing.

"I hope your dad's surgery goes as well as it can," she offered.

"Thanks. He's expected to have a full recovery, and if all goes as planned, he'll still be allowed to fly after."

"He's also a pilot?"

"He's a naval aviator. Flying runs in the family. He's the luckier one, though. I couldn't go back to flying after my injury."

"What happened? If you don't mind me asking," she added quickly.

A pause followed, and then Logan began again, his voice low and solemn, as if he were talking about an incident that had happened just yesterday.

"I was assigned to deliver cargo to various locations," he said slowly. "There was an explosion at a nearby nuclear plant while I was flying, and the blast . . ." he trailed off, the expression on his face one of hurt.

Dawn turned to face him, gently pulling his arm off her shoulder and held his hand in hers. "We don't have to talk about it if you don't want to."

He shook his head and closed his eyes for a second.

"I'm fine as a passenger, but I can't pilot because of my PTSD. I actually miss flying. I got my commercial pilot license before I joined the Air Force, and it's been a while since I've been in any type of aircraft."

"I'm glad you were okay . . . and that you decided to work at the studio."

His smile reappeared. "Me too."

She glanced toward the kitchen, sensing that Marion and Hikaru were still there, deep in discussion. Her aura abilities now allowed her to *hear* fragments of their conversation, something about the tragic death of a CEO in a house fire. She guessed it'd be a while before Hikaru would leave with Logan.

"Want to check out one of CETT's airlift prototypes?" Dawn asked him.

They stood side by side in the garage, admiring the silver aircraft in front of them. It gleamed even in the dark. After a few moments, Logan walked closer to the vehicle and knocked on the metal with his knuckles.

"Strong alloy," he muttered to himself, circling it in a full walkaround.

"So, what do you think?" Dawn asked, watching his scrutinizing eyes.

"Looks like a military-grade glider—for a civilian," he said, a hint of awe in his voice.

Dawn hovered her hand over the sensor, and the door opened in front of him. She motioned for him to step inside.

Without any hesitation, he ducked his head in and sat in the driver's seat, immediately tapping on the controls while Dawn got in from the passenger side.

"Unauthorized driver," said the vehicle's control system. A warning on the control panel blinked red.

"Disable biometrics security," Dawn said, and the warning light disappeared.

"This is impressive. Biometrics, remote access, solar and electric charging, self-driving *and* stealth mode? How much was the sticker price if you don't mind me asking?"

"Well, uh, it was free, because it's just being loaned to us. Jett Pierce is like an uncle to me."

Logan looked at her in disbelief. "Can Jett be *my* uncle when I grow up?"

"It's not what you think!" Dawn laughed. "My dad is obsessive about his privacy, so instead of putting any major assets under his name, he *borrows* them from Jett. He prefers that our family keep a low profile, if you know what I mean."

"I see. It *is* hard to get any real privacy these days," Logan agreed as he reclined his seat. "Does that mean this glider doesn't have a tracker on it? All the military airlifts had trackers, and this one seems oddly familiar."

"No trackers. We also don't usually give out our address, which is why I gave you Hikaru's address before," she said before realizing she had given away too much.

He turned his gaze from the controls and studied her, the silence engulfing them both.

She wished she could tell him the truth—about everything—how learning aura abilities made her head hurt. How she was trying to figure out her dad's riddle to help him, to *find* him. How she wanted things to go back to "normal"—whatever that was now. And how she wished these evenings when Logan was with her could stretch on forever.

"I can tell you're keeping something from me," he said with a flash of his crooked, irresistible smile. "You're the only person I know that has to be on house arrest for a special *project*," he said, cupping his mouth with one hand to mimic telling a secret.

Dawn blanched and opened her mouth to rebut him, but before she could think of an excuse, he quickly added, "Dawn, it's okay. I get it. You can tell me the whole story when you're ready. By the way, you look even prettier this way."

"What?" Dawn asked, her mouth hanging open, completely caught off guard by his last comment.

"Honestly, you looked beautiful the way Sparkle did your make-up and all, but you look even better without it."

She toyed with her amulet, mortified that he knew Sparkle did her makeup at the studio. Since she hadn't gone anywhere in a month, she had forgotten about trying to look presentable.

"I, um," she balked, and her eyes darted away. It had been ages since she had received such a compliment. "Thanks," she said awkwardly.

Suddenly, he leaned toward her, closing the gap between them, and his lips were on hers.

It happened so fast that it took her by surprise. She sprang back, speechless and stunned.

A few seconds passed, each one multiplying the awkwardness permeating the air.

Logan bit his bottom lip. "I shouldn't have done that. I'm sorry—maybe I'm coming on too strong."

"It's fine," Dawn blurted, regaining the ability to speak. "I was just surprised, that's all."

"Are you sure? I really didn't mean to steal that kiss," he said sheepishly. "I just really enjoyed our kiss the other day . . . as well as spending time with you and your family, getting to know you and all. I was thinking, Dawn, even if you stop coming to the studio, could I take you out sometime—on a real date?"

A burst of giggles erupted from Dawn as she scooted toward him, recovering from her instinctive recoil.

"I would love that . . . and I thoroughly enjoyed our first kiss too," she admitted.

She let him pull her close.

"Would you miss me if I stopped coming by your house?" he whispered as his lips traced her earlobe and skated to her neck.

The sensation tickled and sent a shiver down her spine at the same time, forcing her to draw a ragged breath. She turned toward him as his lips continued to drive her mad. Her fingers ran through his hair as she caught a whiff of the faint scent of . . . what was it, spruce?

"I'll take that as a yes," he whispered when she failed to produce words.

She closed her eyes, relishing his boldness, the moment his lips found hers. Their mouths parted and their kiss deepened.

A gentle earthquake rolled through, but neither Dawn nor Logan paid it any mind, locked in each other's tight embrace. When they were together, just for that moment, it was like everything and everyone else disappeared along with all their cares.

It's just me and him, she thought, cherishing their moment and pushing away the decisions that would surely need to be made too soon.

CHAPTER 17

"YOU'RE THINKING ABOUT Logan, aren't you?"

Dawn grinned at Laurel and shrugged. The last few days had come and gone, yet ever since Logan's visit last weekend, nothing could shake her state of euphoria.

Laurel and Lopple had returned—the latter for dinners—like nothing had ever been amiss. In fact, Laurel now accepted the food offered to her and, to Dawn's surprise, occasionally said "thank you." Perhaps it was an Aquavian princess's way of extending an olive branch—at least it was a start.

They had spent all morning in the study, practicing shielding. After lunch, they'd switched gears to do some riddle-solving. With her laptop on her dad's desk, Dawn pulled up the research she had previously compiled with the help of X8. However, every now and then, a thought of Logan caused her to randomly break into an inexplicable grin.

Dawn cleared her throat, willing herself to concentrate on the task at hand. They both looked at the screen projection, which displayed a snippet of Howel's letter:

There is one coveted, rare ingredient, which must be retrieved when the time is right. It is rooted near the river where it's always night. Ripe for picking in the dark, but go not beyond the Ides of March. Past the maw and deep in the throat, it's hard to find and harder to grow. You've once been there long ago. You'll need a guide whose name you'll know. You'll need a guide whose name you'll know.

"Obviously, we know that the ingredient is likely some kind of plant near a river because my dad wrote that it was 'rooted' near one."

Laurel nodded from the comfort of an armchair she was curled up on. "It has to be in a cave system, because your father also said 'it's always night' and it's 'past the maw and deep in the throat.' I've been through tons of underwater caves, and a lot of the deeper systems don't have skylights to let in any sunlight."

"Yes, but this cave can't be completely underwater, otherwise he wouldn't have put 'near the river,'" Dawn said, then swiped the projection. "These are all the known caves with nearby rivers. There are thousands, which is why I narrowed it to the places my dad and I visited."

She swiped again and the screen changed to a much more manageable list.

"When you do that thing with your hand, it looks like you're using en," Laurel commented, sounding a tad impressed.

"Maybe that's why groundlings stopped using en—because technology just became more convenient."

"Could be, but that doesn't mean Lumen don't know how to use technology," she said, crossing her arms. "I just haven't been taught."

"Would you . . . like me to teach you?"

Laurel nodded eagerly, then, as if scaling back her anticipation, nonchalantly added, "That would be nice."

Dawn returned the nod and pointed to a button on her keyboard. "This button projects your screen. You can tap any of the locations I've typed, and it will display the details."

On the projection, Dawn tapped "Heavenly Pit" and another module popped up, listing a detailed description and a digital model:

Known as Xiaozhai Tiankeng

Location: Chongqing Municipality, China

Formerly known as one of the Earth's deepest sinkholes

Formed by an underground river that connects to the Panyang River

Dawn hovered her O-shaped hand over the image, then spread her fingers out. The 3D image zoomed in, perfectly in sync with her hand gesture, filling the study with the breathtaking landscape of the Heavenly Pit.

Laurel swatted her hand at the digital projection, testing whether she had any effect on it, then looked crestfallen to find she didn't.

"Like this," Dawn said, swiping her hand slowly and more fluidly. "You can also ask the virtual assistant, X8, to help if you're not sure what to do."

"It's named X8?"

"I'm listening," an amicable, posh male voice said from the laptop.

"My dad named him. It's short for the infinity AI's version X8.783 . . . er, I think. Ask him something, like this, 'X8, how many of these caves have Howel and I visited?'"

The AI replied instantly, "There are eleven locations."

"But the Ides of March is in a few days," Laurel said. "You can't possibly scout that many places by then—not by yourself."

"I was thinking you and Lopple could help. We could search the places separately and take on three or four places each."

"Me?" she asked, wrestling down her brows. "Angel said I was only to train you in aura abilities."

"She didn't say *where* you had to teach me, right?"

"Right." Laurel nodded slowly, elongating the word. "Except this is just the kind of thing my father would object to."

"You wouldn't necessarily have to go alone." Dawn picked up the journal on the desk, effortlessly activated it, and flipped to the section of colaquases. "I checked my mom's map of colaquases and saw which ones were closest to the caves. Maybe you can take a few trusted guardians or friends from the colaquases."

"What's this?" she asked, after getting up and peering over Dawn's shoulder.

"My mom sketched these maps showing where the underwater cities are."

"How did she know the locations of all our major colaquases?" Laurel asked, her voice shrill with panic.

"I'm not sure. Maybe she was friends with the Aquavians."

Laurel snatched the journal and frantically scanned the pages. "You didn't put this into your computer X8 thing, did you?"

Her slender fingers gripped the pages in a way that looked like she might rip them out.

"No, I didn't! Give that back," Dawn said, lightly slapping Laurel's hands to loosen her grip. She breathed a sigh of relief when Laurel released the journal.

The Aquavian's eyes narrowed to slits, and all friendliness evaporated.

"You were considering putting this into *that*," Laurel accused, pointing to the laptop like it was Pandora's box or some other mythical, cursed object.

"All this tech is CETT-issued and completely secure," Dawn said matter of factly with a glare.

"And what happens if it gets stolen or breached?"

"If it ever gets into the wrong hands, there are fail-safes . . ." she trailed.

The truth was that nothing was ever one hundred percent secure *all* the time. Sure, Jett Pierce's tech was as safeguarded as it could get, but that didn't mean it was hack proof if someone, such as a disgruntled CETT employee, was determined enough.

"I see your point," Dawn conceded. "I won't upload any of this to the system. This journal was one of the few things I have that belonged to my mom. When she died, my dad . . . I mean, Howel . . . continued writing in it, so I mean it when I say I'm going to do everything in my power to keep it safe."

Dawn smoothed out some of the wrinkled pages of the journal, and she heard the princess blow out a long exhalation.

"You *must* strengthen your shielding," Laurel said emphatically. "No Lumen should be able to read this off of you. Promise me you'll keep this secure, both the journal and your thoughts."

"On one condition. You stay out of my head from now on," Dawn warned. "Marion told me the rules of engagement; no more bending them."

"Fine. I have a condition as well," Laurel said crossly. "Stop thinking of me as an Aquavian princess."

"Sold," said Dawn. It was a good tradeoff, and she could see that keeping the colaquas locations a secret meant a great deal to Laurel. Besides, she needed Laurel's help if there was any hope of getting the missing ingredient and completing the mission on time. The Ides of March signified the full moon, which was in three days.

They turned their attention back to the list of locations.

"We need to whittle down this list," Dawn said while drumming her fingers on the desk.

"Remove the ones with skylights, remember?"

"Right. X8, remove the caves with skylights, then sort the remaining caves by shortest distance to a river."

"Here are the five remaining caves," X8 replied after a second.

Dawn's face lit up in relief as she and Laurel scanned the short list:

Tham Khoun Xe Cave — Laos

Río Secreto — Mexico

The Heavenly Pit — China

The Underground River — Philippines

Lost River Cave — United States

"You think someone from the colaquases can help us?" she asked Laurel.

"No. We're searching for a rare plant in the Eretzian realm. I would need a guardian for protection, and requesting aid will raise questions. My father will hear of it for sure."

"What about Lopple? Maybe he can help."

"About that," Laurel said, rubbing her chin, "Now that you can somewhat shield, it's time you knew that he's a shifter."

"You mean, he's Aquavian, like you?"

"No, he's definitely Etheran," Laurel said, pacing the room. "Most use their aura to fly, and it's rare for them to be shifters as well since flying takes a great deal of energy."

"Are you *sure* he's a shifter?"

"I know another shifter when I see one. The face he shows us is not his true form."

Dawn fell silent, lost in her thoughts. Malstrom's soufors were hunting Lopple. Could that be the reason he chose to keep his shifting abilities a secret?

"I couldn't shield until recently, so any Lumen—like the ones I met at the council of Tencho—would've been able to read me and see that Lopple was in contact with me. His constant disguise makes sense, otherwise I might've accidentally given him away."

Laurel furrowed her brow, not entirely satisfied with Dawn's conclusion. "Do you think Marion knows he's a shifter?"

"Not sure, but I know Miss M. trusts him."

"And how about *you*?" Laurel asked, halting her pacing and turning her gaze to Dawn to see her full reaction. "Do you trust Lopple?"

Good question, Dawn thought. Somehow, deciding whether to ask Lopple for help felt like a pivotal decision, one that could ensure their victory or their failure.

"I go back and forth. I can't figure out why my dad didn't share this part of the mission with Lopple, or maybe he did and didn't tell me." Dawn shrugged and finally concluded, "I'll have to ask Marion. It's about time she shared what they've been discussing in their secret meetings."

She turned off the laptop, and the projection disappeared.

Dawn rolled her head from side to side, wishing for a break from the pressure of a looming deadline. "Want to go outside for some fresh air? I met the porus over the weekend."

"Really? Marion told you about *all* the porus?"

"Mm-hmm . . . come on."

Laurel waved her off and flopped back into the armchair. "It's too hot outside, and I've already met Sid's poru and the ospreys. I see them every once in a while when they hunt for fish."

"How does that work, exactly? How can Lumen control their porus?"

"Only Lumen with strong auras can develop a poru bond. Every Valedorian, sangwor, and Aquavian guardian that I know of has a poru. The bond is strong, nearly unbreakable. Although the creature has its own instincts, it will obey and protect its master no matter what."

Dawn sat down in the swivel chair with renewed interest.

"That sounds like loyalty on another level. By the way, you promised you'd tell me a bunch of other things once I learned how to shield, like how you shift."

"Go ahead and take your walk. I'll tell you all about us shifters when you get back."

Dawn returned from her walk in the backyard—sweaty, but with a clear mind. Marion had prepared tea sandwiches (tuna for Laurel) and green smoothies for them. Unbothered by the heat, Miss M. stayed outside to tend to her plants while Hiro lazily watched from shaded spots.

Laurel bit into her sandwich, toasted breadcrumbs clinging to the corners of her lips as she spoke. "Ever since the first generation of Aquavians, our shifting abilities activate shortly after birth."

"You shift right after you're born?" Dawn asked, her eyes growing wide.

"That's right," Laurel said with a full mouth. She paused to chew and swallow, then continued. "We're born in our true, land-dwelling forms. Mothers can give birth in birthing caves, or they can go to a designated Aquavian island. As soon as the newborn takes its first breath, they're taken to the water to shift. This tradition activates their en. After they successfully shift, the mother can choose to spend their first few days on land or in the water."

"That's . . . fascinating," Dawn said between sips of her smoothie. "You're born to swim."

Laurel nodded. "It's been happening like this for almost a thousand years."

That remark reminded Dawn of Malstrom—the thousand-year-old king—and her newly acquired knowledge that she was part of the Aurelian bloodline; she was potentially a lumere just like Malstrom. *Why wasn't I told any of this earlier in life?*

Dawn took a bite of her sandwich and chewed, wishing she knew the reasons behind Howel and Marion's decades-long secrecy, why they thought withholding information from her all this time was the best choice.

"Judging by the face you're making, your sandwich must taste like bilge scum."

"I just remembered you telling me about Malstrom," Dawn explained.

Laurel grimaced before Dawn could finish her sentence. "Malstrom the Merciful," she said with disdain, gesticulating quotation marks in the air.

"Yes, well, I learned that I'm Aurelian. I'm part of a lumere bloodline. Does that mean I can wield a sentient jewel . . . like Malstrom?"

This time, Laurel's eyes went wide. "Finally," the Aquavian said. "I was wondering when someone was going to let you in on that."

"I guess I learned a lot from Marion last weekend," Dawn replied, feeling slighted that even Laurel knew of her lumere lineage. "So, tell me. How does a lumere wield a corgemma?"

Laurel's eyes darted toward the center of the table where a projection of a gold necklace with a shiny emerald pendant appeared floating in the air. The jewel was magnificent, fit for Cleopatra herself, Dawn marveled.

"Corgemmas were priceless to their respective leaders," Laurel said as the projected jewel rotated slowly in the space between them. "The kings and queens who possessed them paid for them with the lives of their loved ones."

A young woman dressed like royalty appeared in the projection, and a bearded man beside her—he was crowned, and adorned like a royal, his hand comfortingly rested on her shoulder. His beloved turned to face him, embracing him and giving him a tender kiss. He held her—too long for a regular goodbye. Tears streaked down their faces as they looked upon each other, each memorizing the other's.

The anguish disappeared from the woman's face as she steeled herself, standing tall and regal. She turned around and faced the floating emerald necklace. With her hand, she reached out toward the jewel. At the exact moment her fingertips grazed the emerald, a flash of white light blinded them.

She was gone. The jewel remained.

The man reached for the necklace, which floated willingly toward him. Upon grasping it, he fell to his knees, sobbing and muttering something unintelligible.

The projection disappeared to reveal Laurel's face, her chin resting atop her hands.

"This was the sacrifice of every lumere," she said. "One of their beloved—usually a spouse or child—willingly gave up their life and infused the jewel with their en."

"That man's wife died when she touched the emerald?"

"Yes, but her aura lives on. That's why they're called *sentient* jewels. The essence of their aura is infused in the jewel, and it grants the lumere even more powers."

Dawn shook her head. "What kind of special powers would be worth the life of someone they love?"

"The power to heal—they saved countless lives when disease ran rampant and modern medicine had not yet been developed. The power to control the earth's elements—to protect their people from natural disasters and till the Earth to grow food. The power to see into the future and prepare for it, and so many other abilities."

"Oh, so it's for the so-called greater good," Dawn said with sarcasm. "Sounds like it's a way for tyrants to gain more power and hoard it, so they can live in the lap of luxury and wage war against all those who oppose them."

"I suppose you think you know better because you were there a thousand years ago," Laurel challenged.

"I didn't need to be *there*, Laurel. History repeats itself."

"You don't get to judge the lumeres," Laurel said evenly, leaning back in her chair as if she'd already debated the topic long ago. "They kept the peace when our realms were divided."

"Is that really what happened? Or is that what you were taught?" Dawn argued, peering out the backyard window.

The ospreys' hawk-like chirps cut through the air, some loud and clear, some faint and farther away.

"It is what I know," Laurel insisted. "Those who were sacrificed gave up their lives *willingly*. The twelve lumeres and their living sacrifices volunteered for the spell to bring balance and prosperity—hence, four lumeres for our three major clans. After it was fulfilled, they vowed to never again invoke the ancient sacrificial spell."

Dawn studied her Aquavian friend, who exhibited unusually reserved behavior. A month ago, Laurel had gotten all riled up talking about Malstrom. But this wasn't about him—and that's when it hit her. Laurel spoke about the lumeres *collectively*. Their intentions were pure; the cost they paid was high. Maybe all would have gone well if it weren't for Malstrom, who was apparently the bad apple of the bunch.

"It still doesn't sit right with me how the lumeres basically killed their family members. And I—*I* am part of their bloodline."

Laurel suddenly turned her head toward the side door, and half a second after, Marion burst through it from the backyard, beads of sweat dotting her forehead. The ospreys' high-pitched calls pierced the air.

"Get to the bridge," Marion cried, panting. "NOW!"

CHAPTER 18

WITHOUT WAITING FOR an explanation, Laurel sprang out of her chair and made a beeline for the bathroom. Dawn bit her tongue, resisting the urge to ask what was happening as she followed suit. Her housekeeper was right on her heels.

The bridge was swirling with metallic blues and grays when Laurel flung open the bathroom door. Before the Aquavian could turn back to ask where they were going, and before Dawn could relish the thought of traveling by bridge again, Marion shoved them through.

Dawn outstretched her arms, stumbling into the dark space. The room was noticeably cooler than her house, and goosebumps quickly rose on her arms. She collided into Laurel's shoulder and grabbed hold of her arm as they shuffled around blindly.

Marion's steps echoed on the hard floor behind her.

We're not alone here, Laurel projected to Dawn.

A small orb of light sprang from in Laurel's free hand, and silhouettes of the three of them appeared. Marion was hunched over, hands on her knees as she panted. She straightened up and wiped the sweat from her forehead.

Dawn gasped as a hooded man, draped in a cloak the color of a storm cloud, stepped out from behind the cheval mirror.

"Do not be afraid," he said, taking a step in their direction, then pulled back the hood of his shepra cloak to reveal his face and short-cropped, fire-red hair.

Dawn recognized his features instantly. While her memory of the council of Tencho was hazy at best, the one thing she remembered vividly was Sid's flaming locks. The man who stood before them looked more like a muscular version of Sid and seemed a good foot taller.

"I opened the bridge for you," said the stranger. "I had to ensure you weren't followed."

"We were not followed," Marion confirmed. Even in the little light they had, Dawn saw her housekeeper squaring her shoulders like a bodyguard. "And who might you be?"

"You may call me Fanto," he said. He stepped behind the mirror, reached for something against the wall, then dim light bulbs flickered on. Laurel extinguished her light orb, and the women took in their drab surroundings, except for Marion, who kept her eyes on Fanto.

The mirror bridge before them was much larger, like a doorway, but plain in appearance, studded with half as many jewels. Dawn whipped her head behind her and spotted a rusty table and a few chairs in the corner of the room. Next to the table were shelves, gun racks, and a pegboard wall with all kinds of weapons. On the other side of the room was an expansive area with partitioned stalls dividing the space.

Dawn was just about to ask where they were when Marion's voice projected to her and Laurel: *Do not speak.*

"We're underground," Fanto said, answering the question they silently asked, "in a worm bunker. You're the only ones here. You can explore it, with caution," he said, as his eyes darted toward the back of the room where the weapons were.

He padded calmly toward them and stopped in front of the mirror. Despite his towering height, he seemed gentle in demeanor. His expression was not menacing.

"You are safe here. This is a locked bridge. I will rendezvous with Sid and the team now. Await further instructions," he said to Marion.

Before Marion could respond, he turned around and disappeared through the bridge. Its metallic hues returned to a solid state, reflecting their disgruntled faces.

"You don't think we should speak to Fanto," Dawn said to Marion, her comment sounding like half an observation, half a question.

"It is my first time meeting Fanto—if that is his real name," Marion said. "Generally, the less Lumen who can recognize your voice, the better."

"And what about you?" Dawn asked. "He heard *your* voice."

Marion shrugged. "I'm just your housekeeper. But he does seem okay to converse with. He bore a resemblance to Sid."

Laurel nodded, whether in agreement with Fanto's relation to Sid or with keeping their voices unrecognizable or both, Dawn couldn't tell.

"What do you think he meant by 'worm' bunker?" Dawn asked.

"Etherans regard humans without aura abilities as worms," Laurel replied.

Dawn scrunched up her face in disgust, clearly offended.

"It's true," Marion confirmed. "I've heard it many times. Most sky dwellers I've met, think humans without aura abilities are despicable, revolting beings. The ignorance has been passed down from generation to generation."

"Etherans don't have a kinder word to describe people who aren't Lumen, but we Aquavians do," Laurel chimed in as she made her way to the table and chairs in the corner. She sat down, resting her elbows on the table and her chin in her hands. "We call them 'regs,' short for regular humans."

Dawn walked to the corner of the room and absent-mindedly looked over the shelf of weapons as she pondered how being a "reg" could be such a despised thing.

"What happened back there with the ospreys?" Laurel asked Marion.

Marion took her time, gathered her thoughts, and explained she had been at the far end of the backyard when she heard the ospreys overhead. They had just made their rounds in the neighborhood and spotted two Lumen. Seconds later, a few of Sid's agents appeared and urged Marion to vacate the premises; the agents stayed behind to deploy a decoy per their protocol.

"Hikaru appeared when he sensed the commotion—he stayed with Hiro and helped with the distraction," Marion said.

Dawn, who had been absorbed in examining the wall of pistols, glanced up at her housekeeper, thinking she heard a flicker of anxiety in Miss M.'s voice. She was not surprised to see Marion exude her usual, confident demeanor.

"I know Hikaru and Sid's agents can take care of themselves," Marion assured.

"What did the Lumen look like?" Laurel asked, sneaking a sideways glance at Dawn, who immediately pictured the soufors—the Inked Man and Blade, his femme partner.

"They didn't say."

"Were they on foot? Or were they flying?" Laurel pressed.

"They didn't say," Marion repeated as she walked over to the table and pulled up a chair, "but it's obvious they're looking for someone."

Her eyes settled on Dawn, who had moved to another shelf, trying on tactical gear.

Dawn rapped her knuckles on the vest she had put on. "Not sure what materials these are made of," she muttered to herself. Next, she scanned an area that had boxes of ammunition. "There's enough gear, weapons, and ammo for a small army. It wouldn't hurt to bring some back with us, right Miss M.?"

When she heard no answer, Dawn looked up to find Marion sitting at the table, staring at her with a far-away look in her eyes.

"I'll bring some, just in case," Dawn said, interpreting Marion's silence for acquiescence.

After a while, Dawn urged Laurel to try on some boots and other gear. When Marion grew restless, she got up, reminded them to be careful with the weapons, then went off "to find a bathroom and see what type of rations are available."

Left to their own devices, Dawn and Laurel surveyed the weapons and found everything from crossbows to swords to massive laser guns—too heavy to carry. By the time Dawn was done, she had stuffed a duffel bag with firearms, a few knives, holsters, and ammo. She doubted any of the blades would be as useful to her, as she'd hardly received training with them. Knives were meant for close combat, and the idea of using them made her uncomfortable. Still, she didn't dismiss the idea of learning to throw them, glancing at the empty stalls.

Laurel followed her gaze. "What are you thinking?" she asked. It was the first time she had asked rather than reading Dawn's mind without permission; Dawn was grateful for their earlier agreement.

"I was thinking it's kind of remarkable there's an underground shooting range here," she said, making her way to one of the stalls. At the far end were paper targets, some with bullet holes in the killshot areas.

On the floor, Dawn picked up something cylindrical that resembled an oversized metal cigar. It was a silencer, she realized, and soon after, she found the handgun to which it could be attached, abandoned on the counter.

A random thought occurred to Dawn. "You know, I hardly ever hear you talk about Ezra—you haven't gotten to spend time with him since you started training me."

Laurel blinked at Dawn a few times but did not respond.

"Do you miss him?" Dawn prodded while loading bullets into the handgun. "Would you have chosen him if it were up to you?"

"No," Laurel said flatly without hesitation. "But nonetheless, we're betrothed."

Dawn looked at her friend with compassion, knowing she had to reach a level of maturity to accept the situation—an arranged marriage for political machinations.

"Why not tell your parents what you really wish for?"

Laurel swatted the air as if dismissing a ridiculous idea. "It doesn't matter. Why wish for something that can't happen? I'll end up disappointed," she said matter of factly, folding her arms. "*You* should stop fawning over Logan. You'll end up disappointed too."

"I'm not fawning. I'm hoping," she insisted, "that somehow, I can find a way to make it work. A couple weeks ago, I didn't even know what aura or en were. Yet, here I am, crossing bridges, learning how to project and shield. Two months ago, I couldn't have fathomed that I'd ride on a giant bird of prey or be in an underground bunker in the middle of nowhere or try on tactical gear with a shifting mermaid. I've done what seemed impossible. So in comparison, pursuing an unlikely romance with a coworker isn't far-fetched to me at all."

"It will never work out," Laurel said softly, in a way that wasn't intentionally rude or pessimistic. She stated it simply as if it were as true as saying the ocean is wet.

"Let's shoot a few rounds," Dawn said, changing the topic, her head tilting toward the target on the other side of the stall.

Laurel narrowed her eyes at her apprehensively, rooted to her spot.

"It's not that hard. I'll show you how," Dawn coaxed.

She found two e-vizors near the stalls and gave one to Laurel.

Whoever stocked this place is well connected—it has everything, she thought, then shuddered as Jett Pierce came to mind. He was known for his high-end tech, but Dawn never took him for a weapons guy.

Dawn showed Laurel where to load the bullets for the handgun, how to turn the safety switch on and off, take a firm stance, aim at the target, and finally, pull the trigger.

The sound echoed through the space upon firing, and Laurel let out a high-pitched shriek. Dawn set the gun down, chuckling at how rusty she was; she'd barely hit the target's edge. She found the Aquavian leaning against the stall wall with her hands covering her ears. Her dusky-toned skin had turned a sickly shade of bluish green.

"Are you okay?" Dawn asked. "Did you want to try shooting it?"

Laurel uncovered her ears and shook her head. "I'm—I'm okay. That was louder than I expected," she said, forcing a smile. "I'd rather watch," she added before retreating to the table.

Dawn practiced shooting for a couple more minutes, improving her aim to the targeted areas with the help of the e-vizor. When she turned around, she caught Marion standing near the table with Laurel, a wistful look in her eyes.

"You look so much like your mother," Marion said as Dawn approached her.

There was a melancholy air about her housekeeper in that fleeting moment—there and then not—Dawn thought she could've imagined it.

"We need to discuss your mission. Time is running out," Marion said, her change of subject feeling disjointed. But Dawn agreed. The Ides of March was fast approaching.

As the three of them sat at the table and huddled, Dawn got Miss M. caught up on their plan to visit the five caves; they agreed that splitting up to search for the missing ingredient would be most efficient.

Then Dawn mentioned bringing Lopple along. To her surprise, Marion *didn't* agree on recruiting Lopple for his help, not because he couldn't be trusted, but because "he was tasked with searching for other rare ingredients for Howel," explaining that they were still hard to find.

Finally, the conversation took a turn that allowed Dawn to ask more about the mission. How would gathering all these ingredients help? What sort of potion was Howel concocting? What was his master plan for her—his adopted daughter—and for the council's Earth-saving measures? The questions rose to the forefront of her mind, like a tangled mass of seaweed washed upon the shore. All Dawn managed to stutter was a single word.

"W-Why?" Dawn asked.

"They've all been difficult to find because—" Marion began, but Dawn cut her off, struggling to translate her thoughts into coherent speech.

"N-no, I mean, why gather these ingredients?" Dawn clarified slowly, willing her tongue to cooperate. "What is my dad going to do with these ingredients if we find them in time? We don't even know where he is."

Marion nodded, taking a second to collect her thoughts.

"Let us first remain focused on obtaining your missing ingredient, then we worry about getting it to Howel. The list of ingredients, or the ones that I'm aware of," Marion explained, "could be used to create a few powerful, restoration jewels. All the plants have regenerative properties, and I think Howel is attempting to restore Earth's atmosphere."

Dawn pursed her lips. "All right, we can cross that bridge when we get to it, but why wouldn't Etherans and Aquavians openly work together to create these so-called restoration jewels if they're necessary in restoring the Earth's atmosphere?"

Laurel scoffed. "Malstrom and his elites would rather watch the world burn before toiling with Aquavians. They've ordered us around for centuries."

"That's not quite it," Marion interjected. "In my discussions with Hikaru and Lopple, we've discovered a pattern of activity that might reveal Malstrom's true intentions. Recently, there have been a series of fatal accidents—or what *seem* like accidents—of high-ranking leaders around the globe, as well as CEOs that have decided to step down from their positions. We think that the leadership replacements have been bought to do Malstrom's bidding."

"That sounds . . . far-fetched," Dawn said skeptically. Miss M. was never one to indulge in conspiracy theories.

"Nearly twenty-five years ago, your mother, father, and Howel realized there was a slew of replacements—from the same corporations that control the world's manufacturing processes, tech, and other companies that directly affect the Earth's environment. This has been happening for the last hundred years."

Laurel's eyes bulged. "Your father is not Howel?" she squeaked, processing the first half of the sentence.

"No, he's not. I'm adopted," Dawn said, on the brink of an epiphany. She stood up from her chair so abruptly it toppled backward.

"The journal!" Dawn remembered. A headline about a corporation—Bright something—and a random executive perishing in a house fire came to mind. "My mom or Howel kept news clippings and announcements of people who retired, left the company, or . . . died."

And the true cause of death might've been assassination. She shuddered at the thought.

"There've been plenty of renaming of companies, creation of shell corporations and new sectors, mostly in the name of reinventing," Marion explained, leaning forward, her hands gesturing animatedly. "Malstrom has infiltrated governing entities and has eyes on the inside to influence powerful people. A lot of these *accidents* were uninvestigated, swept under the rug."

"That's preposterous," Laurel whispered, her eyes wide with realization. "If that were true, the sangwor and Sid's troops would be the first ones to implement this—this insane plot. They're the ones who have trained to assimilate with Eretzians."

Marion nodded slowly. "Thankfully, Lord Angel, Sid, and a small group of Etherans—including some of the sangwor," Marion said, her eyes meeting Laurel's, "have been against the assassinations from the beginning. They're part of the secret council—and they've quietly recruited other Lumen to bring an end to Malstrom's plot."

"It doesn't make complete sense though," Dawn said, righting her chair and settling back in. "What would Malstrom hope to accomplish? He already has control of most of the sentient jewels and the sky kingdom."

"Howel and Lopple think Malstrom's goal was to restore Earth," Marion replied, "but he can't properly wield the Eretzian and Aquavian jewels—they're not in his bloodline."

"Wait—that can't be right," Laurel insisted. "I've seen projections of Malstrom using the other sentient jewels as weapons."

"Yes, he can weaponize them," Miss M. said pointedly, "but to use them for their *restorative* powers, he must have the same bloodline of the lumere that forged it. There's another complication," Marion sighed. "It will take all twelve jewels and their lumeres to restore the entire Earth, but Malstrom's jewel—the twin jewel—was lost . . ."

"When his wife took it and fled the kingdom," Laurel said, finishing Marion's sentence.

"I'm confused," Dawn admitted. "What's the twin jewel?"

"I thought you taught her Aquavian history," Marion chided Laurel.

Laurel rolled her eyes. "Some—I haven't gotten to that part yet."

Miss M. sighed and folded her arms. "There's no time like the present," she said, leaning back in her chair to get comfortable.

"Fine," Laurel conceded, then proceeded to project twelve multi-colored, sparkling jewels floating at the center of the table. "I'll give you the short version. Remember how the twelve corgemmas required sacrificed lives to create them?"

Dawn nodded.

"Malstrom and his wife, Agatha, were part of that sacrificial ritual," Laurel continued as the projection morphed to Malstrom and his very pregnant, golden-haired partner. "His wife was to be the sacrifice, but she was carrying twins at the time."

Dawn gasped, guessing what happened. "The spell took her and her unborn twins?!"

"It did not take Agatha—it only took her twins," Marion said, spoiling the ending and earning a glare from Laurel. "Hence the name, the twin jewel."

"No one expected that outcome—not even Malstrom," Laurel said, her projection changing again to Malstrom and his weeping, childless wife. "Agatha, who was expecting herself and her unborn to be the sacrifice, was distraught with grief. She never got over it. On the day that Atlantis was established, Agatha and the twin jewel went missing."

"There must've been plenty of commotion and chaos that day as your people took to the seas," Marion added. "It would've been easy for Agatha to slip away with the jewel undetected."

Laurel nodded. "It is said she made a pact with the people who first came to be known as the Aquavi that day. She was hellbent on undoing the spell and freeing the en of her twins. No one knows whether she succeeded, but she was never seen again."

"And neither was the twin jewel," Marion said. "To restore the Earth, it would take the power of all twelve corgemmas. Malstrom has searched far and wide for the twin jewel. Since the Last Days have begun, those on the secret council believe Malstrom has abandoned his search and taken a different approach."

"You think Malstrom is trying to control the Earth's resources to prolong the Last Days," Dawn surmised, "while Howel wants to create a restorative jewel?"

"Yes. That's what we—Hikaru, Lopple, King Kameo, and I—believe. Lord Angel's and Sid's focus has been on foiling the plot to assassinate Eretzians. Sky dweller sentiments have been split. Some agree with Malstrom's extremism, while others want a more peaceful outcome."

"I disagree with the first part . . . respectfully," Laurel said flatly, then added the last word catching Marion's unamused gaze. "I've never met Howel, and I think he's wrong about one restorative jewel making a difference. Only a *sentient* jewel could complement the eleven to fully restore the Earth's core *and* atmosphere."

"Restoring the atmosphere alone buys us time," Marion explained wearily. "Even the small change a restorative jewel can bring will make a big difference."

"I think it's a brilliant plan," Dawn breathed. "Malstrom won't be bothered to stop us in creating a restorative jewel. I doubt he even suspects that's what Howel is trying to do. I bet Malstrom underestimates the power of an incremental change."

Laurel stared at her, brows furrowed in confusion.

"Think of it this way," Dawn elaborated. "If a travelling ship changes course by just one degree in the middle of the journey, it could end up somewhere entirely different. This will give us time to make more changes in the future."

"Exactly," Marion said, punctuating each syllable. "Our future generations will benefit. We'll buy time to make technological advancements, and we shall change the Earth's trajectory."

Laurel's troubled expression remained, but she nodded.

The three spent the next half hour discussing what type of plant might be in the caves. After listening to Dawn recall her description of the cave sites, Marion concluded that they should spend their efforts looking for *fairy fern*—a rare plant with regenerative properties.

A projection of the bright green plant appeared at the center of the table. Its leaves looked small and dainty. Bunched together, it could pass as a distant cousin of cilantro.

"Fairy fern may seem delicate, but it's hardy," Marion said, pointing to her projection. "It thrives in cold, wet climates without sunlight."

Two of the sites seemed more ideal for producing this rare Eretzian fern: Heavenly Pit and Lost River Cave. All the caves had plenty of foliage near their rivers, Dawn recalled. But these two were in colder climates this time of year.

The caves required a guided tour to access the sites, and fortunately, Howel had set up private guides when he and Dawn had gone together. X8 could easily access the records and schedule the tours. Dawn and Laurel would travel by bridge and arrange air lifts to get them as close to the sites as possible.

At last, the puzzle pieces were starting to fit together. Marion and Hikaru would leave for the Lost River Cave in Kentucky tomorrow; Dawn and Laurel would head to the Heavenly Pit in Chongqing, China. There was just one thing that Dawn wanted to say, but she hesitated.

"Anything else we need to address?" Marion asked, sensing Dawn's unease.

"I'm going to ask Logan to come with us," Dawn blurted out.

"What?" Marion and Laurel both asked in surprise. "That is not a good idea," Marion continued, as if she needed to elaborate on the emotions playing out on her face.

"He could help us. He could protect us," Dawn insisted.

But the truth of the matter was that she was venturing back into the world as a *Lumen*, of all things. Dawn wanted to go with someone who knew her for her, a normal human being. And besides, Logan was special. She wanted to be with him, and if sharing all of her new world wasn't possible, then she would take him as far as the journey would allow.

Laurel looked at Dawn as if she had sprouted octopus tentacles, but kept her mouth shut.

"If you're worried about staying safe, we could ask Sid to spare an agent or request for one of Jett's guards," Marion protested.

"Why don't *you* request for Fanto to accompany you, and Hikaru can come with me and Laurel," Dawn offered, knowing that Marion would not agree to separate from Hikaru, one of many things she learned during lockdown.

"Hikaru and I," Marion paused, choosing her words carefully, "work better together. I see your point, but how exactly will you explain the bridge to Logan?"

"Don't worry—I already have a plan for it," Dawn said. "If things go sideways, Laurel can erase his memory."

Hopefully, it won't come to that, Dawn prayed.

Marion considered her words and then nodded. "Very well then. The three of you will go together. We should prepare to leave by tomorrow."

"You'll be leaving here right now," Fanto said from the other side of the room as he stepped through the swirling mirror.

The three women stood as he came toward them. He took half a second to survey Dawn's and Laurel's tactical gear before turning to Marion.

"The decoy was successful, and the porus were able to track the Lumen suspects," he said, conjuring a projection of the Inked Man and Blade flying through the air of their own volition.

Dawn blanched at the image.

"Ah, you know these soufors," Fanto observed, then the projection dissipated. "These brazen hounds of Lord Malstrom think themselves above Etheran law. They will not hesitate to create a commotion in the presence of worms and then erase their memories."

Dawn, still trying to recover from seeing the soufors, bristled at the mention of "worms."

"Did you capture them?" Marion asked, commanding Fanto's attention.

"No, we would not engage them unless it is absolutely necessary. Our orders are to prevent *your* capture," he said, glancing from one to the other. "The agents and porus have completed a sweep of the perimeter and determined it is safe to return."

"And what of Hikaru?" Miss M. asked.

Fanto held a blank expression.

"The decoy," she clarified.

Fanto replied with a piercing stare, as if having a silent conversation. Then finally, he said, "The decoy is safe. He led them away from the location and shook them off his trail after a time. Quite impressive to shake a souf—"

"Thank you," Marion interrupted, relief evident in her sigh.

Fanto nodded. "You may return to the property now." He gestured with his hand toward the mirror and the glass began to swirl.

Laurel was the first to leave, walking awkwardly in her thick boots.

Dawn followed, slinging her packed duffle bag over her shoulder. Before she crossed the bridge, she looked Fanto square in the eyes as best she could despite his towering height and, not caring she was revealing the sound of her voice, said, "I'm taking these weapons with me."

He smirked at her, bemused. "They are worm weapons, and they are not mine to give."

"I'm not asking permission," she snapped. "And they're just weapons. Not *worm* weapons."

Dawn crossed through the bridge without so much as a glance back.

As Marion approached the mirror, Fanto's smirk turned apologetic. Realizing his faux pas, he said to her, "It seems I have insulted your people. That was not my intention."

Unlike Dawn, Miss M. had many years to think about Etheran shortcomings—as well as forgive their ignorance. Despite Fanto's blunder, he had done his job and kept them safe.

"First of all, Fanto," Marion addressed him courteously, "we are grateful to you and to all of Sid's agents for keeping us safe. Thank you for your sacrifice."

Fanto lowered his head and gave her a slight bow. "It is my duty."

Marion knew it was his way of saying that thanks was not needed.

"We're all people, Lumen or not. This is a regular bunker—a *reg* bunker—as the Aquavi might say. I suggest you—and your kin—adopt the Aquavian word for a non-Lumen. After all, Aquavians and Etherans borrow many sayings from each others' native tongues, do they not?"

He gave her a curt nod in acknowledgment.

Before she stepped through the bridge, Marion remembered an old-as-time Etherish farewell, meant for parting friends who may not see each other again.

May the stars guide your way, she projected in Etherish, bowing toward him.

A tremor of surprise flashed across Fanto's face, and a smile settled on his lips upon hearing the Etherish expression.

And the moon light your path, Fanto replied, as was the appropriate response. He bowed once more with his head lower than hers—a sign of deep respect. He did not rise immediately after but chose to remain in his bow even after Marion had left.

CHAPTER 19

LOGAN PINES WAS late.

Dawn paced the living room, casting anxious glances at Laurel, who sat idly on a lounge chair, gazing out the window.

"Are you sure he got the note that Hikaru left him?" Laurel asked.

"Yes, I'm sure—I saw him read it on the camera," Dawn answered, feeling her anxiety peak. What if something had gone terribly wrong? Before Hikaru departed for Kentucky with Marion, he had left a simple note for Logan with directions to her house. "Maybe we should've met him at Hikaru's."

"Then the porus would've seen that something was amiss," Laurel reminded her.

"I should've had a drone follow him. Or should've told him our address last night."

"For the love of Calypso! He's only two minutes late," Laurel said in a feeble attempt to give Dawn assurance. "Hikaru agreed that leaving a note was the least risky."

It had not been difficult to convince Logan to come on their last-minute excursion. Dawn had simply messaged him last night, asking for help in finding a rare cave plant during a day trip.

"I'm there," he agreed, without knowing the details.

Dawn then proceeded to tell him that the day trip was tomorrow . . . in *China*. CETT would get them there and back in one day. All he needed to do was pack for a trek through the forest (without any electronic devices) and show up at Hikaru's house for lunch the next day.

The note Hikaru left for him was simple. *Go two blocks west, enter the white gate, and knock at the front door.* Their house was the only one on the block that had an arched, white wrought iron gate with fancy scrollwork. (It was Pierce's property, after all.)

A knock at the door brought Dawn back to the present. She knew it was Logan, not because they were expecting him, but because she could now sense his aura.

"You found us!" she greeted him upon opening the door with a relieved smile.

"Hi!" Logan returned, walking with her to the living room. "Sorry I'm late—I told everyone I didn't feel well before my lunch break, so they shouldn't expect me back."

"Good idea," Dawn said, giving him a once over. "You're already in your hiking gear," she pointed out. "I thought we could have lunch first."

She motioned to Laurel who sat on the armchair still dressed in sweats.

"Oh," Logan said, noticing Laurel for the first time. He set down his rucksack. "I actually thought it would be just the two of us, but this oughta be fun."

"I must've forgotten to mention that Laurel was coming," Dawn hedged. "She's really experienced with cave exploration."

"It's all good," Logan said with a sincere smile. "So, what's for lunch?"

"Finally," Laurel muttered. "I'm starving."

They ate quickly and chatted about their itinerary, but not before Logan swore himself to secrecy. In any case, no one—no groundling, anyway—would believe he had gone to China and back in one day.

Dawn sketched the plant they were looking for and showed Logan, saying that it was so rare that no accurate pictures could be found online. He studied the drawing, remarking that he indeed had never seen anything like it.

After lunch, Logan waited in the living room while Laurel and Dawn changed out of their sweats. When they returned in their hiking gear, he took one look at them and chuckled. "Those are some heavy-duty boots," he teased.

Laurel cackled. "I knew we would look ridiculous!"

"It was all we had for a last-minute trip." Dawn shrugged, but couldn't hold back her laughter when Laurel assumed a power stance in her combat boots.

"Ready to travel?" Laurel asked.

"As ready as I'll ever be," Logan said, donning his rucksack. "My only regret is I won't get to *see* CETT's newest tech."

"Conditions of our agreement," Dawn reminded him. She picked up her own backpack full of snacks and extra supplies.

It was her idea to pretend the bridge was a teleportation device, and plausible enough that CETT would've given her dad a prototype. Marion had suggested they blindfold Logan, and Laurel would project darkness in his mind, ensuring he'd never get a glimpse of the bridge—no contingencies. They had moved the cheval mirror from the bathroom into the garage to make their "teleportation device" story more believable.

Dawn pulled a blindfold from her pocket. Logan stooped down, allowing Dawn to cover his eyes. As she did so, she tenderly tucked his hair behind his ears.

"I need a haircut, don't I?" Logan asked as he straightened back up.

"Well, no . . . I like running my fingers through it," Dawn confessed.

Laurel cleared her throat, reminding them of her presence. "We should get going. It's almost 6:00 a.m. in China."

"It's safe right? You've used CETT's tech before?"

"Yes, it's perfectly safe. I've um, teleported a few times already," Dawn fibbed. She nodded at Laurel to start her projection, then opened the door to the garage.

"You promise you can't see anything?" Dawn asked.

"Not a thing," he said. "I'm completely blind. I think it even got a little darker."

She guided him to the mirror, which was beside the airlift. Laurel activated the bridge, and the glass swirled metallic hues as she focused on their destination near the outskirts of New Hong Kong.

During last night's dinner, Laurel had projected a few bridge maps that Reed had shown her. As the son of the Aquavi's head chronicler, his special privileges granted him access to their map archives. The safest bridge that brought them as close as they could get to the Heavenly Pit was in a nature reserve. While there were other Aquavian bridges nearer to the Pit, they were underwater—too dangerous for them to cross with Logan in tow. As soon as it was decided, Marion had contacted Jett's personal assistant, Gita, and arranged for an airlift to take them the rest of the distance.

"I'll go first," Laurel said, disappearing into the swirls of the glass. The plan was to have her take a quick look around (erase memories if needed) and make sure no one would see Dawn and Logan cross.

All clear, Laurel projected to Dawn. Beyond the bridge, Dawn could see that Laurel was on rugged terrain at the base of a rockface. She tugged at Logan's arm still tightly around hers and moved toward the bridge, instructing him to step over the threshold and duck his head to avoid hitting the top of the mirror frame.

In an instant, they were outdoors in a chilly and overcast environment. They had crossed over to a large alcove, concealed by plenty of vines and shrubbery. The bridge itself was embedded in a dark grayish rock, dulling their reflections. Upon closer inspection, Dawn saw the gems were covered in dried mud. To find this bridge, you'd have to know what to look for.

"We're in China!" she whispered to a still blindfolded Logan, squeezing his arm.

A broad smile appeared on his face as he said, "I can't wait to see it." His breath appeared as vapor in the brisk air, and Dawn felt him pull her a little closer.

As soon as they rounded the hillside, Dawn removed Logan's blindfold and Laurel lifted her projection of darkness. He shielded his face as his eyes adjusted.

"Did CETT make the blindfold too?" he joked. "I couldn't see a thing. And the teleportation tech is amazing. It's like walking through a door, except it's to another country!"

"It really is amazing, isn't it?" Dawn said, taking in the rest of their surroundings.

They stood in a clearing of grass and dirt paths, wide enough for small vehicles to traverse. On the right was a small yet inviting oriental building. Behind it was a gate—the main entrance to the nature reserve. Everywhere else, the paths led to hills and thick bamboo forests. Dawn peeked at Logan's face, which held an expression of awe, probably not unlike how she looked when she first crossed a bridge.

"Well, what are you waiting for?" Laurel called back. She had already started walking toward the structure.

As they approached the building, Dawn admired the curve of the roof and the red lanterns that hung near the front, flanking the entrance. "They must've celebrated the lunar new year recently."

A few other people walked through the main gate, and a couple staff members dressed in matching red and ivory uniforms directed them toward the structure.

The three of them stayed close together and exited the gate quietly. Once outside, they could see the parking lot, which had about a dozen identical carts with CETT's logo on one side, and a smattering of guests' commuter vehicles. A larger silver vehicle, similar to the prototype at home, stuck out like a sore thumb. It was undoubtedly their ride.

Someone is approaching us, Laurel projected.

A man in a dark blue, modernized Tang suit walked toward them. "Good morning," he said upon reaching them and gave a slight bow. "Welcome to the nature reserve. May I ask where you have traveled from?"

Dawn knew this was the CETT rep who was sent to collect them. There would be no exchange of names or identification. Marion said he'd simply await their arrival outside the reserve and ask about their travels. Their exact passphrase, to verify that they were the esteemed guests of Jett Pierce, had been decided upon during Marion's exchange with Gita.

"We have traveled from afar," Dawn replied vaguely, intentionally not answering his question. "Might you have some kudzukan tea?"

Laurel snorted at their poorly scripted exchange, but there was no mistake that only *they* would be asking for kudzukan tea.

"Of course," he said, ushering them toward the silver vehicle. Passphrase accepted.

The airlift had all the same functionality as the prototype at home; this didn't seem to trigger Logan's PTSD, probably because he wasn't the one piloting it. He even winked at her as he got in the front passenger seat. Laurel, on the other hand, glanced nervously out the window and gripped her seatbelt so hard her knuckles turned white.

"Are you all right to fly?" Dawn asked, knowing they didn't have a choice.

Laurel nodded vigorously and took quick, shallow breaths. "I-I'm fine," she muttered.

Logan craned his neck to check on them, then looked back at the CETT rep, who was also their pilot. "Excuse me, sir—"

"Please, call me Captain," the pilot said cheerfully.

"Um, okay, Captain," Logan said. "How long is our flight?"

"It will take forty-five minutes to reach our destination," he said, "weather permitting."

"What?" Laurel squeaked, while Captain pressed a few buttons on the dashboard. The vehicle's propellers moved to position and softly spun into motion. The cabin was soundproof.

Try to breathe normally, Dawn projected to Laurel. *I'm sure it'll be a smooth ride—much smoother than riding a diurlax.*

Laurel cast her a scathing glare.

"Breathe in for four seconds," Logan said, craning his neck to look at Laurel, "hold for four seconds, breathe out four seconds, then hold for another four."

He gestured with his hand to show the rise and fall of his chest. Laurel did as he had demonstrated, and after a few rounds, her breathing had slowed.

"Look at the view," Dawn said, squinting at tiny dots and squares now beneath them.

They glided above patches of land that must be crops and the greens and grays of the trees mixed with the city streets and structures. Dawn saw Logan peering out his window as well, lost in thought. They all sat in silence, admiring the aerial view of the countryside.

It had been more than a decade since Dawn had gone to the Heavenly Pit with her dad—well, *Howel*. She wondered whether she should still call him "dad," and she concluded she would; it brought her comfort. She reminisced about their travels—the countless flights and places they had visited. How she cherished those trips.

"We're beginning our descent," Captain said, interrupting her thoughts.

They landed in the nearly empty parking lot near the visitor center entrance. It seemed that the site had yet to open.

"Enjoy your tour of the Heavenly Pit," he told them when their backpacks were hoisted and they were ready to leave. "I will see you when you're ready to return."

As they approached the Heavenly Pit's visitor center and entrance to the site, an older woman with a white-haired bob came out to meet them. "*Ni hao!*" she said with an enthusiastic wave, then greeted Dawn by her full name.

Dawn ran up to the woman, Mrs. Zi Shi, and returned her greeting, bowing politely. Mrs. Shi looked almost exactly the same as Dawn remembered, except she seemed a little shorter. But that was most likely because Dawn had grown.

"I'm happy you are strong and well," Dawn said in Mandarin as best as she could.

Pleasantly surprised to hear Dawn speak her language, Shi took out her glasses and put them on. They were holo-glasses—fancy CETT specs that translated languages for the wearer.

"Please, speak comfortably," Shi encouraged the three of them now that Laurel and Logan stood behind Dawn. "I'm surprised you remember me! You were still young when you visited. I see you have returned with friends."

"Yes, this is Laurel," Dawn said, motioning to her left, and then to her right, "and my friend, Logan. We work together."

Shi squeezed Dawn's arm and gave her a knowing smile as she took a look at Logan. "Ah, he is so handsome. You are so cute together," she said in Mandarin, clapping her hands together and holding them in front of her.

"Oh, we're not . . . he's not my . . ." Dawn trailed, shaking her head, trying to recall the right word. All she could think of was *lover,* and she dared not say that out loud.

At that moment a man dressed in a white polo shirt and charcoal hiking trousers had emerged from the visitor center and joined Shi's side.

"Do you remember my son?" Mrs. Zi continued in Mandarin, motioning to him. He was a foot taller than Shi and looked nothing like her. In fact, Dawn didn't recognize him at all.

"Good morning," he said in English. "Please, call me Gan. I will be your guide today."

Dawn shared a worried glance with Laurel before smoothing out her expression.

Hoping not to come off as rude, Dawn introduced herself before asking Shi, "Won't you be accompanying us as our guide as well? Like the last time my dad and I were here?"

She shook her head and explained something in an apologetic tone, then contorted her face to a pained expression as she pointed to her knees. Laurel and Logan nodded in sympathy.

"I see, I'm sorry to hear that," Dawn said, secretly projecting to Laurel that she didn't remember Gan. How could he help them find the plant when he was not, as her dad had specified *a guide whose name you'll know?*

"Not to worry," Gan chimed in. "My mother has trained me thoroughly, and I've been leading the tours on my own for years. I've also explored more of the cave's passages."

"I'm sure you're very qualified to be our guide," Dawn said, pulling out the drawing of the fairy fern from her pocket, "but my dad wanted me to find a rare cave plant—critical for his work. I was under the impression that your mother was the only one familiar with it."

Dawn passed the paper to Shi and her son.

"It's called fairy fern."

They studied the paper with furrowed brows. "I've never seen it," Shi said flatly.

Dawn frowned. They were already off to a bad start. The guide who her dad had trusted hadn't seen the plant. What were the chances they'd find it on their own?

She felt Logan give her a comforting side hug. "It'll be okay," he whispered in her ear.

Realizing she had been fiddling with her pendant, Dawn stopped and folded her arms.

"I think I've seen it," Gan said suddenly. He traced the drawing's tiny leaf with his pinky. "I'm not certain, but I think I've seen something similar to this deep in the cave system."

I'm scanning his memories, Laurel projected. *I don't see anything exactly like fairy fern.*

"Would you like me to take you?" Gan asked. "If we descend now, you'll have more privacy. We open to the public in half an hour."

At the very least, they needed to rule this place out. Dawn drew in a deep breath and exhaled slowly. "We're in."

CHAPTER 20

THE OVERCAST SKY had cleared completely, but the cold air nipped at their faces as Dawn and the group descended more than two thousand stair steps to reach the bottom of the Heavenly Pit. Gan fulfilled his role as tour guide by enthusiastically sharing the pit's history: Thousands of years ago, the underground river had formed a massive cave in the rock, which eventually collapsed as a sinkhole. Explorers discovered it, naming it the deepest sinkhole of its time.

Despite technological advancements, the local government refused to install a hydrolift to transport people going up and down the sinkhole. Only those who were physically capable had an opportunity for an in-person visit—a centuries-old sentiment.

The group fell silent as each one focused on steadily going down the stone steps. Some areas were steeper than the rest, slickened by the morning dew. Gan periodically pointed out spindly spiders that wove their webs underneath the railings, the birds that made their homes in the vertical cliffs, and the camouflaged insects in the lush foliage surrounding them.

At the halfway point, they stopped at a small platform for a rest. Dawn took a seat on a bench, stretched her tired leg muscles, and caught sight of Laurel, who leaned heavily on the railings, catching her breath. On Tencho, it was she who had difficulty ascending the stairs in the mountain. *This altitude is different for both of us.*

Logan sat down next to Dawn and took a sip from his water bottle. "This is incredible," he said, gazing up at the top of the pit, "and we're only halfway down."

She nodded, following his gaze. When she said nothing else, he nudged her shoulder with his. "What's going on in that head of yours?"

"After all these years, I'd forgotten what it was like to be here. See how the sun rays illuminate the rock walls?" she pointed out. "When the light hits just right, you can see all the details in the cracks and grooves of the cliffs. Virtual experiences don't do this place justice. I'm lucky enough to be here again—and with you."

She turned to look at him, and he smiled at her, setting her heart aflutter.

"Can I take your picture?" Gan offered, holding up his phone. "If you stand by that railing over there, you'll see the opening of the Heavenly Pit in the background."

"No pictures." Dawn stood up hastily, then realized how she must've sounded and turned to face Logan. "I mean, I *want* to, but this is supposed to be—"

"I know, I know," he said loud enough for only her to hear. "This is a *secret* trip. We're leaving no evidence behind." His eyes twinkled with amusement as he took her hands in his. "I'm good with that. It just means we'll have to come back and document everything *next* time."

Dawn blushed. All she could do was smile stupidly back at him.

Next time. Those words made her feel a little embarrassed, but all warm and fuzzy inside.

Calypso's crab! Laurel projected. *Infatuated people do the most ridiculous things.*

Dawn looked at Laurel who had the biggest smirk on her face. Then her expression changed when she saw there were a few tourists beginning their descent.

"We should be on our way," Laurel called out to Gan, then headed down the steps.

When they finally reached the bottom, the air had cooled considerably, and a mist had formed like a cloud hanging halfway in the pit.

"This place has its own ecosystem," Gan explained. "That's why some species of plants and animals can only be found here."

They walked around, stretching out their legs and peering up at the top of the pit. From where they stood, Dawn felt so secluded from the rest of the world, as if the pit had swallowed them up. Only the lush forest, mist, and sky were in her vision, as well as the occasional speck of birds—eagles, Dawn guessed—flying overhead. The susurration of water rushing over rocks could be heard in the distance, but other than that it seemed almost pristine with the absence of the modern world's skyscrapers, throngs of people, and a digital ad in your face every minute.

Gan led them through the dense forest as they followed a narrow path. The trees towered overhead and there were vines everywhere; he said even though the vines and undergrowth were cut periodically to make way for the path, they grew back quickly.

The roar of the river grew louder as they hiked, then finally, the cave entrance came into view. Gan said he'd ready their boat while the others took a restroom break if needed. As he started to remove the tarp off one of the watercrafts, he looked to the river and dropped what he was doing. "What do you think you're doing?!" he shouted. "It's dangerous!"

Dawn ran out of the bathroom to find Laurel waist-deep in the frigid water.

"I'll swim while you take the boat," Laurel yelled back, unaware of what she did wrong.

You can't shift while we take the boat—they'll see you! Dawn projected.

I wasn't going to shift, Laurel returned, refusing to leave her spot. *I can swim behind the boat to get a better sense of where the river flows through the cave.*

"Come out of the water," Logan coaxed as soon as he arrived at the scene. "Isn't it cold?"

"I don't mind," Laurel said. Then she projected to Dawn. *No matter, I can just erase their memories.* She started wading toward them.

"Wait!" Dawn held her hand palm up in protest.

Logan and Gan sent her a look that made her question her own sanity.

"I mean," Dawn said, putting her hand down, "I forgot to tell you that Laurel is an expert . . . cave diver. So she'll be, um, swimming near the boat. While we're in it." She prayed they'd believe her.

"Right," Logan said, drawing out the word, his brain still processing what she said.

"You're not riding in the boat?" asked Gan, still confused. "You'll get hypothermia without the proper gear."

"Hippo what?" Laurel asked at the same time that Dawn said, "She's wearing the right gear, actually."

Gan looked from Laurel to Dawn questioningly.

"I brought a self-heating towel and extra clothes for her," Dawn added.

After a side-eyed glance at Logan, who shrugged cluelessly, Gan seemed to accept Dawn's resolve. "I know my mother agreed to your terms of a private tour that was to remain completely off the record, but I'm not a cave diver. If she's going to swim, and if anything were to happen to her, you will assume *all* the liability."

"Got it," Dawn said, quickly taking the helmet Gan handed her.

"The three of us will wear life jackets and helmets."

As soon as they had geared up and boarded, Gan started the silent motor and slowly steered them into the mouth of the cave. For a moment, they were engulfed in darkness, then their helmet lights turned on automatically and illuminated their line of sight.

Laurel stayed a good two to three meters behind the boat and kept her head above water so Gan could see her every time he checked. After a few minutes, he seemed to ease up a bit and began pointing out the red-orange stalagmites, columns that looked like cupcakes stacked atop one another, and needle-sharp stalactites.

As her eyes grew accustomed to the darkness, Dawn noticed subtle changes in the cave formations. They took on hues of aquas, purples, and whites; some of them had a sparkly sheen.

"We're getting close to the areas with cave flora and specimens." Gan pointed to a spot ahead where the floor was smoother. "This system branches off to another cavern and eventually opens into the forest."

He cut the motor, and they slowly drifted to the area to alight.

When they had disembarked, Dawn handed Laurel a helmet, courtesy of Gan, and towel from her backpack. *Did you sense anything in the water?* Dawn asked her silently.

If we had continued drifting in the river, the current would have picked up, Laurel told Dawn. *I think it leads to a different cavern.*

"Gan, can we make sure to check that part of the cave before we leave?" Dawn asked, pointing in the direction of the current.

"If you're worried about the strong current, I have experience navigating those areas," Laurel added.

"I'm impressed! You must have explored many caves." Gan pointed his flashlight down the path of the river. "See how the ceiling of the cave gets lower farther down? Navigating that part is tricky. We can do it, but we'll need to allocate extra time."

Dawn nodded. She had come this far. *We'll make time for it.*

They followed Gan through the cave and stopped whenever he pointed out ferns. None matched the drawing. Either the leaves were too small, too wide, or too dead. The only thing keeping Dawn's disappointment at bay was Logan, who seemed to be enjoying himself.

"Come check out this fungus," he called, crouched over a strange, luminescent plant.

"Ooooh," Laurel said. "I think it's growing on some kind of animal poop."

Despite not having found fairy fern yet, Dawn was happy Logan was making the most of their day trip.

"How about we check one more place before heading to the forest?" Gan asked her. "It's through a shaft, but it's an unforgettable view."

He rounded up the group and led them to a hole in the cave wall that was roughly a meter in diameter. It was at Dawn's waist level, and since she was the shortest, Gan said she could crouch and walk through, but everyone else would have to crawl. He went in first on his hands and knees, followed by Dawn, Laurel, and lastly, Logan.

After crouching and crawling for five minutes and only having each other's rears to look at, Gan announced, "We're here. Careful on the entry."

He dropped down about two meters to the floor. Then he helped the others down.

"I have a flashlight," Logan said, rummaging through his rucksack. He pulled it out and placed it atop one of the flatter rocks nearby. Bright light flooded the space and Dawn gasped.

The underground lake, which had been a pretty blue with just their helmet lights, had turned a bold turquoise. They could see straight through to the bottom of its shallow depths.

"What a sight." Logan beamed.

Laurel nodded in silence, and Dawn found herself smiling in awe at the little lake.

After they spent a few minutes checking for any plants to no avail, Dawn (and her loud, grumbling stomach) declared that now would be a good time to head to the forest and take a break. Back they crawled through the shaft, then Gan led them into the forest.

It was invigorating to breathe fresh air once they had emerged. Gan brought them to a clearing with some boulders and a log to sit on, then Dawn shared her jerky and granola with Logan. Laurel was satisfied with her cucumber rolls while Gan munched on energy bars.

After snacking, Gan asked if they wanted to check some ferns in the area. Dawn shook her head. The plant they were looking for was supposed to be *deep in the throat* of the cave.

"It couldn't hurt to look around though, right?" Logan said as he walked over the log to stand behind where she sat. "We have about three more hours left to get back to the pit. That should be more than enough time."

"I guess it couldn't hurt," Dawn conceded.

"You look stressed out," he said as he started to give her a gentle shoulder massage.

The gesture startled Dawn at first, and she declined, trying to twist out of his grip, but he insisted. She sat there awkwardly, but immediately felt her shoulders relax. Dawn closed her eyes and took a deep breath, focusing on the ambient forest sounds around them: buzzing insects, the croak of a frog, a rustle in the leaves, then a faint giggle. Her eyes shot open.

"Did you see that?" Laurel asked, walking over to a shrub at the base of a massive tree.

"I didn't see anything, but I heard laughter, I think," Dawn admitted.

Logan paused his massage, his hands resting on her shoulders.

"What did you see?" Gan asked as Laurel searched the shrub's leaves.

"She was a tiny person, a wingless fairy, I suppose."

"You saw a fairy?" Logan asked, taking a seat on the log next to Dawn. She saw that he covered his mouth with his hand, as if rubbing his stubble, but she knew he was stifling a laugh.

"There are folktales about fairies inhabiting less populated provinces," Gan said very seriously. "My mother told me she saw one when she was a child. She described it as having sharp features—a thin body and short hair. I didn't think to ask whether it had wings or not."

"Did you see it? The fairy?" Laurel asked Gan.

"No," Gan admitted. "Mother said fairies reveal themselves only to children."

Logan shrugged. "It could've been a lizard."

Sighing heavily, Laurel sat down on a rock. *I know what I saw,* she projected to Dawn, who Dawn said nothing but gave her a barely visible nod.

"Well, ladies and gent," Logan said, standing up. "Nature calls. I'll be back in a few." He veered away to Dawn's right, soon out of sight in the dense forest.

"And I'll be going that way," Gan said, pointing in the other direction.

Laurel waited until they were out of earshot, then said crossly, "Gan believes me. He's never seen a fairy, yet he believes. Do *you* believe me?"

"Of course I do," Dawn said, trying to soothe her.

"Then why didn't you try to convince Logan?"

"He seemed to have already made up his mind about it," she returned, absentmindedly fiddling with her pendant. If he didn't want to suspend his disbelief, why force it?

"Because if you want to be together, it'd be much easier if you believed the same things."

"True, but this isn't something in the deal breaker bucket. Not right now, anyway."

"She's *right there*, sitting on the branch." Laurel pointed up to the tree on her left.

"Who?" Dawn asked, scanning the myriad branches among the infinite green leaves.

"The fairy. She's clear as crystal."

Dawn kept searching, but shook her head, surprised at her own disappointment. "I don't see her. Maybe there's a reason she's revealing herself only to you?"

"Perhaps. Uncle Niro says these creatures can project and show illusions like Lumen."

"Can she show you where the fairy fern is—if it's here?" Dawn asked, perking up.

"She just flitted away, probably because they're coming back now."

A moment after Laurel finished her sentence, Logan and Gan entered the clearing. The four ambled back to the cave—slower and more fatigued—checking the ferns along the way.

They weren't having any luck, so Logan and Gan walked ahead, consumed in their own conversation about hiking adventures. Laurel, who was walking in front of Dawn, stopped abruptly, and Dawn collided with her.

"Why did you stop?" Dawn asked, annoyed.

"The fairy—she's back," Laurel whispered.

"Ask her about—"

"Shhh! She's projecting something to me." Then she shared the projection with Dawn: a bird, circling above the treetops—not just any bird, but an osprey. A poru.

Whose poru do you think it is? Dawn asked, worry creeping in.

I'm not sure, but it can't be any of Sid's. Marion said she wouldn't tell anyone our location. I can't track the poru's aura, but that's a good thing. If I can't sense it, that means it most likely can't sense us either.

"We still have a long way to go before we get home. If we get ambushed now, there's no way we'd get help in time. We have to get out of here as fast as possible," Dawn said, wishing she had a way to contact Marion.

As if on cue, the sky thundered, and rain began to pour.

"Laurel? Dawn?" Logan's and Gan's voices rang out from afar. "Where are you?"

"Go, go, go!" Dawn urged, shielding her face from the sudden downpour. She hoped the sound of the rain had drowned out their voices.

We're safer in the cave, in the water, Laurel assured Dawn. *I know some guardian tricks.*

They caught up with Logan and Gan—who looked relieved to see them—but ran past them. Once in the shelter of the cave, Gan took the lead and guided them back to the boat.

Logan pulled Dawn aside as Gan helped Laurel board, then get on a life jacket and helmet. "What happened back there? You scared us when we couldn't find you."

"We saw something that startled us," she said, trying to come up with an excuse. "I think it was some kind of leopard." It wasn't a full lie. She *had* glimpsed a white wild cat passing through the thick foliage, although it had been much earlier during their trek.

"I can see there are a lot of things you won't tell me, maybe not all regarding the plant we were looking for. I hope you know you can tell me anything."

Dawn felt so low. Not only had she completely failed to find what they came for, standing before her was the man of her dreams who'd basically ditched work to go searching for a mythical fern with her, who'd been nothing but supportive; and here she was, lying to his face. Logan, who had every right to feel betrayed, didn't hold it against her. In fact, he was smiling at her.

His smile.

All Dawn could do was nod, weakly smile back, and mutter thanks. *I will tell you everything. In time.* She promised him and herself silently.

The torrent caused by the heavy rain jostled the boat so much, Dawn thought she might get seasick. Thankfully, Gan deftly maneuvered it with proficiency. He wouldn't allow Laurel back into the water, stating that the conditions were too dangerous to explore the other cavern.

Laurel didn't argue. She was exhausted and nodding off in the rocking boat.

Dawn held back her tears. They had missed their chance.

By the time they had reached the pit, the downpour had stopped, but the ascent to the top still proved perilous with the slippery stairs. It took them much longer to get to the halfway point than anticipated. The only benefit was, they weren't alone. Gan had given them standard ponchos to wear. If a poru showed up, they would be indistinguishable from the tourists. Laurel was awake enough to shield their thoughts from any unwanted reading.

It was after 4:30 p.m. (12:30 a.m. for Dawn and Logan, probably 3:30 a.m. for Laurel) when the group had reached the top, panting. Since they were behind schedule, they quickly said their goodbyes, then departed with Captain to the nature reserve.

At nearly 2:00 a.m., Marion welcomed them back through the bridge. A very exhausted Logan left with Hikaru soon after so he could get a few hours of sleep before going to work. Stifling a yawn, Laurel was just about to cross the bridge home, but Marion stopped her.

"There's been a complication," Miss M. said somberly. "Lord Angel and Ezra were trying to get ahold of you and sent multiple messages here through the porus."

Laurel blinked repeatedly, seeming more awake, as if she could sense Marion's grave tone.

Marion continued. "There was a break-in and struggle in Jett's compound—he suffered a minor injury. The sangwor were involved, and unfortunately . . . one of them was slain."

"Oh no," Laurel breathed. "Don't tell me—please, no—Stralla?"

Marion nodded.

Laurel's eyes welled with tears, and she said something indecipherable before disappearing through the bridge.

"What happened?" Dawn asked Miss M., following her into the kitchen.

Marion poured Dawn a hot mug of tea, then pulled up a broadcast report.

They watched in silence as a reporter recounted the break-in at Jett's compound. Despite Dawn's stupor, a few phrases jumped out at her: "multiple suspects" and "an unidentified assailant in critical condition." The segment finished with law enforcement on the scene, who speculated an "alleged attempted murder."

"It hasn't been reported yet, but the assailant died at the hospital," Marion said. "Ezra met with the authorities to claim the body earlier and verified that it was his sister, Stralla. He notified Lord Angel, who sent word to Sid."

Dawn looked into her steaming mug of tea, wishing she'd wake up from this bad dream that kept getting worse. She couldn't bear to look Marion in the eye. "We didn't find anything," she said, unable to suppress her tears and regret any longer. "We didn't even search the whole cave. I wish I'd . . . I should've—"

It was useless. No matter what she felt, she couldn't go back and change the past.

"Hikaru and I couldn't find anything either. The caves were flooded with heavy rains soon after we arrived."

After a long pause, Marion lifted Dawn's chin with a firm yet gentle hand. "We will find a way," she said with encouragement. "We may have a resource problem with Laurel distracted, but we won't give up. The reason I'm telling you all this is so you'll know what we're up against. I'm not sugar coating anything."

"I know. It's just that—" She sighed and wiped her tears. "We're almost out of time."

INTERLUDE 2

"LAUREL, IS THAT you?" a woman called between sobs. She pushed her brown hair streaked with silver away from her eyes and looked toward the door.

In the barely lit main room, Laurel took a moment to catch her bearings, having just crossed the bridge. She recognized Ezra's perpetually frowning father, who nearly collided with her as he flitted out the door. He slammed it shut with his aura.

Ezra, on the other hand, was the polar opposite; Laurel sided with his siblings who unanimously agreed he took after his mother. He approached his betrothed calmly, yet wearied by the burden of grief, eyes brimming with tears. "We've been expecting you."

He led her to his mother's room where she sat, hunched over in the middle of her bed. Like the rest of the castle of Etero, the stone walls were bare and slat gray. The room was, as expected, traditionally plain and austere, as Etherans kept few personal belongings. Their quarters were always chilly, but tonight, it felt like plunging into arctic waters.

"Oh, Laurel," the woman cried when their eyes met. Ezra's mother looked frailer than her own, wrapped in black shawls and shepra silk.

The pain in her eyes accented the finer wrinkles in her face. "Stralla is dead! She is gone!"

When she held out her arms, Laurel collapsed into them, unable to hold back her own anguished sobs.

Letting their grief overtake them, they wept freely in each other's arms. They held each other until their cries subsided, and Stralla's mother had fallen asleep.

Some time after—Laurel couldn't tell if they had been crying for minutes or hours—Ezra gently pried his mother's arms away and tucked her into bed, as if *she* were the child and not his parent.

Laurel could not shed the weight of despair that news of Stralla's death had brought. She wondered if this was how drowning felt—her heart heavy in her chest, every wave of grief pummeling her like Lemuria's bone-crushing swells.

She and Ezra tiptoed back to the main room where a futon was laid out in the center. In her hand, he placed a warm, citrine crystal before lighting a fire in the hearth and activating gems to brighten the space.

"Did your mother know?" Laurel examined the stone she held, its yellow sheen reminding her of Stralla. "Did she *see* that this was Stralla's fate?"

"Of course she knew." His voice carried sadness and bitterness intertwined. His mother was *the* Mina de Somn, the Lady of Dreams. "Her abilities have always been a gift and a curse."

Laurel looked up to find him standing in front of the fire, staring into its dancing flames. He resembled so much of his mother—dark wavy hair, tan skin, and wide eyes that bared everything, down to his very soul. His tears had dried; Laurel's had not. More of them spilled down her already tear-streaked face. She gritted her teeth, anger creeping up from her jaw, flushing her cheeks.

Ezra kept his attention on the fire that cast strange shadows across his face. "Lord Angel and I think that Malstrom sent the sangwor to assassinate Jett Pierce. Malstrom wanted more control over his resources and—"

"Why?" Laurel cut in, angrily.

He turned toward her with a look of resignation. "That was always his plan—more power to have better chances of restoring—"

"I mean, why are you telling me all this? Stralla's death changes everything!" She threw the crystal at him, and he caught it with his en in midair, unflinching. A moment ago, her fatigue and grief had weighed her down like a ship's anchor. Now, she was a volcano erupting with raw, unyielding fury. "Why do you pretend that it won't rip your family apart?!"

Ezra let the crystal float, suspended near his head and turned his gaze back to the flames. He stood there forlornly for what seemed like a long time. If he was angry, he did not show it.

"You are welcome to stay here," Ezra finally said quietly without looking at her, "but you are free to leave at any time. Reed has been asking after you. You should tell him you are safe. I'm going to the healer's ward to collect Stralla's body, then I need to talk to my brothers before making preparations for the burial."

When he left, the crystal clattered to the floor.

Laurel sat on the futon, trying to decide which emotion felt the most overwhelming. Sorrow, apathy, anger? Was it just physical exhaustion? She couldn't decide, but she knew one thing: She couldn't stay here anymore. Not while the Lady of Dreams was here.

Laurel loved Stralla's mother. Or she thought she did. Now, in this moment at least, she didn't think she could ever forgive her. *What is the point of having the gift of prophecy if you don't use it to save your own daughter?*

Ezra would've brought up how being a seer was a great burden, and his mother was doing what she thought was right for the greater good.

Whatever. That sort of logic really scraped the bottom of the bilge barrel.

She got up and took a cloak hanging on a hook by the door, swinging it around herself. The cloak belonged to Stralla, who would no longer need it, Laurel realized sadly. She walked back to the bridge, her whole body aching for sleep, but she needed to see one more person before leaving Etero: her *own* mother.

"It is in the middle of the night. Lady Alcina is still asleep in her chamber," the Etheran attendant told Laurel.

Let her in, her mother's voice reverberated through their heads.

The attendant opened the door for Laurel and she walked in, passing the other glass hyperbaric chambers. Their occupants slept peacefully in them, like they were in groundling coffins. She walked to the back of the room where her mother's chamber was and leaned over the glass to see her sunken, corpse-like face and closed eyes. They had remained shut for *so* long.

Mother's condition did not seem to be getting better, even though her sister Kailani had brought her to Etero, the sky kingdom's capital, for their advanced healing capabilities. Etherans had never taken in subdwellers to their healing chambers, but since Kailani had married an Etheran, and her father was the king of Atlantis, Lady Alcina was the one and only exception.

Mikei, the Orako word for "my child," projected her mother. She continued in their native tongue. *It has been a long time since you have come to visit me in Etero. You disappoint me.*

Her words pierced Laurel.

I'm sorry, mother, Laurel sniffed, although she didn't *feel* sorry about not visiting. She continued in their native tongue. *Father and I have been busy. He has gone on an excursion with Lord Blackfin, and they have not yet returned . . .*

Was she a fool to come here? To assume she'd find comfort in her mother's counsel?

Something has happened. What is it?

Laurel hesitated but continued. "My friend Stralla, the sister of my intended, has died," she whispered, fresh tears springing to her eyes, threatening to spill over.

She was a sangwor, as are her brothers, was she not?

"Yes, mother. She was . . . slain on a mission," she said, her voice breaking.

Why are you surprised? She lived and died by the sword.

Laurel blinked back her tears with great effort.

You are a princess—royalty, her mother reminded her harshly. *Inwardly, your heart may weep; outwardly, you must exhibit strength. What do you have to cry about? You have beauty and blessings in abundance, so much life left to live.*

Laurel nodded silently. She no longer felt her grief overwhelm her. The weight in her heart had come and gone, leaving only emptiness.

Her mother's chest heaved. *I must rest. Go home. Wait for your father.*

Laurel waited in the darkness, not bothering to procure any light. She simply sent Reed a comm and waited. He replied with a barrage of angry words—his way of expressing his frustration without saying anything insulting.

Then he listed reasons why she couldn't stay in this cabin:

"It isn't allowed."

"You're betrothed."

"The patrol guard noticed you."

"You're going to get me suspended from training."

Blah, blah, blah. Finally, he said he was on his way. Laurel hadn't responded to any of it. She simply waited.

A half hour later, she could hear his sarcastic projections through the partition:

Right when I'm in the middle of my morning drills, that's *when you decide to send me a comm? You couldn't comm me earlier with "I'm safe at home now, Reed" or "I've crossed the bridge and am back at the palace?" That's the thanks I get for sharing secret bridge maps. I risked my scales for you . . .*

The partition door slid open and revealed his scowling face. *I should've alerted your fa—*

His scolding stopped abruptly as he caught sight of her in the darkness, her shellshocked figure, huddled in the corner of the cabin floor.

She stared at him blankly. Her eyelids were swollen, and she was sure she looked utterly exhausted.

What's wrong? he asked, his tone of annoyance flip-flopping to one of concern.

Stralla has died. She's gone, Laurel projected morosely.

Stralla—is that Lord Ezra's sister?

Laurel nodded. *I couldn't stay in Etero, and I didn't want to stay in the palace by myself.*

He crouched down beside her, scanning her for injuries; he found none. She could tell he pitied her—again—and although

Laurel abhorred it, she was too fatigued to move, to leave, or to do anything to make him feel otherwise.

You can't stay here, he said apologetically. *The patrol summoned me to remove you from the cabins. Can you stay with any of your friends for now?*

She looked into his blue eyes, which were filled with worry. *Are we not friends, Reed?*

He paused for a moment, seemingly deep in thought, as if pondering what he should do.

Come, he said, taking her arm and pulling her up. *I'll take you to my mother and Uki.*

CHAPTER 21

DAWN'S PHONE BUZZED on her nightstand—a message from Sparkle:

"Yo. Been a while. Your man was gone half the day yesterday, today he looks like garbage. Tired, but happy. Were you guys out late?"

She missed Sparkle terribly. His occasional messages (despite her lack of response) reminded her of the normalcy she longed for.

Dawn sat propped up on pillows on her bed and checked online for news on Jett. All the reports she found confirmed what Marion had already told her. Wanting to stay in bed a few minutes more, she retrieved her mom's journal and flipped through its pages, pausing to examine the different leaf and frond drawings. *Why wasn't there anything on fairy fern?*

She sighed, glancing at her clock, feeling like she was running behind since she'd slept most of the morning. Outside, the sky was overcast, and strong gusts of wind batted leaves and debris at her window.

Dawn drew up the blanket around her to keep from shivering, but she couldn't get rid of the cold dread she'd felt since she had returned from China. Last night, she informed Marion of everything, including the lone osprey poru that Laurel had gotten wind of. Miss M. had listened intently but kept her thoughts to herself; they were to regroup and discuss tomorrow.

As exhausted as she had been, she'd fallen into a restless sleep, dreaming of nonsensical things that she couldn't remember upon waking. She hoped Laurel had gotten better rest despite receiving devastating news. Her thoughts wandered to Logan and how tired he must be at work. She sighed again, feeling anxious, wanting to talk with him about the next caves she needed to scout.

Dawn rescanned the journal, frustrated at not finding anything on fairy fern. There were various plants for healing and restoration, including an herb named moonshade. Apparently, it served as an antidote for aura block, something which Dawn had no idea even existed.

Kudzukan had its own page and drawing, on which Howel had written, "Boil Kudzukan leaves for a more potent elixir."

On the opposite page was "Ambrosia, an Etheran fruit." "Strength of a warrior" was scrawled underneath the sketch that looked like oddly shaped grapes.

Underneath the ambrosia was a drawing that looked like a closed tulip with a short stem. It was the only one that had its roots drawn, which roughly resembled an upside-down hand. It was labeled "Dysprosia—Strong roots. Do not touch," the last three words underlined.

She turned the page to find sangwor shamrock with the inscription beneath the sketch: "Leaves of four, breathe no more." She remembered Lopple's lethal ordeal about a month ago.

Voices from downstairs interrupted her thoughts. She closed her eyes and reached out with her aura, sensing Hikaru and Marion in the kitchen. The others took a smidgen longer to identify; Laurel,

Lopple, and . . . Ezra? She was surprised she could feel their auras more distinctly. What once felt nebulous and fuzzy was now solid, concrete.

A quick jolt of an earthquake shook the house, and she heard someone yelp—probably Lopple or Ezra. She found it all the more amusing that she could *sense* their fear; Lopple was genuinely afraid that the end of the world could happen every time he felt a tremor. This sixth sense of hers was developing with a swiftness she hadn't anticipated.

By the time Dawn had sauntered downstairs, Hikaru, Lopple, and Ezra were seated at the dining room table, opposite Marion and Laurel. Miss M. patted the seat between herself and Laurel, signaling Dawn to sit. A somber air permeated the room despite the celebration-worthy spread, including soft-shell crab, sushi rolls, sashimi, and an assortment of Korean side dishes.

Dawn scooped a generous helping of japchae noodles on her plate and whispered to Laurel, "How are you holding up?"

"I'm fine, thanks," the Aquavian replied automatically. Her eyes had dark circles underneath. Ezra's eyes looked slightly puffy as well. Both were dressed in linen Etheran clothes similar to the ones they'd worn the first day Dawn met them.

Dawn's eyes caught Ezra's who sat across the table. "I'm sorry to hear about your sister."

"I appreciate that." He managed a fleeting smile before turning back to Lopple who he must've first met that morning. They continued their conversation. Something about a volcano.

Lopple seemed his usual talkative self, but he had a cut on his forehead and the tips of his fingers looked blackened.

Dawn piled sushi on her plate and noticed deep-fried, soft-shell crabs in front of Laurel.

"Courtesy of the Aquavi fishermen," Marion remarked, who followed her gaze. She looked to Laurel and asked, "Soft-shell crab happens to be your favorite, isn't that right, Laurel?"

Laurel, who was looking down at the barely-picked-at crustacean on her plate, startled at the mention of her name. "Oh—yes, they're delicious," she said without looking up, then let out a long and deep exhalation. "I'm not very hungry at the moment. Please excuse me— I'll wait in the living room."

After she left, Marion broke the awkward silence. "Ezra is here to see Laurel, to talk about his sister's burial arrangements."

"I see," Dawn felt compelled to respond. "Well, uh, feel free to use the study for privacy," she said to Ezra.

"They already did that," Lopple offered.

"Since Ezra was here," Marion continued, "I told him what transpired yesterday. He offered to accompany you and Laurel on your next cave-scouting trip. We're short on time, and you spotted a suspicious poru yesterday," she said, eyeing Hikaru, and trailing off.

Dawn struggled to unpack what her housekeeper was getting at. It was clear to her that Ezra was not *asking* to go with them; he must've been concerned about Laurel. "Did you already check with Sid if that poru was one of hers?"

"It wasn't any of her agents," Marion confirmed. "No one from Sid's team, including her, knew about your trip yesterday. Somehow, there's an unidentified Lumen out there who's gotten wind of your whereabouts. If anything were to happen, Ezra would be able to keep you and Laurel safe and call for reinforcements."

Dawn took a piece of sushi, dipped it in soy sauce mixed with wasabi, and slowly chewed as she thought. If Ezra wasn't asking, she wasn't asking for Logan to go either, groundling or not. After she swallowed, she said, "Thank you, it does sound like a good idea. Logan is still coming, if he's available."

They ate the rest of their lunch in awkward silence. Afterward, Marion insisted that Dawn check on Laurel while the others help tidy up. Translation: They wanted to have a discussion without Dawn, who didn't think it worth the effort to argue anyway.

"What happened to your sweats?" Dawn asked Laurel, who was curled up on the couch, staring off into space.

"I . . . don't know," Laurel said morosely.

"I'll get you more comfortable clothes," Dawn said, then leapt up the stairs as her aching calves screamed in protest. She returned to find Ezra standing in front of Laurel, speaking to her, although he might as well have been addressing a statue. He fell silent as Dawn approached.

"You can change in the bathroom. No need to go upstairs to my room," Dawn said, handing Laurel her clothes. "We climbed *a lot* of stairs yesterday," Dawn explained to Ezra.

"Yes, she mentioned," Ezra said tersely.

Without a word, Laurel took the clothes and headed to the bathroom, leaving Ezra and Dawn alone in the living room. They stood there, staring at the closed bathroom door as they waited for Laurel. It was one of those instances wherein thirty seconds felt like an eternity. She risked a glance at Ezra and caught him glaring at her.

His expression was somewhere between a frown and scowl—"the stink eye," Sparkle would've said. Ezra instantly schooled his features and broke eye contact.

"Is there something on my face?" Dawn swiped a hand over her mouth.

"You're different," he blurted out. He shook his head, as if that wasn't what he meant to say. "Your aura, I mean. Never mind, it's nothing."

She watched him as he folded his arms across his chest, then looked down at his feet. He closed his eyes, gently rubbed his eyelids, and pinched the bridge of his nose. His discomfort and grief were as palpable as Laurel's.

Ezra cleared his throat again and opened his eyes. "I must be on my way to continue with Stralla's arrangements," he said more to the bathroom door than to anyone in particular.

Then he strode to the garage, where they had left the mirror last night. Dawn felt his presence disappear and she knew he had crossed the bridge.

"Laurel, are you okay?" Dawn asked, padding over to the bathroom door.

Laurel opened it and stepped out wearing the sweats Dawn had given her. She silently walked back to the couch, hugged her legs close and leaned against the soft backing.

"Ezra gave me a comm stone," she said, holding her wrist cuff up where the stone was hidden. "He'll contact me when he needs to."

"Look, I know you're . . . going through a lot," Dawn said, sitting next to her. "You don't have to be here right now. When Miss M. and I figure out our next locations to scout, we can send you a comm. So, if you want to go home—"

"I don't want to go home," she cut in sharply. "Anyway, there's something you should know. Ezra spoke to his two younger brothers, who are also sangwor. One of them was on the same mission as Stralla. Their orders were to assassinate Jett Pierce."

Dawn froze. *The sangwor attacked Jett?*

"His bodyguards fought back. But Stralla wasn't planning to go through with the assassination. Or that's what Ezra *said* he found out—I'm not sure what I believe anymore," she said, throwing a hand up. "Ezra's family is a mess. He and his siblings are, or *were*, all sangwor—loyal blood warriors. His mother is a seer, and Malstrom calls upon her at times for her gifts of prophecy."

"Wait—what?" Dawn asked, attempting to process all the new information.

"When Malstrom started the assassinations, it caused a rift between Ezra's parents," Laurel explained wearily. "His father is a staunch supporter of Malstrom's plans, while his mother was not. All four children served as sangwor during a time of peace.

When Malstrom's directives became more . . . violent, Ezra stepped down and took over his father's non-combative role in the sky kingdom. But Stralla and their two younger brothers had no excuse, and no reason to disobey their orders."

Laurel paused. Dawn sensed that merely saying Stralla's name was painful to her.

"They could have killed Jett easily, you know," Laurel said. "They are trained to use aura weapons, needles poisoned with sangwor shamrock."

"Touch leaves of four, breathe no more," Dawn whispered, recalling what was written in the journal under the shamrock sketch.

"How did you know?"

"My mom—or dad—wrote about it in the journal. The plant looks like butterfly wings."

"It would seem," Laurel said, carefully measuring her words, "that Stralla died by her own poison. I don't believe she *wanted* to kill Jett, but she and her brother needed to make it *seem* like they attempted."

As she recounted what Ezra had relayed, Laurel wrung her hands. Stralla and her brother had planned to create an explosion using one of CETT's vehicles, then leave. But there was another person on the premises—a masked Lumen of short stature and small frame—an adolescent, they assumed, who dragged Jett out of his room and closer to the explosion. The blast knocked him unconscious. As Stralla and her brother felt Jett's aura dissipate, they doubled back. The masked Lumen attacked them and said something in their Etheran tongue, which translated to: "Finish the job you came to do."

They fought up until the authorities came. The mysterious Lumen was a formidable fighter and had struck Stralla's brother down. Seeing that he was about to receive a deathly blow, Stralla had used one of her needles laced with poison and aimed it toward the attacker. Her plan backfired when the Lumen shielded and deflected it, sending it right back to her.

"I'm not sure I'm understanding," Dawn admitted. She gently placed a hand over Laurel's, whose fists were balled so tightly, her knuckles were white. "Was this masked Lumen there to also assassinate Jett? Was he a sangwor?"

"That remains a mystery," Marion said, entering with Hikaru and Lopple. "He was obviously as skilled as a sangwor warrior, as Ezra's brother attested, yet he didn't kill Jett. This, however, is something that Sid will investigate. She has a team guarding Jett and another to track the attacker." Marion turned her gaze on Laurel and assured her, "It's only a matter of time before the assailant is captured."

"Right now," Miss M. said, turning her attention to Dawn, "our focus needs to be on finding that last ingredient, and Lopple has an interesting theory to share."

"I know I haven't been exactly forthcoming with you, Dawn," Lopple said, stepping forward with a slight limp, "but now that your aura has been activated, I trust that you'll be able to shield properly—most of the time. You can feel it, right? How you can sense our auras and porus."

Dawn nodded, recalling how she could *feel* who was in the house when she was upstairs.

"The very essence of your aura has changed. You're a completely different person from the Dawn that I met at Jett's hangar. I'm sure you remember when I so rudely placed my hand on your shoulder. I could barely clock your aura without doing so." He gingerly sat down on the opposite chair to relieve the weight on his leg. "This is just the beginning—your metamorphosis is not yet complete."

Dawn eyed him, curiously, recalling Laurel's words: *I know a shifter when I see one.*

Lopple's eyes flicked to Laurel for half a second, then back to Dawn. "Howel is *not* searching for fairy fern," he revealed with a sly smile.

"I'm listening." Dawn regarded him cautiously.

"Howel is looking for dysprosia, a root with symbiotic qualities." With a flourish of his hand, he conjured a projection of the bulbous plant, similar to the one in the journal. The roots resembled an upside-down hand with overgrown fingernails. "The person who touches its roots is imbued with enhanced Lumen abilities—including the gift to wield a sentient jewel."

"I thought wielding the jewel required the right bloodline," Dawn said flatly.

"It does. As I said, it *enhances* the ability." Lopple stretched his bad leg out, sucking in a breath through his teeth.

"If you're so familiar with dysprosia, then why aren't you tasked with finding it?"

He held out a hand, cradling the projection in his palm. The roots reacted, coiling around his fingers and arm. "It *feeds* off you, makes your desires come to fruition."

Although he wouldn't look directly at her, there was a murderous glint in his eye—or so Dawn thought, filing it away for later.

"Let's just say I and dysprosia don't mix. Howel and I came to the understanding that I'd be of better help finding the other ingredients, hence my many injuries," Lopple said, rubbing his singed fingers together tenderly. "Howel wants *you* to find the dysprosia."

"In any case, there's something Howel wrote in the letter for you," Lopple continued, "something only *you* would know. Finding the right location was not supposed to be based on Marion's experience."

Dawn fiddled with her pendant, realizing he was right. Something had been off from the start at the Heavenly Pit. She had not known Gan's name before they met, and Howel's letter clearly stated, *You'll need a guide whose name you'll know*—twice.

Dawn let out an exasperated sound and retrieved her laptop, then asked X8 to display the short list, minus The Heavenly Pit:

Tham Khoun Xe Cave – Laos

Río Secreto – México

The Underground River – Philippines

Lost River Cave – United States

"We don't have *time* to visit all of these," Dawn said, pacing the room. They couldn't even cross off the Lost River Cave since it had been flooded. "The letter said 'go not beyond the Ides of March,' and that's in two days!"

"Don't panic," Marion said. "Why don't you read the letter again? Maybe there's something—"

"I know the letter by heart, and I know all the guides' names at each of these places." Dawn kept pacing and saw that Hikaru had taken a seat at the bench near the bay window; Miss M. walked toward him to join him; Lopple was drumming his fingers on his knee, muttering his thoughts to himself; and Laurel was dozing off on the couch.

None of them seemed to be as concerned as she was that she was getting nowhere. Her plan was falling apart, and her self-doubt was crippling.

"Guys, a little help, please?" Dawn said, feeling herself break into a cold sweat. "Was there anything else that Howel mentioned to any of you that you think might be helpful?"

"How about you sit down and tell us what you remember from these caves?" Marion suggested. "What were they like and what was the most memorable thing about each trip?"

Dawn nodded and sat down. She went through each cave, stated the guides' names, and her most profound memory about each trip. She remembered Río Secreto in the most detail, since it was the most recent excursion. Recalling her trip to the Underground River proved the most difficult, as she had only been fourteen years old at the time of their visit.

They peppered her with questions about the colors of the cave, the weather, the flora, the scents, and on and on. Two hours later, Dawn was pacing the room again, and everyone else agreed that none of the details were a telltale sign that the dysprosia would be there. It didn't help that for roughly half their questions, Dawn's response was, "I don't remember."

"Let's take a break," Marion suggested, heading toward the kitchen. Hikaru followed.

Lopple stood up and stretched his arms over his head, then hobbled over to the bay window and looked at the backyard. "There has to be something else that you're not recalling," he said to Dawn with his back to her, "something significant."

"Something significant," she repeated with a sigh. "To be honest, I have doubts about the short list. Everything I'm recalling seems trivial. But what if there's a place outside the short list that seems more *meaningful* to me?"

"How many places were a match according to the computer?"

"Eleven, and we've only scouted one," Dawn groaned.

Lopple turned around to face her, thoughtfully rubbing his goatee. "Before we consider these other locations, I recommend we try one more approach."

"Sure," Dawn said. "I'll try anything."

"You might not like this," he warned. "I suggest that you let me *read* you—have a look into your memories. There were many things that you said you couldn't remember. That doesn't mean they have left your memory completely; they're simply harder for you to access."

Dawn grimaced at the thought of Lopple rummaging through her memories, especially the ones of Logan. "What are our other options?"

"What about Laurel?" Lopple asked, arching an eyebrow. "Will you let *her* do it?"

Dawn looked toward the Aquavian. Sure, they had their little spats, but she *trusted* Laurel. She had blocked her secret memories of Logan from Laurel before; she was confident she could do it again.

"Do what?" Laurel yawned. They had to re-explain it, but she agreed to do the reading.

Laurel and Dawn sat facing each other.

"Close your eyes," Laurel instructed. "You'll see what I see. Think only of the caves we're targeting."

Dawn closed her eyes and tried to relax. A rush of memories flooded her mind, like someone trying to watch four different videos at the same time. Laurel zoomed in on one—the Tham Khoun Xe Cave. They entered where the river flowed through the cavernous maw. Dawn saw her kayak, following the craft with Howel and their guide Tai Nguyen as she showed them the gorgeous cave formations. For a moment, she was there, taking in the sound of the roaring waterfall and admiring the cerulean waters.

Her memory skipped through portions of the journey, lingering on moments that seemed significant—Howel pointing out plant life within the caves, recordings he took in different parts of the cave system. Her memories faded and blurred from one to the next.

They were on their way to the Underground River in Palawan, an island of the Philippines. Dawn watched as the journey sped up and slowed down under Laurel's manipulation. One moment, they were boating from one shore to the next, and in a split second, they were trekking through the forest, following Jericho Buteras, who wore flip flops instead of hiking shoes.

Dawn heard Howel's voice as he called out to their guide. The scenery started to change to the brown, brackish water of the underground river, then the memory paused.

Who was Howel speaking to? Laurel asked, her voice reverberating in Dawn's head.

Jericho Buteras, our guide, she heard herself say. It sounded weirdly unfamiliar.

The memory skipped back to Howel's voice, calling out to the guide who had walked too far ahead of them. *Why isn't Howel saying his name?* Laurel asked.

Dawn listened to her dad's voice. "Echo! Wait a moment, we're looking at the most peculiar lizard!" he called out with hands cupped around his mouth.

His nickname is Echo, she recalled. *Yes, we called him Echo, short for Jericho.*

The letter! Dawn gasped. *It specified "a guide whose name you'll know" twice to make an echo.*

"He was writing about Echo!" She jumped from the coach, bursting with euphoria.

"You found it!" Laurel said, overjoyed, also springing to her feet. The two embraced each other and squealed, ecstatic to have finally solved Howel's riddle. Despite Laurel's grief, her genuine happiness for Dawn was palpable, and Dawn blinked back tears, suddenly overwhelmed with gratitude.

"*We* found it," Dawn beamed.

"Well done," Marion said, a relieved smile on her face. She had returned during Dawn's reading and laid out the coffee, tea, and mini pastries—and Lopple was already digging in.

Miss M. walked over to Dawn and threw her arms around her so tightly, squeezing the air out of her. "I knew you'd figure it out," her housekeeper whispered before releasing her.

A weight lifted from Dawn's heart, and joy swelled in the room—a room full of people who were supporting her. When she was nearly exasperated from frustration, they were the ones who stuck around. It meant more to her than they knew. She turned to face Lopple. "You should come with us," she urged. It wasn't a question.

"If you think I'll be of help, I will accompany you," he said while gobbling a profiterole. Then his face darkened. "But I will not be taking hold of the dysprosia."

"Agreed." She took a chocolate croissant for herself. First things first, she'd celebrate this victory, which brought them a step closer to completing the mission.

Marion and Dawn spent what the was rest of the chilly afternoon on chores and making preparations for the trip to the Underground River the next day. They decided to leave late afternoon in consideration of Stralla's burial; Ezra sent a comm to Laurel informing her that Stralla's ceremony would commence at sunrise. Laurel gave in to her exhaustion and napped on different couches while Hikaru tended to Lopple's injuries.

As night fell, the wind's howls grew louder and more violent, swaying the trees and swatting small twigs against the house like a belligerent ghost. Both Lopple and Laurel stayed for dinner, the latter with more appetite this time. Laurel projected the bridge maps when they discussed plans for the next day. They decided to arrive at an uncharted island south of Manila.

Marion called Gita and made the arrangements for an airlift from there to the Underground River. Miss M. and Hikaru would remain at the house and stay in contact with the porus. Besides, seven passengers seemed admittedly excessive.

With their plan all set, they chatted and shared travel stories; Lopple was back to his jovial banter, projecting his adventures, such as exploring active Icelandic volcanoes. The night eventually winded down after a few rounds of dessert: Marion's decadent, dark chocolate lava cakes. Even Laurel, who said it was "just okay," ate every last bite. As rain began to pelt against the house, Lopple and Hikaru sleepily went their separate ways on full stomachs.

"Did you need something before you head out?" Marion asked Laurel, who lingered as she put leftovers away.

"I want to ask a favor," Laurel said, abashedly looking down at her folded hands. "Would it be all right if I spent the night here? I'll be leaving for Stralla's burial early in the morning."

"Of course," Marion said with sincerity, delighted to accommodate her. "The guest room is already prepped. I'll get an extra blanket for you."

"Is everything okay at home?" Dawn asked.

"Yes, I'm just too tired to go back and forth." Laurel waved her hand dismissively.

Dawn's aura could sense a spike in Laurel's weariness, exhaustion, and fresh wave of grief. She wondered whether experiencing the emotions of others was part of her metamorphosis.

After she retrieved some oversized clothes for Laurel to sleep in, she laid them on the guest bed while Laurel was in the bathroom. Then she got herself ready for bed. When she was in the privacy of her own room, she sent a message to Logan:

Hi there. Miss me? I'm going on one last cave exploration trip tomorrow afternoon. Wanna come? I won't go home empty handed. I have a lead this time.

In less than a minute, he replied:

I'll go anywhere with you. I just need to be back by Sunday morning. It's my last weekend to train for the marathon next weekend.

Dawn loved how he had committed himself even before he knew *where* they were going. She had completely forgotten about his marathon training, though. If all went according to plan, perhaps she'd get to meet him at the finish line of his race. She thought for a while, then replied:

"We'll be back in time for sure, and I'll be cheering you on in your marathon. Dress for humid weather tomorrow. Thanks again for being there for me."

His response:

"What are friends for if not to tag along on free trips around the world? Can't wait!"

Full of giddiness, she danced around her room while reading his last message.

A faint knock at her door interrupted her thoughts. "Dawn?" Laurel's voice called from behind the door. "Um, mind if I sleep in your room tonight? I'm not used to staying by myself in reg rooms."

"Come on in!" Her spirits were high as she swung the door open.

Laurel waltzed right in with a fluffy comforter and pillow in tow, dumped them at Dawn's feet, then crawled into her host's bed.

"Please, go right ahead," Dawn said dryly. "I'll take the floor."

"Thanks," she yawned, ignorant of the sarcasm. "I'm so tired."

Dawn adjusted the comforter, folding it over like a sleeping bag. Then she turned off the lights and lied down. In the dark, she could hear Laurel fluffing her pillow and tossing in bed. Outside, a heavy clap of thunder shook the sky, followed by heavy rain pelting the house.

"Dawn?" Laurel asked, when she was finally settled, "Who's your closest friend?"

That was unexpected, Dawn thought, but she closed her eyes and pictured her friend with pink-tipped hair. "His name is Sparkle."

"What makes him your closest friend?"

"Hmmm." She opened her eyes and stared pensively at the dark ceiling. "I've known him since high school, er, like a decade ago." *Back when teachers were still calling him Sang Ook Kim,* she thought, but didn't say out loud. "We have the type of friendship that transcends space and time. It doesn't matter how long it's been since we've seen each other. Every time we talk, we pick up right where we left off."

Silence followed. Laurel was thinking about Stralla, and it made Dawn reflect on how lucky she was to have a friend like Sparkle— someone who was on her side no matter what. Someone who kept her honest when they didn't see eye to eye. She missed spending time with him, his humor, their chats about nothing and everything; she realized then she had taken their friendship for granted.

Laurel sighed deeply. "I don't know if I'll ever have another Etheran friend like Stralla. I don't know if I *want* to," she choked out as a sob escaped her. "I miss her."

Dawn, now wide awake, knit her brows and squeezed her eyes shut as her friend's grief weighed upon her. She hesitated to say something, fearing it might come across as insensitive. Obviously, to Laurel, the late Stralla was a confidant, a sister, a motherly figure, and more. Yet, here was Laurel, trying desperately (and failing miserably) to suppress her heartache.

"You are grieving," Dawn said, her own voice breaking. "The depth of your pain is a reflection of your love. The fact that you feel brokenhearted speaks volumes of how you valued the time you spent together."

"I thought . . . we'd have so much time . . . to spend together," she managed. "After I married Ezra, I was gonna be . . . part of his family. Stralla was gonna be . . . my sister."

Dawn fumbled in the dark to find a tissue box on her nightstand and handed it to Laurel.

"I'm grateful, though." Laurel loudly blew her nose. "I truly am—that I got to know her. She was a light to me in some of my darkest moments."

Dawn wasn't sure of what more to say, so she said nothing, and hoped that just being available to listen was enough. Hours passed before Laurel's soft cries subsided. Finally, she began to relax, and the sound of the steady rainfall lulled Dawn to sleep.

Interlude 3

LAUREL FACED HERSELF in the mirror and adjusted her stark-white wrap dress, making the neckline appear more modest. Her wavy, waist-length locks were neatly pinned back, and she deemed her appearance acceptable for an Etheran celebration of life. She checked her face and her eyes, which showed no signs of her crying. Ezra's mother, on the other hand, had deep, dark circles under her eyes—the result of her constant weeping over the last two days.

"Ready?" Ezra asked as he stepped into the living room with his mother.

Laurel nodded, seeing their reflections behind her in the mirror. He looked dashing as always, even in his plain white garb. The short, well-groomed stubble of his beard suited him. It was the closest to clean shaven she had ever seen him. His mother clung to his arm to steady herself, the white shepra silk flowing over her frail, specter-like silhouette.

"Don't forget—no spoken words, or you'll break decorum," Ezra reminded Laurel yet again. "The entire ceremony will be conducted in Etherish. This is not any ordinary Etheran burial, but a sangwor celebration of life—"

"I know, I know," she muttered. "All sangwor will be there, and so will Malstrom."

"*Lord* Malstrom," he corrected. "Try not to draw attention to yourself."

Laurel scoffed. Ezra's "reminders" did nothing to ease her qualms about attending Stralla's funeral. She wanted to be there, but as an Aquavian, she did not *belong* there. Burials were for family members and Etherans only; it didn't matter that she was betrothed to Ezra.

She was an exception. The sole reason she was *allowed* to attend was that her sister Kailani and her Etheran husband of high rank were approved to go, and Laurel would be attending as Kailani's proxy. She was to remain silent for the duration of the ceremony.

Easier said than done, she thought. Her emotions were haphazard, making every effort to shield her true thoughts and keep a placid expression more difficult. Ezra had insinuated that she would dare to draw attention to herself. The insult stung like saltwater in a cut, but Laurel bit her tongue, holding back an acerbic barb.

Silently, they each donned their shepra cloaks and pulled the hoods over their heads. Laurel looked into her betrothed's stoic eyes, wishing he'd say something comforting before they crossed the bridge, even the overused Etherish saying, "Do not be afraid."

Instead, he muttered, "Leave your shoes here."

The morning sky consisted of a dark blue mixed with gray on the horizon as dawn started to break. The sky was the only thing Laurel found as beautiful as the Atlantean waters, and she admired being closer to it in the Etheran realm.

While all Etherans had the ability to fly, it was custom for them to process barefoot to the place of burial outside the castle grounds. It seemed like a lot of trouble "to be one with the Earth," as she recalled Ezra saying. Not wanting to project her complaints, she gritted her chattering teeth, her sensitive, bare feet enduring the biting cold of the City of Etero.

As they walked, other Etherans joined them, filing behind in singles or pairs. She looked at the growing line behind her and spotted Angel, Dalton, Sid, and Fanto among others.

The procession ended at the center of the capital where a giant tree stood, looking as ancient as time itself. The attendees formed a half circle around it, and for a moment, Laurel imagined its gnarled branches and exposed roots reaching out toward them.

In the corner of her eye, she spotted Kailani's husband beckoning her, so she discreetly slipped past Ezra and his mother to stand in her place.

As she gazed at the massive tree, she realized she had seen it before—in a projection, during one of her history lessons with Reed's father. All she could remember was that he carried on and on about the roots, that they go deep into the ground where the Jewel of the City is buried. And something about how the jewel keeps the sky city suspended by feeding off the tree, while the tree itself is sustained by . . . the Etherans buried there? She wished she had paid more attention to her lessons.

Before she had time to ponder it further, she caught sight of the grave close to where Ezra and his mother waited. Next to it was a mound of dirt.

Laurel heard movement behind her, and she turned to see about twenty masked sangwor, solemnly treading toward the tree. Their formal white raiments swished in unison as they walked, and their masked faces had blank expressions etched upon them. The skin on the back of Laurel's neck prickled at the eerie spectacle.

At the front of the sangwor procession, four white-gloved pallbearers carried Stralla's body on a bed decorated with ornate gold and silver filaments. Laurel recognized one of the pallbearers—Stralla's father, who had heavy-set eyes and a hard line for a mouth. The other three carrying Stralla were masked sangwor, two of who had to be Ezra's brothers.

Laurel's breath hitched when they passed, and she caught sight of Stralla's veiled body. Although she was clothed in her white raiments, identical to the ones worn by her fellow warriors, she seemed much more regal and stately, even in death. Small white flowers adorned her unbraided hair, and her folded hands held a simple bouquet.

Laurel remained so focused on Stralla as the pallbearers made their way to the tree that she didn't notice an unmasked man walking at the end of the procession until he passed right in front of her. She did a double take—*it was Malstrom!*

A silver crown embellished with jewels sat atop his head. He was cloaked in the finest white shepra silks and linens that moved gently with his royal gait. She managed a glimpse of his face. Dark eyes and those striking Valedorian features, the same sharp jaw she had seen in Ezra. Malstrom's steely eyes swept the crowd from side to side, his head unmoving.

Laurel met his gaze for a split second, then she tore hers away and drew a sharp breath. Her stomach lurched as she looked down at her feet thinking, *act normal, act normal.*

Are you all right? Kailani's husband discreetly projected to her, noticing her discomfort.

Laurel nodded but broke into a sweat despite the near-freezing weather. She closed her eyes and practiced the breathing exercise Logan had taught her on the airlift. *This is a ceremony to honor Stralla.*

Pull yourself together, she told herself. She exhaled, then slowly opened her eyes.

Malstrom stood at the front of the tree, facing the small crowd, silently commanding attention. To his right were Stralla's father and mother; at Malstrom's left stood the other brothers.

Stralla had been right—Malstrom was alive and well. Youthful, even—well, for a thousand-year-old monarch. Standing next to Ezra's father, it was plain as day Malstrom looked young enough to be Ezra's older brother. *How in the seven seas had he not aged?*

The Sky King held his hands behind his back as he projected in Etherish. *Today, we honor sangwor Stralla Valedor, who perished fulfilling her duties. May her memory live on with her father, Lord Ezekiel, her mother, the Mina de Somn Teborah, and the rest of her kin.* He nodded solemnly at both of them as his voice reached the minds of all present. *Let us Lumen remember: we are dust, and to dust we shall return.*

His words, Laurel knew, were neither meant to comfort nor console, but to serve as a reminder of mortality, a revered Etheran sentiment. She wondered if he truly believed those words himself. Did *Malstrom* consider himself mortal? Was he, too, awaiting the day he would breathe his last?

Malstrom turned around, took a handful of dirt from the mound and let it fall from his palm into the grave. All the attendees lined up to pay their respects in the same manner.

When it was Laurel's turn, she cleared her mind of all thoughts, refusing to be distracted by Malstrom. This moment was for Stralla. She followed her brother-in-law to the front, grasped a handful of earth, then tossed it into the grave. It was dark and deep in the pit where Stralla was laid. Her face was no longer visible, and perhaps it was for the best—to remember her the way she had looked when she was alive and vibrant, with an insatiable thirst for adventure.

'Til our currents cross, my friend. Laurel's heart whispered the Orako saying. She dared not project it. Inhaling deeply, she caught a subtle, sweet fragrance in the air, then she turned toward Stralla's parents and bowed to both of them in sympathy.

Although her eyes were still swollen from her tears, the Lady of Dreams looked into her eyes, reached out to Laurel, and clasped her hand. *Did she ever tell you what her name meant?*

Laurel replied, *She told me you named her Stralla, Evening Star, because she was your light in the darkness.*

The woman smiled wistfully. *You will come to our quarters after this and eat with us,* she projected. It was not a request or command, but a statement. Knowing she could not refuse, Laurel nodded and took her place once again next to her brother-in-law.

They waited while the remaining attendees paid their respects, and the ceremony seemed to come to a close. The processing sangwor hadn't placed dirt into the grave; instead, they positioned themselves around everyone, encircling the attendees and the tree. They all stood, silently waiting. *What now?*

The sangwor suddenly raised their hands to the sky, palms up. The motion, which was done with impeccable military precision, was so abrupt, Laurel clutched her heart in surprise. From their palms shot out blue flames, reaching skyward. The heat surrounded her. Mesmerized, she watched as they carefully adjusted their palms to combine their flames to form four pillars of fire surrounding them and the tree.

Again, the sangwor, still rooted to their spots, shifted their palms, each to their right, and with the coordinated push of their auras, the sangwor combined their flames and created a whirlwind of fire that burned a deep, rich blue.

It was a sight to behold with the backdrop of the breaking dawn. The gray heavens had turned a pinkish hue, but it began to glow brighter. The flames were changing color, Laurel realized. From blue, to a crimson red, then to a blazing orange. Laurel lifted her head skyward as the beautiful inferno warmed her back, then the tip of her nose, all the way to her fingertips and toes that had gone numb from the cold merely moments ago.

She turned her attention back to the grave. Malstrom had gone—to where, Laurel didn't know—but in his stead was Asher Elkhorn, the Etheran historian who looked just as sickly pale as the last time she'd seen him.

Stralla's brothers and parents stepped to either side of the grave, facing one another. As they held out their hands, the mound of remaining dirt moved at their will to fill Stralla's final resting place. When they had leveled the earth, Laurel could see previously obscured woven baskets of white gardenias—the source of the sweet fragrance.

Ezra's mother flourished her fingers and a blanket of flowers cascaded over Stralla's fresh grave. The act was so tender, as if she were tucking her child into bed for the last time.

With that final gesture, the sangwor extinguished their whirlwind of fire, revealing the morning light's pink hue in the sky. The warriors solemnly brought their hands down as the brisk chill returned to the air.

CHAPTER 22

DAWN WOKE UP to find herself alone in her room, her bed unmade. She got up from the floor and stretched, her neck popping as she rolled her head from side to side.

After folding her blankets and making her bed, she activated the cleaning bot and watched it silently scamper around the room. It was unusually quiet throughout the house, no voices coming from downstairs.

Reaching out with her aura, she sensed two Lumen and five porus—outside. She peeked around the window shades. Dark clouds loomed in the sky, casting shadows everywhere; the rain had stopped for now, but hail had been forecasted later. Marion slowly stepped around her garden in rainboots, taking care not to slip in muddy areas. A gardening bot hovered beside her, carrying a basket half full of fruits and vegetables. Hiro padded behind them, and Dawn sensed Hikaru's aura nearby, maybe in the greenhouse minding his healing herbs.

Knowing that the weather had plummeted, Dawn dressed and bundled herself in a thick jacket before heading to the backyard with her own basket to lend a helping hand. Outside, the chilly yet refreshing air nipped at her face. She and Marion filled two baskets of lavender and various herbs from the greenhouse before spending the rest of morning preparing for the trip to the Underground River. Hikaru went back home to wait for Logan soon after they left the backyard.

"Miss M., have you seen my knives?" Dawn yelled from the living room as she rummaged through her duffle bag, searching for the three she had taken from the bunker.

"They're here on the counter," Marion said from the kitchen. "Polished and dried."

Dawn strode in and examined Marion's work. "Thanks. I also couldn't find a lot of my clothes upstairs."

"I moved them to our new lodgings," she said while slicing an apple.

"We're moving? Already?" Their conversation about relocating had happened weeks ago, although it felt like yesterday. Marion hadn't specified where they'd be moving, but Dawn trusted her housekeeper to reveal the location at the right time.

Miss M. put an apple slice in her mouth, its red skin an uncanny match with her headwrap. "Yes, we're ready to relocate. We've been moving things little by little—food, supplies, medicine, some weapons, and other essentials."

"Who's *we*?"

"Hikaru and I. He'll be coming with us."

"Right . . . of course." She retrieved a jar of dried lavender from the pantry and added some newly picked stems to the dehydrator. Out of habit, she made herself an oat milk latte while she thought.

Miss M. and Hikaru have been inseparable lately. Or did I simply fail to notice until recently?

It was naive to think Marion didn't have any personal relationships outside their family. Hikaru had followed wherever Howel and Marion had gone, except this time it'd be without her dad.

Dawn sprinkled dried lavender on her steaming latte and took a long, comforting sip. Relocating meant she'd be saying goodbye to Logan soon. Whether or not that meant the erasure of his memory was still up in the air.

Tap, tap, tap, the sound of knuckles rapping on glass. She sensed Lopple awaiting entry through the bridge. Marion went to the garage to let him in.

A second later, the doorbell rang. Hikaru had arrived with Logan in tow. Dawn abandoned her coffee and sprinted to the door, swung it open, and beamed up at Logan. Hikaru waltzed straight in to find Marion without so much as a side-eyed glance.

Logan beamed, stepping inside and wrapping his arms around her. "Miss me?"

"Mmhm," she said with her face against his chest. Her voice came out muffled. "You're supposed to say, 'I miss *you.*'"

They made their way to the living room as she breathed in his scent of spruce. She closed her eyes and couldn't resist hugging him again—although she struggled to get her arms around him with his rucksack on his back.

"Ahem," a loud voice harrumphed. She recognized it as Ezra's.

Dawn and Logan broke apart to find that Ezra, Laurel, and Lopple had entered the room.

"Oh! Uh, they arrived just before you," Dawn said to Logan, a little flustered. She glanced at Ezra and Laurel, who looked exhausted in their formal, white clothes. Lopple was already dressed for the hike, and he moved nonchalantly to the lounge chair.

Without skipping a beat, Logan approached Ezra and held out his hand for a shake. "I'm Logan, by the way."

"Oh my days!" Dawn said, realizing it was their first time meeting. "Yes, this is Ezra—Laurel's fiancé."

Ezra slowly took his hand and gave it one solid shake. "Nice to meet you," he said stiffly.

"Did both of you come from some sort of occasion?" Logan asked Ezra and Laurel, looking over their outfits.

"Yes. A funeral," Ezra replied. "I brought a change of clothes with me."

Marion poked her head into the living room. "You can use the guest room," she said, pointing in its direction.

"I'll change later," Laurel said, dropping her tote bag on the floor.

The smell of pizzants wafted in the air, and Marion insisted they all have lunch first. Lopple wasted no time getting to the dining room while the others filed in after him.

Logan stayed a second behind and put his rucksack on the floor near the couch. "Is that a new look for you?" he said as his eyes swept over Dawn.

She became self-conscious that she hadn't bothered to put on a smidge of makeup or fix her hair, then shrugged dismissively. "We won't be taking pictures anyway. I'll change out of my sweats before we go."

He put his arm around her and brushed her wind-swept hair out of her face. "You've got quite an entourage for this hike."

Dawn nodded. "We're not leaving without the plant this time."

She looked up at him and he gave her shoulder an extra squeeze, as if letting her know that everything would be all right.

After a quick and quiet lunch, the group settled in the living room while Marion and Hikaru cleaned up. Miss M. encouraged them to rest; they still had two hours before their scheduled airlift.

Attempting to lighten the mood with banter, Logan asked, "Anyone have plans for the weekend?"

Dawn thought it endearing that he kept trying to strike up a conversation despite Laurel and Ezra's somber vibes. Lopple shared his plans to check out a coffee shop in Long Beach.

"I've heard they have the best pizzants—but I haven't tried any that topped Miss Marion's. She must have a secret ingredient."

"Onions," Dawn said.

"What was that?" Lopple asked, cocking his head to the side.

"She knows you like onions, so she always adds extra to your food."

"That would explain the extra crunch, and they do create an irresistible warmth!" His eyes went wide, considering this for the first time. "And what about you? Any plans for the weekend?" Lopple asked Logan.

"I'm training for a marathon after tomorrow."

"In this rain?"

As if on cue, thunder rumbled in the clouds.

"At the gym."

"Oh, of course." Lopple said.

Another moment of awkward silence followed. Dawn curled up her legs onto the couch and watched as Logan looked around the living room. "Is that a piano?" Logan asked, craning his neck toward the reception area.

Dawn saw the rectangular piece, covered with a cloth and a vase on top. "Yeah—I actually forgot it was there."

"You never told me you played," Logan said, walking over to it and opening the keylid.

"I don't anymore. It's been a long time since my piano lessons."

"Mind if I play?" he asked with an impish grin while taking a seat at the bench.

"Be my guest."

His fingers gently moved over the keys as a melancholic tune filled the room. It sounded beautiful and slow, a nostalgic song like heartbreak from missing someone.

Dawn's mouth dropped open in surprise at how well he played. The others had perked up as well, listening intently.

"It's a rendition of 'Smile' by Charlie Chaplin," Logan said as he played a swell of arpeggios. "It's one of my parents' favorites. Mine too."

"I thought Chaplin was a comedian," Dawn said, pulling her knees under her chin. "The melody sounds so . . ."

"Sad?" Logan asked while he continued playing. "It is. He was known for his comedic acting in old films, but he also wrote songs to entertain."

After a few minutes, the song slowed as Logan finished with an arpeggio and deeper-pitched notes for a final flourish.

"It really was lovely," Ezra commented. "I've always been amazed by music's power to ease one's spirit. Won't you sing something for us, Stralla?" Ezra asked, turning to Laurel.

She flinched, and a pained expression appeared on her face at the sound of Stralla's name.

"Who's Stralla?" Logan asked as he got up and returned to his spot next to Dawn.

"I'm sorry," Ezra said, shaking his head and blinking rapidly as if his eyes had deceived him. "I meant *Laurel*. I'm merely tired."

"Stralla was his younger sister," Laurel said to Logan, devoid of emotion. "She passed away recently, and we had her funeral today."

Logan's eyebrows shot up. "I'm so sorry to hear that," he said sympathetically.

"Thanks." She rose from her seat. "I think we're all a little tired and on edge. I'll sing something to help us rest."

Logan put his arm around Dawn's shoulders and searched her eyes, seeming to ask if Laurel was really going to sing. Dawn offered him a small shrug; she didn't know either.

The Aquavian's ethereal voice rang out in a language that Dawn couldn't place, immediately putting her into a trance-like state. Dawn's eyelids and limbs felt heavy. She could barely turn to look at Logan, and when he finally came into focus, he was passed out.

It took greater mental energy to draw up her aura shields, but she managed to do it, willing some of her fatigue to subside. She sat up to survey the room. Lopple and Ezra looked sleepy, but they weren't knocked out like Logan. Dawn yawned, still feeling unusually relaxed. Laurel stopped singing, and the drowsiness dissipated.

"What did you do to him?" Dawn asked, brushing a strand of hair away from Logan's peaceful face.

"I put him to sleep."

Dawn shook him gently, trying to wake him. "You did this with your singing?"

"It's siren song," Laurel said. "Learned it when I was young. Don't worry, he'll only be out for an hour."

"She has the ability to make people feel a certain way by using the sound of her voice," Ezra explained. "It's different from projection and works better on groundlings because they can't shield."

Laurel nodded and took a seat on the same couch but kept her distance from her betrothed. "Siren song can make people feel calm, terrified . . . you name it."

"So you're a siren?" Dawn asked.

Lopple snorted. "Groundling perceptions never cease to entertain me."

"I'm not a siren," Laurel said, leaning back comfortably on the couch. "Sirens are shifters who prey on seafarers. They mate with them, then eat them. Sirens can *choose* to have female offspring . . . and the cycle continues. They prefer to live on islands."

"You seem to know quite a bit about them," Dawn said, an eyebrow arching upward.

"How do you think I learned siren song? I spent time with them when I was young. Not all of them are vicious."

"As fascinating as this is, can you lull me into a short nap?" Ezra interjected. "I'm exhausted, and we have a long day ahead of us."

"So if you use siren song on us, when will our sleepiness wear off?" Dawn asked Laurel suspiciously.

"I can control the timing. We can all wake up in an hour—same time as Logan. Nothing to worry about," she assured.

After a tentative nod from Dawn, Laurel sang again. This time, Dawn didn't fight it. She fell into a deep and dreamless sleep.

Wake up.

Dawn's eyes fluttered open at the sound of Laurel's voice. Beside her, Logan was still knocked out. Lopple was curled up on the couch in a fetal position, and Ezra was sleeping with his arms crossed.

The steady rain outside was an appropriate ambience with the soft snores of the three grown men napping in the living room.

"How much time do we have before they wake up?" Dawn whispered.

"Half an hour." Laurel picked up her tote bag with her hiking clothes and pointed at the stairs leading to Dawn's room.

Dawn got up and they both tiptoed to the stairs. When they reached her room, she shut the door gently. "I didn't want to ask this in front of everyone else, but how was the funeral?"

"It was . . . different," Laurel said, looking at her bare feet. She quickly recapped the details, including meeting at Ezra's parent's place in the Castle of Etero afterward. "It turned out to be a rendez-vous for some of the secret council members. Angel stopped by briefly. Do you remember Asher—the historian?"

"The pale guy? He was there?!"

Laurel's face darkened. "Not at their home, but I saw him at the funeral. I suppose he'd have reason to chronicle it as the head historian."

Dawn rubbed the side of her neck, recalling the unpleasant vibes from their encounter on Tencho. "I remember him asking me about my mom. He was rude."

"Perhaps, but Angel has faith in him. He's the council's inside man in Malstrom's circle, and Asher told her that Malstrom got wind of you learning to shield. The soufors have a lead on where you are and are planning for your capture . . . as ordered by Malstrom."

Dawn paced the room, disturbed by the news. "If that's true, there must also be a mole in one of *our* inner circles. It could be one of Sid's agents."

"I wouldn't rule Lopple out yet either," Laurel whispered as she and Dawn changed into their hiking gear.

"I hate to admit it, but it could also possibly be a breach in Jett's tech. Miss M. made a call to Gita yesterday to set up our airlift from the bridge to the Underground River." Dawn pulled her hair into a ponytail and fiddled with her crystal pendant, willing herself to stay calm. "This isn't good. Marion has been planning our relocation for a while. We're supposed to move any day now."

"Ezra projected everything I just told you to Marion as soon as we arrived. He made sure Lopple didn't hear." Laurel sat down on the floor, a nervous look on her face. "You should sit. I have some-thing more . . . upsetting to share. Something Ezra's mother saw in her visions."

Dawn's eyes went cloudy as Laurel shared her projection. It was Howel—withered, thin, and gaunt. Sunken eyes and a fatigued appearance. He was hunched over, hands shaking as he inspected something in a beaker.

"Dad?" Dawn's voice trembled as her breath hitched.

He faded as his makeshift lab morphed into darkness.

Dawn found herself in the expanse of space, viewing Earth from a nest of stars. Darkness coiled around the planet like a snake, squeezing the life out of it. She heard the screams—of mankind and beast alike—and the destruction of cities and forests. All was consumed by the darkness, the end of the Earth.

"No!" Dawn said out loud. She opened her eyes and found herself sitting on the floor of her room, tears streaming down her face. She swiped them away, and looked at Laurel, sitting beside her. "How can that be?"

"We haven't found the ingredient yet."

"But we will! I'm going to find it in time!"

Laurel nodded only once, her mouth set in a hard line. "We still have time to change this outcome."

There was weight to her words. Dawn knew it from the way she said "we," instead of "you." While there was nothing her friend could've done to save Stralla, Laurel would help her save Howel and alter the world's fate. They sat in silence, breathing. A calmness stilled Dawn's racing heart and filled it with firm determination. Failure was not an option.

"How are you and Ezra holding up? You both seemed kind of distant."

"He's . . . okay. We ate at the castle, so we didn't have much of an appetite when we arrived. I let him know the plan with how we're keeping the bridges a secret from Logan. Then I broke off our engagement."

"You what?!"

"I know it's terrible, *terrible* timing with the funeral, but it felt weirdly right. He took it rather well, actually. It felt . . . mutual. It'll be a pain to tell my father, but Ezra said he'd help."

"Are you disappointed?" Dawn asked after recovering from her initial shock.

"A little. We didn't love each other, not romantically, anyway, but I thought perhaps one day we might," Laurel said, putting on one of her socks. "I'm still kind of angry with his mother."

"Because she didn't tell you about Stralla's death?"

She shrugged and put on her other sock, not meeting Dawn's eyes.

"I can't imagine what it'd be like to accept the future death of her daughter."

"She didn't *have* to accept it," Laurel argued, her voice shrill.

"I don't know what else Ezra's mom saw, but my guess is that Stralla's death must . . . affect other things in the future. I'm sure his mom is hurting, you know?"

Laurel started for the door. "We should go downstairs. They're waking up now."

Dawn steeled herself, determined to remain focused on the mission, before heading downstairs.

"How was your nap?" Dawn asked Logan, arriving in the living room with a tray of espressos.

"Best nap I've had in a while," Logan admitted as he stood from the couch and stretched. He took a cup and sipped the hot liquid. "I didn't realize how tired I was."

Laurel's lips twitched.

"Let's get going," Lopple said, sharper than before, "while it's still early."

He, too, picked up a cup and drank it in one gulp while glancing at his wrist watches. Ezra, who was standing near the window and frowning disapprovingly at the downpour, gave him a curt nod and walked toward the garage when Marion stepped into the living room.

"Dawn, can I speak with you, please?" Miss M. asked her. "In the kitchen."

Dawn followed her and nearly collided into her housekeeper when she spun back around to give Dawn a hug.

"Oh!" Dawn yelped in surprise. She saw Hikaru behind the kitchen counter, thoroughly absorbed with grinding herbs using a large mortar and pestle. He didn't look up at them, on purpose, Dawn suspected.

The Ides of March is in two days, Marion projected while taking food packs from the fridge and stuffing them in the nearly full backpack on the counter. *Ezra told me that Malstrom's soufors have a lead on your whereabouts. It is only a matter of time before they find us.*

"It's going to be fine," Dawn whispered. "I can shield now and—"

We are moving tonight. Hikaru and I will move the rest of our essentials while you're searching for the dysprosia. As soon as you have it, come right back. I gave Lopple a comm stone so he can contact me when you're ready to cross the bridge.

You gave one to Lopple? Dawn replied voicelessly. *Laurel said—*

I know why Laurel has her reservations about him, but trust me. He's on our side.

But you haven't cleared out the greenhouse yet—

Marion walked right up to Dawn and gripped her shoulders, holding her at arm's length.

Listen to me. Marion paused, an intensity in her gaze. *I didn't clear the greenhouse or the garden. It would raise suspicion. No one except Hikaru knows that we're leaving tonight, not even the porus. You. Cannot. Tell. Logan.*

Dawn was about to argue but felt her housekeeper's grip on her shoulders tighten. "Okay! Miss M., you're shaking."

It is safer for you and him if he does not know. I promised your mother—before she died, I promised her I'd keep you safe. I am the Keeper of House Aurelia . . . tell me you understand.

Marion's palpable resolve and near desperation caused her to take ragged, shaky breaths.

"I—I understand." Relief flooded her lungs as soon as Marion released her shoulders.

Soon after, Dawn left with the group for the Philippines with a backpack full of snacks and her head spinning with thoughts about Marion's role as *housekeeper.*

CHAPTER 23

THE SOUND OF roosters crowing at first light greeted Dawn, Laurel, Ezra, Lopple, and a blindfolded Logan as they emerged from the flat side of a karst mountain known as Elephant Cave. The night before, Laurel had explained that Lumen created bigger bridges for moving large items. Historians chronicled this one as being used to transport animals the size of a diurlax, as well as vehicles. If Jett's pilots were Lumen, they could cross with airlifts.

For the most part, they were out in the open, except for some shrubbery and wild brush that helped hide the bridge in plain sight. A few nipa huts, flat lands, and rice fields filled Dawn's vision, and she removed Logan's blindfold so he could see for himself.

Only one thing was out of place in the picturesque scenery: a lone airlift and the woman standing next to it, staring at them expectantly. The dirt beneath Dawn's boots gave a satisfying crunch as she and the others walked toward the attendant, who was dressed in a gray blouse and black slacks—Jett's assistant.

"Good morning." Gita held her hands clasped in front of her as she assessed the group. "You keep curious company, Miss Farringdon."

Dawn greeted her cheerily, not giving away hints for the true reason of their trip. "My friends and I are here to enjoy a much-needed excursion."

"Of course. Care for a cup of kudzukan tea?" Gita asked, ushering them toward the airlift. She froze for a moment.

Dawn and the rest of the group saw what had caught Gita's attention: a malnourished little boy, crouched in the tall grass a few feet behind the vehicle. When he was certain that he had been discovered, there was no point in hiding. He stood up, revealing his threadbare shirt and shorts.

The boy walked toward them barefoot with an outstretched hand and an apprehensive smile. He had an adorable mess of bedhead black hair and seemed nearly skin and bones.

I'll erase his memory, and we'll be on our way, Gita projected. She moved her hand, palm up, in the direction of the boy's head. He stopped in his tracks.

He does not need erasure, Laurel replied, her disembodied voice in her head. *He's no threat to us.*

"He probably just wants coins," Dawn said out loud, searching her pockets.

"I have some," Logan offered. Dawn realized he was oblivious to the silent exchange that had occurred. He gave the boy his spare change, and a full grin (albeit with several missing front teeth) bloomed on the kid's face.

Dawn exhaled her held breath in relief as the boy took off running toward the huts, and Gita lowered her hand.

"Come. There'll only be more of *them* if we delay," Gita said with a hint of disdain. By *them*, Dawn was certain Gita meant groundlings, although her comment could've been misconstrued by Logan to mean child beggars.

Getting ready for takeoff gave Dawn déjà vu. Anxiety emanated from Lopple, Ezra, and Laurel combined. Once they were in the air, Dawn noticed their nerves had calmed considerably, but Lopple, who was sitting behind Gita, kept eyeing the dashboard.

"Are you piloting this . . . thing?" Lopple asked Gita.

"No," Jett's assistant replied calmly. "There was no time to re-schedule a licensed pilot to take you, as I received a call for your travel plans late last night."

"Then who's flying the airlift?" Laurel asked, gripping Dawn's seat from behind.

"George is," Gita smirked.

"Who in the seven seas is George?!" Laurel shrieked.

Logan chuckled. "Autopilot," he and Gita said at the same time.

"Don't worry," Gita soothed. "It's a short flight."

"You took commercial flight lessons?" Logan asked Gita.

"I did but didn't complete my training." Gita's eyes didn't stray from the sky in front of her. "Mr. Pierce had me prioritize . . . other initiatives."

"How is he, by the way?" Dawn asked. The backs of the front seats displayed infotainment screens for the passengers seated in the back, and it showed a camera view of the passengers in the front and vice versa.

"Healing up nicely. Not long before he's fully recovered." Gita looked directly into the camera. "He is a strong man." *For a groundling,* she projected.

Time passed rather quickly, and it felt like only a minute later when they began their descent. The airlift landed on a dirt path near the shoreline. Everyone except Gita disembarked, and she assured Dawn she'd find a discreet place to park the vehicle.

The group walked toward the shoreline, scanning the empty huts that lined the area to offer beachgoers shaded places to sit and eat. Vendors were arriving, setting up their carts for the day to sell their wares, including waterproof holo goggles, sunglasses, and towels.

"Where to?" Logan asked Dawn, using a handkerchief to wipe the sweat from his brow. The sun was just peeking over the horizon, but the air was already warm and humid.

Dawn pointed to the docks, where boats of different sizes bobbed up and down in the choppy water.

"Are those some sort of canoes?" Ezra asked.

"I think they're called *bangka*." Dawn recalled how locals fashioned bamboo poles on both sides, parallel to the boat to keep them stable.

"They look ancient," Lopple remarked.

Before he could speculate on its safety or lack of it, a man waved to them from the docks and started jogging toward them. When he reached them, Dawn could see that he was the same man from ten years ago, from his thin frame and dark-brown skin to his worn-out flip flops and faded jean shorts. Echo. The only things different were that his raven-colored hair was streaked with gray and that he had a few fine lines on his face.

"It's good to see you, Miss Dawn," he said, catching his breath. He glanced at her friends. "Where's Dr. Howel?"

Doctor? Laurel repeated silently.

"He couldn't make it," Dawn said. "Since he's been preoccupied with his work, we're visiting the Underground River to get some plant samples for him."

"I see. Miss Marion did say it would be you and four others—I apologize for assuming Dr. Howel would be joining us today since he's visited every few years."

"Oh, no need," she assured him. "Just take us to the same spots you took my dad."

"Of course. Do you know what plants you're looking for in the caves?"

Dawn pulled out a piece of paper from her pocket, unfolded it, and shared it with Echo. "Only this one. It's called dysprosia."

"Very few plants grow in the caves," he said with a frown. "I don't recognize this one."

She had not anticipated this response when Howel's riddle clearly referenced *him* as their guide. "Are you sure? I'm certain this grows deep in the caves."

Logan put a hand on her shoulder, his way of saying not to worry.

"Well," Echo started, glancing at the expectant faces of Dawn's friends, "I *have* seen Dr. Howel arranging rocks inside the caves. Maybe he left markers."

"Then we'll take a look at those spots first."

A smile returned to Echo's face. "Before we continue to the docks, can we speak privately?"

Dawn nodded and walked with Echo to get out of earshot. Logan wouldn't be able to hear, but the others could if they used their Lumen abilities.

"I hope you don't mind me asking," he said when they were far enough, "but are your friends . . . how do I say this . . . *gifted?* Are they *doctors,* like Dr. Howel?"

"I guess you *could* call them *gifted.*" She considered the term, disliking how it insinuated that regs were inferior. *Could that be the reason Howel used the term "doctor?"* "Well, all except for Logan, the one who was standing next to me. He's not a *doctor,* but he's kind of . . . more than a friend. Why do you ask?"

Echo smiled. "I *knew* it from the way he looked at you. But I was asking about the others because the area I'm taking you to is dangerous. Are the three others your guards?"

"I don't remember it being unsafe last time. What exactly is dangerous about the caves?"

"Well, there are different creatures that inhabit the areas around the caves during this season. I-I've only seen them from afar. Dr. Howel always brought another *doctor* this time of year to keep us safe."

"The men are trained guards," Dawn said with a quick nod toward the group. *At least, I'm counting on it.* "I'll give them a heads up."

"Everything okay?" Logan asked once they rejoined the group.

Dawn fibbed that they had ironed out some details for the trip. She took a moment to introduce them all to Echo and to project to Ezra and Lopple to be on high alert, relaying what she and Echo had discussed.

I'll send a comm for a few "doctors" to join us, Ezra projected.

They arrived at the docks, and Echo helped them into a large bangka with a covered top. Dawn watched as he deftly kept his balance, walking around the swaying boat with only flip flops on. Lopple looked ready to puke two seconds after he boarded; he sat down and gripped one of the poles holding up the covered top.

As they sped off toward the caves, Dawn looked out over the dark blue waters, remembering they were less cloudy the last time she had been there. The trip was brief, but choppy; Lopple managed to hold down his lunch.

They docked at a beach with a visitor center and a couple gazebos. A lush and dense forest lay ahead of them, its treetops still blanketed with the grayness of the morning light. No other tourists had arrived yet, and unseen birds welcomed them with their morning calls.

A dirt path lined with wooden handrails cut through the foliage. Echo led the way, and the group followed him in pairs. The unrelenting humidity lengthened the minutes they walked, silencing their voices, forcing them to conserve energy. Lopple was limping but wasn't complaining.

Echo stopped when they reached a bend in the course. "From here, we will stray from the path. Try not to touch anything with your bare skin," he cautioned, hopping over the railing.

They trekked slowly for a few minutes to avoid tripping over exposed roots. As they went deeper into the forest, the birdsong, insects, and skittish creatures scurrying about grew louder. Logan kept ducking under low-hanging vines, and everyone else swatted pesky mosquitos that hovered around them.

"We're being followed," Ezra whispered. *By beings who know how to conceal themselves*, he warned silently.

The group came to a stop and grew quiet, listening. Lopple gave a barely noticeable nod as his eyes darted about.

I sense it too, Dawn projected. It was an odd sensation, like the tickle in her nose before a sneeze. Or the prickling on her neck when someone was behind her and she hadn't seen them.

I don't see anything, Logan mouthed.

Laurel shot him a glare and held a finger to her mouth in a silent shush. Then her eyes grew wide as something caught her attention on a tree branch behind him.

A stifled giggle, which was barely discernible from the sound of a trickling stream, came from the trees. Dawn caught a glimpse of a small person running atop the length of a bough, disappearing amongst the leaves. Another giggle. Her eyes searched for the source, this time at the base of the tree a few feet away, where fallen branches, leaves, and protruding roots lay. It was a whimsical sound, like the susurration of wind whistling through forest.

A tiny, delicate face appeared, partly obscured by the greenery.

Dawn gasped. "Did you see that?" she whispered.

"See what?" Logan asked, his voice barely audible.

Echo, Ezra, and Lopple looked to Dawn, anticipating her answer. She debated internally whether she could say out loud what she truly saw. She blinked and the face had disappeared, but in the space behind it, she saw something larger, slowly moving toward them.

"Um . . . there!" Dawn pointed and whispered. "I saw that, that . . . thing."

A giant lizard emerged from behind the tree, blinking its glassy eyes and sticking out its split, black tongue. It crawled around, scraping the forest floor with its long black nails as it foraged. They watched in awe as it turned and scampered away.

Echo looked relieved. "Well, that was a water monitor lizard. There's more of them near the water on the tourist side," he said. "Let's keep going."

Laurel's and Dawn's eyes met for a second; both knew what the other had actually seen.

Why didn't Lopple and Ezra say anything? Dawn projected to Laurel.

They didn't see the fairy, who can choose who they reveal themselves to, Laurel replied, *but Ezra suspects it was something other than the lizard.*

Finally, they reached a clearing where the dense foliage opened up to a sandy shore. Rippling waves of murky water rolled in gently.

Echo asked for assistance with two large, upside down CETT canoes on a nearby rack. It wasn't difficult to turn them right-side up and push them into the water, but the effort soon had them drenched in sweat.

This would've been a lot easier if we could use our abilities, Lopple huffed voicelessly. Yesterday, they had promised to use their abilities only in case of emergency, since both Echo and Logan were regs.

"I'll steer one," Echo said. He looked at Lopple and Ezra expectantly. "Who wants to drive the other?"

They both stared at him blankly, and Dawn figured that neither of them knew how to use motorized groundling canoes. These older models had the motor and steering in the back of the boat, and they lacked AI-assisted and self-driving tech. They were similar to the one she'd used during her first visit, when Echo taught her how to use them.

Dawn volunteered. She, Logan, and Ezra shared one canoe, while Echo, Laurel, and Lopple took the other. Echo ensured they brought extra paddles, helmets, and flashlights, then they set off. As Dawn drove, Logan watched her adjust the speed settings in an effort to learn.

Echo pointed wordlessly across the water to a land mass of jagged rock. As they neared its base, he slowed to an idyllic pace and Dawn did the same. They all fastened their helmets in silent anticipation. As they entered the cave to the Underground River, darkness swallowed them completely. In the cave, it was *always night*, Dawn thought as she recalled her dad's letter:

Past the maw and deep in the throat, it's hard to find and harder to grow.

She wished they could go faster. This is where they'd find dysprosia—the root that was the key to completing the mission. The key to finding and saving her dad.

"Take this flashlight," Echo said to someone in his canoe.

A bright light appeared in front of them and illuminated the river's path as Lopple held the light steady.

Logan turned on his own flashlight and passed it to Ezra at the front of their boat. One by one, they switched on their helmet lights, casting eerie shadows on the slick walls. As they drifted deeper into the cave, otherworldly rock formations towered in columns from the cave floor and ceiling. The water looked darker than kudzukan tea but reflected movement above. Dawn looked up at the ceiling of the cave, teeming with hundreds of hanging bats that squeaked and fluttered in disturbance.

Ew, Laurel mouthed, peering upward.

"Keep your mouth closed," Echo said with a laugh.

Large insect wings brushed against Dawn's face, and she shrieked as she swatted at what looked like giant mosquitoes. She switched off her helmet light, thinking they were attracted to it. There was plenty of light from the others anyway.

"Over there," Echo said, using his flashlight to point at white, flat rocks that were piled atop one another.

They stalled the boats next to the cave floor, as close as they could get it to the rocks.

"I'll check," Dawn said, getting up. Logan offered his hand to help her out of the boat.

Once her feet were on solid ground, she walked as quickly as she could without slipping on the rocks and crouched down to examine the surrounding area with her flashlight. There were some fissures in the floor, but no signs of plant growth. She scanned the rocks again and noticed a few that had fallen out of place from the stack.

"Echo," Dawn called out. "Have there been any earthquakes here recently?"

"Only a couple tremors. Perhaps every other week, but not strong enough for a cave-in," he said. "Why? What did you find?"

"Nothing," Dawn replied, puzzled. "Lopple, come take a look."

Lopple scrambled out of his boat and made his way to Dawn. After scraping at the dirt in the fissures, he came to the same conclusion.

"There's nothing," Lopple confirmed. "Or whatever was there has died."

They returned to the boats. This time, Logan volunteered to steer. In a matter of minutes, Echo pointed out another pile of rocks. Both Dawn and Lopple checked again, finding nothing. They returned to the boats.

"How many more areas did my dad frequent?" Dawn asked, fiddling with her pendant.

"Two more," Echo said, "but he explored them on foot."

My Etheran friends should be in the area soon, Ezra projected.

Dawn gave him a curt nod, relieved he was silently communicating with other Lumen.

"See that tunnel ahead?" Echo pointed his flashlight to the far right of the cave system where the path of the river didn't flow. "If we continue down the river, it flows out at the other end of the cave. The tunnel on the right does not. Howel has explored both tunnels."

"Did Howel still have to go through the cave to get back?" Lopple asked.

"Yes, so it's a matter of which route you want to check first."

Something caught Dawn's eye—a glint of light, like the shine of a gem—in the tunnel on the right. She heard a faint fairy giggle, like the enchanting sound of tiny jingling bells.

"Let's split up," Dawn suggested. "You take the river path, and our boat will take the tunnel."

"No," Ezra said. It was the first time he had spoken louder than a whisper. "It would be wise to stay together."

"We'll be faster if we split up," Dawn insisted.

"We stay together," he reiterated. "We have time."

Dawn saw Logan's eyes narrow at him, but he didn't say anything.

"All right," she conceded, not wanting to argue. She blew out a slow breath trying to remain calm. "Let's take the tunnel first."

After they got out of the canoes armed with their flashlights, Echo secured their boats with rope and tethered them to a thick stalagmite. Then he guided the group through the tunnel; Ezra was the last to follow, guarding their rear.

The tunnel was tighter than Dawn expected. Everyone but her, the shortest in the group, had to stoop while they walked to avoid hitting the ceiling. Logan had entered alongside Dawn, but the passage grew narrower, forcing them to single file.

Even with everyone using a flashlight, they couldn't see much beyond the person in front of them. Whenever Dawn looked past Echo, however, she could see the glint of light she had seen from the boat. It seemed like it was moving, keeping the same distance between them. She wondered if anyone else could see it.

"I see it too," Laurel said, behind Logan. Dawn realized she must've asked out loud.

"See what?" Echo asked as the tunnel opened to a cavernous space. He came to a stop, waiting for everyone to enter the chamber. The glint of light disappeared as Dawn entered.

"It's nothing," Dawn said, as her eyes settled on the dark blue body of water in front of them.

"The river flows through here when it rains, so I don't think Dr. Howel laid rocks here." He pointed his flashlight to the other side of the lake. "He usually inspects *that* area."

Dawn broke into a brisk walk around the lake to get to the opposite side. Logan and Lopple were right behind her. When she reached the area, she slowed and swept the floor with her flashlight, looking for any plant life.

A few deep fissures appeared in the ground, like cracks in a dried swamp, and the three of them followed the rough, black lines to their length; there was no visible plant life.

Now what? Fairy, a little help, please! Dawn cried in her thoughts.

Another glint caught her eye, and she walked to the area of the fissure where it sparkled. She crouched down on her knees and inspected the ground closely, hesitantly running her fingers over what looked like a crooked cord. It had a hardened, wiry texture, and its base was still buried somewhere in the fissure.

"What is it?" Logan asked, kneeling next to her.

Dawn removed her backpack and retrieved a small shovel. "It's a dried stem!"

Thank you, fairy!

Across the lake, Ezra and Laurel pointed their flashlights into the water, silently discussing something. *Have they also found something?* Dawn wondered. Echo kept his distance, patiently waiting near the entrance of the tunnel.

Dawn turned to Logan, pointing at the stem, "I'll need your help with this—you too, Lopple. Hold your flashlights over here."

She took her shovel and wedged it between the cracked, rock-hard ground, then wriggled it back and forth. She tried a few more times, and slowly, the fissure widened and a few more cracks appeared around the dried stem. A drop of sweat trickled down her temple.

"Let me try," Logan offered. Dawn handed him the shovel while she held the flashlight, and he took a turn.

"I think I can create more cracks around the stem," Lopple said, after Logan's attempt yielded minimal results.

Lopple took the tip of the shovel, aimed it at a spot next to the fissure, then raised the shovel above his head with both hands. He brought it down with force, using his sheer strength (coupled with his Lumen abilities, Dawn sensed) to stab the ground. Despite all that effort, only a small pock mark appeared where he struck.

Lopple repeated this a few more times, striking different spots around the fissure until he had encircled the stem with small dents in the ground. It looked like he had chiseled dots around the stem. He breathed heavily but took one more stab at the spot he had first struck.

It was just enough force for the rock to crack, connecting the dots he had made around the dried stem.

"It worked!" Dawn cried, her voice echoing through the chamber.

"Finally!" Lopple stood and staggered to the wall, leaning against it as he caught his breath.

She took the shovel and handed her flashlight to Logan. Whatever was under there *had* to be dysprosia. She wedged the shovel underneath the pieces and see-sawed it until the rock pieces came loose. Once removed, it revealed a dark patch of dirt where the dried stem originated.

It took some strategic digging and scraping, but Dawn managed to loosen the dirt around the stem.

"Let me dig it out," Lopple insisted. He had put on latex gloves and once again crouched beside her. She handed him the shovel and looked through her backpack to retrieve a clear container with a lid, which she gave to Logan.

Lopple successfully unearthed the plant's roots without destroying it in the process. There were still clumps of dirt around it, but Dawn could make out the brown bulbous root that sort of resembled a baby's hand.

"This is indeed the root of dysprosia." Lopple beamed. He set the shovel aside and held the flashlights for a better view. "Use your hands to lift it out of the dirt."

Dawn nodded and cupped the root, immediately noting how strange it felt. Small and raw like a potato, yet warm, as if it were alive.

The dysprosia pulsated in her fingertips, its roots curling around her fingers and hands. She gasped, fighting the urge to drop it. "Gross!" she shrieked, quickly placing it into the container Logan held. He sealed it with the top.

"Gross?" Logan asked, peering at the unmoving plant through the clear container.

They got up and dusted off their knees and legs. Dawn took the container from Logan and shined her flashlight into it, staring at the mass inside.

"It . . . moved," she said. "Or, er, I thought it did."

She shivered, thinking there might've been worms in the dirt, but there were no signs of movement in the container.

It won't be alive for long, Lopple projected to her. *Howel's been preparing a lab and the right conditions to preserve the dysprosia until it's ready for use.*

Dawn secured the container in her backpack, then the three of them made their way back around the lake to rejoin the others.

Ezra stood near the edge of the water, watching Laurel, who had bent down and stuck her hands in it.

"What are you doing?" Dawn asked when she reached them.

Laurel straightened up and shook off water from her hands. "There's something over there." She pointed to the center of the lake where the water looked darker and deeper.

"Do you think it's another plant?"

Laurel shook her head. *Ezra and I think it's an uncharted bridge*, she projected. *This chamber could've been used by Aquavians before.* "I'd go in to check, but this water is brackish, and there are some other . . . disgusting things in it."

Dawn shivered, thinking of worms again.

"Did you find dysprosia on the other side?" Ezra asked.

"Yes! We found one root," Dawn said, unable to hide the excitement in her voice. "Let's go back now."

"What about the other path?" Echo chimed in.

"I think we can leave with this plant for now, and if my dad needs another, we could come back to search the other path."

And we could cross the Aquavian bridge to go on our own, Laurel added silently.

The boats were right where they left them. Logan offered to drive, giving Dawn a moment to relish the relief and excitement that stirred within her.

They would meet the Ides of March deadline. Dawn had breathing room to plan next steps after their move tonight. She wouldn't tell Logan she was moving, but she was determined to find a way to meet up with him for his marathon. After all, he had done so much to support her. *It's the least I could do*, she thought.

CHAPTER 24

THE MORNING SUNLIGHT momentarily blinded Dawn and her entourage as their boats emerged from the Underground River. After their eyes adjusted, Echo picked up speed and Logan followed. They were halfway to the forest when Lopple spotted black birds in the sky, silhouetted against the sun. "We have company," he said, alarm in his voice. He turned toward Ezra, and something else caught his attention that made him mutter under his breath.

An uncanny similarity to foreign curse words, Dawn thought.

Echo slowed the boat, and Logan nearly collided with him before he changed course.

"Head back toward the cave," Ezra instructed calmly.

Echo immediately obeyed, while Logan struggled to reorient the canoe.

"What is it? The soufors?" Dawn guessed. She couldn't sense their auras. She looked up, using her hand to shield her eyes, and saw that the three silhouettes approaching from the forest were the size of humans. They *weren't* birds. Each creature had the wings of an eagle, a woman's face and body covered with feathers, and talons for feet.

"They're sirens!" Laurel shouted.

Dawn spotted Echo hastily fishing something from his pocket, putting them in his ears. The sirens were nearly upon them. She unzipped a pocket in her backpack and pulled out a firearm with the silencer attached, then handed it to Logan.

"Just in case," she told him.

"What's going on—what did she call them?" Logan asked, trying to steer while looking back at the winged creatures.

"I'm not sure . . ." Explaining what they were wouldn't make any sense to him, Dawn knew. They had not quite reached the shelter of the cave when Dawn saw what Lopple had cursed at: Two birds of prey came into view, flying toward them from the direction of the cave.

Diurlaxes. And their hooded riders—the soufors!

The riders swooped down at them and banked a hard left. Dawn caught sight of their menacing faces—the Inked Man and Blade.

Everyone in the canoes ducked for cover, and Logan and Echo had no choice but to cut the motors; they couldn't see where they were going.

We're dead in the water! Dawn's heart pounded so rapidly she thought it might burst.

"What the hell is happening?" Logan yelled in confusion.

The sirens swooped toward them, talons grasping, narrowly missing their prey.

"They're here!" Ezra said, pointing to another pair of diurlax riders hot on the tails of the sirens.

Dawn recognized them instantly, relief giving her a brief respite: the woman with the braids on the council . . . and Dalton riding Fenno.

The boat rocked violently when Ezra and Lopple took to the skies of their own power. Two coils, unsprung. Logan stared at them, open mouthed.

Lopple can fly—he's Etheran, Dawn realized.

"Cover your ears!" Ezra barked from above. "Laurel, into the water!"

Without hesitation, Laurel dove into the murky water, leaving Echo alone in the boat as it swayed dangerously. He fell to his knees, curling up tightly and covered his ears.

Dawn was still seated facing Logan, clutching her backpack, when a piercing siren cry cut through the air. She felt a shield of aura envelop her—unsure if it was her own—but the screeching sound still hit her like shockwaves from a blast. She cried out as her head throbbed from the splitting pain. Losing her balance, she fell backward and landed on the life vests.

Logan was not so lucky. He had no shield of aura, and he hadn't covered his ears in time.

Dawn heard him cry out in agony. She gazed up at the sky in a daze, trying to get her bearings. It hurt to breathe. It hurt to move. Above her, shadows of riders, diurlaxes, and sirens embroiled in battle blurred together. Some hurled explosive fireballs, while talons and hooked beaks reached for their enemies. It was impossible to recognize friend from foe.

A blade sailed through the air, hitting the wing of a diurlax. The grayish-white bird shrieked as it flailed in the sky and retreated for land. The rider, who was smaller in stature, dismounted and took to the skies, refusing to leave the dogfight.

It has to be Dalton.

Logan groaned again. *Move*, Dawn willed her limbs. With her head still throbbing, she managed to sit up and peer at him. He was unconscious, lying on his side, head on the seat; blood trickled from his ear. Although his eyes remained closed, he grimaced.

In the fray, someone ordered, "Stay down!"

She felt the breath knock out of her as she hit the life vests again. Above, the sharp talons of a siren reached for her and missed their mark. Instead, they grabbed hold of Logan, piercing his shoulder and pulling him skyward.

Dawn watched in horror as his limp body ascended. She was alone in the boat—but not defenseless. She crawled to where Logan lay and found her gun, aiming it at the creature who was flying away with him.

The boat was still swaying, and the winged woman was gaining altitude, but Dawn steadied herself on her knees. She squeezed the trigger, and a pop rang through the air. The piercing screeches of the siren let Dawn know she hit her target.

The creature released its unconscious prey from her taloned grip, and Logan fell like an anchor into the water. The siren escaped to land, its flight erratic.

Dawn holstered the gun and stood up, about to dive into the water after Logan when she saw Laurel surface.

I got him, Laurel projected. She swam in mermaid form with swiftness and ease, keeping Logan's head above water, pulling him toward the cave.

"Get to the cave!" someone ordered from above as a sumatok blasted a diurlax out of the air and into the water.

Dawn sat back down shaking, adrenaline and shock coursing through her in equal measure. She started the motor, then followed Echo, who was just ahead.

Glancing back, she saw two more diurlax riders advance toward the fight. That seemed to be Ezra's and Lopple's cue to leave, and both flew toward the boats as Laurel reached the mouth of the cave.

"My friends will hold them off," Ezra said without looking back.

Blade broke away from the fray, her diurlax on Lopple's heels as she called out to her partner, enraged, "They're getting away with the girl!"

A fireball took form in her hand, and just as she was about to hurl it at Lopple's back, a series of powerful jet streams of water shot up, hitting her and her diurlax. The surprised bird halted in mid-air, causing Blade to lose balance and nearly fall off.

The water had extinguished the energy blast, and before the soufor could reform it, she was forced to conjure shields to block sumatoks from a red-haired rider.

Go! We'll hold them off, projected a voice that belonged to Fanto.

Laurel disappeared into the cave first with Logan in tow.

Echo yelped as Lopple dropped into his moving canoe, while Ezra descended more gracefully into Dawn's. Both were glistening with sweat, but they were unscathed.

"Let's get Logan back into the boat!" Dawn cried.

"There's no time," Ezra said.

Laurel agreed. "Siren talons are poisonous—the water will wash some of it out."

The cave's darkness engulfed them. Echo turned on his flashlight, but Lopple and Ezra used bright orbs procured by their en to light the way. There was no point in hiding their abilities after everything Echo had seen.

Their orbs floated ahead of them, and their light was so bright that the bats chirped and fluttered about, confused by the sudden disturbance.

Dawn and her friends moved quickly, listening for sounds of the battle. Even Echo pulled out his earplugs and stuffed them back in his pocket.

"The soufors are advancing toward us," Ezra said. "Dalton and the others must be having a hard time with the sirens."

"Wh-what are we going to do?" Echo's voice quivered.

They had reached the fork in the cave, when a scraping sound—like talons against rock—could be heard in the distance. Dawn sensed the soufors' auras as they entered the cave with their diurlaxes.

"We'll take the tunnel," Ezra said, flying out of the boat and landing on the cave floor.

"That's a dead end," Echo protested.

There's an Aquavian bridge, I'm sure of it, Laurel projected to everyone except Echo.

Lopple nodded and tossed his wrist cuff at Ezra, who caught it. *My comm stone*, he projected, *Comm Marion to unlock the bridge.* He wiped the sweat trickling from his temples. "Echo, you and I will follow the Underground River and exit the cave in the back. The huntersss are after Dawn."

Ezra lifted Logan out of the water with a simple wave of his hand while Laurel shifted and got herself out. As Logan's comatose body floated gently to the cave floor, Dawn grabbed her backpack and scrambled out of the boat.

"This wasn't supposed to happen," she whispered, kneeling at Logan's side and taking his hand. He looked pale and his shoulder wounds oozed blood, but his chest was rising and falling slowly.

"Th-This isn't my first time seeing sirens," Echo admitted. "I've seen what they've done to men. No one could survive such an attack. You should leave him here. He'll slow you down."

Dawn blinked back her tears and cast him an incendiary glare.

"We won't leave him behind," Ezra assured, before she could get a word in. Then, using his aura, he lifted Logan upright into the air. Dawn stood, still clutching his hand.

"I'll carry him." Ezra knelt down and Dawn helped secure Logan on his back, the same way he had carried her on Mount Tencho.

Ezra rose to his feet as they heard more noise coming from the path they had taken. The diurlaxes couldn't have gone far into the cave, but the soufors were gaining on them despite being pursued by the other Lumen.

Before they went their separate ways, Dawn offered Echo her gun. Despite his lack of faith in Logan's condition, she didn't wish Echo any ill will.

"I hope you get home safely, Miss Dawn," Echo replied to the gesture, hesitating once before taking the weapon. Then he and Lopple sped off in the canoe.

Laurel led the way as the group shuffled through the tunnel as fast as they could. Despite Logan's weight and Ezra having to crouch down even further to avoid hitting the low ceiling, they burst through the chamber's opening and into the lake without a moment to spare.

They were waist-deep in the water when Laurel stopped them from going any deeper.

"I'll go first to activate the water bridge," Laurel panted. "It's deeper than it looks."

A loud pop reverberated through the cave, making Laurel flinch.

"Hurry. Take Dawn with you," Ezra urged. "I've commed Marion to tell her you're crossing soon."

"No, take Logan," Dawn insisted.

Ezra hesitated.

"Logan. Goes. First," she said with ferocity.

Ezra gave in and lowered Logan into the water, his blood making the water even murkier. Laurel shifted into her Aquavian form, wrapped an arm around Logan's neck, and descended with him into the lake.

More gunshots rang through the cave, and shouts and yells followed.

Dawn watched, completely unsettled, as Laurel's mermaid fin disappeared from view, then reappeared again as her orb of light illuminated the water's depths. As she counted the seconds that passed, she prayed Laurel kept track of how long Logan was without air.

Their figures got blurrier, then they seemed to hover near a spot that glowed green.

"It's been more than thirty seconds," Dawn whispered. *A damn eternity.* "What's taking so long?!"

Ezra looked back at the tunnel's opening. Dawn could feel anger coursing through him—or was it her own panic? Someone was making their way to them, their light growing brighter from the tunnel. Taunting voices echoed in Etherish through the passage, followed by derisive laughter. Ezra extinguished his orb light and grabbed Dawn's arm.

Deep breath, he projected. Then they plunged headfirst into the water.

In the darkness, Dawn could barely see, but she could no longer sense Laurel and Logan. The backpack helped weigh her down, and she kicked with all her might to descend at the same pace as Ezra. Her head and ears ached, the mounting pressure worsening every second.

Ezra's grip tightened around her arm as he pulled her deeper, then he let her go as he turned back toward the surface. *Keep going!* he projected.

Dawn sensed movement above—the soufors were in the lake! She was out of breath, fighting the involuntary urge to inhale. The pain in her ears intensified and she tried to ignore it. Something glowed green. She reached out with her hand and made contact with a smooth rock wall—the bridge! It began to swirl, connecting the space between two places. Blurring the lines between reality and dreams.

The soufors' hateful aura—shaped as spears—pierced through the water, heading straight toward them. Dawn braced herself but never felt the hit. Their aura spears collided with Ezra's shield—warm and reassuring—which encircled them. A glowing sphere that could not be penetrated.

And yet, it was too late. Darkness closed in on Dawn, and the last thing she felt was water entering her lungs.

CHAPTER 25

OVERLAPPING VOICES TWISTED and tumbled around the corners of Dawn's mind. She struggled to open her eyes, stuck between the world of the dreaming and the awake.

"Are you sure you got all the water out of her lungs?"

"Yes. Look. She's regaining consciousness."

"What was that noise?"

"The porus are being attacked—we're being ambushed!"

"It's Reed. He commed me . . . my father has returned!"

"Go to him. Tell him everything that's happened."

"Laurel, you can't come back here. We'll comm you when it's safe."

After an extraordinary amount of effort, Dawn managed to open her eyes. She tried to sit up, coughing and sputtering, but was only able to prop herself up on one arm. Pain shot through her chest, her lungs ached with every breath, and a bitter metallic taste lingered in her mouth. She found herself on the living room's cold hard floor, her clothes still soaked from the lake.

Ezra helped her sit up and wrapped a warm blanket around her.

Outside, sounds of screeching and explosions were loud enough to rattle the windows.

The cheval mirror had been moved into the living room, next to the laundry room door. A smeared trail of blood came from that room, and Dawn's eyes traced it all the way behind her. She turned to find where it led, and saw Marion crouched near Logan, obstructing his upper torso from her view.

"Logan!" Dawn screamed, ignoring the pain in her lungs and crawling around Marion to find him unconscious and shirtless on the floor.

Hikaru held Logan's arm still. Scissors lay on the floor, along with a pile of wet towels, a cut up shirt, and blood-stained gauze. Marion poured something clear into Logan's wound that fizzed as rivulets of blood trickled from his gaping shoulder wounds. Logan's eyes stayed shut, but he winced as he groaned.

A tapping sound on the window momentarily distracted Dawn. She whipped her head to check where the noise came from and saw white hailstones against the night sky, pelting the glass.

"We're disinfecting his wounds," Marion said, maintaining her composure, yet a tremor of panic in her voice gave her away. "Laurel removed the siren poison, but he's lost too much blood."

More shouts and explosions erupted outside. Dawn glanced at the window again to see people in hoods—the sangwor—flitting through the air, hurling fireballs and aura weapons at Sid's agents on site. A diurlax sailed by as a whirlwind of hail swept past. The scene outside was just as chaotic as the one they had left.

"We need to get out of here." As Marion spoke, a golf-ball sized hailstone smashed through the bay window.

Dawn flinched as shattered glass shards and hail rained on them, but Ezra had shields up in an instant. He flitted toward the window while muttering a comm to someone.

Hikaru kept his attention on Logan, waving his hand over the pierced flesh; the healing crystals he held in his other hand shimmered. Dawn watched in awe as Logan's wounds healed and closed rapidly. The skin that had been punctured just moments before was now new, pink flesh with a fresh scar.

"We can't bring him with us," Marion said.

Hikaru turned to Dawn. "He needs an emergency blood transfusion—I can take him to a hospital."

Dawn pleaded with them. "There must be another way. We have to take him with us!"

"You already know what must be done," Marion reminded her.

Right. Erase his memory and leave him here, Dawn thought bitterly. She looked upon Logan's pale face—he winced, yet his eyes remained closed.

Taking his hand in hers, she leaned in close to his ear and whispered, "I'll make a way for us. I promise."

She straightened, still holding Logan's hand, and looked at Hikaru. On the verge of tears, she gave him a single nod.

Hikaru waved his hand over Logan's head, and at once, his grimace smoothed to a peaceful expression. "I'll erase his memory at the hospital. We need to go."

"You'll have to drive him." Marion's voice rose above the sumatoks from outside, which grew louder and more frequent. "There's no way you'll be able to fly out of here."

Hikaru darted toward the garage. With a flick of his hand, Ezra floated an unconscious Logan to follow the healer, as if he was wheeled away on an invisible stretcher. Dawn was forced to let go of his hand, hoping this wasn't the last time she'd see him.

"We're leaving, Dawn!" Marion said, pulling her up by the shoulders.

Another window shattered and a hooded flier, who stood outside of it, spotted Dawn. He raised his hand toward her, but Ezra flicked his wrists and sent the piano smashing into their foe. A cacophony of notes, splintering wood, and breaking glass filled the living room.

Dawn yelped as Marion shielded her with her own body, dropping back to the floor. Dawn scrambled to her feet in time to see the vehicle vanish in stealth mode as the garage door facing the street opened. The hail and rain pelted the car, creating a barely visible outline as Hikaru sped away.

The garage door closed, but not before two sangwor slipped inside and flew right toward Dawn.

"Why are you still here?" Ezra shouted at Dawn, soaring to clash with the intruders in the air. He sent two aura blades whirling, faster than the wind, striking the assailants.

"I need the journal!" Dawn sprinted toward the study, flung the door open and spotted the cognac book on the desk next to the ormolu clock. As she grabbed the journal, the window in the study exploded. She raised the journal to cover her face as glass shards went flying.

A second after, Dawn risked a look at the window. Ezra was already there, fighting the intruder.

"Get out of here!" He turned his head and raised his hand toward her. "Marion, the bridge!"

Dawn clutched the journal, her feet lifting off the ground. She was flung backward toward the mirror. Ezra's hand was still outstretched toward her, and within that millisecond, things seemed to move in slow motion.

The sangwor behind him seized this window of opportunity. He raised his hands above his hood, and where there was nothing a fraction of a second ago, appeared a long, pointed dagger of aura.

Dawn's eyes widened as she witnessed the sangwor sink his aura blade deep into Ezra's back. There was no time to shout a warning, let alone think it. Dawn hadn't even blinked.

Immediately, Ezra's aura dissipated, replaced with a sense of realization and pain. Dawn braced herself as she hit the living room floor and rolled. Sharp pain from the clutter stung her arms and back, but she forced herself up on her knees and palms, sucking a breath in through her teeth as broken pieces of glass cut deeper.

Turning toward the study, Dawn saw Ezra had recovered—at least momentarily—to dodge two of the sangwor's punches at break-neck speed. The sangwor's fists were a blur as he pounded the hickory floor, causing the hardwood boards to break and crack.

Against the odds, Ezra had rolled back on his feet, to the other side of the room, but the sangwor sent a powerful aura kick that plowed into Ezra.

Why didn't Ezra shield himself?!

Still on her knees, she picked up a piece of debris—a wooden plank with nails poking through—and took aim to hurl it at the intruder when something round and small smacked the sangwor in the back. A cloud of fine powder released on impact. It didn't injure the sangwor, but the dust sent him into a dazed stupor. Before the cloud cleared, Marion hurled another sack of her mystery concoction at him.

Dawn threw the debris, but at the same time, Hiro nudged her, demanding her attention and throwing her off balance. The plank missed the sangwor, who shook his drowsiness off and once more catapulted himself toward Ezra. With anger renewed, he picked Ezra up from the floor and tossed him against the ceiling like a rag doll. There, Ezra stayed pinned, clutching his throat as the sangwor used his aura to choke the life out of him.

Marion pulled Dawn up to her feet and toward the bridge. "We must leave!"

"He's going to die!" Dawn said but knew Marion was right. If they stayed, they'd only be putting themselves in harm's way. What good would their deaths do with a failed mission?

Ezra's feet stopped kicking as he gasped for air and his eyes rolled back in his head—the kind of thing that happened in exorcism movies.

A hooded flier came crashing through what remained of the window to the study, delivering a powerful aura kick to the sangwor, and all three of them fell to the floor. Hiro bounded to Ezra and pulled him by his cloak away from the scuffle.

The flier's hood fell back to reveal fire-engine red hair—*Sid!* Dawn was so relieved to see her, and even more surprised that she had landed three heart-stopping punches on the sangwor before her hood had fallen all the way back.

"Let's move!" Marion ordered, forcefully pulling Dawn toward the bridge. Marion stepped through clutching Dawn's arm.

Wait—the dysprosia! Dawn pointed to her backpack that was out of reach, laying in the rubble on the living room floor.

Hiro! Marion projected as she pulled Dawn through the mirror.

They stumbled onto the floor of a room she didn't recognize.

Dawn stared, panic stricken, at the swirling bridge—its movement was slowing down. The plant they sacrificed everything for was left on the other side. Just before the last swirls turned solid, Hiro leapt through with Dawn's backpack, its strap secured in his mouth, and collided with her on the floor.

"Hiro!" Marion half-sobbed, half-laughed in relief as she and Dawn hugged the loyal husky.

After taking a few minutes to collect themselves, Marion stood and gingerly helped Dawn up, gently brushing off shards of glass and debris from Dawn's clothes and hair. She explained what happened while Dawn was passed out.

"I commed Ezra and Sid to destroy the bridge after we crossed. Hikaru will need to find another bridge." Marion's calm and steady voice could not hide the worry gnawing at her heart. "There's something you should know about Hikaru. I've been able to stay in contact with him through Hiro. Hiro is his poru."

Dawn stared at her housekeeper with mouth agape. When the shock subsided, she admitted, "I *did* find it unusual Hiro had lived so long—I thought he was the healthiest husky! But now it makes sense that he's been sharing human years with someone. Hikaru has been with you all along."

"He's been with *us* all along." Marion bent down to pat Hiro on the head, scratching behind his ears. "It looks like Hikaru has already left the hospital, and he'll be on his way here soon."

"And where is *here*?"

"Copenhagen, Denmark."

Dawn turned around, taking in her surroundings. The room they were in was nearly empty except for a tan sofa bench. Beside it lay a cushioned bed for Hiro, and the canine had already found his way there to occupy it.

Morning light filtered in through the sheer curtains draped over the floor-to-ceiling windows across the room. The walls and minimal lighting cast a soft hue around the space. Dawn turned to examine the bridge they had crossed—a framed, square mirror, extending from the floor to about eight feet high.

Large enough for a horse to go through, she mused.

It took up most of the dividing wall. The gems embedded into the wooden frame served as the room's only embellished piece, a stark juxtaposition with the space's monochrome tans and soft whites.

She frowned, letting out an exhalation heavy with misery and guilt. *Here I am, safe and sound, while Logan is in the hospital, Ezra is fighting for his life, and Lopple . . .*

She looked at her reflection, abandoning her train of thought. The woman staring back at her was unrecognizable. A face full of cuts and scrapes, a tangled mess of hair, torn, damp clothes, and bits of glass and debris still clinging to her from head to toe.

"What happens now?" Dawn asked Marion.

"We wait," her housekeeper said quietly. "Waiting is the hardest."

While they waited, Marion urged Dawn to get cleaned up and rest. They would be most helpful to the others if they were refreshed and thinking clearly. As Dawn's adrenaline spike waned, she found herself exhausted, body aching, and stomach grumbling. She forced herself to shower, dab ointment on all her cuts and scrapes, and change into clean clothes.

Both women sat in the dining room, sipping hot tofu soup. They didn't utter a word to each other until they were finished.

"Miss M.," Dawn started, after taking a sip of her freshly brewed kudzukan tea, "now that we have the dysprosia, how will my dad contact us?"

"He has a way of contacting you when the time is right. The Ides of March is tomorrow. He'll get in touch soon. I placed the plant container in the pantry for now to keep it in the dark."

Dawn nodded. "I miss him."

"Me too. He's been preparing the lab to harvest the plant. My best guess is he's taking advantage of the full moon."

After a moment of sipping their tea in quiet contemplation, Dawn reached for a piece of fudge. It was one of Marion's specialty desserts, perhaps to remind them of the comforts they had although things were in a moment of transition. Dawn sunk her teeth into a corner of the decadent confection, wondering what Lopple would say if he tried it. "I should tell you everything that happened in the cave."

"Let's wait for Hikaru to arrive so he can hear it too. Laurel did give us, I assume, a very condensed version of what happened." Marion took a fudge square for herself and eyed Dawn for her reaction. "There's something else I wanted to tell you. Hikaru and I are married."

"What?!" she coughed, after just sipping some tea.

"We'll be celebrating our tenth anniversary in a few months."

Dawn stared at her housekeeper, speechless. In all her life, she had known Miss M. to be devoted to her work and had only recently discovered she did indeed have a personal life—one that apparently very much included their family healer, Hikaru Kawasaki.

"H-how did . . . er, when did this all . . ." Dawn sputtered, failing to form coherent sentences.

Her housekeeper smiled warmly. "I met him shortly after I met your mother. He taught me all about plants, healing herbs, and balms. I was a slow learner, but he was kind and patient. He was fascinating. A man of few words, and I hung on every one of them."

"I guess it's time I started calling you Mrs. M.!"

Marion chuckled, then her face transformed into a more serious expression as she recalled more of her past. "When your mother found me in South Africa, I was sixteen, on the streets, barely surviving. She saw something in me." Marion shook her head slightly, doubting her own statement. "She took me in and got me to the right doctors. I was so ill at the time; I needed surgery."

Marion stared into space, reliving the trauma and pain of her past.

"We don't have to talk about it if you don't want to," Dawn said softly as she put her hand over her housekeeper's clenched fist. "We've been through enough this week."

A quiet laugh escaped the woman's mouth as she relaxed her hand.

Marion shared a few more stories about her and Hikaru, how he always appeared with sunflowers for her, the way he'd tell her he missed her even though he saw her every day, how he relocated to live nearby whenever they moved (which was a lot), and the myriad things he did to make her feel special.

Dawn was happy her housekeeper had found love despite not being aware of it all these years. A tinge of envy was also at play, but it gave Dawn hope. *Miss M. and Hikaru managed to make things work despite Howel's relocations. I, too, will find a way for me and Logan*, she vowed.

CHAPTER 26

AFTER LUNCH, MARION gave Dawn a tour of the penthouse, which had five suites on the top three levels of a luxury skyscraper. Exhausted and sore, Dawn dozed off in the great room waiting for Hikaru to arrive.

It felt like she had just closed her eyes when she was awoken by the healer's voice. She sat up on the sofa to find Hikaru and Marion standing in front of the bridge in a tight embrace, as if they hadn't seen each other in ages. Outside, the late afternoon sun still shone brightly, bathing the room in its golden hour light.

Their joyful reunion, however, was short lived. Marion pulled away with an alarmed look. "Sid commed! Ezra and his parents need refuge immediately . . . and Ezra needs a healer."

Hikaru sprinted upstairs as Marion activated the bridge. The mirror swirled in front of her, and she took a step back as a hooded man came through supporting a barely conscious Ezra. Hiro whined from his dog bed.

Anxiety and shock flooded her senses as she leapt up from the sofa. Ezra was a wreck—covered in blood and bruises. Hikaru had returned with his medical bag, and he and the hooded man removed Ezra's cloak and laid him down where she had been sitting a moment ago.

Before the bridge returned to its mirror state, a tan-skinned woman stepped through. Her mere presence overwhelmed Dawn with grief. They locked eyes, and the woman rushed into Dawn's arms, sobbing uncontrollably.

Taken by surprise, Dawn let the distraught stranger hug her and cry into her shoulder. Marion shot Dawn a questioning look that asked, *You know Ezra's mother?*

I've never seen this woman before in my life! Dawn countered.

With a small pocket knife, Hikaru cut through Ezra's shirt. As the fabric fell away, Dawn saw from the corner of her eye what looked like first-degree burn marks on his chest and neck.

"Let's get him into the room," Hikaru said urgently.

"Use Dawn's suite," Marion said. "The other room has a futon that isn't set up yet."

Hikaru and the hooded man quickly hoisted Ezra up and out of sight. "Marion," Hikaru's disembodied voice called from the room, "I'll need a pitcher of water and plenty of towels . . . and brewed moonshade leaves."

Marion sprang into action. Dawn and Ezra's mom were left standing in the great room, with Dawn awkwardly patting the woman's back. A minute later, Marion dashed into the room with Hikaru's requested supplies and out came the man, shutting the door behind him. He pulled back his hood, revealing his tired, lined face.

He approached Dawn and gently pulled the sobbing woman away. "We are Ezra's parents," he said with a thick accent Dawn couldn't place. He held his wife's shoulders as she continued to weep. "I'm Ezekiel, and this is Teborah, known in the Etheran realm as the Lady of Dreams."

Dawn drew in a shaky breath, recovering from her shock. "I-I'm Dawn," she said, considering whether she should say she was a friend of Ezra. After all, it was *her* fault that he was injured. Ezra had joined *her* mission, and he had been at *her* house, fighting with the sangwor so she and Marion could escape. "I'm so sorry about Ezra. If it weren't for—"

Ezekiel held up his palm. "There's no need to apologize. Ezra merely fulfilled his duty."

Teborah, who had her face buried in her hands, cried louder upon hearing her son's name.

"Please pardon my wife," Ezekiel said softly. "She is still grieving for our daughter, Stralla, and to see our firstborn in this state is . . ." He paused, patting his wife's back to comfort her. "She is a seer and gets confused sometimes. There are . . . occurrences she has seen that have not yet come to pass. Befriending you was likely one of those occurrences."

Dawn nodded, still slightly confused.

"Is there a room where she can rest for a while?"

Dawn ushered them toward the empty suite. "Do you need help with the futon?"

"We'll manage. You have our thanks," he said as he and his wife entered the room.

Sitting back on the sofa, Dawn caught her reflection in the mirror—haggard and unsettled. Leaning forward on her arms on her legs, she let her head hang, closed her eyes, and tried to slow her breathing. It didn't do much to help the overwhelming sadness and anxiety that worked over her. A door opened and she looked up.

Marion emerged from the room with an empty tray, closing the door behind her. "Ezra has some broken ribs, and he is carrying negative en that's blocking his own aura . . . but he'll live." She looked Dawn over. "You look pale. What's wrong?"

"I'm just catching my breath." She attempted to stand but sat back down when her legs threatened to give way. "Ezra's parents are in that suite for now. I hope that's okay."

"Of course." She scanned Dawn with concern. "How about we get some fresh air on the balcony after I prepare more supplies for Hikaru?"

Dawn swallowed and nodded.

The late afternoon air chilled Dawn to the bone even with outerwear, and her teeth chattered the second she took a breath outside.

The side of the balcony opened to a spacious patio to host outdoor festivities. There was an expandable dining table, as well as heating lamps, a grill, and various nodes and plugins for virtual entertainment. Dawn followed Marion as she walked around the balcony, then up a flight of stairs that led to the roof.

When they reached the top, Dawn took in a flourishing garden full of hardy, winter plants—it must've taken her dedicated housekeeper months. She opened the greenhouse door for them, and they rushed inside, where it was considerably warmer.

"I should've brought a scarf and gloves," Dawn chattered, rubbing her hands together.

"We'll get used to the weather soon enough," Marion said. She motioned for them to sit on a bench that gave them a view of the Copenhagen skyline. "Besides, we don't know how long we'll be staying here."

"How did you find this place? Does Uncle Jett own it?"

"No, I am in contact with his property manager—one who understands Lumen travel methods, hence, the bridge. Jett doesn't know where we are, and it is safer that way."

They sat in the quiet of the greenhouse as the golden hour transitioned to twilight. The city that surrounded them roused to life—lights glowing, air and ground traffic bustling.

Marion broke their silence. "I've heard that Ezra's mother is a prophet of sorts. Is that why she recognized you?"

"I think so . . . Ezra's dad said something about that. It felt both strange and familiar being hugged by her . . . like she's known me for a *long* time." Dawn chuckled.

"Do you feel better now?"

"Yes, but I can feel everyone's emotions much more. The grief of Ezra's mom is . . . overwhelming. My shielding doesn't seem to help," she explained, hugging her own arms. "Is this normal? Did this happen to you when you were learning to shield?"

"I cannot say that I experienced others' emotions in an over-whelming sense, but Hikaru may have some thoughts on it. You can ask him when he's done treating Ezra.

Another thought came to her. "Earlier, you said that Ezra had negative en that blocked his own aura. What does that mean?"

Marion hesitated, her eyes hinting that she didn't want to add to Dawn's burden.

"Miss M., tell me. Please," Dawn urged.

Marion conceded. "When Ezra fought the sangwor, he must've been hurt by their negative aura, and it blocked his own. He's unable to use his own aura abilities."

Dawn pictured the moment Ezra got stabbed in the back with an aura blade. He had absorbed all that negative energy, she realized. "When will he recover?"

"It is hard to say. Healing takes time. For now, he is a regular human being."

A regular human being. The words haunted Dawn. Going from Lumen to reg—Ezra's injuries were *that* debilitating, and Dawn knew it was *her* fault. Her thoughts strayed to Logan; she couldn't guess whose injuries were worse, but she was certain of one thing: People were getting hurt *because of her*.

"Dawn, you mustn't blame yourself for what happened," Marion soothed.

"And what about Echo and Lopple?" Dawn shot back. "There were gunshots and—"

"Look at me," Marion said both sternly and gently. "I'll say it again: You mustn't blame yourself. I *know* Howel—he would've made sure that both Echo and Lopple knew the risks. They made their choice."

Dawn nodded as she looked at her housekeeper but couldn't dispel the guilt that clung to her like her own shadow. Did Echo truly consider he might not've survived the day? Was giving him a gun all she could've done to keep him safe? And what about Lopple? She had doubted him, thought him untrustworthy at times, but he had bought her, Logan, and Ezra time to escape . . . and sacrificed his life in doing so.

It's all. My. Fault.

When Hikaru finally trudged out of Dawn's room, he seemed like he had aged ten years. Fatigue made the fine lines on his face look more pronounced. Dawn approached him before he could get to the dining table, where Marion had a bowl of hot soup waiting for him.

"Hikaru," she started, intending to ask about Logan.

"Ezra is doing fine," Hikaru cut in, "but I've depleted my healing aura on him. Your cuts and scrapes will have to wait until tomorrow."

Instantly self-conscious, Dawn's hand flew up to cover the cuts on her face she had forgotten about. "I, uh, actually wanted to ask you about Logan. How was he when you left?"

"Ah, right," he said, rubbing his eyes. "The blood transfusion was successful. He is in a deep sleep to get the rest he needs to recover. He should wake in a few days."

"And his memories?"

Hikaru gently patted Dawn's shoulder. "I removed his memories of us starting with your trip to the Heavenly Pit."

That was better than Dawn had hoped. At least Hikaru hadn't erased her completely.

"How did you explain his injuries?"

"I told the hospital staff that he was poisoned from some kind of bug bite on a hike, and that he collapsed and hit his shoulder," he said, shuffling to the dining room. "I created a different memory and projected it to him. It will be hazy, but it should stick."

He *created* a memory for Logan, she realized, filing it away. *Is creating memories an aura ability that I could learn?*

She followed Hikaru. "I never got to thank you, Hikaru, for everything. Thank you for healing Logan and for taking care of me and Miss M. all these years."

Marion, who was preparing tomorrow's meals in the kitchen, stopped what she was doing and smiled at them.

The healer seemed taken aback. He simply responded with a short, "un," a Japanese way of acknowledgment.

Marion smirked. "I told her about us. And that Hiro is your poru."

"Ah," Hikaru said, nodding and facing Dawn with a look of sincerity. "I do regret that we couldn't tell you sooner. Only Howel knew. We kept our relationship hidden from everyone else; it was too great a risk that Malstrom's spies might find out and leverage this against us, and we couldn't have others inadvertently revealing it to you."

"I understand. Truly."

Marion brought tea to the table and sat next to him, brushing her shoulder next to his—her way of telling him that the three of them were fine. There were no grudges to be held.

Past midnight, Dawn tossed and turned on the sofa, unable to find a comfortable spot. While the blankets were soft and she was physically tired, she still felt mentally unsettled. On the floor, a few feet away from the sofa, Marion and Hikaru were sound asleep on their futon. (Marion thought it best that everyone stay on the same floor for the night.)

Dawn's tired eyes looked upon them with envy. They had so quickly fallen asleep that she was convinced they had used their aura abilities. There was only one other person in the penthouse who was still awake: Teborah, the Lady of Dreams.

The greenhouse had provided respite from Teborah's grief. Now, it had returned, welling up inside both Teborah *and* Dawn like an endless, flowing river. Worse still, Teborah's other emotions were complex. A whirlwind of resentment, gratitude, relief, wishfulness, and more; experiencing them simultaneously was driving Dawn nuts. She wished she could shield herself from them, but exhaustion—or maybe bridge lag, in her case—had taken its toll.

Dawn sat up and let out an exasperated sigh. She decided to get the journal and go out to the balcony. A distraction was what she needed, and anything was better than staying put.

Silently, she rose from the couch and tiptoed to the door of her room, careful not to wake Hiro. She very slowly turned the knob, opening it just a crack. When she was sure no one had heard her, she turned on her phone flashlight and slipped inside. Trying to make as little sound as humanly possible, she held her breath and scurried to the bedside table, shining her light on the spot where she had left the journal.

In its place was a small tray that held a colorful assortment of Hikaru's healing crystals.

Dawn scanned the area, and her eyes landed on Ezra's silhouette, who was slightly propped up with pillows. In the light of her mobile device, she could see the burn marks on his chest and neck, as well as the skin that had turned a bluish purple—bruises from the beating he took. Her eyes met his. He was squinting at her, adjusting to the light.

She inhaled sharply, surprised to find him awake. The scent of menthol flooded her nostrils. "I-I'm sorry to wake you," she whispered. "I just came in to get the journal."

Ezra closed his eyes, then opened them again lethargically. "Are you all right?" he asked in a voice so soft, Dawn wasn't sure whether he had actually spoken.

"What?" she responded automatically.

"Are you all right?" Ezra whispered again, his lips barely moving.

Did he really ask if I'm all right, considering the condition he's *in?* The absurdity of it almost made her scoff out loud. "Yes, of course I'm all right," she breathed, after too long a pause.

He closed his eyes sleepily.

Dawn opened the single drawer of the bedside table and found the book she was looking for. As she carefully shut the drawer, she checked Ezra again. His eyes were still closed, and he hadn't moved. She thought about how he'd selflessly fought to get Logan and her to safety—a sacrifice that had brought immense pain to his mother and robbed him of his Lumen abilities for who knows how long.

"Thank you for saving Logan and me," Dawn whispered, unsure if Ezra was still conscious. "We owe you our lives."

Ezra's neck bobbed as he swallowed, but he remained silent, and his eyes stayed closed.

Before she left, she grabbed her dad's cloak from the closet, its cloud-like colors changing as the light struck it.

The shepra fabric was much warmer than her winter coat despite its weightlessness. The only parts of her body still cold were her hands and face, as they were exposed to the frigid gusts of wind. She turned on a heating lamp, then sat at the outdoor dining table with the journal.

Today was the Ides of March. Her heart rate doubling, she turned to the page she dog-eared—the entry on dysprosia. The sketch and scrawled caption looked as bare as it did before: "Strong roots. <u>Do not touch.</u>"

But I did touch it. It moved—pulsated, she shuddered as she remembered the sensation. *Lopple didn't want to use his bare hands. Did it change me?*

After scouring the page for more words along the margins, and finding nothing, she gave up. Howel would have to explain this unsolved mystery.

Medicinal plant references interested her for a few minutes. As expected, moonshade was listed as a remedy for aura block. She squinted at the tiny sketch—a leafy, veiny plant.

"X8, where do moonshade leaves grow?" Dawn asked, trying to keep her voice down.

"I'm not sure," the AI replied on Dawn's mobile device. My knowledge bank doesn't have an exact match to moonshade. Would you like me to run an online search?"

"Sure."

"My search didn't return any exact results," X8 said a moment later. "But I can tell you where moon*shadow* flowers and other similar plants grow."

"Never mind," Dawn whispered as she closed the journal. She looked up at the cloudless night sky, expecting to see darkness and twinkling lights, but gasped at the shimmering sliver of green and purple that illuminated the heavens.

She stood up and walked to the edge of the frameless balcony glass, marveling at the view. A few minutes passed, and the sorrow that weighed her heart down ebbed ever so slightly.

"It is beautiful, isn't it?" a woman asked behind her.

Dawn jumped and clutched her heart, then whirled around to find Ezra's mother in her own shepra cloak. She stood in the dark like a spectral figure.

"In Etero, the aurora borealis is a wonder to behold, unlike any-thing you've ever seen," Teborah said. She took her place next to Dawn, still gazing at the ethereal lights. "It is comforting to see them from down here too. We are all under the same sky."

"Yeah, um, yes," Dawn said, finding her voice. "I had no idea the northern lights could be seen from Copenhagen."

"Copenhagen . . . so that is the name of where we are," Teborah replied, sighing wistfully. "It is my first time in the Eretzian realm, although I've had many visions of it."

Dawn turned to look at Ezra's mother and saw a woman displaced by circumstance, ravaged by grief. Despite her frail appearance, she sensed a warrior who was both vulnerable and unbreakable underneath the surface.

"You can't sleep either?" Dawn asked.

Teborah shook her head and pursed her lips. "Insomnia is but one curse of my clairvoyance. Although, it is not too late in Etero right now. The sun would just be setting. It hasn't even been a full day since . . ."

The end of Teborah's sentence died on her lips, but Dawn knew she was going to mention Stralla's funeral.

"I heard you buried her today—your daughter," Dawn offered. A wave of grief rolled over them and tears pooled in Dawn's eyes. "I'm so sorry for your loss. I'm also sorry that Ezra was injured . . ."

A tear slipped down Teborah's cheek. She nodded and brushed it away. "Thank you for sharing my burden," she said as she pulled something from her pocket and held her hand out toward Dawn. "I came to give you this."

Dawn curiously extended her hand, and Teborah placed a ring in her palm. A shroud of calmness settled over Dawn the moment the ring made contact with her skin. Its design was elegant yet simple—a silver band with three dark-colored crystals clustered at the center.

On closer examination, Dawn saw that one of the stones was smooth and black—obsidian, she guessed. The second stone was also black but had a roughly hewn texture with striations. The third, she realized, was not black at all, but a sparkly, deep purple.

The ring was charged with a different kind of aura, one that brought instant relief from the roiling emotions of others. Dawn's shoulders relaxed as Teborah's grief subsided. She blinked at Teborah with surprise.

"It's an empath ring. And you are an empath," she said as if it were the most obvious thing in the world. "It is why you can sense and experience others' emotions."

Dawn opened her mouth to say something but closed it again. She had felt countless emotions within the last few days alone and wondered how much of the inner turmoil was her own: Laurel's resignation and sadness, Marion's anxiety, Hikaru's mental exhaustion, and most recently, Teborah's grief.

"It can be a dangerous thing," Teborah continued, "to know others' emotions and be swayed by them, especially if you are unsure of your own. In time, you shall learn to strengthen your own en, enough to not need the ring."

Dawn swallowed, her throat dry. "Are you also an empath?"

"No, but this ring was gifted to me by an empath, and it is now my gift to you."

It must be of immense value, Dawn thought. "When I've strengthened my shielding, I'll return this to you. It wouldn't be right for me to keep it."

"In my culture, it is an insult to reject a jewel freely given. I ask for nothing in return."

The woman's lips curled up at the ends, yet Dawn wasn't sure if it was a deceptive smile or her reaction to an insult. Either way, Dawn couldn't find a polite way to refuse the gift. She thanked Teborah and made a resolution to repay her somehow.

After Teborah left, Dawn slipped the ring on her index finger and let out a long exhalation as the last traces of grief dissipated. Relief at last.

CHAPTER 27

DAWN.

Dawn, the voice called again.

She stirred, still sound asleep on the sofa. *Here I am,* she thought. *Is this a dream?*

Dawn! Howel's voice said a third time.

Dawn gasped in her sleep. *Dad!*

That voice sounded so clear, yet so far away.

Darkness surrounded her, and she realized she was still lying on the sofa with her eyes closed. *I must be dreaming.*

It's not a dream, the voice said. *I'm truly here. Remember Jack? He visited me recently.*

Ah, yes. Our code name. He was safe.

I'd like to see you very soon, Howel said. *Bring the dysprosia.*

Dawn sat up suddenly, jolted out of her sleep.

"Dad?" She squinted and held her hand out to shade her eyes. Shafts of bright sunlight poured into the great room. Her aching body reminded her of yesterday's events, so she got up slowly and walked toward the delectable aromas coming from the kitchen.

"Did you say something, Dawn?" Marion asked.

Her housekeeper was sitting at the dining table with Ezra's parents and Hikaru, and it looked like they had just attended a fancy luncheon. Ezekiel wore a blue collared shirt and black slacks, while Teborah wore a classy, dark blue dress with a floral design. Hikaru sported his usual business casual, but Marion flaunted an artfully folded gold and lapis blue headwrap that complimented her full-length dress.

Dawn looked at the sweats she wore and immediately wished she could vanish. "I, um, thought I heard my dad," she mumbled, tucking her bed-head hair behind her ears.

"It is just us here," Marion said, sounding concerned. "You slept most of the day. It is already four o'clock in the afternoon."

"Yeah, I think I'm jet lagged. Er, bridge lagged. Please excuse me," Dawn said with an awkward smile and dashed to the bathroom.

Marion followed her. "Dawn," she said in a hushed voice, "Hikaru and I bought Ezra and his parents some clothes—a bot delivered them this morning. His parents might be with us until Ezra fully recovers. Are you okay? You seem a little disoriented."

"I'm positive I heard my dad's voice."

"Do you think he sent you a comm?"

"A comm . . . wouldn't I need a comm stone for that?"

Marion eyed Dawn's protection stone, and a second later, Dawn registered the meaning.

"Oh! I forgot this was a comm stone!" Dawn said with a burst of excitement. Howel must've had a piece of the same cut.

Dawn activated her pendant and heard Howel's familiar voice. "Meet me at the bridge with the ingredient when you receive this." It was followed by a series of pulses, some short, some long.

"He wants me to meet him," she told Marion. "There's a bunch of pulses, like morse code or something."

"Bridge coordinates. May I hold it?" she asked, eyeing the protection stone.

Dawn passed the jewel to her, and in seconds Marion knew where to send Dawn.

After scarfing down a granola bar and getting ready, Dawn looked at her reflection in the bathroom mirror. The sun exposure in the Philippines had slightly darkened her complexion. Ezra was still sleeping when she snuck into her closet and dug out slacks and an ocean-blue blouse that reminded her of Laurel. She was worried about her and made a mental note to get in touch soon after seeing her dad.

Despite looking put together, Dawn's insides were a bundle of nerves. She carried the empath ring in her pocket, deciding it was best to be fully present, to take in her dad's emotions as is.

Marion clasped her hands together in satisfaction when Dawn exited the bathroom. "Amazing what a decent outfit and a brush can do."

Dawn had to agree. She'd been wearing comfy sweats for weeks, and her hair was either in a messy bun or ponytail; the transformation made her nearly unrecognizable.

Marion handed her the dysprosia container and a pastry box with a folded note attached. "Cookies. For Howel," she explained as they made their way to the great room. "I'll hold on to your protection stone. Howel will comm me when you're ready to come back."

"You've really thought of everything. Thank you," she told her housekeeper.

"Ready?" she asked when Dawn was in front of the bridge.

Dawn took a deep breath and nodded. This was the moment she'd been waiting for. Everything she'd worked for, the aura training, the mission, and the sacrifices she made led her to this. She'd finally get to see her dad.

The glass swirled in front of her, and her reflection disappeared. She stepped through the bridge, and there he was, standing in front of her, beaming. With his arms outstretched, Howel beckoned her for a bear hug.

"It really *is* you!" She embraced him, confirming he wasn't a figment of her imagination.

"Look at you!" He held her at arm's length. "Dressed like a proper adult! And your aura . . . my little girl is gone! What happened to your face? You look like you got in a scuffle."

"I'm all right, really," she laughed as she set down the box and container on the desk nearby. "I missed you so much. I even missed hearing your British accent."

He ushered her toward the swivel chair. The room looked exactly like his study in California. Dawn spotted the ormolu clock on the desk, and puzzled by the uncanny similarity, gingerly touched the ornate design. It was solid and . . . real. The Monte Carlo rug on the floor had the same scuff marks. Everything was the same, down to the books on his recessed bookshelves—except for a strange red hue in the room.

"Where are we? Your study was destroyed last night."

Howel shoulders slumped a bit as he took a seat in the armchair next to her.

"I saw the broadcasts, loads of them, about the attack on Jett and what happened to the house," he said with a click of his tongue. "Is Jett all right?"

Dawn nodded.

"It's a shame about our house though. We had lovely memories there. This room is a projection construct, made to look like a familiar place—home. It would've been too great a risk to bring you to the lab."

Dawn narrowed her eyes at him. He was wearing the same sweater vest the last time she saw him in person, and she warily considered that *he* might be a projection. He looked different somehow and she couldn't quite put her finger on what it was.

Were the lines on his face always so pronounced? Was his frame the same, or did he lose some weight? Maybe Hikaru should visit him and check.

"Are you . . . well?" Dawn asked suspiciously.

"Healthy as a horse, considering my circumstances," he said with a warm smile. "I could really use a latte from time to time, but I can't complain. Despite the demise of the house, I'm glad you're unharmed. Things are just things after all. I take it Marion, Hikaru, and Lopple are doing fine too?"

"Mrs. M. and Hikaru are doing well—"

"It's Mrs. now, is it?" he laughed. "I should've known you'd find out. What about Lopple? I haven't heard from him in a while."

Dawn shook her head and recounted their entire ordeal. She also tried her best to include everyone she had met and all pertinent details, starting with her trip to Tencho, from spending weeks in aura training with an Aquavian princess named Laurel, to her friendship with Logan, then explained last night's chaotic events. How Logan got impaled by a siren and had his memory erased by Hikaru. How they barely escaped the house while Ezra bought them more time. How he was beaten within an inch of his life and aura blocked. And how he and his parents were staying with them at a new safehouse.

Howel listened intently, nodding every so often. After a half hour of talking and reliving the past two months of her strange new Lumen life, Dawn was utterly drained.

"I know this mission took a toll on you," Howel said with a pained expression. "Tell me again, how do you know Lopple and Echo perished if you didn't *see* them?"

"I heard them . . . I mean, I heard the gunshots," Dawn said. She looked down at her hands, wringing them. Her voice dropped down to a whisper. "I know they're dead because . . . I couldn't feel their auras anymore. I'm so, so sorry—it was my fault."

Howel took her hands in hers and wiped the tear she hadn't noticed tracing her cheek.

"No, my dear, it wasn't your fault. No matter how much you think it is, it wasn't." Howel sighed, taking out a handkerchief and blowing his nose. "Echo was a trusted friend, and I implemented something of an insurance plan long before he got involved with the more perilous parts of my work."

"An insurance plan?" she asked, mid sob.

"Every time he was scheduled to work with me or any of my Lumen associates, he was to clock in with my designated agent before *and after* the assigned task was completed. If he failed to clock in after," he sighed wearily, "he would've been assumed dead—no questions asked. A generous compensation would've been paid out immediately to his beneficiaries."

Dawn's grief had morphed into shock. She stared at her dad, aghast that Marion was right. Still, nothing he could say would release the hold that guilt had over her. There was no point in arguing with him. *She* was the one with Echo that day, and it was on her to seek atonement for what transpired.

"Did Lopple have this same plan in place?"

"No," he said with a shake of his head. "Lopple knew exactly what he was getting into. His real name was Gabriel Rockwood."

He got up, put his hands in his pockets, and began slowly pacing the room.

"What?" Dawn asked, her eyes following him.

"He was a very talented shifter, and it's quite rare for Etherans to have that ability, even moreso control it to the extent that he could.

He is Lord Angel's father. Last year, he was sentenced to death for conspiring against Lord Malstrom, but he successfully fled the Etheran realm using his shifter abilities. Gabriel never admitted it, but exacting revenge consumed him."

"I knew something was off," she said after collecting her thoughts. "Laurel *sensed* he was a shifter. Lop—I mean, Gabriel, said he was aiding you . . . to create a restoration jewel."

"I let him *think* I was creating a restoration jewel. The ingredients needed are powerful on their own, and I reckon Gabriel thought he could help me and also pursue his vendetta simultaneously."

Howel carefully lifted the container of the dysprosia to eye level, examining its contents. "When you took hold of the dysprosia, did you feel . . . a surge of power?"

Dawn nodded and shuddered, remembering its roots curling around her hand. She was perturbed that she and Marion had guessed the ingredient incorrectly—twice. Her dad wasn't planning on creating a restoration jewel, which left only one other option: a corgemma.

"The ingredients are for a sentient jewel," he said, following her train of thought.

"Now that you have the dysprosia," she said, pointing to the container in his hands, "someone in Ezra's family—or another Valedor in the Etheran realm—can wield it, and then you can come home, right?"

"Dawn," he said gently. "I'm here, in this moment with you, and *you're* home. Safe with Marion and Hikaru. Surrounded by people you trust and love. My mission—*our* mission—is not yet fulfilled. The Ides of March is when the moon is at its most powerful. Tonight, I will expose the dysprosia to it and begin the months-long process of extracting its en . . ."

Howel continued to drone on, but Dawn was no longer listening as her hastily formed thoughts revealed a new reality: *He's not coming back. Not yet.* Dawn's eyes flicked to the folded note Marion had attached to the box of cookies, and a feeling of resignation came over her.

"Are you cross with me?" he asked. "I'm truly sorry I left the task to Marion to explain your biological parents. Your mother was a powerful empath as well. I can't recall if that was something Marion knew."

Dawn shook her head. "I'm not angry . . . it was all such a shock, finding everything out at once. How did you know I was an empath?"

"I suspected it." Howel set the container back on the desk. "Did you ever wonder why you learned languages so easily? You know Tagalog, Chinese, Korean, some Japanese, and enough European languages to get by."

"Is this another one of your riddles?"

"I believed your affinity for picking up languages is due to your empath abilities. Sure, they weren't manifesting as strongly as they are now that your aura has awakened, but I reckon that much of learning languages has to do with understanding context, feelings, and emotions."

He stuck his hands in his pockets, waiting for her reaction. When none was given, he offered, "You know I love you as if you were my own daughter, right?"

"Of course. You're the only one dad I've ever known, and I'm grateful for all you did for me growing up. I just wish things could go back to normal. Being an empath is . . . I've just been having a hard time managing everyone else's emotions," she sighed. "Why didn't you tell me about everything sooner when you had the chance?"

"Dawn, you're so, *so* young! I wanted to give you as normal a life as possible . . . you know, give you a chance to find yourself first. If you would've found out any sooner about your parents, aura abilities, or the prophecy—everything, really—I'm not sure how you would've reacted. Your prefrontal cortex was still developing—"

"Oh, come on!" She broke into laughter. "I can't believe you're joking about this!"

"It's a gift to find humor in all circumstances." He winked.

"Anyone would've reacted the way I did when I found out the world was ending," she said, considering the council of Tencho. "Can you tell me . . . what happened to my mom? And who is the woman you're in pictures with—the one whose pictures I have framed and who supposedly died from a rare form of cancer?"

"Both your parents died fighting for control over a sentient jewel. That jewel is now in possession of Lord Malstrom."

The words hit her like a slap in the face. Her real mom and dad had sacrificed their lives to fight a losing battle.

"The woman in the pictures," Howel continued, "is just a friend of mine . . . her image was altered and used to create portraits, along with a fake identity. Very few knew that Kathryn's baby survived. Many thought she had a miscarriage—and we encouraged that idea. So we created a persona to help hide your lineage."

"Who's 'we,'" Dawn asked through gritted teeth.

"Myself, Marion, Hikaru, and Jett Pierce."

It all started to make sense, Dawn thought. Jett was the one who had means to access the global database. He could make up people, hide people, and find people . . . which meant that a leak in his company would be catastrophic for her. There was only one person from his organization that knew of her whereabouts over the past week. *Gita.*

"There's something more I need you to do," Howel said, interrupting her thoughts.

Her breath caught in her chest. She had barely gotten out alive with the dysprosia in time.

"First," Howel said, "stay hidden. No more putting Logan or your groundling friends at risk. Second, wait for my instructions. I have an Eretzian friend who will aid you in the next task."

Dawn frowned, slightly offended. She had never *planned* to put her friends at risk. Indeed, Logan had been through enough, but she also didn't desire to give up her groundling life. Shouldn't she have a say in this? It was *her* life, after all. She pursed her lips, weighing Howel's words. What he was asking of her was important—*saving-the-Earth* important.

"Sure, I'll do what you ask if it means we have a viable world to live on in the foreseeable future. But I have one condition," she hedged.

His smile radiated warmly. "Always thinking a few steps ahead, just like your mother. What is your condition?"

"No more secrets."

As far as she could tell, everything still felt shrouded in mystery. She had learned of her biological parents (one of who was an empath), her aura abilities, and the Lumen realms within the past few months. There *had* to be more that she wasn't aware of.

"Agreed," Howel said. "I'll be forthcoming, all in due time."

Dawn blinked and her surroundings began to look hazy. The reddish hue in the room glowed brighter.

"The moon is rising," Howel stated with an air of sadness. "This dysprosia needs to be tended to."

"You're . . . leaving?" she asked, squinting at her dad's blurry outline. "This was so fast. Can you give us one more minute?"

"The projection construct is fading. I've commed Marion to let you cross over," he said, sounding far away. "And I'm sorry. I'm sorry it has to be this way." His voice trembled as he struggled to hold back tears. "If we don't meet again, remember that I love you—have *always* loved you as my own flesh and blood."

Dawn found herself standing in front of the mirror in the great room, her reflection staring blankly at her. She had more questions unanswered than when she started. There was an uneasiness and sorrow her dad carried deep within, and she knew in that moment that things would never go back to the way they once were.

CHAPTER 28

IT WAS TWILIGHT when Dawn returned. The fading light cast a somber air about the safehouse occupants, who were, for the most part, quiet. They spoke only when needed, whether due to the subconscious fear of finding themselves amidst another ambush or because they were each lost in their own thoughts, she wasn't sure. Ezekiel and Teborah isolated themselves in their suite, leaving Dawn to lounge in the great room with Hiro as company.

Marion and Hikaru prepared dinner, and soon after, mouth-watering aromas of garlic and savory dishes called everyone to the dining room—except for Ezra, who remained in Dawn's room, resting.

At the dinner table, the heavy ambiance gave way to warmth and comfort. Marion explained the special ingredients she'd used to bring to life the flavors in each entree: a tofu and eggplant stir fry, rotisserie chicken, and a hearty garden salad with nuts and thinly sliced apples. Smiles replaced frowns and pursed lips as they listened to her talk about umami and simple seasonings. Such was the magic of delicious food.

As they ate, Ezra's parents engaged in lighthearted conversation and took turns sharing their nostalgia-inducing home-cooked meals, including a maple-sweetened bread called panab and khordeer tongue. The latter was the late Stralla's favorite. Dawn fiddled with the empath ring on her finger, relieved she was no longer overwhelmed with their family's grief.

With their stomachs full and their spirits lifted, Hikaru delved into the previous night's events and asked the Valedors how they came to need refuge.

Ezekiel spoke first. "After Stralla's funeral, Teborah and I were visited by members of the secret council. The historian, Asher, said there was someone who provided a lead to the soufors on your location." His eyes flicked at Dawn, then back to Hikaru. "We learned later—through our sangwor sons—that Lord Malstrom planned to question us."

Teborah's expression turned sour, as if recalling the taste of a dish gone rancid. "We decided not to appear for the summons. Better for us to keep silent than to give Lord Malstrom a chance to read us. He had dispatched some knights to arrest us. At that time, we tried to contact Ezra, but he did not respond. So we sent comms to Sid."

"That must've been when Ezra was aura blocked," Marion said, pouring her a cup of Kudzukan tea.

"Yes," Ezekiel responded, rubbing the stubble of his beard. "You were ambushed and outnumbered. Sid informed us of that—but who from her agents would betray the cause?"

"I'm not sure, but I do know that Gita was the only outsider who knew we were going to the Underground River," Dawn answered with gritted teeth. "*Not* one of Sid's agents. She's Jett's assistant."

Realization hit Marion and Hikaru like a ton of bricks.

Marion grumbled something in Afrikaans under her breath. "I contacted Gita to arrange for flight transportation on both trips," she fumed.

"That's why Laurel had sensed a poru on our trip to the Heavenly Pit!" Dawn seethed. "She must've tipped off the soufors and sirens at the Underground River."

"There were sirens?" Teborah asked, aghast.

The group erupted in explanations of what took place, speaking over one another.

Marion continued a string of what the others assumed were obscenities in Afrikaans, then nearly shouted, "She was a double agent this whole time!"

"Do you think . . . it has to be her!" Dawn recalled. "She was the masked sangwor at Jett's!"

"I'll kill her—I'll kill her myself. She murdered Stralla." Ezekiel said in a chillingly soft voice of controlled rage.

"It is as the prophecy states," Teborah's voice rang above the others, silencing them. "'In the Last of Days, there will rise a lumere, who many shall oppose. A light in the dark, a voice for the groundlings, to unite the three realms and restore the Earth.'"

The room fell eerily silent as Teborah continued. "'The One will pass through the fire—born again—and the crown of the sky will wither like the dying grass.'"

A chill crept up Dawn's spine as she drew everyone's gaze. Her throat went instantly dry, and she reached for her glass of water to take a sip.

"It is you, *you* are The One, my child," Teborah said, erasing all doubt if there was any.

Dawn choked on her water, gasping and coughing as Marion patted her back. There was no more running from the truth—after meeting with Howel, she *knew* the sentient jewel he was creating was for her.

"Are you all right?" Marion asked after she finally stopped sputtering.

"Yeah—I mean, no," she sighed. "I think . . . er, I *know* dad is creating a *sentient* jewel, not a restoration one—"

Marion cut in. "I assumed incorrectly, and I only wanted to protect—"

"Dad said he let Lopple think that as well. He also said Lopple was a shifter whose real name is Gabriel Rockwood."

Marion's eyes widened. "Gabriel," she repeated. "I do remember meeting him once. He had a different look, a different face."

"Gabriel." Ezekiel whispered. "He married my cousin, and he was Lord Angel's father. It was announced he was executed, but there have always been rumors that he escaped . . ."

"He, um, died in the Underground River cave," Dawn said, pulling at her pendant. "I'm so sorry . . ."

Teborah took his hand and gently rubbed his shoulder. "These last few days must've been overwhelming for you too, Dawn. How did the rest of your meeting with your father go?"

"Yeah, 'overwhelming' is a good way of putting it. Talking with my dad about everything . . . was a lot to take in. I think what worries me most about being this prophesied lumere," she said, gesticulating quotation marks in the air, "is that I don't have a clue of what I'm supposed to be doing. I'm just waiting for dad's next instruction, the next mission."

"That is very Howel-like of him." A soft laugh escaped from Marion. "Most people, including myself, have no clue of what they're supposed to be doing at any stage of life. The ones who do are the fortunate few, but most of us are figuring it out as we go."

"She is right," Teborah admitted.

A look of surprise passed over Hikaru's face. "Surely as a seer, you could guide her steps, show her what will come to pass."

"It is true that I can *see*, but not all things are revealed to me. Now that the moon is full, my abilities are amplified. There are still many uncertainties, but it is clear as crystal that Dawn is The One."

Dawn squirmed uncomfortably in her chair. "In the prophecy, you said The One will 'pass through the fire.' What does that mean?"

"It is an Etherish saying that means you will undergo great tribulations," Ezekiel said, his eyes revealing he did not envy her.

Teborah quickly added, "It is also prophesied that you will encounter mountains of challenges, which will crumble before you."

"Would anyone else like to volunteer to be 'The One?'" Dawn asked under her breath.

Marion placed an assuring hand on her shoulder. "We won't always have all the answers, but I'm here—we're here," she said in Hikaru's direction. "We'll figure it out."

Dawn instantly felt her housekeeper's calm energy radiate in the room, like a light that couldn't be dimmed. *Hope*, she thought.

The noise of the espresso machine was a welcome distraction to drown out Dawn's negative thoughts. She breathed in its rich, complex aroma with notes of chocolate and vanilla—*home*. With her mood improved, Dawn's mind drifted back to her meeting with her dad.

What good does it do to dwell on uncertainties? He was safe and well. He had the dysprosia. He could contact me through the protection stone, and Marion will teach me how to read bridge coordinates.

Gratitude swelled in her heart; despite being completely out of her element for the past few months, she held onto the hope that her family and newfound friends provided.

"Hikaru! Get the go bags!" Marion's disembodied voice interrupted Dawn's thoughts and carried an urgency that frazzled her nerves.

"What's wrong?" she asked, running to the great room.

Hikaru sprinted up to the suite with Hiro on his heels as Marion rapped on Ezekiel's and Teborah's door.

"I received a proximity alert—Hikaru and I put them on the nearest bridges to tell if anyone crossed them," Marion explained. "Teborah! Ezekiel! We need to leave!"

"We're ready," Ezekiel said as he opened the door and stepped out with his wife.

"Do you know who crossed?" Dawn asked, hoping it was a mistake.

Marion took Dawn's hand and put it over her wrist cuff. It pulsed, and the aura passed through Dawn. In an instant, she could tell it was the Inked Man . . . and then another pulse . . . his partner Blade—the soufors! "H-how did they find us here?"

Hikaru returned with his backpack on and handed his medical supplies and Marion's go-bag to Teborah. He and Ezekiel went to get Ezra.

Marion dashed to the kitchen with Dawn behind her. "I do not know . . . this is a safehouse," she said, removing bags of dried herbs from the pantry. "I have not connected any online devices to CETT systems . . ."

Dawn gasped, covering her mouth. "*I* did! I activated X8 from my mobile device last night, and he went online . . . I shut it down right after. I can't believe this!" She muttered her apologies as she followed Marion back to the great room.

"It can't be helped now. We have a contingency plan and another safehouse," Marion explained to the group. "Teborah and Ezekiel, I've commed Sid. She has a place in Etero where she can hide you, and it might be safer if we split up."

"What about Ezra?" Ezekiel asked, holding up his barely conscious son with Hikaru supporting his other side.

"He can stay with us," Hikaru replied. I'll be able to treat him until he regains his strength."

Teborah turned to Dawn. "The time has not yet come for us to return to Etero. Our place is with you right now."

"You don't want to go back to the Etheran realm?" Dawn asked her, picking up her bag next to the sofa. The journal and her dad's shepra cloak were already in it.

"Even the roses in Etero have thorns."

"Very well," Hikaru said, as the glass on the mirror bridge began its familiar change of color. "My friend on the other side has unlocked the bridge for us."

Hikaru, Ezra, and Ezekiel crossed first. Teborah followed.

It was Dawn's turn next. She looked back at Marion with Hiro at her side. Reaching out with her aura, she felt her housekeeper's assuring presence. *I'm here. I'm right behind you.*

Dawn faced forward. It's time to embrace this, she knew. Lean into who she was to become if they were to succeed in navigating the journey ahead. She straightened up, pushed aside her thoughts of uncertainty, and—without hesitation—stepped through the swirls.

"We're too late. They're gone," Randen Silvers sneered into his comm stone. The tattoos on his neck seemed to pulse as anger and hatred worked over him. He loathed the worm he was hunting. Hated how he and his partner Knives were always so close, yet grasping at air. Hated the treacherous lumen who were aiding her—worms and subdwellers alike.

"Are you sure this was the location that was pinged?" Nekra Clove asked.

"Positive," Gita answered through the comm stone. "You should've gone earlier, like I said. Lord Malstrom is going to—"

"Shut it, you little runt," Randen snarled. He shuddered with the thought of the pain he'd have to endure. All for a stupid worm. He stared at the little cup of espresso that was left on the kitchen counter. With his gloved hand, he touched it, confirming that it was lukewarm at best. *The little worm had known they were coming.*

"You better check if that traitor, Dalton, knows of any other leads or safehouses," Nekra threatened.

"I've read him thoroughly. I've gotten everything I could out of him, and if it weren't for what he overheard from Sid, we wouldn't have gotten the first safehouse location," Gita answered pointedly.

"Do. As. I. Say," Nekra bit off each word. "Take his other eye if you have to!"

There was a pause before Gita's reply. "No. I'm done doing your dirty work. This is *your* job and you're ridiculously useless at it!"

"ENOUGH!" Randen roared. "I'll torture him myself. We'll be there at first light."

He severed the comm connection, then unleashed his pent-up frustration in a sumatok that decimated the pantry. Herbs and splintered wood went flying.

"Silvers!" Nekra yelled, annoyed that he couldn't control his rage. She made an exasperated sound and went back to the great room to check the bridge.

Randen stood alone in the kitchen for a few moments as the cloud of dust settled. He didn't care that Nekra was annoyed. He had to let it out, and he felt better instantly. He worked better and his mind was sharper, too, when he could wield his aura violently. He inhaled deeply and caught a whiff of mint and something else. *Moonshade.*

He laughed as he entered the great room where Knives was inspecting the bridge jewels, attempting to get a pulse of its last coordinates.

"Wherever they crossed was a closed bridge—*always* a closed bridge. They're cautious." She caught his snickering reflection in the mirror. "Care to share what you find so amusing?"

"Moonshade. Remember that sangwor who said he aura blocked someone? He was here. He's with them."

Nekra wheeled around to face him, smiling. "It'll slow them down. Looks like we're hunting two worms, now."

Acknowledgments

I'm eternally grateful to God and His master plan. It was a long journey bringing this book to fruition, but every person I met over the years and every challenge I had to overcome have shaped this labor of love.

To my editor Jamie Ryu, I appreciate your expertise and all the time and energy you've poured into *Last of Days*. Thank you for your guidance and for patiently answering all my questions—I learned so much and know this experience will help me continually grow as a writer.

Gigi Rosenfeld, my sister, thank you for your feedback in the earliest stages and for all your help in this seemingly impossible passion project.

Eileen Apostol Pingol, mare, your musical talents and language-learning superpowers never cease to amaze me. Your music and lyrics are forever part of the fabric of this book. From the bottom of my heart, thank you for inspiring me to chase my dreams.

To my beloved husband, for believing in me from the start and encouraging me amidst all the chaos of life. You are a dream come true.

To my son Loki, for all your love, steady and true. *Mahal na mahal kita.*

To Mom, for instilling in me the value of grit, keeping the faith, and exploring the world. Your sacrifices as an immigrant have given me endless opportunities you never had growing up, and they have made all the difference. I love you.

To Dad and Grandma Rosalina, for your love and our bonds of family. I look forward to the day we'll be reunited with Grandpa Herman Sr.

To my dearest friends who cheered me on in all the stages of this book, thank you. You've brought me immense joy with your gentle coaching, curiosity, and sometimes shameless promotion! Most importantly, you've helped me make a way for my art.

ABOUT THE AUTHOR

Photo by Janely Abigail Duran

Lizerne Ventura graduated from the University of Southern California with a degree in Journalism. She spent most of her professional career in various content roles for movie sites and software companies. Now she's telling her own fantastical stories inspired by her love of travel, K-dramas, and anime. When she's not writing she can be found spending time with her family or lounging at libraries and coffee shops—near her home in SoCal and around the world.

Visit her online at lizerneventura.com.

www.ingramcontent.com/pod-product-compliance
Lightning Source LLC
Chambersburg PA
CBHW020557120726
47903CB00001B/291